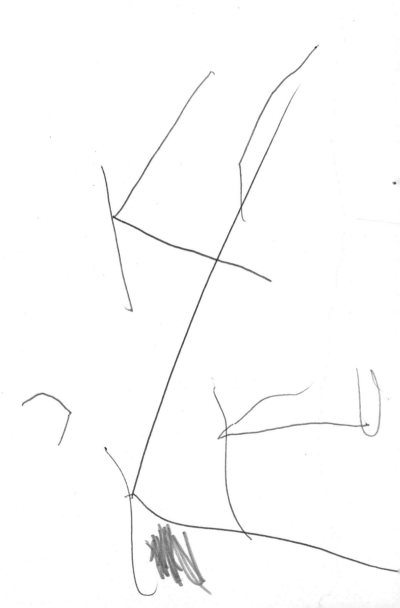

Crossing the Line

Steve Dewey
Kevin Goodman

An original publication of watwo

Crossing the Line

ISBN-13: 9780993222221
ISBN-10: 993222226

http://cometodereham.co.uk
http://www.watwo.me.uk

Cover design: Paul Vought

watwo, marlborough, wiltshire, uk

Steve thanks Lizzie for her ears and eyes

Kevin dedicates this book to the memory of
Helen Goodman (1956-2003)

Prologue

Hardly a day seemed to have passed since he last saw her face, and now she was dead. Evening had slowly stolen the light from the room as he sat in the armchair, his mind numbed by the newspaper article in front of him. The head-line blared out at him. It never changed, no matter how many times he read it.

He'd been away from the flat for a month. On his return he'd picked up the Sunday newspapers from the table in the hallway where his cleaner had placed them. He read them in the living room, while drinking his coffee. Nothing of interest had happened in the world, he had thought, so he read the newspapers desultorily, starting with the most recent, flicking through the pages. Then, in the second paper he read, the headline to a short article, tucked away on page seven, caught his eye.

UFO Girl Takes Own Life

He found himself reading the report again, just able to make out the type in the failing light.

> Peta Shepherd, 20, was found dead on Saturday at her home in the small Wiltshire town of Dereham.
>
> Miss Shepherd moved to Dereham last year following her interest in the flying saucer mystery that has excited so much curiosity.
> Richard Patterson, local reporter for the *Dereham Gazette* and UFO expert, was a friend of Miss Shepherd's. He said she was a kind, caring girl, and

that he had been shocked and dismayed by her death. When asked if her suicide was related to the flying saucer mystery, Patterson said that she had been an earnest seeker after truth, but she had been depressed before her death after a bitter break-up with her boyfriend, Archie Conn, 30.

The cottage Miss Shepherd lived in is owned by Lancashire-based businessman, Philip Creighton, manager of the rock group, The Gentleman Farmers, who recently had chart success with their second LP, *Here We Are Again*, and the single from that album, *Flocking Birds*. Creighton was unavailable for comment about the tragedy.

Local police have ruled out foul play, although they wish to speak Mr. Conn.

There was a photograph of Peta beside the article, a small blurred picture of her smiling face. The paper was a couple of weeks old now. She was already lying in the cold, dark earth. Harry quickly leafed through the other newspapers, and found another article. He skipped the introductory paragraphs, and then read:

Peta Shepherd had been involved with a UFO contactee group based in a London nightclub, *The Purple Parrot*, where she met had Mr Conn. The two of them moved to Dereham a little over a year ago.

Miss Shepherd left the family home in Hagley, near Stourbridge about two years ago. It is not clear why she left. Her mother, Jane Shepherd, who is separated from her husband, refuses to answer any questions about her daughter.

Peta has a sister, Molly, who is two years her junior. Locals remember Peta as a friendly, bubbly, individual, who always had time to talk and was always helpful. 'Peta Shepherd was a loving, care-free girl. We're all suprised and saddened by what has happened,' said Eileen Thompson, proprietor of Hagley's post office.

Harry knew there would have been no articles at all had Peta not been tenuously linked to celebrity, through Creighton, and mystery, through Dereham.

Harry Roberts, who Peta had known as Colin Butler, swallowed against the hard lump in his throat. His boss, Mick Edge, had known what was happening, knew that he had fallen for Peta, and had recalled him to London before he became a liability.

Harry had assumed the Dereham file closed. Surely, it would be reopened now? He stood slowly and went to the kitchen to make a strong cup of tea. He heard Peta's voice. *Hot sweet tea, that's what you need for a shock, my old Gran would say.* She loved her gran's sayings.

He smiled sadly, switched on the kettle, and leaned against the work surface. He pressed the palms of his hands into his eyes in an attempt to hold back tears. Instead, he squeezed out a sob.

1

Harry had no authorisation for what he was about to do. A remembered Peta smiled at him, urging him on. He crossed the busy road and headed towards a small side street. The street was narrow, gloomy, and grey under a grey autumn sky. A white Ford Transit was parked close to the doors of a large building. *Willis Signwriters* was painted, in a flowing, italic script, across the back doors of the van. Two ladders leaned against the walls of the building. At the top of each ladder was a workman, one of whom, Harry guessed, was Mr Willis. The two workmen struggled to screw a new sign across the old one. Harry stopped. There was just enough of the old sign visible to make out that it had said *The Purple Parrot*. The new sign had only one word: *Peta's*.

Harry had found Len Stone's club, the place where, perhaps, Peta's journey towards tragedy had begun. A chubby man with a round face came out of the club, limping slightly, a cigarette dangling from his lips. Harry didn't need to ask who it was. Peta had spoken fondly of Martyn Harris many times.

'That looks right bostin', lads.' The broad Birmingham accent confirmed the man's identity. 'The guv will be pleased with that!'

Martyn glanced at Harry. 'You all right, mate? Can I help you?'

Harry looked up at the sign again. 'Yes. This is, sorry, was, *The Purple Parrot*?'

Martyn nodded. 'Yes. We're changing the name. A tribute to an old friend who worked here. Why the interest?'

Straight to the point, Harry thought. No chit-chat, no pleasantries.

'I thought I should...' Harry felt his resolve weaken for a moment. His job involved dissembling, lying, trickery, but he didn't always like doing it. He didn't want to do it now, not here, not with Martyn Harris, Peta's old friend. 'I thought I should visit. You see, I am... I was... Peta's cousin.'

Martyn was silent for a moment, and peered at Harry intently, his brown eyes narrow. 'Her cousin?' He was suspicious, Harry could tell. 'She never talked about a cousin.'

Harry had anticipated that. 'I guess she didn't talk about her family much at all, did she?'

Martyn shook his head. 'No. No, she didn't.' Martyn assessed Harry for a few moments more; then his face softened. 'Do you want a cup of tea, mate?'

'That would be nice, thanks.'

Martyn opened the door of the club, and led Harry down a flight of stairs that ended in a small foyer. Here, a pair of heavy wooden doors opened onto the floor of the club. Martyn held a door open, and gestured for Harry to enter. Harry looked around him. He was slightly surprised. The club was not as he'd expected. Peta had often joked that it was little more than a glorified cellar. Archie Conn, Peta's boyfriend, had been vitriolic in his opinion of the club. 'That dippy hippie shit-hole,' had been his favourite description.

Nothing could be further from the truth. Stone had obviously spent a great deal of money improving the club after Peta had left here and moved with Archie to Wiltshire. The colours were cool. There were subtle lights around the bar, above tables, and in the small barred windows. There were potted plants – bamboos, yuccas and figs. He felt the leaves on one of the plants. Silk. He smiled to himself. High quality imitations. Of course, they would have to be artificial, down here in this dark hole in the ground where there was very little natural light. There were leather benches and corner seats against the walls. The tables were clean and shining. Peta had given Harry the impression that the place had been a frantic, hedonistic, hippie den, full of drunks and potheads. This seemed rather... restful.

Harry followed Martyn towards the bar.

'Stay here for a mo,' Martyn said. 'I'll get us a cuppa. Milk and sugar?'

'Just milk, thanks.'

Martyn disappeared behind the bar.

Alone now, Harry's doubts resurfaced. He wondered what he was doing here. *What would Edge say?* Mick Edge was only five years older than Harry, but a university graduate on the fast track to higher office. Edge was keen to make his mark within the department, but had little or no experience of fieldwork. Edge found it hard to understand why Harry had allowed himself to become smitten with Peta. Perhaps Edge had been right. Perhaps he had become too close to Peta. He certainly wasn't thinking straight at the moment.

Harry's thoughts were interrupted by a door opening to one side of the bar. He looked up, expecting to see Martyn. It was somebody else, a well-built man dressed in a blue business suit. His hair was dark, shoulder length; flecks of grey showed in it. Harry thought the man to be in his early or mid-thirties. Harry wouldn't want to mess with him. The man looked at Harry closely, with steely grey eyes. From what Peta had told him this could be only one man – Len Stone.

'Who are you?' The voice carried with it a certain authority. 'And, more importantly, what are you doing in my club at this time of the day?'

'Somebody let me in. I assumed he worked here.'

'Portly bloke with a limp?'

'Yes, that's the one.'

'Ah, Martyn.' A small smile played around Len's mouth 'It seems he's caught my habit of taking waifs and strays off the street.'

Harry said nothing, although he knew that the waif referred to was Peta.

'Sorry, that's a private joke.' Len held out his hand. 'I'm Leonard Stone, owner of this fine slice of London nightlife. People call me Len. And you are?'

'Shepherd. Colin Shepherd. Nice to meet you.'

Len's grasp had been firm until Harry had provided his name – or rather his invented name. Then, Harry had noticed the grip weaken.

'Shepherd?' Len stammered. 'Are you related to Peta?'

'Yes,' Harry said. 'Her cousin'

Martyn came back into the bar, carrying two mugs. He handed one to Harry.

Len looked at Martyn. 'You know this man is Peta's cousin?'

'Yes, he told me,' Martyn said.

'Colin Shepherd, pleased to meet you.'

'Martyn Harris, glad to make your acquaintance. I'd shake yer hand, but...' He indicated the mug in one hand, a freshly-lit cigarette in the other.

'So what brings you here, Mr Shepherd?' Len asked.

'Please, call me Colin,' Harry said. He sipped his tea. 'I only found out about Peta's death recently. I wasn't invited to the funeral. I suspect few relatives were. I didn't know what to do. I had one letter from her, a while back. She mentioned this place. She said she worked here. She seemed... happy.'

A faint trace of grief flitted across Len's face. 'Where do you live, Colin?'

'London.'

'London? Why didn't she come to you when she ran away from home?' Martyn asked.

'Oh, I only moved here recently. Because of my job. I work in the City. I've been meaning to get here for a while, to chase her up, see what was happening. But it was a new job, a new city, time flew by. Now... now, of course, I'm too late.'

'You'd have been too late, anyway,' Len said quietly. 'She left here a year or more ago. She moved to Dereham, in Wiltshire.'

'Yes, I saw that in the paper. She moved down there with her boyfriend, yes?'

'Archibald Franklin fucking Conn,' Len said.

'What was he like?' Harry asked, knowing anyway.

'A smooth-talking, arrogant shit,' Martyn said.

They talked some more, Harry playing the part of the long-lost cousin. He didn't know why he was here, really, but did know that he was looking for information about Peta and Archie. Particularly Archie. This seemed like as good a place to start. And even thought he and Peta had spoken so often while he had been living with her - observing her - in Dereham, he hoped to find out more about her. Len and Martyn provided him with nothing new, which wasn't surprising, really; he probably knew more about Archie and Peta than they had ever done.

When he had finished his tea, he thanked Martyn and Len for their time. 'Nice place you've got here, Mr Stone.'

'It's gone upmarket in the last year.'

'Yes, in her letter Peta said that this place was a bit of a psychedelic hippie dungeon.'

Len smiled. 'Yes, I suppose it was.'

'Well, I'll have to get back to work. My lunch break has already extended beyond what I told my boss.'

'I'll walk you to the door.'

'I'd better get back to work, too,' Martyn said.

'Pronto, Tonto,' Len replied.

Harry's heart skipped a beat. That had been one of Peta's sayings.

Len stood in the dingy side street with Harry. An October wind lifted newspapers in the gutter. 'Nice to meet you, Colin. I hope you'll visit the club.'

'I certainly shall, Mr Stone.'

They shook hands.

Even with the voices of the World Service talking gently in the background, Harry found sleep once again eluding him. All he could see when he closed his eyes was Peta's face. Her voice sometimes came to him. *Am I being haunted by her?* Throwing the bedclothes aside, he made his way to the kitchen, knowing that he wouldn't sleep now. Should he make himself a coffee, or reach for the bottle of Southern Comfort? The spirit at least allowed him some relief from Peta.

He had to be back in the office in the morning. Edge was efficient, and expected all those in his team to work diligently. Just after Harry had arrived back in London from Wiltshire, Edge had drawled in his Scottish accent that *the country needed solid, reliable operatives* – the implication being, of course, that Harry was no longer solid and reliable, and should, perhaps, be moved out of operations. Edge never liked personal issues to intrude into the ordered and efficient running of his department. When he'd returned to London, Edge had assigned Harry a tedious watching job. When that had finished, Harry had been set the task of checking the backgrounds of the hopefuls applying to work at GCHQ. It was a waste of his talents. Edge, Harry thought morosely, no longer trusted him. Had Edge never felt the pangs of love? *No, not Edge.* He lived for the job. Perhaps a search of his file might disclose a weakness. *But even if I found anything, how, or why, would I use it?* Harry realised then how much he hated the tasks Edge had set him. The stupid idea of trying to gain access to Edge's file was proof of that. And although Edge could be hard, Harry actually liked him.

Peta had affected Harry more than he knew. He *had* fallen in love – with someone he'd been sent to watch, to spy on. *Why do I feel this way? Was Peta so special?* He remembered the train journey back to London, how he had told himself that he would now be able to move on, that he always did, that a new assignment would come along and offer new places, new faces, new opportunities. But he hadn't moved on. Only after leaving her had he realised how deeply he felt about her. The news of her death had only intensified those feelings.

A loud rumble of thunder woke Harry. Heavy rain slapped against the window. He was sitting in the armchair. The table lamp beside him was still switched on. He was cold. Harry looked across the room to the clock on the mantelpiece. Six forty five. He went to the bathroom. A cool shower washed away the residue of fatigue. Shivering, he dressed quickly, looking at his reflection in the mirror. He knotted his tie. *Acceptable I suppose.* He'd have to pull himself together, otherwise Edge would kick him out of the Service or put him behind a desk for the rest of his career. The latter prospect filled him with dread. He was no Edge. He'd rather leave than be a desk-jockey.

He arrived at work to find an in-tray overflowing with new files to be checked, and the out-tray empty. He anticipated the tedium of the morning ahead. He gazed out of the window to the city beyond. Concrete, brick and steel met his gaze, a stark contrast to the lush rolling hills of Dereham. He felt as if he'd left a part of himself there. *Pull yourself together.* He reached for the first file in the tray. As he opened the buff folder, his heart sank. It wasn't, as he had expected, another file on another applicant. It was, instead, his report on the Dereham assignment. Edge's thin, spidery writing was all over it.

He felt a hand on his shoulder. Looking up, he found Mary, Edge's secretary, smiling down at him.

'Off with the fairies again, Harry?' Mary asked.

Harry gave her a blank look. She reached across and removed a sheet of paper from his typewriter, and handed it to him.

'I put this there so you'd see it first thing. But you're obviously so conscientious you only have eyes for your in-tray.' She lowered her voice. 'I'd act on this right away, Harry.'

He read the brief note. *Please see Edge as soon as you get in.*

Harry sighed. 'What have I done now?' he asked, his voice heavy.

'I don't know. He's keeping this very close to his chest. Better get it over with, eh? Watch your back.'

Harry knocked at the door to Edge's office. Harry had been expecting the usual barked *Come in*, but to his surprise, the door was opened by a thoughtful looking Edge. 'Get your sorry arse in here now!' he said gruffly.

Edge moved behind the large oak desk, and sat in a leather chair. He ran a hand through his short hair. When Edge spoke, Harry was again surprised. Harry had been prepared for a tirade; instead, Edge simply said, 'Sit down, Harry. This isn't going to be pleasant. Not for me, at least.'

Harry did as he was told. Either Edge was keeping his temper under control, or things had gone far beyond a simple mauling.

'I think I need to apologise to you,' Edge said. He picked up a folder, opened it, read nothing, closed it, and then straightened it on his desk. He didn't normally fidget, Harry knew. 'You see,' Edge continued, 'until about ten minutes ago, I was going to kick you out of the Service.' He paused, and tapped the folder. 'But, after this landed on my desk, I reconsidered. It's an analysis from the psych boys. I might have made a bad call. Perhaps I should have told you about Miss Shepherd as soon as knew what happened.'

Edge had, of course, become aware of Peta's death while Harry had been assigned to the boring watchman job in Slough. Edge had thought it best not to trouble Harry with the news. Harry had already rowed with Edge about that. Perhaps that was why Edge had assigned him to tedious desk jobs.

'But, I have to say,' Edge continued, 'you aren't exactly helping yourself with the stunt you pulled yesterday afternoon.'

Harry was confused. An apology from Edge was one thing, but the man now appeared to be talking in riddles. 'I'm sorry, sir... Yesterday afternoon? I don't quite follow you.'

Edge handed Harry a glossy, eight-by-ten, black and white photograph. Harry studied it. The photograph was pin-sharp. It showed him shaking hands with Leonard Stone on the pavement outside *The Purple Parrot*. Then he remembered it was *Peta's* now.

'As far as we're concerned,' Edge said, 'the Dereham case has been closed. But other agencies are still taking a close interest in Mr Stone and his activities.'

'Six?' Harry asked.

'Possibly. But this comes from our friends across the pond. They have asked for my comments. It seems, Harry, you might have inadvertently kicked over a hornet's nest.'

'The Yanks are keeping Stone under surveillance? Why?'

Edge cleared his throat, and moved the folder around the desk again. 'I've done a little digging. It would appear that Mr Stone has a new woman in his life. Emily Freeman. Nominally, a literary agent–'

Harry interrupted him. 'Emily Freeman? Ed Freeman's daughter?'

'That's the one. I take it you did some extra-curricular reading while in Dereham.'

'Peta had Freeman's book. *Panlyrae–A Message for Mankind* it was called. I read it while I was staying at the cottage. Somehow, the book seemed to be involved in what was happening to Peta. And to Stone. Didn't Emily Freeman send her father's notes to Stone after his death?'

'Yes, she did. Much to the disappointment of our allies.' Edge now fiddled with a pen. 'But there's more to Miss Freeman than meets the eye. She was also a United States Air Force officer, with connections to the security services in the States.

'CIA? FBI?'

Edge shrugged. 'Who knows? Whatever her status, and whomever she ultimately worked for, it seems that whatever was in her father's notes should *not* have been handed willy-nilly to Stone. Our trans-Atlantic cousins are, it seems, a bit twitchy regarding certain security issues relating to those notes.'

'So, why don't they just steal them?'

'Och, do you think they haven't tried? But Stone is a canny lad. Wherever those notes are, they aren't at his club.'

'His house?'

'He doesn't have a house. He lives at the club.'

Of course. Harry remembered now what Peta had told him. A dismal bedsit had adjoined Stone's office in the club.

'But what has this to do with me?' Harry wondered. 'I

admit going to the club, I wanted to see it for myself, and meet Stone if I could. He had been important to Peta.' Harry looked at the photograph again. 'So the Yanks know all our movements?'

Edge gave a rare laugh. 'No. They do not know *our* movements, Harry. They know *yours*. They don't know you work here, and I'm not going to tell them. What I *am* going to do, instead, is send you back under cover. I want you to get close to Stone, and find out why those sneaky bastards are so interested in him.'

'Because of the notes Emily Freeman sent him, surely?'

Edge's scepticism came out in a sharp little laugh. 'Hah! The deranged ravings of an alcoholic alien contactee? Why would that be important?'

'Somebody wanted to know what Peta knew,' Harry reminded Edge.

'And I don't have to remind you I thought that chasing after Miss Shepherd would be pointless. No, there's something going on here. And I won't have the Yanks working on *our* patch without *my* consent. There's something weird about this.'

'Well, I do like field-work, as you know,' Harry said. He felt excited about going back into the field.

'I thought you'd like the idea. But, Harry, note this. You'll be on your own out there. You'll report only to me. If the Americans suss you out, I'll deny all knowledge of this. You'll be a deranged civilian seeking an answer to Peta's death. Which, let's face it, you nearly were.' He paused for a moment, looked into Harry's eyes. 'Perhaps still are.'

Harry would not gainsay him.

Edge leaned back in his chair, placed his hands behind his head. 'As I said a few minutes ago, I made a bad decision in sending you back to work. I should have given you some time off, time to get over her, time to grieve. The girl, Peta...

I didn't realise how close you'd got to her. She was obviously deeply disturbed, and you genuinely wanted to help her. But all I'm interested in is what the Yanks are interested in. This is a personal thing for the two of us. I need someone I can trust, someone the Yanks don't know. And you, I think, need closure on Peta Shepherd.'

Harry nodded. 'Yes, I do.'

'For what it's worth, I'm sorry about how the Dereham job turned out. But I must warn you, this is not a chance to seek revenge, or retribution, or absolution, or whatever other nonsense you have in your head.'

'No, of course not,' Harry said.

Edge rose from his chair. 'Right, get down to Documents and get a full set of papers drawn up. What did you say your name was when you saw Stone yesterday?'

'Colin Shepherd, Peta's cousin.'

'*Colin* again, eh?' Edge arched an eyebrow at him. 'Do you know why you always choose *Colin?*'

Harry shook his head. 'No, sir.'

Edge tapped the folder in front of him. 'I do. One day, I might tell you.' He let the words sink in. Then he said, 'Right, get some documents in that name, and collect a car from the pool. Nothing flash mind you.'

'I didn't know we had anything flash.'

Harry returned from Documents to find somebody else already at work at his desk, labouring through the folders. All Harry's personal belongings had been moved to a desk nearer Edge's office. The phone on his desk rang. He picked up the receiver.

Edge's voice and demeanour seemed different now. 'Are you settling in okay?' Edge asked.

'I've only just found my new desk.'

'Well, don't take any shite from your new colleagues.' Harry could hear a smile in Edge's voice. 'They're all flash and no shine. I've set the wheels in motion, so get your arse into gear. I'll expect updates on a regular basis.' With that the line went dead.

Harry looked at his new documents. A driving licence, birth certificate, and various other papers. *Colin Harold Shepherd.* He did some paperwork relating to this new case, opening a file, making some notes, and thought about the days ahead. He then went to the car pool, where he picked out a red Ford Cortina. This evening, he would get to know Mr Stone and *Peta's*, the place that had become so important to him since Peta's death.

He was now Colin Shepherd. He wondered, with a mounting feeling of excitement, where this new persona would take him.

2

When the door to *Peta's* opened, Harry was greeted by the round face of Martyn Harris.

'Hello... Martyn?' Harry said.

'Ah, Colin. Nice to meet you again. Come on in. The guv is in his office.'

They walked down the stairs to the club. Martyn's limp was more pronounced today. 'Your leg, Martyn...' he said. 'Are you okay?'

Martyn grimaced. 'It hurts like fuck.'

'Should you be working?'

'When the days grow shorter, damper and colder, the pain gets worse. If I didn't work because my leg hurt, I'd be sitting around from October to February.'

'What happened to it?' Harry knew why Martyn limped, of course; he'd heard about it from Peta.

'I fell off a ladder, and broke it. Funny thing – my leg reminds me of Archibald Franklin Conn. Not that Archie caused me to fall off the ladder. No... But Archie came as quickly as he could when I fell. He soothed me and shushed me while we waited for the ambulance. That's what this leg sometimes reminds me – that even the Archibald Franklin Conns of this world have some humanity in them.' They walked out onto the floor of the club. 'And yet everything that happened... to Peta, to Len, to this club... Everything seems to have happened because of that moment.'

'What do you mean?'

'While I was in hospital, Len relied on Archie to do my jobs. Archie was given too much responsibility, too much freedom. He had easy access to the office and to Len's bedsit.' Martyn shook his head. 'Stupid, stupid.' He looked at Harry. 'Would you like a drink? Tea? Or something stronger?'

'Tea would be great, thanks.'

Martyn took Harry behind the bar, to a small kitchen. He switched the kettle on, and busied himself finding mugs, and milk. 'When Archie first came for his interview, I wasn't sure about him. Even little Peta thought he was a bit too smooth.'

'Yet Mr Stone still employed him?'

'Len believes in second chances. Archie was thrown out of the Army after fiddling accounts. Len had once worked for the Manley Boys - have you heard of them?'

Harry nodded. Of course, Harry had heard of them.

'Len used to run errands, and do a little security work. When Len was provided with the chance to go straight with this club, he grabbed it. He saw something of himself in Archie, I think. He wanted to help another person living at the margins back onto the straight and narrow.'

'Very noble.'

'Len is a good man. Hard, but honest. Of course, not everybody's like Len. Employing Archie set the dominos tumbling. Poor Peta was the last domino to fall. Len still mourns her.'

'We all do.'

'True enough.' Martyn finished making the tea, and handed Harry a mug. He led the way out of the kitchen and back into the club. 'Find yourself a place to sit. I'll fetch the guv.'

Martyn left him. A few moments later, Len came through the door at the side of the bar. He walked over to him and shook his hand. 'Nice to see you, again, Colin.'

'And you, Mr Stone.'

'Len, please.' Len shook a cigarette from a packet, and lit

it. He offered the pack to Harry, who shook his head. For a while, they made small talk. Martyn came back with tea for Len, and sat down with them.

Martyn looked at his watch. 'Trudie's late again,' he said to Len. 'She's spending more and more time with her boyfriend.'

Len sipped his tea. 'That's the guy who plays bass for The Mighty Ones, isn't it?'

Martyn nodded. 'If this carries on, we'll have to fire her.'

'That's your job, Martyn.'

Martyn laughed, and turned to Colin. 'It still boggles me that I have the authority to do such things. Len made me co-owner of the club only a few weeks ago. Me! Co-owner of this club! When Len made me the offer, I jumped at the chance.'

Len smiled. 'You always were a good man, Martyn, and you worked hard. You deserved it.'

'Sometimes I feel overwhelmed, though. All the responsibility! I lack Len's killer instinct.' Martyn smiled at Len.

Harry could see and feel the good-natured relationship between the two men, an amity that wasn't just about the business.

'So,' Harry said, looking around the club. 'Do you own all this?'

'I do. Well, we do. I've paid off my debts.'

Harry knew to whom Len had been indebted. He'd already checked Len's financial status, and Len was, in fact, still in debt; but to the banks. When he talked of paying off debts, it could only be to the Manley Boys. 'Well, I'm impressed,' Harry said. 'Peta gave the impression it was a dive.'

'So much has changed since those days,' Len said.

Martyn laughed. 'Oh, even Len's changed in the last

couple of months. The kaftans are all gone. He's trimmed his hair. He's now the very model of a sharp-suited businessman.'

'Somebody has to meet the bank managers and accountants, the agents and AR men. I can't trust you with them now, can I Martyn?' The gentle ribbing between the two spoke of trust and warmth.

Then the kind of question Harry had expected arose.

'Peta never really spoke of her extended family,' Len said.

This was it, Harry thought. *This is where the lies have to come easily.* 'I'm a cousin on her father's side,' he said. 'My mother is Peta's father's sister. We moved to Kent when I was young.'

'That explains why you don't have a trace of Black Country accent,' Martyn said.

'Yes. Peta's mother and grandmother were from Yorkshire, of course.'

'She loved her grandmother,' Len remembered.

'Yes. Sadly, Granny Shepherd died a few months ago.'

That was the first statement that by Martyn or Len could check – and it would stand up. Harry had already researched Peta's family.

'I'm sorry to hear that,' Len said.

'Did you see much of Peta?' Martyn asked.

'When we very young, yes. But... There was a falling out. You see, nobody in the Spencer family liked Peta's father. And even the Shepherd's weren't that keen on him to be honest. My own mother supported Peta's mother, my aunt, more than she did her brother. My mum said something to Peta's mother about him, and... Well, Peta's mother was very defensive about her husband. Whatever my mum said must have been bad. But nobody talks about it.'

And now, Harry was lying. But he knew, and guessed that Len and Martyn would also know, that there was something happening in Peta's family that had finally driven her away.

'What was she like, when she was young?' Martyn asked. 'Peta, I mean.'

'Oh, Peta was good laugh. She had her hair in pigtails, and was a bit of a tomboy. We used to go to the river and catch sticklebacks, and chase each other through the fields. Little Molly would be there, of course, chasing and running as well, and my sister Sarah. We all had fun. It all probably seems impossibly dreamy and idyllic now, but that's how it was.'

That was how Harry had hoped Peta's life had been, or would have been had he, in fact, been Peta's cousin. And he had lied in this particular way for effect. Harry could see that his words had worked. Both Martyn and Len were misty-eyed, imagining a frolic through the fields in which they had played as little part as she had.

Len dragged on his cigarette. 'How have Peta's family taken the news?'

Harry sighed. 'Because of the... disagreement, we're not close to Peta's parents, I'm afraid.' Harry affected a stuttering, indecisive mien. 'You have to understand... I suppose Peta might have told you something of... but her father...'

Stone nodded. 'Peta told me some of the treatment she'd received from her father over the years. It's not surprising she left home. But she forever worried afterwards that little Molly would become the focus of her father's attentions.'

'We all worried about that, I suppose.' Harry shrugged. 'But what could we do, Len? '

They were interrupted by the arrival of Trudie, the barmaid.

'Let's continue this in my office, shall we? Follow me.'

Len stood and walked towards the door beside the bar.

'I'd better get to work,' Martyn said. 'Nice seeing you again, Colin.'

'You too, Martyn,'

Martyn went behind the bar with Trudie. Harry followed Len through the door. They walked down a short corridor to another door. They entered the office. He noticed a door in the office, painted the same colour as the walls. He guessed that this led to the dingy bedsit that Peta had mentioned.

Len took his seat behind the desk. 'Take a seat, Colin.' Harry sat opposite him. There was sadness now on Len's face. 'You said yesterday that you didn't go to the funeral,' he said.

'No. It was for close family members only. The divisions that run through our families are very deep now. I'm afraid the wounds will never heal.' Harry knew that he could tell some truth now. 'Peta was buried in a Roman Catholic Cemetery just outside Stourbridge. I intend visiting her grave soon. It's the least I can do.'

'Well, that's something I didn't know. So Peta was brought up a Catholic? That might well explain a few things. She was always... spiritual. She took to... what we were trying to do... like a duck to water.'

'Took to what?'

'Peta and I, we–' Len stopped and smiled. 'You'll think we were barking mad.'

'She hinted at something in the letter she sent to me. Communications, contacts, or something like that.'

Len gave a deep sigh. 'Yes. Peta and I were in contact with... aliens, I suppose you'd call them. Either that, or some form of spirit. She was such a natural, that girl. I'd never seen anything like it before, not even when I was out in the East.' Len paused, and then gave Harry a calculating look. 'You're not with the fuzz are you?'

'Good Lord, no,' Harry laughed. 'I think I told you yesterday, I work in the City.'

'That's okay, then. It's just that, to initiate these contacts, I

28

needed to use some strong grass. Not the kind of thing you'd want to admit to the fuzz. Peta, however, could go into a trance at the drop of a hat.'

'And you contacted... something?'

'Yes, we contacted something.'

'Do you still do this?'

'No. I began to lose interest after Peta left.'

'Why did she leave?'

'Oh, she loved her boyfriend, Archie. Did you hear about him?'

Harry shook his head. 'His name was mentioned in the newspaper. What was it... Archie Conn? But her letter... It must have been written before this fling with Archie. Martyn was talking about him while he made the tea. I think he thought I knew about him. Seems you all have a reason to dislike him.'

'Yes. Archibald Franklin Conn. Or, as he's known around here, Archibald Franklin Fucking Conn.' Len smiled ruefully, and shook his head. 'Archie manipulated Peta. He was good. He convinced her to run away to Dereham, to become part of the UFO scene down there. Before they went, Archie stole a huge stash of my grass.'

'Do you think Peta knew what he'd done?'

'For a while, I thought she did. But in the end, changed my mind. I went down to Dereham, after her picture appeared in the *News of the World*.'

Harry acted surprised. 'She was in the papers?' Of course, he knew she had been. He was living with Peta and Archie at the time. His mind conjured up a picture of the living room of the cottage in White Street, on the road to Copsehill, with its view over Derebury Hill and The Tump. Sometimes he strongly missed Dereham.

'Yes. The paper did an article about the UFOs down there.

Her picture was in the paper. It was then I realised where they'd run to. Why I hadn't made the connection before, I don't know.'

'Perhaps you hadn't wanted to.'

Len lit another cigarette. 'Perhaps. Who knows? Anyway, I went down there to find Archie, but he'd already dumped Peta and blown the scene.' Harry noted the phrase. Len might dress like a businessman, but he was still a hippie at heart. 'Peta told me what had happened. I was angry. But she said she didn't know about the stash, and I believed her.'

'You left her there?'

'She left me, sitting in a café, and stormed out in a huff. I came back to London later that day.'

'Did you never visit the town again?'

'A week or so after she died. I went to the hill she always went to, sat on its slopes, and smoked a joint. I relaxed. Copsehill. It's a very beautiful place.'

Harry knew, and felt the pang of loss. 'That must have been sad.'

'It was. But–'

'Yes?'

Len looked a little embarrassed. 'She spoke to me.'

Harry was, for the first time in the conversation, surprised. He didn't have to act. 'She *spoke* to you?'

'You have to remember, Colin, that communicating, contacting, is what we did together. When I smoked dope and relaxed, that's what I was waiting for. But I didn't expect to hear Peta.'

'What did she say?' Harry was intrigued, wanted to know what important message Peta might have delivered.

'Nothing much. It was a trifle. She was just... amusing. Asked me about Emily.'

Harry feigned a blank look.

'Oh, Emily is my girlfriend. Peta said I should marry her.'

'Have you heard her voice again?' Harry wished he could hear her voice, her real voice, not the dream voice that followed him around.

'No. I think I would need to go to Dereham to hear it. And, anyway, it doesn't matter anymore. That one last conversation with her was all I needed.'

'Where did you meet Emily?'

'She's from the States. I met her when she was visiting once. She's in the process of moving over, in fact. We're going to live together. I miss her when she's not around.'

'And what about this Archie? Do you still want to find him?'

'I want to see him. I used to think I'd break his legs. But... I left that world behind me a long time ago. I just want to see him. To confront him with the things he's done.'

You and me both, Harry thought.

Harry was surprised at Edge's choice of meeting place. He had imagined his boss the kind of man to choose one of London's many gentleman's clubs. Instead, Edge had chosen a small bar near Trafalgar Square. When Harry entered, Edge was already there, sitting with his back to a large glass window that looked out over the busy thoroughfare. Edge sat sideways in his seat, looking out of the window at the people scurrying by. Although late in the afternoon, shoppers and tourists scurried by. He caught sight of Harry, and waved him over.

Harry sat opposite his boss. 'This bloody country,' Edge muttered. 'It gets more like the States every year. I sometimes wonder how long it will be before we become a twenty-four hour consumer society. I give it ten years before we're another state of the union.' Edge's dislike of the Americans

31

and their culture was no secret; the cause of this antipathy was unknown. 'And how's it going with you, Harry?'

'I've made contact with Stone,' Harry said. 'He still thinks about Peta Shepherd. She certainly had an affect on people.'

Edge grunted, and studied Harry. 'How true that is,' he said. He raised his hand and called a waiter over. 'Scotch for me ... And for you?'

'Coffee.'

Edge pulled a face. 'This isn't the continent you know. You can have some alcohol if you want. '

Harry looked up at the waiter, who was hovering at a respectful distance. 'Just a coffee thanks. Strong, only a little milk.'

'Suit yourself.' Edge grumbled. Edge waited until the waiter had moved away to the bar. 'This meeting is totally off the record, of course.' Harry nodded. 'So, have you met this Freeman girl yet?'

Harry frowned. 'No. She's on her way back from the States as we speak. I got the impression from Stone... no, from Martyn Harris, Stone's assistant, that she was finalising a permanent move over here. I might well see her the next time I go to the club.'

'Good. Get close to the pair of them. Get their trust. My opposite number in Six tells me that *something* is going on. This girl seems to be important to *somebody* in the American government. I wish I knew why. My contact tells me that some Yanks are looking at this almost as if she's defecting to a hostile foreign power. So the CIA may well feel emboldened to operate in this country without official sanction. I cannot, and will not, allow that.'

The drinks arrived, and Edge took a sip of his scotch, pulling a face. 'Cheap foreign shite, probably brewed in Japan. Cheeky sods charge full price for it, too. Perhaps I should have gone for a coffee as well.'

32

Harry was puzzled. 'Are you concerned about Emily Freeman?'

Edge shifted in his chair, and lowered his voice, making it difficult for Harry to hear what he was saying over the general hubbub of the bar. 'You know, she's a bit of a mystery that woman. I've done some more digging. Officially, she was nothing more than a public relations officer in the United States Air force. But her rank was *lieutenant*. A high rank for what is, essentially, a civilian position. In addition, she only worked part-time. It's all very odd.'

'Perhaps she's in love, and has genuinely resigned so she can live with Stone,' Harry pointed out.

'But I need to know. And that's your job.'

Harry thought for a moment. 'I can't be sure that I'll ever get close enough to Stone and Freeman. Although I'm pretending to be Peta's cousin that might not be enough to gain Len's trust.'

'What happens if an actual member of Shepherd's family comes down to London also looking for Stone? Your deception could fall apart.'

Harry smiled. 'I learned a lot of things while undercover with her, of course.'

'Of course,' Edge conceded.

'The chances of another relative turning up are very slim. Peta had severed all ties with her family, except for her grandmother. Peta's mother and sister had moved away and, as far as I know, the father is well out of the equation. The grandmother died a few months ago. Becoming a relative seemed the best way of getting close to Stone. I knew Peta well enough. I have enough background knowledge to keep up the deception. I can find out more, if required.'

'Just don't take any unnecessary risks. I'm out on a limb here. My neck will be on the block if it all goes wrong. If my

33

neck is for the chopping block, yours will follow soon after. You get my drift, Harry?'

'Crystal clear, sir.'

'Right, so what do you propose to do next? Nothing rash I hope?'

'As a matter of fact, it is rash, sir. I intend suggesting to Stone that we visit Peta's grave.'

Edge shook his head. 'Is that wise?'

'I need to gain Stone's trust. He's never visited the grave. By taking him there, I hope he'll begin to think of me as a friend.'

Edge sighed. 'Do you think this will work?'

'Of course it will.' Harry wished he felt as confident as he sounded.

Len Stone parked his Austin 1100 in the Heathrow Airport car park. He was an hour early. Emily's flight didn't land until 13.45, and it would be at least another three-quarters of an hour before she could clear customs. For the first time in months, he felt nervous. Not the kind of anxiety he would once feel when meeting the Manley Boys, or when brokering a deal for the club. This was different. A jitteriness that was almost *pleasant*.

He remembered when he first met Emily, over a year ago now. She had been babysitting her father, Ed Freeman, during a book-signing for the reissue of *Panlyrae–A Message for Mankind*. Len had, of course, gone to Foyle's to get his book signed. He'd been surprised when Emily had talked to him, a silly conversation about a book dealer he knew; that she already knew who he was added to his surprise. He was even more mystified when she later asked to meet him at the Carlton Hotel.

At the signing, Len could see that Ed Freeman was unwell; that he was a heavy drinker had been obvious. Soon after

Emily and her father had returned to the States, Freeman's damaged liver finally failed. He slipped into a coma and died a week later. Emily was alone. Her mother had committed suicide when she was young, and her brother, Ed Jr., had dropped out and followed the hippie trail. She sometimes received postcards from him, from somewhere exotic like Marrakesh or Afghanistan or India; but she hadn't seen him for years.

Emily had contacted Stone a few days after the funeral, and a telephone friendship had ensued. A month or so later, she had been sent over to England on official Air Force business, and they had met up. Within a few days they had slept together. After a few weeks, they both knew they were in love.

As the lift doors opened into the arrivals area, Len remembered the night when Emily had decided to move to England. She had been lying in his arms and talking of the future. Her life in the States was heading nowhere, she said. She should resign her job and move in with Len. The idea had excited them both, and they spent the rest of the night planning their new life together.

Len checked the arrivals board, and noted that her flight was ten minutes ahead of schedule and would land at 13.35. He smiled; his new life with Emily would start ten minutes earlier than expected. He went to the airport café, bought a paper and a coffee, and sat down in a quiet corner. He lit up a cigarette. Emily didn't approve of his smoking, his only vice these days; he'd made her a promise that he'd try to give it up. He scanned the paper. He smiled when he found an article story about the Dereham UFOs on one of the feature pages. He read it with interest, and was unsurprised to see Peta's name, and Richard Patterson's. The article writer had tried to connect Peta's death with a 'UFO cult'. Patterson was quoted in the article. No, he said, there was nothing mysterious about Peta's death; she had committed suicide because she had been depressed about splitting up with her boyfriend. Then appeared the name that made Len's skin crawl. Archibald Franklin Conn. The boyfriend who had run away. The past seemed determined to intrude on the present. Len looked at the arrivals board again. Emily was up there, probably stacked in a holding pattern. So near and yet so far away. He needed her with him now.

He looked back at the article, skipped the paragraph about Peta, and found himself becoming absorbed again in the Dereham mystery. He remembered when Peta had first shown him articles about it. She had found those stories so exciting. No wonder Archie had found it so easy to lure her there.

His thoughts were interrupted by an announcement over the Tannoy. Emily's flight had landed. He drained his now cold coffee, and picked up the newspaper. He walked to the arrivals gate and took a seat. His eyes never left the doors that led from customs; he willed the time to go faster. Half an hour dragged by; then, finally, the first passengers began to filter through. Each time the doors opened, Len's heart missed a beat. More and more people came through, but there was still no sign of Emily. Soon, the numbers began to dwindle; there was an emptiness in his stomach; he felt like a teenager again, stood up on a first date.

Another fifteen minutes passed. Len was on the verge of checking with the airline to see if Emily had boarded the flight. Then the doors opened again. His heart skipped beats, absurd butterflies lolloped in his belly. She was there, just as he remembered her – the full figure, the round face, the snub nose, the blue eyes, the full lips. She didn't look happy. He rushed to greet her. 'You know, I was beginning to think you'd bailed mid-Atlantic.'

She gave a weak smile. 'No way, lover boy! I'm here for the long haul. I'm goddamn pissed at your customs boys, though. They weren't exactly welcoming. Seems I drew the short straw...' Emily finally smiled and dropped her hand luggage to the floor. She threw hers arms around Len. She whispered in his ear. 'Sorry, Len. How I've missed you!'

He hugged her tightly to him. Emily was here. Here to stay. With *him*. 'Come on, let's get back. I've a little surprise for you.' He picked up her heaviest bags, and steered her towards the exit.

The traffic was heavy on the roads around the airport. Stone glanced across at Emily. Her eyes were closed, and he assumed she was dozing, the jet lag catching up with her. He concentrated on the road ahead. When she finally spoke, it was slowly, thoughtfully. 'Y'know – maybe I'm being paranoid, but I really think those customs goons were on the look-out for me. I think I was the only person on that flight who was searched.'

Len glanced across at her. 'Perhaps you *are* paranoid – but then again, perhaps not. After all, until a couple of weeks ago you were on the payroll of the United States Air Force. Perhaps Uncle Sam wants to make sure you haven't taken any secret documents away with you.'

Emily lapsed back into silence.

Half an hour later, Len parked the 1100 in the street in front of a smart, pre-war, semi-detached house in Hayes. Emily's eyes were still closed. Without a word, he exited the car, and walked around to Emily's side. Len opened the door quietly, and gently shook her awake. 'We're here, Emily, we're home.'

Emily opened her eyes, and spoke sleepily. 'Back at the club already? That didn't take long.'

'No, not the club.'

Emily sat forward. Len could see her looking at the tree-lined street with wide eyes. 'This ain't no club, Len Stone. What are we doing here?'

'Welcome to British suburban life. I thought a new life required a new home. Let me carry you over the threshold.'

'Carry me?' Emily said. 'We're not even married! There'll be no carrying until we're married!'

Len took Emily's hand, helped her from the car, and then led her down a short crazy-paving path to a house with a dark blue door onto which the brass numbers 38 were screwed.

'Where are we?' Emily asked.

'South Avenue, Hayes. We're just a train ride from the centre of the city. Now I'm a respectable businessman, I thought I'd better start acting like one. So, while you were away, I went house-hunting. Fell in love with this place as soon as I saw it.' He took a set of keys out of his pocket, and handed them over to her. 'Go on, open the door.'

She took the offered key. 'Len, you did all this...for *me*?'

Len held her free hand. 'No. For *us*.'

Emily placed the key in the lock, and turned it. The door opened on to an ornately tiled hall, with rooms off to the left. At the end of the hall was a kitchen. On the right was a wooden staircase. Hesitantly, she moved inside the house. Len quietly closed the door behind him. The sun shone through the stained glass windows of the front door, bathing the hall in diffuse light. Len moved past Emily, and opened the first panelled door on the left. 'This is the living room.' He moved along the hall, and opened the second door. 'This will be the dining room. The door under the stairs leads to a dry cellar. And ahead, as you can see, is the kitchen. The house needs some sprucing up, but with my contacts, it won't take long.'

Emily's silence confounded Len. 'You do like it, don't you?'

She looked at him then, and Len saw the tears in her eyes. 'Len! It's... it's... Wonderful! Thank you.' She put her arms around him, and her lips met his. Then she pulled away and smiled at him. 'Now, you'd better show me where the bedrooms are...'

She took Len by the hand and, laughing, pulled him towards the staircase.

Edge was in his office, dictating a letter to Mary when the telephone rang. Irritated by the interruption, he picked up the receiver and barked into it. 'Yes?' When he learned the name of the caller, he said, 'Please hold a moment.' He dismissed Mary with a gesture. Once the door had closed behind her, Edge spoke again. 'Well... Did you search her?'

'We did as you instructed, sir. All her luggage was taken from her, and opened. We checked through it thoroughly. We X-rayed the contents, and the suitcases themselves. We found nothing out of the ordinary.'

'Was she met by anyone?'

'Indeed she was. Based on the photographs you sent us, I would say she was met by Mr Stone. I had them tailed after they left the airport. I hope I did right, Mr Edge.'

'You did. Are they home now?'

'Yes sir. Not at the club you mentioned, though. They went to a house in Hayes. Lots of lovey-dovey on the doorstep.'

'Thank you.' Edge replaced the receiver. 'Damn!' he said to the empty room. He ran his fingers through his hair. This had not been what he expected to hear. The girl, it seemed, was clean. Why had the Yanks let this woman go so easily, yet remain interested in her enough to set a watch in this country? Something didn't feel right.

3

When Harry arrived at *Peta's*, the door to the club was unlocked. It was a bright autumn Saturday, and the street and the club looked less grim in the sunshine. He pushed the door open. It was early afternoon, and clubs like this came alive at night. Somebody was already working. Harry suspected it would be Martyn Harris. As he walked down the stairs, he could hear raised voices. The loudest, he could tell by the accent, was Martyn's. He stopped at the closed double doors that led onto the floor of the club and listened to the argument that was taking place inside.

'You're supposed to give me a week's notice!'

The second voice was female. He remembered it – the barmaid, Trudie. 'I've told you, I'm finishing at the end of this shift, and that's that!'

'But look, if it wasn't for this club, you'd never have met Dave!' Martyn's tone became conciliatory. 'I understand you want to go on tour with him, and that's fine. But surely a week won't make any difference, will it?'

The girl's voice grew softer. Harry strained to hear what she said next. 'Oh, Martyn, I've given this a lot of thought. The tour is going to be a real blast! I'm sorry, but my mind is made up. I love Dave. I'm going with him *today*.'

Martyn laughed. 'Love! What do you know about love? Twenty years of age, and you think you know it all.' His voice softened. 'All right, Trudie. Who am I to stand in the way of young love? I envy you a little. Touring around Europe sounds fun. I'll get your wages drawn up at the end of trading tonight. Although what Len's going to say, I don't know.'

Harry took that as his cue to make an entrance. He opened one of the heavy double doors and called out cheerfully. 'Good afternoon!'

Martyn looked over. 'Good afternoon, Colin. What brings you back here?'

'I like the look of your club, Martyn. How much does it cost to get in?'

'Hah, you probably wouldn't have thought it was so nice a couple of years back. It's a quid a night. If you think you'll be popping in every weekend, then you'd best become a member. You pay a flat fee and that's it. Works out cheaper than paying on the night each time. We're usually open Friday, Saturday and Sunday, and sometimes one night during the week, depending on the bands.'

'I think I'll join up, then. Has your clientele changed much since you improved the place?'

'Not so much, really. We get a few more businessmen, like you, than we used to. And some members of less well-known bands. But it's mainly weekend hippies, if you know what I mean.'

'Also a bit like me,' Harry said.

'I wouldn't like to pass judgment,' Martyn said with wry smile. 'Hang on there while I get some forms for you to fill in.' He left the bar through a door that opened into the corridor to Len's office. Harry watched through the safety glass in the door from the dance floor as Martyn limped down the corridor.

Harry moved to the bar, which Trudie was preparing for the evening. 'Too early for a drink then?' He gave her his best smile, hoping that the girl would open up to him.

'I'm afraid so.'

'Have you worked here long?'

'A year and a bit. Since the girl before left... Peta.' Trudie looked up Harry sharply, frowning. 'Oh, you're Colin, aren't you. You're her cousin. I heard Martyn and Len talking about you yesterday.'

'I hope it was all good.'

Trudie looked away. 'Yes, I think so. I didn't hear much that was said to be honest.'

'So do you like it here?'

'Oh yes. Len and Martyn are good people. I'm going to miss this place. This is my last shift, Colin. I'm leaving tonight. My *boyfriend*, well, he's in a rock group, The Mighty Ones. Have heard of them?'

Harry nodded. He knew nothing about them, but wanted to maintain rapport with Trudie.

'Well,' Trudie continued, 'they've been offered a European tour supporting one of the big rock bands. Dave, my boyfriend that is, wants me to go with him. Problem is, it's a last minute arrangement, and they leave the day after tomorrow.'

'Now that is too good a chance to miss. You go for it.'

The girl smiled at him. 'Yes, Martyn said he envied me.'

Harry was gaining her confidence. 'Despite what people think, being in the insurance business doesn't pay that well, especially for clerical oiks like me. I did a little bar work back home when I was a student. I could fill the breach until the bosses get a full-time replacement.'

Trudie's eyebrows knitted together. 'I don't know. I'll be honest with you, I did hear a bit more yesterday. Martyn's a friendly bloke, even if he does sometimes look like he's chewing a wasp, but I have to say, he's got a bee in his bonnet about you. Have you done something to upset him?'

Harry shook his head. 'I don't think so.' Harry was surprised that Martyn, who had appeared so affable, had taken against him. 'I've only met him twice.' Harry couldn't remember saying anything untoward on either occasion they had met.

His thoughts were interrupted by the doors from the stairs opening. Len breezed in. He held the hand of a woman who walked confidently beside him. That, Harry thought, must be Emily Freeman.

'Colin, good to see you again', Len said. 'Trudie, get the man a drink.' He smiled. He seemed happy. That, Harry thought, was the obvious effect of having Emily Freeman next to him.

'Thanks, Len,' Harry said. 'I'll have a G and T.' He had surprised himself by asking for a gin and tonic. There was something of the gin and tonic drinker about Colin Shepherd, Harry supposed.

'I'll have a scotch,' Len said.

'And I'll have a bourbon,' Emily said, in an easy American drawl. It had been months since Harry had read the book Peta had lent him, the book written by Emily's father, and he couldn't remember where in the US she'd grown up.

'Colin, I'd like to introduce you to Emily Freeman.'

Harry shook her hand. 'Pleased to meet you, Miss Freeman.'

Len took a swig of his scotch. 'Now, what brings you here again, Colin?'

Harry smiled his winning smile. 'Well, I like the look of your club, Len. I thought I'd sign up.'

Len smiled back. 'Not as square as you look, then?'

'Oh, no. I like discovering new bands.' Perhaps then, Harry thought, he might actually find out what The Mighty Ones sounded like.

Martyn came out of the door beside the bar.

'Here're the membership forms,' he said to Harry. He nodded at Len. 'Hello, guv.' He leaned over and kissed Emily on the cheek. 'Always a pleasure to see you again, Emily.'

Emily laid a hand on Martyn's arm. 'And you Martyn. And we'll be seeing much more of each other from now on.'

'I'm looking forward to it.'

Len looked at Harry. 'Emily has moved from the States to live with me.' He also kissed Emily's cheek. 'I'm so happy.'

'You look it,' Harry said.

'I've even bought a new house in the suburbs. I must be growing up.'

Emily rubbed Len's arm affectionately. 'You can buy a house for us, Len, but don't grow up.'

Len laughed, and looked into her eyes. There was love there, Harry could see it. He wondered if Len had put Peta firmly in his past. Would his plan to tempt Len to Peta's grave work now that Emily was here? At least Trudie's decision to follow her Dave to Europe had provided Harry with a way into the club. Working at *Peta's* would enable him to get closer to Len and Emily.

Martyn quickly brought the subject up. 'Len mate, Trudie's leaving us.'

'When?'

Trudie industriously wiped the top of the bar, and refused to meet Len's eye.

'Tonight,' Martyn said.

Len directed himself towards Trudie. 'What about your notice, love?'

Trudie looked at Len sheepishly and explained the situation.

Len smiled. 'You're in *love?*' he said. 'Then, of course, you must go Trudie, you *must*. I can't stand in the way of love when I'm a fool for it myself.'

Trudie lit the room with a broad smile. 'Thanks, Len. I'll miss this old place. And you and Martyn.'

'When you get back, look us up. We might be in need of a barmaid again.'

'I will, Len. But hopefully Dave will be stinking rich by then.' Trudie at last stopped polishing the bar top and went to the kitchen, humming happily.

'So we'll need somebody behind the bar tomorrow,' Len said. 'Better get onto the agencies, Martyn.'

Harry spoke quickly. 'No, wait, hold on Martyn.'

Martyn paused, one hand on the chrome handle of the door to the corridor. Harry explained about his lowly job, and how he'd worked as a barman before.

'That sounds ideal,' Len said.

Martyn rubbed his cheek and ummed-and-ahhed.

'What's the problem, Martyn?' Len asked.

'I'm not sure, guv.'

Len looked at Harry, then at Martyn. 'Let's all go to my office to discuss this.'

Len sat behind his desk. 'So, what's the problem, Martyn?'

Martyn sat in the chair on the other side of the desk to Len. He glanced at Harry. 'Don't take offence, Colin,' he said. He looked at Len. 'He's a Shepherd for chrissakes! Remember what happened last time?' He turned and looked at Harry, who sat on the sofa that was pushed against the wall. 'Sorry mate.'

Len fiddled with a pencil. 'All right, Martyn. I understand. But let's face facts.' He began to count off on his fingers. 'One. Trudie *is* leaving. Neither of us wants to stop her, right?' Martyn shook his head. 'Two. We need a replacement, quickly. Three. Colin might be related to a Shepherd, but I don't think he'll run off with our doorman, as we don't have one, or need one these days.' Len smiled mischievously. 'Unless, of course, you have designs on him yourself?'

Martyn's eyes widened. 'Bad joke, Len.'

Len looked genuinely sorry. 'Apologies, Martyn.'

Harry understood the unspoken implication. Martyn was a homosexual. *Well, that's one for the files then. Chalk one up for me, Edge. There's something you didn't know.*

Len attempted a compromise. 'Look, I promise I'll find a replacement as soon as possible. After all, this club is really happening right now. We'll have no problem filling the position. But it is the weekend, and we probably won't get a replacement until at least Monday. With Colin working here, we won't need to give the job to the first person who comes along. We all liked Trudie, right? And she was good with the punters. I'd like to replace her with somebody as sharp as she was. I reckon a week or two, tops. How does that sound to you?'

Martyn shrugged. 'OK, one week,' he said. There was reluctance in his voice. Harry would have to mollify Martyn.

Len smiled. 'Good. Harry, get yourself a drink from the bar, on the house. It may be your last chance.'

Harry left the office, making sure that as the door swung behind him, the latch didn't catch. He glanced back at it to check that it was slightly ajar. It was. He walked a few paces along the corridor with a heavy step, then turned and walked quietly back to the door where he stood, holding his breath. From where he was standing, he could just see Martyn, who had now moved to the sofa.

'I still don't like it, Len. That family is bad news. Peta really screwed you up. Now another member of that family turns up.'

Emily, who had been leaning against the wall, behind Len, spoke for the first time. 'You mean he's related to Peta Shepherd? Man, that's well weird!'

Martyn grunted in reply. 'Bloody cursed by 'em, that's what we are. I tell you, it'll end in trouble.'

'But, hey, come on, folks,' Emily laughed. 'He seems, so...

nice. Quite normal in fact. A bit square for my liking, but you know...' Harry saw her for a moment, as she moved beside Len. At least Emily and Len were on his side. He would have to charm Martyn.

Harry walked down the corridor stealthily, and opened and closed the door at the end quietly. He popped his head around the corner and found Trudie back behind the bar, refreshing the spirits in their optics. He smiled at her.

'Have you got the job?' Trudie said.

'I think so. Len said I could have a drink.'

'Another G and T, Colin?'

'Yes, please.'

Trudie handed him his drink. Then she leaned in towards him, her elbows on the bar, speaking quietly. 'I'll tell you something. I came in as Peta's replacement. Len was in a hell of a state when she left with that Archie bloke. When she died... he was almost beside himself. He blamed himself for what happened to her.'

'It wasn't his fault though, was it? There was nothing he could have done.'

'No, of course not. But for a while, he didn't see it that way.'

The doors to the club opened and some people wandered in.

'Excuse me,' Trudie said. 'I'll have to do some work.'

Harry took a sip of his gin and tonic. He didn't really like it that much. He would have preferred a scotch. But this was Colin's drink. He moved to a table near the stage. Everything was, he thought, coming together nicely; he was getting closer to Len and learning about the relationships between Martyn, Len, Archie and Peta. Soon, to keep Edge happy, he would have to have to get close to Emily Freeman and find out why the US secret services were so interested in her. For the moment, there was little else he could do. He leaned back in his chair, and watched the people begin to trickle in. He indulged himself in his favourite hobby. People watching.

4

He lay flat on his stomach, underneath a large bush, a rhododendron he seemed to remember, at the edge of the lawn. The light rain had now stopped, and although he'd been out here, hiding, watching the house for two days now, he didn't feel the cold or damp. He had closely watched the occupants of the house over the last forty-eight hours. The male left at eight in the morning, and returned just after five-thirty in the evening. The woman left at nine, dressed in riding gear, and came back just after eleven. She then spent the rest of the day either pottering around the large and expansive garden, or walking the two Labrador dogs. *Nice life if you can get it*, he mused.

He knew today was the day to act. He had until five thirty at least to get into the house. He checked his watch. It was now just after three in the afternoon. The woman had returned from walking the dogs about half an hour ago, and wouldn't go out again. From his vantage point, he could see her working in the large conservatory, already setting the table for the evening meal. The dogs were housed in the large kennel near the swimming pool, out from under her feet.

He raised the binoculars to his eyes, and carefully scanned he house and gardens, then studied the long gravelled drive that sloped down from the lane beyond. The house sat in a natural bowl. He sometimes wondered if that accounted for the cold and damp that were distinct childhood memories. From his vantage point on the rim of the bowl he checked

49

the lane at the head of the drive in both directions. He'd done this regularly throughout the afternoon. He'd seen only three cars pass in the last hour. Probably rich mothers and nannies, he thought, collecting brats from school. Everything was coming together. He felt a thrill in his stomach; the anticipation of what was to come quickened his senses.

He packed his binoculars and flask into his knapsack, and stealthily moved to the small copse to one side of the house where he'd made his camp among the trees. There had been no coppicing here since his father had died. The woodland was thick with vegetation, and no paths had been made through it. He took a different route to his camp each time so that he would leave no obvious trail to his hiding place. He reached into his tent, and removed the items he needed. He picked up a bottle of cola he'd bought yesterday, and took a swig. The cola was flat and tasteless. He felt stale and sweaty. He needed a bath. He would be able to have one later, and he looked forward to it.

He put the rope and gaffer tape into his knapsack. He waited another ten minutes, breathing slowly, replaying a Bach cantata in his mind. Then he slipped on a pair of thin driving gloves, and stood.

He made his way quietly through the copse, towards the house. He approached the garden at the house as stealthily as he could; still the dogs began to bark. The kitchen door opened. He stopped behind a tree. The woman called out 'Buster! Archie! Shut up! Dinner won't be long!'

Archie! Bloody hell. He was so going to enjoy this. He smiled as he heard the door slam shut. The dogs quieted for a moment, but as he walked through the gate into the back garden, the dogs started their noise again. He walked to the back door, and knocked on it. The woman opened the door. He could hear a radio crackling in the background.

Reception here had always been bad, he remembered, because of the surrounding hills.

The woman's voice was plummy, revealing no trace of her Welsh upbringing. 'Yes, can I help you?'

She sounded bored, as if waiting to rid herself of a salesman, or a beggar. He probably looked like a tramp, he thought. Then, she finally studied the man in front of her. He saw recognition dawning. The stubbly, unshaven face and the unwashed, unkempt hair couldn't hide who he was. Not to her. 'Oh, my God!' she finally said. 'Archie!'

Archibald Franklin Conn smiled back at her. 'Hello, sis. Long time, no see.' He punched her hard and square on the nose. She fell backwards, against a kitchen table and a chair, and then to the floor, cracking her head on the red quarry tiles. He knelt down beside her. Her nose was already bleeding profusely. He took her head and shoulders in his arms. She opened heavy eyelids and moaned. 'Archie? What are you...'

Archie smiled down at her, and tightened his arms. 'I can't say it's pleasant to see you again, you hideous bitch.' With a short, savage twist, he broke her neck.

Archie moved the dead woman to the kitchen table, and sat the body of his oldest sibling in one of the heavy wooden chairs, with her back to the kitchen door. He pulled her head back and cleaned the blood from around her nose and mouth with his handkerchief. Once he was happy with the position of the body, he went out of the kitchen and across the hallway into the living room.

He looked around him. Little had changed since his father had died. Archie could hardly believe eighteen months had passed since then. The same faded flock *fleur de lys* wallpaper, which was once a vibrant red but had now faded to a shade of brown; the mahogany inlaid settee that had tea stains on the fabric and cigarette burns on the side rails. He crossed the room to the heavy, pre-war armchair in the corner. He pulled it to one side. He lifted the rug it had been sitting on and threw it onto the chair. There, set into the floor, was the family safe. It was the same old safe, and, he hoped, the same old combination.

He turned the dial on the door backwards and forwards, stopping at the numbers he remembered. There was, finally, a satisfying mechanical *thunk*. He pulled the heavy door of the safe up and open. A smile creased his face. The safe was packed to the top with neatly bundled bank notes of every denomination. Just like dad, he thought. *Money for a rainy day. But it always fucking rains in Wales, and they never spent any of it.* He slipped the knapsack from his shoulder. He took from it the rope and gaffer tape and placed them on the coffee table. He stuffed the notes into the knapsack until they reached the top. He wished he'd bought another bag with him. He didn't want to take one from the house. He wanted everything in the house to remain as it should be, with one or two exceptions. At the bottom of the safe he found a service revolver, and two boxes of bullets. He put these on top of the notes in his bag. He then slammed shut door of the safe shut, and spun the dial.

'Now, where would they keep their wills?' he muttered to himself. Against the wall was an ancient bureau. His father would pull down the walnut front and write a cheque there, or sit on the teak and leather campaign chair and write a letter to one of his Army *chums*. Archie opened the bureau, and searched the small shelves built into it. Nothing but old letters, cheque books, and bric-a-brac. He began to rifle through the drawers. He soon found the two unsealed brown envelopes that contained the wills. He read them quickly, and realised that, of course, both his brother and sister continued to acknowledge his existence by ignoring it; his name was in neither document. He wasn't surprised – there had been no provision for him in his father's will, either. He took two similar envelopes from his coat pocket, and placed them in the drawer in which he had found the wills. Cultivating a bent solicitor had been worth the money.

He could forge his brother's signature perfectly, but as a precaution he'd left his sister's *new* will unsigned. He found a number of documents in the bureau that had her signature on them, and spent the next half an hour practising her lazy scrawl, until he was happy with the result. He signed his sister's fake will with a flourish. He screwed up the sheets of paper on which he'd practiced, and then picked up the original wills. At the far end of the living room was a fireplace that still contained the ashes of the previous night's fire. He knelt down and put the pieces of paper and the wills into it, struck a match, and set fire to the pile of paper. He watched the papers burn. When only black and grey ashes remained, dancing in the draft being drawn up the chimney, he raked them into the dark gritty remains of last night's coal and wood. He stood and looked at his watch. He still had about an hour until Giles returned home. He decided to have the bath he'd promised himself.

As Archie dried himself, he looked out of the bedroom window at the garden. All of this would be his. Once he'd disposed of Giles, and played the part of the grieving brother, he planned to sell it all – the house, the antiques – and cash in any bonds and insurance policies. He would live the high life. He regretted having to put his dirty clothes back on. He thought for a moment of raiding Giles's wardrobe, but thought better of it; there might a cleaner, an *au pair*, a housemaid, who would notice missing clothes. As he returned to the living room, he heard tyres on the gravel of the driveway. Giles had arrived. Archie slid his hands back into his gloves, grabbed the rope and gaffer tape, placed them on top of the gun and money in his knapsack, and then carried the knapsack to the kitchen, where he put it out of view on the floor in the kitchen. He picked up the heavy, black, cast iron doorstop, and hid himself behind the kitchen door that opened onto the hallway. A key scraped into the Yale lock, and the door creaked open.

Then Archie heard the voice of Giles for the first time in a long time. 'Lou! I'm home! Is supper ready yet?'

Giles' footsteps came closer, and then stopped. Archie knew his brother was standing in the doorway, staring at his sister. She still remained in the seat on which Archie had placed her, upright, her back towards the door, although her head now tilted forward, and her chin rested on her chest.

Giles sighed. 'Have you been at the bloody sherry again, you old soak?' He walked into the kitchen. Archie gave one swift blow to his brother's head with the door stop. Giles collapsed to the floor. Archie lifted his brother and dragged him onto another of the chairs by the kitchen table, opposite his dead sister. 'Christ, Giles old lad, I really think you've put on weight.' Archie tied him to the chair, and then put a strip of gaffer tape across his mouth. Archie sat next to his sister and waited for his brother to regain consciousness. He closed his eyes, and tried to recapture the fugitive melody of Bach that had played in his mind earlier.

Ten minutes later, Archie heard a small, muffled moan. He opened his eyes, and watched as Giles slowly opened his. Giles shook his head; then he saw Archie, and then his sister. He tried to say something. Then he tried to get up from the chair. The chair came with him, and Giles fell back into it. The muffled cries from Giles became more urgent.

Archie frowned. 'You might as well calm down, Giles. You won't get very far.'

Giles looked at Archie, then fell still and silent. Archie watched him for a few moments. Then he nodded, reached over and took the tape from Giles's mouth.

'Archie! What the hell are you doing here?' Giles looked at his sister. 'Lucinda... you killed Lou, didn't you!'

'You always were quick off the mark, weren't you, Giles?'

Giles swallowed. 'What the fuck do you want?'

'Simple, dear *brother*. My inheritance, nothing more.' Archie smiled bitterly.

The colour drained from Giles face. 'Is that what all this is about, money?'

Archie stroked his sister's cheek. He thought for a moment. 'Money is one part of it. The other is...' He shrugged. 'Do you remember how mother died?'

Giles nodded. His fleshy, round face puckered into a sour frown. 'She was an alcoholic. The booze killed her.'

Archie shook his head. 'Sadly, that's not quite true. She found out about father's little affairs, and wanted a divorce. True, she turned to the booze, but it was father who killed her. He spiced her bottles with neat alcohol. Tasteless, she would hardly have noticed it in the gin and sherry. But over the years, it finally damaged her liver irreparably.'

'You're lying!' Giles spat back.

'And when the old goat began to goad me with this, well, I did what I thought best at the time. I left. It would've been nice, had father – or you – subsequently acknowledged me in any way. You might have been saved from all this... unpleasantness. I found out about father's death from a local paper. I still pick up the papers from down this way. You can find them in Bristol. And Cheltenham. I like to read them. To remind me of–' Archie gave a cynical little laugh. 'Home. That was the first I'd heard of it. I waited for somebody to get in touch. I *do* have a phone number, after all. I *am* on the

55

electoral roll. I thought a solicitor might find me eventually. But guess what? Although you know the answer, don't you.'

'Is that all the reason you needed for... for this? Christ, Archie, you're unhinged!'

'Only because you, Lucinda and father made me this way. You know why he hated me don't you? Why he treated me like a bastard!'

'Because you *are*. You are a bastard.' Giles snarled. Then his head dropped. 'So you know that then? When did you find out?'

'Oh, father loved telling me that I wasn't his. That you and Lou weren't my real brother and sister. Poor Mother. She was trapped in a loveless marriage with him by her love for you two... brats. Little wonder she sought solace in another man. And I was the result.' Archie paused, momentarily in a past world. 'I remember the night he told me... It's as if it were yesterday. The look on his face... He gloated, taunted me.' Archie sat silently for a moment, remembering the humiliation, the pain, the loneliness.

'And then, of course,' he continued, 'there's the money. You *owe* me. You *all* owe me. For the last eighteen months I have been poor. I don't like being poor. Being a part of the Conn household taught me the proper love of money. I've tried different ways of getting my hands on it, but they never made me quite enough to live in the style I'd become accustomed to. Then one night I got to thinking about you, and Lou, and the man who wasn't my father, and how you had all fallen on your feet, while I was poor, rejected, alone, a part of nobody's family. And then I realised – I *should* have some of the family's money. But you would never have given me any. Let's face it, I wasn't even in the wills I destroyed this afternoon. So, I thought it best to steal *all* the money. To do that would mean killing you two, but...' Archie shrugged. 'I won't miss you. I wonder who will?'

Archie stood up. 'Still, enough reminiscing. I found Father's old revolver in the safe. I could shoot you, Giles. It would be... *merciful*. But it would also be messy and... incriminating. I have a much better plan for you, my *dear*, *loving* brother... The brother who kicked seven shades of shit out of me, day in, day out. The brother who made my life hell, while the lovely Loulou stood by and watched... And laughed.' Archie looked across at his sister, then jabbed a finger at Giles. 'You think I'm mad? Well, if that *is* the case, then you and this whole fucking family made me that way.'

Archie crossed the kitchen to a cupboard. 'Drink? If I remember, you were always partial to a good malt.' He poured two generous measures, and looked around the room. He placed the tumbler on the kitchen table, just beyond his brother's reach. 'Good health, Giles.' Archie took a long swig from his own glass. He looked at his brother. 'Oh, you can't reach yours, can you? Poor Giles.'

Archie undid the knot at one of Giles's wrists. 'No funny business,' he said.

Giles reached out to the glass, his hand shaking, and fingered it. 'Why would I want to drink with you when you're going to kill me anyway?'

'Because it will buy you time in which I might change my mind.'

Giles picked up the glass, and drank the malt in one impulsive gulp.

Archie smiled. 'Just what the doctor ordered, eh?'

Giles nodded. Archie tipped Giles's chair backwards, and allowed it to fall. He cursed as his head hit the floor, and then began flailing at Archie with his free arm. Archie pinned the arm down with his knee, then bent over Giles. He reached into his jacket and took out a hypodermic syringe. He held it in front of his brother. 'Do you notice something about this syringe, Giles?' Giles shook his head. 'It's empty,

57

full of air. An air bubble in the blood – quite often fatal, and very difficult to trace.'

'Archie, please... Don't do this. Please'

'Ah, the begging. Well, you never listened to me when I begged you to stop kicking me. So I don't think I'll listen to you now.'

Giles yelped as Archie twisted his hand, gripped one finger tightly, and inserted the needle beneath his fingernail. Giles yelped again. Archie depressed the plunger, and then stood up, releasing his brother's arm. 'At worst,' Archie said, 'You'll suffer a massive stroke, and become nothing more than a drooling vegetable. At best, you'll be dead in a few moments. Nice and clean. Whatever happens, your new wills provide for either possibility.' He gave a laugh. 'I wonder if Father knew, when he drove me away into the arms of the military he so loved, that I'd learn so much, so many ways to kill a man – and bring it home with me?'

Giles' body suddenly arched against the back of the chair. His eyes widened, and a strange, unnatural gurgle passed his lips. He twitched a couple of times, and then was still. Archie studied Giles for a few moments, then bent down and put two fingers to the artery at Giles's neck. He could feel no pulse. He stood, poured himself another tumbler of whiskey, and raised it upwards. He looked first at his dead sister, then at his brother. 'Cheers, me dears.' He downed the whiskey in a gulp.

Archie pushed his sister from her chair. He untied his brother, and dragged him closer to Lucinda. *Brother struggles with sister, strangles her then has a heart attack. Shame, but it happens.*

He looked at the position of the bodies. They looked haphazard enough. He examined Lucinda's broken nose, and the bruises on Giles's head. He considered the fingernail beneath which he'd inserted the needle of the syringe. He could see a small drop of blood. He picked up the door-stop, and smashed it into Giles's hand. A sensible counter-measure, Archie thought; no forensics expert would consider that droplet anything out of the ordinary now, set against broken fingernails and mashed bones.

Archie needed music. He switched on the Roberts radio on the window-sill, and tuned it to Radio 3. He'd been brought up listening to classical music. His father had never had time for big bands and rock and roll. Classical music was the only thing his family had ever given Archie. In a happy coincidence, one of his favourite pieces of music was playing. He turned up the volume, and conducted *Bolero* for a moment. Then he set the kitchen chair upright, put the rope and gaffer tape in his knapsack and zipped it up. He made one final check of the room, and then went to the living room. He replaced the rug and armchair, and shut the bureau door he'd left open. He checked the fireplace again, and looked around him. All seemed as it should be. He left the house, leaving the radio playing and the backdoor unlocked, and made his way to his tent.

He packed the tent into a rucksack. He picked up litter and anything else he thought might signal his presence, and put it all into a carrier bag. He removed his gloves, and added them to the rubbish in the carrier bag. He scuffed across the ground where his tent had been, raising the crumpled weeds, then dragged fallen branches over the same spot. Confident that his occupation of the site could now only be detected with the most detailed examination, he left the copse the opposite way to which he'd entered, carrying his rucksack on one shoulder, the knapsack on the other, and his carrier bag of rubbish in his left hand. He knew this countryside well, and walked out into a field. He looked like any passing hiker. Twilight was falling. He crossed a fence into another field where he knew there was a public footpath. Here, he followed the path to the lane that led back to the family house. The house that would now be his. After a few yards, he turned to his right, up a rutted track that was soon hedged on both sides by wide spinneys. A few tens of yards up the track his Land Rover lay hidden deep in the trees, covered by the camouflage netting and cut branches he'd placed over it two days ago. The chances that anybody had seen his Land Rover were small; he'd chosen this location with great care. The land on which he'd hidden the car was detached land belonging to his family. No, he corrected himself, it belongs to *me* now. He threw the branches and brash aside, quickly bundled up the netting, unlocked the back door of the Land Rover, and placed the netting, rucksack and carrier bag inside. He then unlocked the driver's door, climbed into the car and placed the knapsack on the passenger side of the bench seat. He started the Land Rover, bumped down the track back to the lane, and then headed to the main road that led to Cardiff. Within a few hours, he'd be back in Reading, where he'd fled after his failure to swindle the dozy flying saucer freaks in Dereham.

Archie turned on the radio, which was tuned to Radio 3. The Ravel had finished while he had been removing all trace of his camp-site and walking the fields. Now, the soothing sounds of a Beethoven symphony filled the car. He smiled to himself, lit a cigarette, and glanced at the knapsack. He had enough money to tide himself over until the wills had been read. Then he would be a rich man. How long would it take for the bodies to be found? Knowing how reclusive his half-brother and sister were, he reckoned it wouldn't be until Monday at the least. It was already late Friday afternoon; it was unlikely cleaners would be in at the weekend.

Archie wondered why he hadn't considered killing his brother and sister sooner. He had made more money today than he ever had in any other way, straight or crooked. Archie began to hum contentedly as the Land Rover whined along the road.

5

The telephone rang. Michael Edge picked up the handset. 'Yes?' he barked. It had not been a good night for Edge – rumours of terrorist cells, gun-running into Northern Ireland, missing explosives.

A throat was nervously cleared at the other end of the line. 'Is that Michael Edge, at the Security Service?'

'Yes, it is. Can I help you? I was about to go to lunch.'

'Mr Edge, this is Detective Inspector Owen Evans of South Wales Constabulary. I think I have some information that might be interest you.'

'Well, Detective Inspector, get on with it.'

'I'm calling about a notice, circulated to all police forces by your department.'

'Have you any idea,' Edge said, tiredly, 'how many notices we send out a week? Especially in the current political climate?'

'This hasn't anything to do with terrorism. Well, I don't think so, anyway.'

'Let me be the judge of that, Detective Inspector.'

'The notice contains a request for information regarding an Archibald Franklin Conn. I quote: 'Any force that has reason to believe they may have the above person in custody, or know of his movements, should–'

Edge finished the sentence. 'Should contact this number immediately. Blah blah blah... I *am* aware of the file's contents. I wrote the bloody thing. So Detective Inspector, what do have for me?'

'Early this morning the bodies of Mr Conn's brother and sister were found at the family home, by their cleaner. The female, Lucinda Conn, appears to have been strangled by her brother. The brother's body was found close to his sister. A cursory inspection seems to indicate that he died of natural causes. There are no signs of a break in.'

'Hold on, Detective Inspector.' Edge leaned back in his chair and thought. He pinched the bridge of his nose and rubbed his tired eyes with his free hand. A few moments passed. Edge returned the receiver to his ear. 'Where are the bodies now?'

'Still in place. After I read the contents of your notice, I had forensics leave everything as it was, and left a bobby to keep watch over the house.'

'Good thinking. And what of the cleaner?'

'She's in hospital, being treated for shock.'

'Keep her there for now. We should keep a tight lid on this.'

'You make what seems a case of domestic violence very mysterious. Can I ask what all this is about?'

Edge gave a little laugh. 'You can, but at this moment even I don't know.'

There was a knock at the door. 'Come!' Edge barked. Paul Morrow entered the office. Morrow was an almost gaunt man in his late forties. Edge nodded at him, and then returned to the phone conversation. 'Thank you, Detective Inspector. I'll be sending some of my people down later today. I'd appreciate your full co-operation.'

'Of course. Thank you.'

'Goodbye.'

Edge grimaced, and then looked up at Paul Morrow. 'Is my life to be one continual round of confounding confusions, Paul?'

Morrow nodded at the phone. 'Who was that?'

'Owen Evans, a detective from South Wales Constabulary.

This is an interesting diversion. Murder most foul. And somehow connected to Archibald Franklin Conn.'

Morrow's thin face narrowed in a puzzled frown. 'Who?'

Morrow would be good for this job, Edge thought. By training, he had been a forensic scientist. No Valleys woodentop could learn more from the crime scene than Morrow.

Edge clasped his hands together and pinched his chin between his forefingers. 'Paul, you entered my office at an opportune time. Drop whatever you're doing. You're off to the rainy valleys of South Wales. Take a radio car and your box of tricks.' Edge stood and walked to a secure filing cabinet. He unlocked it, opened a drawer, and removed the file It was a thin file. 'Everything you need to know about Archibald Franklin Conn is in there. The plod seems to think this is an open and shut case but, as it involves the elusive Mr Conn, nothing can be ruled out. I want you to do your usual thorough job. I want to know if Conn was responsible for this. If he is, I want him brought in.'

Morrow would normally take Ted Davies with him on a job like this. 'Davies is on leave, sir,' Morrow said.

'On leave, eh? Take Liz Carter, then. I want you there in less than four hours. I also want a report from you by midday tomorrow. You can omit the details; just the basic facts will do.' Morrow turned to leave. 'Oh, and Paul?' Morrow turned back to Edge. 'Anything you need while down there, requisition it. You have my authority to do what you feel needs to be done.'

Morrow nodded. 'And if we find this Conn?'

'Nothing heavy. Get the plod to bring him in.'

'Okay, sir. I'll get moving.' Morrow left, closing the door behind him. Edge sat back in his chair, deep in thought. He wondered if he should appraise Harry of this surprising turn of events. Both cases were linked, after all. But Harry would only ask to be taken off the Stone assignment and demand to be sent after Conn. Harry was still fragile after the Dereham job. The psych evaluations showed it. *If I do keep him out of the loop, and he then finds out I've withheld this from him, it could alienate him.* Edge didn't want that to happen. Harry showed promise.

Edge sighed. Everything that had happened since Harry had been assigned to Peta Shepherd in Dereham was confusing, Edge thought. The reason for that assignment in the first place were flap-doodle, horse-shit, so much nonsense. *UFOs. Shite.* Edge had assigned Harry to Peta because somebody, somewhere, thought there might be something in all this contactee nonsense. Northern Ireland was at war with itself, the paramilitaries were bringing the conflict to the mainland, and still somebody in this building thought the telepathic messages Peta Shepherd received from aliens was of equal if not greater importance. After all, the argument went, there might be useful information in those messages. A novel technology. Information about political activities here on Earth. The secrets of peace forever. Some crackpot in the upper echelons of the Service had sanctioned the operation. Some crackpot who believed in UFOs as much as the crackpots in the street. It would be foolish to pretend the intelligence services had no such crackpots. Of course they did. The occupants of offices such as these were only human, after all. There were Tories and Lefties and Marxists and Trots here. There were Catholics, Protestants, anarchists and Anthroposophists. There was every human possibility. And their occupation, their very special occupation, made them naturally suspicious, inquisitive, secretive, and conspiracy-minded. Is it any wonder that somebody, somewhere in this building, somebody at a higher grade than Edge, actually thought there was substance to this UFO nonsense, somebody who actually believed that ordinary folk were contacted by aliens on a regular basis? Was it any wonder that some of these *contactees* were known to those crackpots in the Service with an interest in that sort of thing? Edge wondered if the crackpot was in Defence Intelligence; somebody in Scientific and Technical, perhaps. Flying saucers seemed like their kind of thing.

Len Stone had never made a secret of his interest in UFOs, the occult and other esoteric subjects. His club had been a well-known meeting place for others who shared his beliefs – among whom, according to the files, was the drop-out Lord, Philip Creighton. A dope-smoking, Saville Row-suit wearing, acutely self-promoting band manager who invited to his parties the rich, famous and well-connected – rock-stars, barons and baronesses, diplomats and politicians. It was hip to be at Creighton's parties, where the sex, drugs and alcohol came freely and easily. It was little wonder the security services worried that such well-connected and stellar partygoers might talk to the wrong people at the wrong time. There was always somebody from the Service at Creighton's parties. Thus, it would be wise to assume there were also representatives of the CIA, KGB, Mossad, DGCE and all the rest. Len Stone was often at Creighton's parties. Creighton managed bands that performed at Stone's club. Stone had at one time run a UFO contactee group that Creighton sometimes attended. Peta Shepherd had been the foremost contactee of that group. And then Len Stone had then become romantically entangled with Emily, daughter of well-known American contactee Ed Freeman, whose book *Panlyrae–A Message for Mankind* had been a bible to Stone.

Edge ran the palms of his hands over his stubbled cheeks. He felt tired, and he still hadn't eaten lunch. What a tangled web. No wonder Five had wanted somebody close to Peta Shepherd. Harry had been that man. And then, inevitably,

Harry had fallen for her. Edge had seen the picture of Peta Shepherd, published in the *News of the World* to accompany an article on the Dereham phenomenon. She was a cute kid. Too young for him. Probably too young for Harry. But too late now. Peta had been living in Dereham with Archibald Franklin Conn, a minor criminal, a chancer. Conn had left, Peta had died. Now Harry believed that Conn had somehow caused her death. He wanted revenge. Meanwhile, the crackpot in Five who sat above Edge and controlled him, who believed in UFO shite and contactee bollocks, was afraid that Conn had learned something from Shepherd, something that could be sold to the highest bidder. And so the web became ever more tangled.

And now, Edge thought, the bloody Yanks were on *his* patch, without authorisation, watching Stone and Freeman. Another strand to the web. So Edge had begun his own operation to discover what the Yanks up to. He was in the middle of the web. *I have to make sense of it all.* If he could maintain control, he might untangle himself from the web – he would be free. Things could go badly wrong, however. Harry was a danger, Edge knew it. Poor old Harry. Lovelorn, starry-eyed, vengeance-seeking, fucked-up Harry.

Edge pushed back his chair, and stood up slowly, stretching, yawning. He opened the office door. 'Mary,' he barked. She was sitting at her desk.

Mary smiled at him. 'Yes, Sir?'

'Contact Morrow before he goes. Tell him to take Harry.'

He had made his decision. He needed lunch. And a drink, a quick snifter. Or two.

Harry sat with Detective Inspector Evans beside the hospital bed of Meg Dawkins. Morrow was with Liz Carter at the Conn house. The odd sob still bubbled out of Meg Dawkins, and she would then dab a tear from her eye with her folded handkerchief.

Harry looked at the middle-aged lady, and said softly. 'How are you doing, Mrs Dawkins?'

Meg Dawkins spoke quietly. 'It was so lovely this morning, wasn't it, the weather?'

'It was,' Harry said. It had been a lovely morning. The sun had been bright in a blue sky, but autumn cool on leaves turning to yellow and gold on the trees. Even now, the weak autumn evening sun shone through the curtains of the hospital room. 'Shame it was spoiled for you.' Harry shifted slightly in his seat, leaned in closer to Mrs Dawkins, his voice soothing. 'So you've been cleaner for the Conn family for... how long?'

'Nearly twenty years.' Mrs Dawkins dabbed at her eyes. 'I worked for the Major first, you know, their father. Well, when he died, Giles and Lou, that's Lucinda, they kept me on. It was easy money, you know, because Lucinda was neat and tidy. Giles... that was another matter. He was lazy. But I only had to clean up after *him*, not the two of them. As I say, Lou was tidy, enough. It was easy. I liked working there. Mr Dawkins, he has... well, he *had*... a proper job, down in Swansea. I do cleaning jobs for the extra you know, so we can have a proper holiday, like. We went to the Lake District just last week.'

'Did you notice anything as you approached the house?'

'Not really. I went through the side-gate, like I normally do. On a fine day like this, Lucinda would normally have the back door open, and the dogs would have run around to say hello to me. But there weren't any dogs, and the back door was closed. The dogs were still in their kennels, which I thought was odd.'

'Were the doors locked?'

'The back door was unlocked. But that's as it should be. When I arrived I tried the handle of the door, and the door swung open. If Lou was out with the dogs, she'd always lock the door. Lou normally leave the backdoor unlocked during the day when she's home. So I called out, *Lou, love, it's me!* But there was no reply. Just silence, see. So I put my head around the door. And...' Mrs Dawkins stifled a sob with her hanky. 'Then I could see... them... both. On the floor. I couldn't make sense of it at first. Why they were lying there like that.' She paused to dab again. 'In the morning the sunlight comes through the kitchen window lovely, I always liked washing up in the mornings, looking at the birds in the garden.' Again she sobbed. 'I walked closer to them, but I could see things weren't right. There was blood...' The sobbing became louder.

'I'm sorry, Mrs Dawkins. And that's when you realised....'

'They were dead, yes. I knelt down to check for a pulse... or something... I don't know what I was looking for really. Lou wasn't breathing There was blood all over one of Giles's hand.' Mrs Dawkins let out a long wail. Evans turned away and looked out through the new curtains, into the sunlit garden.

Harry waited for the crying to stop.

'I liked Lou,' Mrs Dawkins said. 'After a while I pulled myself together, and knew I had to phone the police.'

'You haven't cleaned anything up, moved anything?'

'No, everything is as I found it this morning. Oh, except I turned the radio off.'

'You said you liked Miss Conn. Did you like Mr Conn?'

'Not really. He was a bit of a pig, as I said. Slovenly. He was also selfish. Like a grown-up teenager really. Except he didn't like that pop music. Always listening to classical music. You know, I remember the radio was on when I

69

walked in, playing classical music. It was surprising.'

Evans spoke then. "Oh, really? If they always played classical, surely it was no surprise that the radio was switched on.'

Mrs Dawkins looked at Evans, then at Harry. 'That's right, that wasn't a surprise, no, it wasn't that. It was that it was so loud. They wouldn't normally have it loud.'

'Perhaps Mr Conn was trying to cover up the shouting,' Evans said.

'Perhaps,' Mrs Dawkins said. 'Although we're miles from anywhere.'

Harry spoke again. 'Now, the Detective Inspector here believes that Giles Conn killed Lucinda, and then had a heart attack himself. Do you have any idea why Mr Conn would kill his sister?'

'No, not really. They'd lived together a long time. And Giles relied on Lou. She used to cook his dinner and... she was like a wife in a way.'

Harry raised an eyebrow. Mrs Dawkins had obviously spotted it, and blushed.

'No, I don't think in *that* way,' she said. 'I think I'd have known if there was anything... odd... about their relationship. She was simply devoted to him.'

Harry smiled warmly. 'Thank you, Mrs Dawkins.' He looked at Evans. 'Do you have any more questions for Mrs Dawkins?'

Evans shook his head. 'We already have a statement from Mrs Dawkins. Everything she's told you matches with that statement.' Evans stood, and looked down at the pale woman. 'Now, Mrs Dawkins, you rest here for the night. You've had a nasty shock.'

'Thank you, Detective Inspector.'

Harry pushed his chair back, and stood. 'One more thing

before we go. What happened to the other brother? Archibald, isn't it?' Mrs Dawkins nodded. 'Do you know where he is?'

'I don't. Lou and Giles didn't like him. Giles especially. I think Archie was glad to get away.'

'Did you like him?'

'He's a rogue, Mr Roberts.'

'A lovable rogue?'

'He can be a charmer, certainly; but lovable? He was too cold and distant for that, I think.'

Evans drove Harry back to the Conn house. Morrow and Liz Carter had finished there, and were waiting for Harry to arrive. Something was niggling Harry. At the moment, he couldn't put his finger on it. Evans was tapping his finger on the steering wheel to Tom Jones singing *Delilah* on Radio 2.

Harry leaned over and turned the radio down a little. 'Why would Mr Conn want to kill Miss Conn? Mrs Dawkins said that Miss Conn had been a devoted sister, and what with Miss Conn cooking the dinner and Mrs Dawkins tidying up after him, it seemed as though Mr Conn had an easy life. '

Evans shrugged. 'Mrs Dawkins can't know everything. After all, she only worked mornings. Perhaps it was something simple; perhaps Miss Conn had some annoying habit that drove Mr Conn over the edge. Perhaps she hummed all the time. Perhaps she nagged. Perhaps she watched rubbish on the television and prevented Mr Conn listening to his classical music. You never know, really, what might cause somebody to lose their temper, or their reason.'

Harry considered this. The Security Service wasn't tasked with solving murders; it was only interested in this case because Archibald Franklin Conn might somehow be involved. Evans was much more likely to know what triggered violence and murder.

'Do you like classical music?' Harry said.

'I've never got on with classical music. I don't like modern pop music, either. It's all been downhill since The Beatles released *Sgt Pepper's Lonely Hearts Club Band*. Now, Tom Jones singing *Delilah* – that's something I do like. Something I can sing along to.'

'Do you know Mrs Dawkins?'

'No, this is the first time I've met her.'

'You sounded very friendly with her.'

'You learn to be sympathetic and empathise with people in this job. Sometimes you have bad news. Sometimes you need information.'

'I suppose you have to adapt, find the best approach for people in very difference circumstances.'

'You do. To be honest, though, empathy has never been my strong point.' He looked over at Harry, as if seeking a challenge, or a confirmation. 'I'm not a very feeling person, and if I'm not asking questions, or getting to the point, I get bored.' Evans concentrated on the road. 'I sometimes think my lack of empathy is why I haven't progressed any further in my career.'

Harry knew that he was being told this because he was safe. He was MI5; Security Service didn't just blab people's secrets. 'Has this always been your patch?'

'Yes. I was a beat bobby. I've made my way up through the ranks. But I'm fifty now, and I know I won't get any further up the ladder.'

'Still, Detective Inspector is a pretty impressive. You must know what you're doing.'

'I like the job. I like to be involved, help the community, you know? At the same time, retirement seems so close now.'

Evans smiled at the thought of the retirement ahead. 'I do like to fish. And do some wood-turning in the shed.'

'I still have some way to go before I reach that happy state,' Harry said.

They reached the house. Evans stopped in the driveway, behind Morrow's car. He and Harry got out, and began the short walk up the gravel drive to the front door. Harry spotted a cigarette between the grey stones. It looked fresh. He looked at the brown paper around the filter. It was a Rothmans. He found another as they neared the door. He asked Evans if the brother and sister smoked.

'I don't think they did,' Evans said. 'The house doesn't have that smell, you know.' Harry nodded. 'And Mrs Dawkins doesn't, either.'

They entered the house. Harry found Morrow, and gave him the two cigarette ends. 'Well spotted, Harry,' Morrow said.

'That man you're looking for, Archibald Franklin Conn. Do you know why he's named that?'

'What do you mean?'

'*Franklin* Conn. Mrs Dawkins called the brother and sister by the single surname *Conn*. But the other brother is called Franklin Conn.'

'Oh, yes. I see what you mean.' Harry frowned; the copper had caught a small detail that he had missed. 'No, I don't. Do you?'

'No idea. It might just be an affectation, you know?'

'It might be.'

'And then again,' Evans said, 'it might be the key to whole mystery.'

6

Carl Cleaver could smell the newsroom before he even entered it. As he pushed open the door, he prepared himself. This might not, he decided, have been the best time to stop smoking. It was late on Monday afternoon. He had been out of the office, at a supermarket opening. There had been a buzz there about some murder that had happened over the weekend.

The door to the editor's office was open, and Carl made a bee-line for it. He entered the office where Tom Hughes sat behind his desk. Hughes looked up and smiled at him. 'Jesus! You look like you need a holiday.'

Carl sat opposite his editor. 'I've just had one.'

'Oh yes, of course. I remember now. It's been so very peaceful here, I knew there had to be reason. Still, you don't look like you've just had a holiday. You look... mournful.'

Carl smiled in turn. 'Never give up smoking, Tom.'

'Where did you go? Swanage, wasn't it?'

'Yes, that's right. Nice weather for the time of year.'

'November?`

'Half-term. We thought it would be good to get away.'

'But still, November?'

Carl shrugged. 'Better than the summer holidays. Too hot. Too many kids.'

His wife, Jenny, had actually suggested the break. It would be good for their marriage, she'd said. In that case, it would perhaps have been better to leave the twins with their grandparents. They had been a handful, and ensured that he and Jenny had little time to talk. He'd managed to find a kind of refuge in the local boozer. That had, unsurprisingly, made Jenny's foul moods even worse. He knew he shouldn't be doing it. But he couldn't help himself.

Hughes broke into his reverie. 'Still, I have a nice story for you. The sort of story we don't see much of on the South Wales Evening Clarion. A nice juicy murder.'

'I've been hearing rumours while out and about.'

'Thought you might like to do a bit of real reporting.'

'Was it anybody important?' Carl asked.

'The Conns at Lanbier Manor, the big house out Crynant way. Brother and sister.'

'The Conns, eh?'

'You knew the younger brother, didn't you? You would have been at school with him.'

Everybody knows everybody around here, Carl thought. Sometimes he wanted to get out of Swansea. 'Archie? Yes... I was at school with him for a time. Not seen hide nor hair of him since, I was, oh, about eighteen.'

'The boys in blue think it's an open and shut case. Brother breaks sister's neck, then has a heart attack from stress, or anger, or the effort of killing her. It might make a good human interest story.'

Carl stroked his chin. 'Archie Conn, yes. He was a rum one. Always arguing with his dad, and his brother and sister. The girls liked him though. He was a handsome lad. Played rugby for the school.'

'Do you think there might be more to this business?'

Carl shrugged. 'Who knows?'

'What happened to him after school?'

'He attended sixth form with me, in Swansea. Then he joined the army. He was a charmer. He's probably a senior officer by now.' Carl shook his head. 'I can't see him murdering his brother and sister, though. I can imagine him being a con-man, if he isn't still in the army.'

'Con-man, eh? Right name for it.'

'He was always trying something on at school.'

'I knew you were the right man for this story. Find out what you can, and make of it what you will.'

Hughes lit a cigarette. Carl envied him. 'I don't know much about him, really,' he said. 'Some school anecdotes. We hung out together a little, and I went out to the Manor a few times. But we moved in different circles, particularly in sixth form.'

'Well, work something up. Ask a few questions. You think he was dodgy, so you never know what you might find out. Just because the plods think it's an open and shut case, there's no need for you to skimp on some leg-work.'

'When's the inquest?'

'Friday, I think.'

Carl stood up. 'I'll make some calls.'

At his desk, Carl phoned police officers he'd talked to before, and friends from school. Meg Dawkins, the cleaner at the Conns, was unable to take calls, her husband said. She was still recovering from shock.

During the week, Carl followed some hunches and talked to some people. He discovered nothing new. Like him, his friends from school had lost touch with Archibald Conn. None of them believed Archie could be a murderer.

Carl sat in the public gallery during the inquest. He looked around him. There were fewer than a dozen people present. He couldn't see Archie Conn. There were no other newspapermen. He'd attended numerous inquests in his career, and this one seemed no different to the others. The evidence presented seemed straightforward enough. Lucinda Conn had died of a broken neck. Giles Conn appeared to have died of natural causes; either a heart attack, or an embolism. The coroner stated his findings, and was more circumspect than the police had been. He noted that though Miss Conn had a broken neck, she might perhaps have fallen; perhaps she'd been pushed in anger by her brother. That Miss Conn had a broken nose, and Mr Conn broken fingers on one hand, might indicate an altercation. This in turn might indicate that Mr Conn was indeed angry, and, in the colloquial phrase, about to burst a blood vessel; hence the embolism. Equally though, the coroner noted, nobody saw an altercation, nobody saw Miss Conn fall, or Mr Conn attack her; it was possible, then, that somebody had entered the house, killed Miss Conn, and attacked Mr Conn, who had then died of a heart attack. The coroner recorded an open verdict.

As the few attendees rose, Carl noticed Detective Inspector Owen Evans slowly shaking his head. Obviously Evans thought something was wrong. Carl quickly made his way to the exit, and waited to intercept Evans. It was a cold, grey, wet day in Swansea. When Evans emerged into the street, he opened his umbrella and began to walk towards the car park. Carl followed, and then quietly sidled up to the oblivious detective.

'You didn't look happy, Detective,' Carl said. 'Did you not get the verdict you expected?'

Evans looked at Carl. 'Oh, it's you Cleaver. Sorry, nothing to say. The case is closed now, put to bed.'

'It was an open verdict. Surely the police will continue working on the case?'

Evans stopped walking and faced the reporter. 'You heard the result of the inquest in there. Giles Conn went off his rocker, that's all. A family argument went too far, perhaps. Domestic violence. It happens.' Evans began to walk again.

Carl hurried after the detective. 'The investigation seems

to have reached a conclusion very quickly.'

'You didn't see the bodies, Cleaver. They were so close together. And our SOCOs found nothing to implicate anybody except them. Nothing was missing. There were no fingerprints, other than those we would expect. Everything was as it should be. It was almost too clean.'

'Archibald Conn?'

Evans turned his head and eyed the reporter shrewdly. 'You're a good reporter, Cleaver, I know that. But take a bit of friendly advice. Drop it. It was a tragedy perhaps, but it happens. Not often around here, I grant you, but not exactly worth losing your job over.'

'Why would I lose my job over this?'

Evans continued walking, and said no more.

Carl stood in the street, the rain coming down harder now. What Evans had said sounded like a threat, he thought. Yet he had known Evans in a professional capacity for years, and Evans had always been amenable. There was something unusual going on here. He looked across the road and saw a newsagent's. He wanted a cigarette, and he was going to have one. And then, after that, he was going to get to the bottom of this mystery.

Carl walked back into the newsroom, still deep in thought, smoking an Embassy. He had considered ways in which he could get further information about the case. Before he reached his cluttered desk, the editor's door flew open. He heard the voice of Tom Hughes across the hubbub of the newsroom. 'Carl, my office, *now*.' The tone of Hughes's voice made it perfectly clear that Carl's presence was required immediately.

'Shut the door,' Hughes said as Cleaver stepped over the threshold. This wasn't a good sign, Cleaver thought. Once the door had been shut, and Cleaver had sat in the proffered chair, Hughes handed over a manila envelope. 'This arrived by motorcycle courier a little while ago. Read it. Go on, read the contents. Then tell me what in heaven's name you've been up to.'

Cleaver opened envelope, and removed the papers inside. 'It's a D-Notice...'

Hughes sighed loudly. 'Yes. And, what's more, I had a telephone call from the Chief Constable this afternoon. It seems you've been bothering Detective Inspector Evans.'

Cleaver frowned. 'That was bloody quick. A D-Notice? I only left Evans an hour ago.'

'Look, Carl, as your friend, I'd advise you to drop this.'

Cleaver knew his boss of old. 'And as a fellow journalist?'

Hughes gave the Carl a sly look. 'What you do in your time is your own affair. If you were to carry on, it would be without my express consent, and therefore you would be acting outside the remit of your job here.'

Carl understood. D-Notices were not legally enforceable; they were only advisory. Still, as general rule, newspapers took D-Notices seriously; it was in their own interests not to upset governments without clear and compelling reasons. 'I still have a few days holiday owing. I know I'm just back from two weeks off, I was wondering if...'

Hughes held up a hand. 'Oh, absolutely. You seem to be a little stressed about your marriage.'

So, Carl thought, Hughes had been listening to him all those times down the pub.

'Take another week off,' Hughes continued. 'We'll call it compassionate leave to keep the bean counters happy.'

'Thanks. Jenny will be... uh ... pleased.'

Hughes leaned forward over his desk, talking quietly.

'Listen, I don't like the state getting heavy and trying to stop us doing our work. Someone wants this Conn affair forgotten. I want to know why. So you find out. Be careful. You do have a wife and kids to provide for.'

Cleaver nodded. 'I'll make a start by interviewing the housekeeper. I'll also try to find out what I can about Archie Conn. That'll keep me busy for a while. I'll report back when I have a lead or two.'

Carl had found the address for Mrs Dawkins in the telephone directory. The door to her house was answered by a surly-looking man in his late fifties. His gruff 'Yes?' was almost a bark. His attitude would have shamed a German shepherd dog.

Carl was by now polished practitioner of the introductory conversation. He smiled warmly. His tone was charming. 'Hello. My name is Carl Cleaver. I'm a reporter with the *Evening Clarion* and we're doing a piece on the *very* sad events up at the manor. I was wondering if I could speak to your wife, if possible.' Over the shoulder of what he assumed to be Mr Dawkins he could make out the figure of Mrs Dawkins at the end of the dark hallway.

Mr Dawkins's face became more hostile. 'She's very upset. I'll thank you to go away.'

As the door was about shut in Carl's face, Meg Dawkins called out. 'That's enough of that, Charlie.'

Mrs Dawkins pushed aside her husband, and opened the door wider. She ushered Carl into the hallway. Her husband stormed off down the short hallway. Carl heard a door slam, and then there was silence.

'Now, young man,' Mrs Dawkins said. 'What is it I can do for you?'

Carl explained again the reason for his visit as Mrs Dawkins opened the door to the living room, and gestured

Carl inside. 'He's been fussing around me since... well, you know... After all these years of married life, I find it quite sweet, really.'

Carl sat down in the offered armchair. 'I really don't want you to think that I'm being disrespectful to the Conn family. But news is news, and people will want to know some details. Can you tell me anything about them? What could have triggered such a tragic event?'

Meg sat on the settee opposite him, and told Carl what she had already told the police. When she talked of first seeing Lucinda she broke off, her eyes filling with tears. 'Oh God! When I think of her, all pale and still...'

Carl reached over and touched Meg's hand gently. 'It's all right, Meg. Let's not go down this route, shall we? Let's chat about them as people, the way you want to remember them.'

She nodded in between quiet sobs. She told Carl how she had come to work at the Manor, about Giles's untidiness and Lucinda's devotion to her brother.

Carl had a thought. 'You must have been working for the family when Archie was around? The younger brother?' He smiled gently at her, hoping to coax a revelation from her. He didn't know what. 'You know, I went to school with Archie for a while. Very quiet lad, kept himself to himself,' he lied.

Mrs Dawkins actually laughed. 'Oh, and pigs would fly, Mr Cleaver. You're as smooth-talking as he is.' To his surprise, Carl felt himself blushing. 'Yes, young Archie...' she continued. 'He always seemed to be a square peg in a round hole. Never seen the like of it, you know? At times it was like a family at war. The old man and Giles would give the lad merry hell. No wonder he joined the army as soon as he left school. I hardly saw him after that. The family never spoke much about him. Even after his father died, nobody called him to tell him. He wasn't at the funeral.'

'Good for Archie,' Carl said. 'Sounds like there was no love lost there. Any idea which regiment he joined?'

The door of the living room was flung open. The large frame of Mr Dawkins filled the opening. 'Enough of the chat! he just wants gossip for the local rag!' Mr Dawkins grabbed Carl, and dragged him to the front door. Mr Dawkins opened the door and pushed Carl through it. Before the door slammed shut, Carl caught sight of Meg Dawkins, her face flushed, her hands covering her mouth. He then heard children laughing, and looked around. Carl smiled at them, and then turned to walk back to his car. The children scampered away. At least he now had a lead to follow. He would see where Archie Conn might lead him. Investigating Archie's military career should be a simple enough. Carl remembered now that Archie had been a member of the Combined Cadet Force while at school. He wondered if Archie had been trying to impress his father. A simple telephone call to the present commander-in-chief, or whatever his title was, of the Cadet Force might provide information on which regiment Archie had joined.

Mrs Dawkins was loyal to the Conn family, that was clear; but she couldn't hide the tensions within it, particularly those relating to Archibald Conn. Carl started the car and pulled away. What skeletons would be exhumed?

7

Skinner could feel sweat on his neck as he waited for Len Stone and Emily Freeman to leave the house. The rear of the van was warm and stuffy on this muggy, misty November night. Three British mercenaries sat with him; they were skilled in electronics. He hadn't thought it worthwhile risking his own men on this operation. If this job should go wrong, the consequences hardly bore thinking about. He would have to fall on his sword. Major Ellis, back in the States, would continue the project – Project Flashlight, as it was officially known; or Project One-Watt, as it was unofficially known, even by Skinner. Humour and sarcasm brightened the dark corridors of black ops. Skinner knew he had to be here tonight. That was okay by him, though; he still liked fieldwork. The mercenaries knew that, if caught, they should muddy the waters. IRA, DGCE, Mossad: they could claim to be working for anybody. Easier if they were Brits. This team came highly recommended through channels. Two of them would fit bugging devices inside Stone's house. The third would tap the phone line. They would do their jobs efficiently and quietly. The bugs were standard US devices, but the mercenaries knew how and where to fit them. They had read the manuals, and been trained by an unwitting CIA agent who had no idea why he was training Brits. He had probably asked back at Langley what the Air Force guy was doing. He wouldn't find out. Very few people knew what Skinner did, or who he answered to. Skinner allowed himself a wry smile. That was because he only really answered to himself. Setting up Operation

Flashlight had been his original role. Now, keeping it secret was his primary task.

'What are you smiling about, Skinner?' one of the mercenaries said.

'None of goddam your business, Barnes.'

Barnes was a big guy. He looked more like a thug than an electronics expert, Skinner thought. He should be running around in some African country with a machine gun over a well-muscled arm, kicking in doors and blasting away. He had probably done so. Skinner had never asked for detailed information on these mercenaries. He had allowed a subordinate to select the right men. Still Barnes looked like he could handle himself if his team found themselves in a tight corner. If Stone returned home early from his club there might be trouble; he had been a bruiser in the past, had done some unpleasant jobs for the Manley Boys.

Hah, the Manley Boys, Skinner thought. There was a crime outfit with a sense of humour. Manley Boys. Especially when everybody in every intelligence agency and police force knew Tim Manley to be a homo.

Skinner looked around as the window between the rear of the van and the cab slid open. Skinner could make out the driver's face, lit by the orange streetlights. 'That's them gone,' the driver said, quietly.

'Okay.' Skinner turned to the mercenaries. 'Give them five minutes, and then get to work.'

The mercenaries merely nodded in reply. Skinner returned to his thoughts. He needed to know what Emily Freeman was saying to Len Stone. Who knew what she might have told him already? Freeman knew she was bound to secrecy; it had been one of the prices she had paid to be near her father. But her father was dead now, and perhaps that had loosened her tongue. Perhaps that was why she had come to England to live with Stone. Eventually, she would become a British citizen, and enjoy the protection of British law. What would the Brits do if they knew about Project Flashlight? Sure, the Brits and the Yanks shared defence information; but not about Flashlight. Project Flashlight had put the US military so far ahead of all other nations it was a strategic advantage that had to be kept secret, even from their allies.

'Time to go,' Barnes said.

Skinner gave them a reassuring smile. 'I know you guys will do a good job. Keep it tight, keep it clean.'

'Don't fuck up, basically,' Barnes said. 'We don't need a lecture. We don't fuck up.'

Barnes opened the rear door of the van, and the others followed him out. Barnes was, Skinner realised, the *de facto* leader of this team. Good. Skinner trusted Barnes. All Barnes had to do now was break into Stone's house, in the early evening, when most of the neighbours would still be awake. At least it was dark. They had a cover story ready, of course, if an inquisitive visitor should come knocking. Should a suspicious neighbour phone the police – the Old Bill, as Barnes called them, which Skinner found amusing – the story wouldn't bear scrutiny, anyway. Barnes and his fellow mercenaries would be in like Flynn and out again. They could probably finish the job before the police arrived. Through the sliding window and out of the front windscreen, Skinner could see one of the team, wearing a purloined GPO jacket, already ascending the telegraph pole in front of Stone's house. The tap would be wireless, transmitting a signal to a safe house Skinner had already rented down the road; home for the mercenaries for the next few... whatever. Weeks, months. Years? Skinner was paranoid about security. How long would he wait before thinking

Freeman was safe, was unlikely to talk about her past life? He knew he would always worry that the moment he sent the mercenaries home and emptied the safe house of surveillance equipment, Freeman would spill her guts. He wished he knew if she already had. That gap in his knowledge bothered him.

And another thing still bothered him – the identity of the man the CIA had photographed meeting Len Stone outside his club a couple of weeks ago. The CIA had sent the photograph to MI5, but it had taken MI5 a week or more to reply. Some Joe Soap, they said. Somebody named Colin Shepherd. No criminal record, worked in the city. No big deal. But one of Skinner's own agents, tasked with checking out Stone's club, told him that Shepherd was now working there, behind the bar. Why would a businessman from the city need to work a bar in his spare time? There were, of course, two reasons why MI5's reply to Skinner reply might have been tardy. Perhaps Colin Shepherd was so harmless, so anonymous, that the Security Service could hardly bother itself to deal with the query. Alternately – and this was the possibility that bothered Skinner – perhaps they had needed to create a cover story for him. If this Shepherd was an MI5 agent, why would *they* want him in Stone's club? Sure, Stone smoked some weed, and sure, patrons were snorting charlie in the toilets. But that was a police matter. MI5 wouldn't be involved. Skinner was left with the worrying notion that MI5 also wanted to get close to Stone, and through him, to Emily Freeman. That was, of course, assuming that Colin Shepherd was not simply an anonymous city worker. In this business, paranoia could run out of control.

Skinner had no jurisdiction here; there were limits to what he could do. And there were also limits to what he could ask Langley to do; he didn't want to arouse the CIA's suspicion.

86

There were only certain things he could ask Langley to do for him, without arousing their suspicions. In the end, he had asked a private dick to check out Shepherd. The dick knew the ways of the British system – electoral rolls, telephone directories, utilities, discreet questions of friends in the tax offices and social services. Still, the dick had only reiterated what MI5 had told him. Shepherd's address, telephone number, social security number, and National Health Service number all tied up. The dick had followed him to his city office. Shepherd seemed to have strange working hours, and had taken a lot of leave lately. Still, to phone Shepherd's offices – which provided the kind of secretive private banking service that warranted its own high levels of security – and ask the kind of questions that Skinner wanted answered would itself have aroused suspicion.

'Mason's finished,' the driver said.

Skinner looked through the windscreen again, and saw the mercenary climbing down the pole. He looked at his watch. Barnes and Britten should be finished soon. He was becoming impatient now. He wanted the job done, and Freeman and Stone to come home, so he could begin listening in to their conversations and phone calls. He was tempted to pray that Barnes and Britten would get out safely, now he knew that Mason had completed his job successfully. He thought that praying would be an abuse of his relationship with God, whose blessings he had always received with gratitude – particularly over the last fifteen years, since he had joined Project Flashlight. If there *were* aliens – which was possible, although he knew that the UFO stories he had heard and seen reported in the press were hokum, especially as he had planted many of them – he wondered how they had been brought to God. Had Jesus appeared on each planet when God deemed the alien races ready to receive His wisdom, the good news? It would have to be Jesus – otherwise the Holy Trinity would be the Holy Infinity. Unless the Holy Trinity was only local. Perhaps the Father and Holy Ghost were a spiritual Duality permeated the universe, while the Son differed on every planet. He wondered whether he was being heretical for thinking this. His theological musings were interrupted by the rear doors of the van opening. Mason clambered in.

'Any problems?' Skinner asked.

'Receiving loud and clear,' Mason said. He passed a small instrument to Skinner. It showed the strength of the signal being received. The signal was strong.

'Good work,' Skinner said.

The doors to the van swung open again, and Barnes and Britten climbed in. Before Skinner could speak, Barnes said, 'Check the signal, Mason.'

Mason turned a dial on his instrument. Skinner knew that it changed the receiving frequency. 'Perfect signal,' Mason said.

Skinner nodded, and then looked at Barnes. 'Good. You left the house as you found it?'

'Of course,' Barnes said.

Skinner tapped the window to the cab. 'Get us out of here, Oldrey.'

The diesel engine of the Ford van chugged into life. Oldrey drove the van two hundred yards down the road, where he turned into another street. Oldrey found a space between parked cars and pulled into it. Skinner and the mercenaries exited the van, and walked a few yards down the road to a house similar to Stone's.

Skinner unlocked the door. 'Welcome to your new home, boys,' he said. 'Enjoy it – it's costing the US tax-payer a pretty penny.'

Oldrey went to the kitchen to put the kettle on. Skinner and the other three mercenaries went upstairs. The back bedroom had been turned into the kind of high-tech surveillance studio unlikely to be found in the London suburbs.

Britten pressed various controls, and green lights flickered on across different devices. Loudspeakers hissed into life. 'The signals are good,' he said.

All they now had to do was wait for Freeman and Stone to return home. The three mercenaries were focused on the state of the art equipment in front of them. Now, Skinner thought, while their attention was not on him, would be an opportune moment to offer a quick prayer to the God who continued to watch over him.

8

Edge and Harry had a plan for Len that required him to visit Peta's grave in Harry's company. Harry was at the cemetery now, checking out the location, seeing how busy it was on a weekday. When Edge had suggested Harry visit the site, he had been eager to go, as soon as possible. He *needed* to go. He had, of course, never visited Peta's grave. Edge had held up his hand. 'Say no more. Of course, of course. I know your time with Miss Shepherd left you with unresolved feelings. Go to the Midlands, say what you need to say to Peta.'

'Thanks, Mick. I'll be back tomorrow.'

'You'd better be,' Edge had said.

Harry was down on his haunches before the still fresh grave of Peta, feeling a little foolish. He didn't know what to say. He wasn't an atheist, as such, more of an agnostic. He hadn't prayed since he was a kid. He didn't think anything he said now would be heard by Peta. He continued to crouch beside the grave, looking at the black, recently-turned soil in front of him. And then he realised that what he wanted to say wasn't for Peta, and certainly not for God, but for himself. He wanted to say out loud what he'd been thinking. By saying it, it would become real. He lived in a world of lies and shadows, of deception and dissembling. If he *spoke* the truth, he would know it to be the truth.

He dropped his head, as if unable to face the imaginary Peta as he spoke. 'I loved you, Peta,' he said. 'I wish I'd told you at the time. But I couldn't. You loved Archie. And... And it wasn't my job to fall in love with you.'

He started at a voice from above him. 'What *was* your job then?'

Harry turned towards the voice The face he saw there surprised him. He fell backwards slightly, putting out a hand to steady himself. The same round face, the same small nose, the same big brown eyes. The chestnut brown hair was longer, and framed the face differently. Harry could hardly speak. 'Who are you?'

'I'm Molly. Molly Shepherd.'

Harry stood and faced the girl. She was taller than Peta, a good four or five inches taller. She didn't have Peta's delicacy, but she had poise, and, to have approached Harry so stealthily, a certain grace. 'Molly,' Harry said, echoing her. 'Molly Shepherd. Peta's younger sister.'

A fine eyebrow lifted on Molly's face. 'Yes, her younger sister. Margaret. Or Molly. I prefer Molly, and so did Peta. Who are you?'

Harry was caught. He couldn't be Colin Shepherd, could he? What if there was already a relative called Colin? And yet it wasn't time to be Harry. 'Colin,' Harry said. He smiled. He was always Colin. 'Pleased to meet you.'

Molly was not easily charmed. 'Colin who?'

Harry thought fast. 'My surname is only usually winkled out of me over coffee.'

'I don't drink coffee with mysterious strangers,' Molly said. 'I don't winkle.'

'I'm... sorry to hear that.'

'Well, there you are. Now, I'd like to be alone with my sister.'

Harry turned, and walked down the path towards the gate. He glanced over his shoulder, to find Molly also glancing over hers. He continued down the path to the entrance. Here, he sat on the wall and waited. He shivered in the cold. Ten minutes passed before he heard the sound of boots on the path. He turned as Molly approached.

'Molly?' Harry said. 'I'd... I'd like to talk to you. About Peta.'

'Colin No-Name? I'd like to talk to you too. And specifically, what you meant when you said it wasn't your job to fall in love with Peta.'

Harry examined the face again. Molly looked away, discomfited by this scrutiny. He was trying to see into her, to understand what she already knew. 'I was with her,' Harry said quietly. 'I left a few days before she died.'

'You knew her then?'

'Pretty well. We got on together.'

'But you didn't get together. Otherwise you wouldn't have said what you said just now.'

'No, we didn't.' Harry rubbed his hands together. 'Look, Molly, it's cold. Let's go and have a coffee. You won't have to winkle anything out of me. I'll tell you what I know.'

She nodded, and Harry guided her towards the car. Why he was doing this, he didn't know. There was nothing in it for the Service. Peta and Molly had been separated by circumstance for about two years. Molly hadn't been involved in all the ufological nonsense, and certainly knew nothing about Archibald Franklin Conn. Yet Molly was a connection to Peta, the only connection he now had. And there was that striking resemblance.

Harry took two mugs of coffee to the table where Molly sat. As he sat down he gave her a smile he hoped was reassuring. He had decided to be honest with her, in a way he couldn't be with Peta.

He sipped his coffee, and smiled at her again. 'Peta was a lovely girl.'

'Woman,' Molly said. 'She was a lovely woman. I'm the girl. She was older than me.'

'Yes, I know. She was two years older than you.'

'Eighteen months,' Molly said. 'But close enough.'

'I was watching her,' Harry said.

'Watching her?'

'Yes, watching her. I lied to you just now. My name isn't Colin. It's Harry Roberts. I work for... *people*... who had an interest in Peta. She knew me as Colin Butler.'

Molly narrowed her eyes. 'Harry? Colin? Colin, Harry? What should I believe? I don't trust anybody or anything. Show me something with your name on it.'

Harry took his driving license from his wallet, and handed it to Molly. She unfolded it, and studied it. She then reached down to her handbag, and took out a pen, put it on a napkin and slid them over to Harry. 'Sign the napkin.'

'You're very careful.'

'I know.' Molly looked at the napkin, and then at the driving licence. She handed the licence back to Harry.

Harry folded the licence and put it carefully back into the wallet, then slipped the wallet inside his coat. 'Luckily, I have *my* wallet with me today, rather than Colin's, otherwise we would both be confused.'

'Okay, so you are who you say you are. But who do you work for?'

'I'm afraid I can't tell you.'

'So, the... what do you call them... secret services?'

Harry shook his head. 'I want to be honest with you, but there are some things I can't say. So I will say – I can neither confirm nor deny that I work for such a service.'

Molly picked up her mug in both hands, lifted it to her mouth, but looked intensely into Harry's eyes. She took a sip of her coffee and then placed the mug carefully back on the table. She shook her head. 'But I don't understand. What was Peta mixed up in?'

'Nothing serious. She wouldn't have been arrested or locked-up. It was thought she might have...' He approached

93

the word carefully, knowing it was ambiguous, and uncertain of what Molly already knew. 'Contacts. Contacts with information.'

She raised the eyebrow again. 'Contacts? You mean flying saucer contacts?'

'Yes. How do you know about that?'

'I don't, really. When Peta... died... mum went down to Dereham, of course. The only person who really seemed to know Peta was the flying saucer... expert.'

'Patterson? Richard Patterson?'

'Yes, that's him. Mum said he was kind of other-worldly, that he didn't seem to care too much about day-to-day things. He was off in the stars, she said. All he knew was that Peta had been depressed. She'd been dumped by her boyfriend, he said. Oh, and that her other friend had left her, unexpectedly.'

Harry knew that his face showed his hurt.

'Oh,' Molly said. 'Mum said the friend that left her was Colin somebody. That was you, wasn't it?'

Harry nodded. 'Yes,' he said sadly.

'Bastard,' Molly said.

Harry looked at Molly intently. 'Honestly, Molly, I didn't know how depressed she was. She was, as you said, a woman. A grown-up. I didn't know how much she had been hurt by Archie leaving her.'

Molly shook her head, but more as if she was shaking something away from her than denying Harry. 'I'm sorry, Mr Roberts. I don't know what happened down there. I'm wrong to blame you in any way. Even that Archie–'

'Oh, you can blame him all you want,' Harry said. 'Archibald Franklin Conn was a devious, manipulative shit.'

Molly frowned. 'That Patterson bloke didn't seem to feel quite as strongly as you.' She shrugged. 'Mum said he thought Archie was all right.'

'Patterson tends to see the best in people, especially if they say they believe in flying saucers. It was different for me. I got to know Archie well, I knew what he was like. I lived with them, you see. I was their lodger.'

Molly smiled sadly. 'And that was when you fell in love with Peta.'

She was intuitive, Harry thought. He put his coffee down on the table and sat back in his chair. 'Yes. That's right. I fell in love with her.'

'Is that why you left?'

'In a manner of speaking.'

'What does that mean?'

'My... boss... He could see what was happening. He ordered me back. I had to go.'

'But if you'd stayed...'

Molly was right, Harry thought. What if I'd stayed? Would Peta still be with us now? Even if she hadn't loved me, would my support at least have helped her through that difficult time? He believed that Archie had triggered the events leading to Peta's death. But what if it had been *his* actions. What if Peta had finally broken when her last friend left her? He thought back to the cottage in Dereham. Without him and Archie there the small house would have seemed too big, empty and quiet. She had lived on the streets for so long before moving to Dereham. Had she harboured dreams of domesticity, of a settled life, that had been shattered by Archie's, and then his, departure?

'Mr Roberts, I hope you don't blame yourself. She *was* an adult...'

'Yes, but a fucked-up adult.' He looked at Molly. He wanted to know what she knew about Peta and her father, but it was a difficult subject to broach. 'Peta told me she ran away from home to get away from her father'

Molly, who had seemed until now so open, retreated inside herself. 'Yes,' she said quietly. 'Dad was a pig.'

'Can you tell me...?'

'No, I can't. It's not as bad as you think, nor was it in any way good. I don't think Peta told you everything?'

Harry shrugged. Peta *had* told him everything, in those dark days after Archie had left her.

'I can't tell you. It's not my place. I don't know if what she said has bothered you, but don't let it. As I say, it's not as bad as you fear, but is worse than you could know.'

Harry nodded, but he had learned now that Molly didn't know everything. Peta had been guarded in what she had told him, but what she had told him had been as bad as he had feared. Molly didn't know. Another secret. Had Peta been sacrificed by her mother to protect Molly? It was a question he knew he couldn't ask. 'You seem... different.'

Molly looked around her, then back at Harry. 'I was stronger than Peta. I know that now. And Mum did finally leave Dad. I've had time to recover. I've used that time to help myself. I realised that the problem isn't *me*. The problem is Dad.'

'You are more assured. Less timid,' Harry agreed. But it conflicted with what Peta had told him. Molly was weak and nervous, Peta said. Had she been lying? Perhaps not lying, he thought - exaggerating, dramatizing the situation? How much, then, of what Peta had told him that night was true?

'I am stronger, I think,' Molly said. 'Ironically, that probably comes from Dad. Mum would have left him years ago if she had been... *more assured.*' She smiled and then looked down at her mug. She ran a finger around its rim. 'But when we did finally leave, that's when we lost touch with Peta. We didn't hear from Peta for a long time. She wouldn't talk to mum. She did phone Granny Shepherd, though. I think that was her way of talking to mum, you know? Then Granny Shepherd died, and new people bought the house. Peta phoned them before she... died. But the woman at the house said Peta put the phone down before she had time to give her mum's new number. Once Granny Shepherd died, it was like we disappeared from Peta's life. When Peta phoned Granny's house and heard a different voice, I think she panicked, thought she'd lost us forever.'

'Lost *you*,' Harry said. 'Lost *you*. She was always talking about you. I think she resented your mother for not protecting her. She was worried about you, though. She wanted to find you, and get you down to Dereham with her. She talked about it all the time.'

'Why didn't she phone when Granny Shepherd was still alive?'

'She wanted to. But she'd just moved to Dereham, she was in love with Archie, everything was new and exciting. I think time passed too quickly.' Harry looked at the windows of the café, which were covered in condensation. 'Anyway, your grandmother might have already died by then. She would still have felt she'd lost you.'

Harry looked back at Molly. There were tears in her eyes. 'I wish I could have helped her, Mr Roberts.'

Harry took one of her hands. 'Please, call me Harry. Believe me, there was nothing you could have done. Perhaps I could have helped, if I'd stayed. But she *was* depressed. I didn't think she would...' He shook his head, and looked down at the table. He could feel tears in his eyes too. 'If that bastard Archie hadn't used her, then tossed her aside...'

'You sound bitter... Harry. Angry, even.'

Molly was right, Harry thought. He was angry. Angry with Archibald Franklin Conn. Conn had known her history as well as he had. To toy with her, to use her in the way he had, and then to leave her, *dump* her, had been *cruel*. Conn should also suffer. 'I'm going to get him,' Harry said.

Molly moved her hand, so that she could squeeze his. 'Go get him, Harry.' She smiled at him.

That smile, so like Peta's, encouraged him. And thrilled him, in a way it shouldn't.

9

As he wiped down the top of the bar, Harry reminded himself that the object of this assignment was Emily Freeman, and not Archibald Franklin Conn, despite what he had said to Molly. Yet the urge to find Archie was strong. Morrow had found tyre tracks cut into a track near the Conn house, and leading out onto the road. The tyres had the typical pattern found on a four-wheel drive vehicle, like a Land Rover. Might have been a local farmer, Morrow said. Could it have been Archie? If Harry found Conn as a result of this operation, that would be a happy coincidence. He had talked to Len and Martyn about Conn, had they had no idea where he was, that much was clear. Harry wasn't even sure what he wanted to do even if he found Archie. Hit him? Talk to him? Cry with him?

Len was in a good mood this morning, which was fortunate. What Harry was about to suggest would require tact, and a complaisant Len. Harry wasn't comfortable with what he was going to do – he liked Len, and he liked Emily. Still, *liking* never usually got in the way of the job. *Liking* people was an inevitable consequence of gaining trust. He would have to do what he needed to do soon, however. This job was, after all, temporary. Once the new bar-hand started, he would see less of Len.

Harry had gone through the plan with Edge again the previous evening. Edge still thought the scheme risky and perhaps unnecessary. But Harry had reminded Edge that they needed access to Emily soon, and their only avenue was through Len. Len needed to be compromised. Harry knew that his plan would create that compromise. It *was* a risk, but a risk worth taking. It would deliver up Len, and thus Emily, quickly. Although he still had reservations, Edge gave Harry permission to carry out the plan. He said he'd call Harry once the arrangements had been made. Harry had nervously waited for an hour after he arrived home, fidgeting around his spartan flat, before Edge rang to confirm everything was ready, and that he would provide contact details in the morning. Edge had finished the phone call with less than positive encouragement. 'Don't screw it up, Harry.'

Harry put down the cloth and turned to the optics. Len was happy, now Emily was finally here and living in his house. They were *shacking up together*, as Len put it. She was, he said, in town, shopping for what she had called the *finishing touches* to the house. 'I warned her not to spend too much,' he had said, but Harry could see he didn't mean it. There was a twinkle in his eye, and he hummed to himself as he walked across the dance floor of *Peta's*, straightening up tables and chairs, before heading to his office. His life was good, Harry thought, replacing a whiskey optic. Income from the club was increasing, he had Emily, he'd cut his ties to the Manley Boys. Len was at peace with the world. *Shame, then, that I'm going to ruin all that.*

Martyn came through the door behind the bar. 'You all right, Colin? You seemed miles away.'

'I'm fine,' Harry said. 'I need to talk to Len though.'

'You go on, mate. I'll finish the optics.'

Harry thanked Martyn, and then walked out of the door into the corridor that led to Len's office. He knocked at the office door, then poked his head around it. 'Len, can you spare me a minute?'

'Sure, Colin. Sit down.'

Harry sat in the chair opposite Len, and thought for a

moment how to begin. Len had obviously been thinking about things unrelated to work, and spoke before Harry could. 'You know, Colin, when I changed the name of the club from *The Purple Parrot* to *Peta's*, I laid a few ghosts to rest.'

Mentioning Peta's name was a happy coincidence, Harry thought. He would let Len carry on talking. This frame of mind played into his hands.

Len fiddled with the leaves of the spider plant on his desk. 'But this office is still the same.' He paused. 'I should do something about it.'

'Perhaps you should, Len,' Harry said.

'I will do. Soon. There are too many memories in here.' He glanced at the spider plant in its antique pot. He smiled, and nodded to the pot. 'I used to hide my stash in there.'

Harry laughed. 'Where do you hide it now?'

'In a money box in the safe. I learned my lesson after Archie stole all my grass.'

'From the pot?'

'No, he stole a bigger stash, hidden in the barrel in the bedsit. You know the one?'

'The one by the bed?'

'That's the one. Do you want a coffee?'

Harry nodded. Len stood and went to the kitchen in the bedsit where he switched on the kettle. Harry could see and hear him through the door. He turned back to Harry, leaning against the worktop. 'Yes, that pot has to go. And that sofa. I used to sleep on it when Peta stayed over. After the contact sessions, you know? Before she ran off with that shit Archie.'

He turned away and spooned coffee into a mug. 'The office could do with a dab of paint, too.' The kettle boiled. Len finished making Harry's coffee, and returned to his chair behind the desk. He handed over Harry's coffee. 'Sorry, Colin, I'm rambling. But with Emily here now, I feel like shaking off some of my past. What is it you wanted?'

'Well, I don't know how this will fit with your current mood of positivity, but I'm going to visit Peta's grave. I thought you might like to come.'

'Oh.' Len fidgeted in his chair. 'Really?'

What Harry was to say next, he'd rehearsed last night. 'Yes. Don't ask me why, but while I was asleep it seemed... well...' He thought a dramatic pause seemed apt. He looked away from Len, and took a sip of his coffee. 'You know, it seemed as if she was calling to me.'

Stone's mouth set into a straight line, and he clasped his hands, almost as if he was in prayer, in front of his chin. 'What do you mean, she *called* to you?'

Harry shrugged, and had another sip of his coffee. 'Well, it seemed more like a dream, I don't know, it was just so vivid, so... so, real.' If that doesn't work with Len, he thought, nothing will. Harry knew about the contact sessions, how they had worked. He had heard it all from Peta. Len no longer had contact sessions; he had, it seemed, left all that esoteric nonsense behind him. Yet Harry suspected that Len had not yet become a sceptic, that he still believed in paranormal phenomena – in ESP, and telepathy, and spirits and the like. 'I guess,' Harry continued, 'I feel like I never said goodbye properly. We were so close when we were young, before the family... split.' It was true that he had never said goodbye properly. He often didn't in his job. 'It's been on my mind for a while. Being here with her old friends has brought it all back.'

Len studied Harry for a moment. Harry knew he was almost there. 'Go on Len, come with me. You knew her so well. You helped her off the street when she was in trouble.

102

And I could do with the company. Martyn was saying that you hadn't had a decent break in months.'

Len's face had been so serious, but now broke into a smile. 'Yes, why the hell not? Mind you, I'd have to clear it with the other half first. I could always call it a business trip. I was thinking of expanding my little business, anyway. I could look at some properties for a club in Birmingham. When were you thinking of going up there?'

'Well, today's Monday, the club is normally closed on Wednesday and Thursday, so I thought then.'

'Thought this out, haven't you?' Len grinned. 'Okay, but on one condition. You come back to my place with me tonight. If I tell Emily while you're there, chances are she'll agree.'

Of course she would, thought Harry. Poor, kind, Emily.

As Len's small car passed through the tree-lined streets of West London, Harry thought how well Len had done for himself. Granted, the foundations of his small empire had been built on a debt to the Manley Boys – second-tier East End gangsters – but to give Len his due, he'd paid back his debts, broken his ties with them, and was now, as far as he and the service knew, an honest, law-abiding, honest-to-god hippie businessman.

Len swung the car into the drive of a smart, semi-detached house. 'Home sweet home,' he said. They got out of the car, and Len led the way up the path.

Emily opened the door as they approached. 'Hiya, babe.' She noticed Harry walking behind Len. 'Hi, Colin. Hey, Len, you bringing work home with you now?'

'Kind of. Colin has given me an idea. I'll explain once you've got the coffee brewing.'

Emily's mouth shaped into a mischievous grin. 'So, a

103

couple of weeks in Limey-land, and now I'm the dutiful little lady, huh? What next, cute little cucumber sandwiches on the terrace? Come on then, let's hear your *idea*.'

Len and Harry followed Emily to the kitchen. Harry looked about him as he moved through the house, his professional senses alert. 'Nice place you have here, Len,' he said as Emily handed a coffee to him.

'Well, it's a place to sleep' Len answered.

'Yeah, sleep... And other things too...' Emily teased Len, a glint in her eye.

Harry was surprised to feel a blush creeping over his cheeks. Emily noticed. 'Jeez, you Brits, you're so hung up over a bit of hanky-panky. It was a joke, Colin, just a joke.' She chuckled. 'We don't have sex really.'

Harry felt the blush re-start, and then he laughed. 'You're right, we Brits are so hung-up. Unless it involves a whip and a horse.'

Emily laughed again. She turned to Len. 'Right then, lover boy, what's the news from the front line?'

'Well–' Len began, but was interrupted by Emily.

'Sorry, Len, I've just remembered something weird I just have to tell you. You know that ring you bought me, at the weekend?'

Len lifted her right hand and looked at it. 'The eternity ring, yes?'

'Yeah, that's the one. Well, I couldn't find it this morning. I thought I'd lost it.' She held it up for Harry to see. 'An eternity ring, see? He loves me.' She quickly kissed Len.

'Is that it?' Len asked. 'Not much of a story.'

'What? Nooooo. No, what's weird is this. I'm sure I put it on the table on my side of the sofa last night, after I took it off.' She looked at Harry. 'I don't want to wear it to the club, Colin. I don't want to get booze and Fairy Liquid all over it.'

Harry found himself wondering if they had Fairy Liquid in the States, as Emily began speaking again. 'Anyway, when I looked this morning, the ring wasn't there. It had moved all by itself. It had teleported.' She looked at Len. 'No, wait. What do *you* call it, honey? *Apported*, that's it. Perhaps it *apported* all by itself.' She laughed, and spoke to Harry again. 'I do like to rib Len about his crazy old notions.'

'Where was it, then?' Len asked.

'On the other table, the one on your side of the sofa.'

'Perhaps you forgot which table you put it on.'

'Oh, no, Len, I never forget something like that. I never forget where I put my jewellery.'

She was a woman, Harry thought, of course she wouldn't.

'Let's make ourselves comfortable,' Emily said. She led the way through to the lounge. Harry sat in an armchair that was positioned at a slight angle to the settee Len and Emily occupied. There were interesting objects around the room – a Buddha on the mantelpiece that looked as though it had come from India and an ornate wooden joss-stick holder. Harry knew that Len had travelled the hippie trail, back before he had met Peta, searching for some form of enlightenment. The walls held interesting modern art. Artists came to the club, and Len had probably bought them there – or settled drinking debts with them. On the wall above the Buddha was a poster from The Gentleman Farmers' last tour, signed by the band. At both ends of the settee were the tables Emily had mentioned. They were small, and ornate, carved in an Indian style – something else from his travels?

'So what's happening?' Emily said.

Len looked at Harry. 'Well, Colin had this idea that he'd like to visit Peta's grave.'

Emily's looked at Harry, concern on her face. 'Oh, Colin! Haven't you visited it yet?'

Harry cleared his throat, as if embarrassed. 'Well, there are... problems... in the family.'

'Yes, you've mentioned them, honey. Well, don't let them put you off. You must go and see her and say your farewells.'

Len put a hand gently on Emily's arm. 'I hope you don't mind, Em, but I'm going to take Colin up there. I want to look around some business premises in Birmingham. I'm thinking of expanding my modest empire.'

'Aww, Len. Of course you can take Colin up. And you can also stop and say goodbye to Peta.'

Len stuttered. 'I didn't mean, uh, that I wanted to... you know...'

'It doesn't matter if you didn't. When you get there, you'll want to, and that's okay by me. I know you didn't love her like you love me, and even if you did, of course it would be okay to say goodbye to a friend.'

Len leaned over and kissed Emily on the cheek. 'You are a fine woman, Emily Freeman.'

She laughed. 'I know I am.'

She certainly was, Harry thought. And bright and vivacious. Sometimes, his job could be so cruel.

'When are you going?' Emily asked.

'Oh, the club is normally closed on Wednesdays and Thursdays,' Len said. Harry only half-listened as Len spoke; he was scrutinising the room again. 'So I thought we'd hit the road early Wednesday morning. That okay with you both?'

'That's okay by me,' Emily said.

'And by me,' Harry added.

They made small talk. Harry noticed that Emily sat on Len's left-hand side. They probably always sat that way. Couples became comfortable with a certain handedness – same side of the bed, same side of the sofa, same side of the dinner table, same side when they walked down the street. Len and Emily were talking about what she had bought in town; lampshades, a throw, cushion covers, a duvet. They were laughing about the duvet, how un-British it was. That was true. Harry still slept beneath blankets and sheets. He thought he should try one. His previous train of thought came back to him. It would be natural for Emily to put her eternity ring on that table, on what would naturally become her side of the sofa. So how would it end up on the other table, six feet away? Len was talking about the hippie trail, as Emily joshed him about his *objet d'art*. Harry smiled politely. Emily's table had a table-lamp on it. The table-lamp had a pine, barley-twist stalk with a faux Tiffany lampshade, all red and green glass. Behind and below it was a double-gang electrical socket. Only the table-lamp was plugged into it. Len was talking about the band playing at *Peta's* this week, a return visit for The Gentleman Farmers. Booking them was quite a coup, given their recent successes in both the singles and album charts, but they had made their start at *The Purple Parrot*, and Len had been instrumental in growing their fan-base in London.

'I like them,' Harry said. Indeed, he had one of their albums, their second. He ought to buy their first. He looked over at the television. It was plugged into the wall opposite the settee. No trailing wires there. The electrics in the house had been neatly arranged. If the ring had moved from Emily's table to Len's table, perhaps Len had moved it. But then... They would have come back from the club late last night, and Len came into work this morning alone. He probably got up, went to the kitchen, made himself a coffee, and then went to the club. Harry doubted he would have gone into the lounge and sat on the settee. There was nothing worth watching on television at that time of the day.

He realised quickly that Len was addressing him. 'Where did you say Peta is buried?'

'Hagley,' Harry said. 'Up Brum way,'

'Yes, she was a Black Country girl.'

Len explained the Black Country to Emily. What, Harry thought, if somebody else had moved the ring? Emily hadn't moved it. Len *probably* hadn't moved it. Then somebody else must have moved it. Len hadn't mentioned a break-in this morning, and they both appeared too happy now to have been bothered by such an incident. Anyway, if there had been a break-in, given the sensitive nature of Emily Freeman's presence – both on this side of the pond and in Len's house – and the interest of at least two intelligence agencies, Harry was sure Edge would have heard of it, and relayed the information to him. No, there had been no burglary. After all, Emily's ring had not been stolen; it had merely mysteriously moved tables. He focussed again on the table on Emily's side, as Len explained Martyn's Brummagen accent and its relation to The Black Country. His eyes moved down to the plug behind the table. It was, he thought, the obvious place for a bug. Had the Yanks been in here? It was a possibility. He wanted to get closer to that socket. He wanted to unscrew it, and see if anything lurked behind the faceplate.

He imagined then, that a team had been in, leaving bugs in appropriate locations. There were sockets in here, in the kitchen, and in the bedroom. No sockets allowed in bathrooms – oh, except for shaver sockets. Perhaps one of the team, tasked with bugging the lounge, had moved Emily's table before noticing the ring. The ring had slid off the table, onto the carpet, and rolled closer, perhaps, to Len's table. When they had all finished, they had checked the house one last time. They wouldn't have hurried, but they would have felt the pressure of time. Somebody had checked the room, seen the ring on the floor and put it back on the wrong table. It was a possibility. It should be investigated.

Harry glanced at his watch. It was 1.30 in the morning. 'I'd better get going, Len.'

'I'll give you a lift home.'

'No, you snuggle up with Emily. I'll get a taxi. There's plenty up on the main road.'

Emily showed Harry to the door. 'Hey, Colin, tell you what. Why not come over tomorrow night after work with Len and stay over? Then you can get off to an early start in the morning.'

'Are you sure that's all right?' Harry said. 'I don't want to impose on the two of you.'

Emily placed a hand on his arm. 'No problem. Besides, it makes perfect sense. The sooner you two leave, the sooner you'll be back.'

Harry walked a couple of hundred yards to the junction, where South Avenue met the main road. There was a telephone box across the road.

The phone was answered within three rings. After the usual security protocols had been observed, Edge came on the line.

'Sorry it's late, boss,' Harry said.

'Och, don't worry about it. I've been studying the movements of some of the local CIA operatives. You know, I'm beginning think that it's not Langley pulling the strings. Whoever it is that's interested in Emily Freeman is... well, somebody else... Somebody using Langley for their own ends, perhaps.'

'Any ideas who?'

'Not at the moment. But Freeman was nominally attached to the Air Force. Makes you think, doesn't it? Anyway, are you all set for your wee jaunt to the Midlands?' Edge almost seemed in a good mood.

'All done. I'm staying over with the happy couple the night before. I think their house might have been bugged, though.'

'Why do you think that?'

'Emily's ring moved from one table to another.'

Edge laughed. 'That's why we spent all that time training you, to notice the small things, the connections, the things out of place.'

'It would be worth checking out Stone's house, I think.'

'Sensible idea. Now, everything else is in place, so just stick to your plan. And remember, if it all goes tits up, it's your head on the block.' With that, Edge termimated the connection.

As Harry walked along the road, keeping an eye out for a taxi, he thought about his head on the block. The simple but high-stakes plan he'd come up with could go wrong. If it did, everything would be compromised. If Len found out he and Emily had been the subject of an MI5 investigation - before Harry's plan had come to fruition, at least - there would probably be a major diplomatic row with the Americans. This was a clandestine operation, unsanctioned and with no higher authority than Edge. Harry knew he would be the fall guy. He would be out on his ear. No contacts, no intelligence, and the ultimate goal of finding Archibald Franklin Conn out of his reach.

10

The club had been quiet. Unusually for a weekday, *Peta's* had been competing with the opening of a high-profile movie with attendant celebrities, and a major rock concert at the Hammersmith Odeon. A bomb scare on the District Line had also kept punters away; recent terrorist activity by the Provisional IRA and Black September had made people nervous. By midnight, only a few regulars remained at the club. Len decided to close early; he had a quiet word with the punters, who quickly drifted into the night.

By one o'clock in the morning, Harry was in the guest room at Len's house, preparing for bed. Emily and Len were also in bed. He had heard the bedroom door shut a final time. He looked at the electrical socket on the wall. He fumbled in his jacket pocket for his Swiss Army knife. After a minute, he had removed the faceplate of the socket. Nothing seemed amiss. The Anglepoise light on the bedside table was connected to a single socket behind the bed. He tried moving the double bed. It was too heavy to move quietly. He could reach the plug of the Anglepoise; he could even pull it out; but he couldn't easily unscrew the faceplate of the socket.

He would leave it as a problem for Edge to sort out. Edge would be able to get an expert into the house with tools and detectors. If the house had been bugged – and Harry's gut instinct told him it had – then he and Edge would have find out who had planted the devices. Edge suspected Langley were out of the loop, except, perhaps, for providing materiel.

So who else might be bugging the house? No other intelligence agency, Harry suspected, would be at all interested in the frankly weird information he'd been tasked to elicit from Peta Shepherd. That was a pet obsession of somebody high up in the Service. Yet the Yanks did have in interest in Freeman, whose father had also been a contactee. What that interest was, Harry found difficult to imagine. Although her father had been a contactee, and had a written a book on that subject, Harry already knew Emily had no interest in UFOs. He'd sounded her out on the subject. She thought it was, she had said to him, all bunkum.

Emily had worked for the Air Force part-time as an administrator, or clerk. Emily was always vague on the actual tasks involved. She made her job sound mundane, work-a-day. The rest of the time, she was a literary agent for her father, whose book about his contacts, *Panlyrae–A Message for Mankind*, was something of a cult classic. She had accompanied him on book-signings, which had taken him all over the world. She had needed to be with her father, she said, because he was an alcoholic – he had, in fact, died from his addiction. Her Air Force employees had been very tolerant, Harry thought, of her leave arrangements, although Emily said she had arranged most book signings for the weekends. Still, that aspect of her life, the crossing the line between the paranormal world of her father and the mundane world of the USAF, perplexed Harry. Something didn't ring true there. He didn't think that Emily was lying; but he wondered if Emily's job in the USAF was somehow connected to her father's alien contacts.

Harry climbed under the duvet on his bed. It was an odd sensation at first; he kept thinking it was going to slip off him. Yet as he tried to assess the connections between Emily, her father, the USAF, and an obvious intelligence interest in

Len Stone, he found himself snuggling into the warm duvet, making a nest, he thought, and then dozing off.

The house was hot; Harry now knew it for certain. He had woken early, and crept downstairs to the kitchen. There, with his Swiss Army knife, he had removed the faceplate of one of the two double sockets. Tucked into the corner of the wall-box was a small bug. It was very modern – transistorised, with a miniature radio transmitter; it took power from the wiring in the socket. Nifty. Harry had heard about them in briefings. Five were expecting to get them soon. Somebody had them already, and the obvious suspects were the Yanks. Unless... There was always Six, of course. Six was, after all, the agency charged with international security. Perhaps they too were worried about Freeman. Or Stone. Yet to add Six to the mix would, Harry thought, make the whole thing – whatever this *thing* was – even more complicated. Harry screwed the faceplate back onto the socket and plugged the coffee percolator back into the socket. He put water, a filter and coffee into the percolator, and switched it on.

Len finally arrived, unkempt, with a prominent five-o'clock shadow across his cheeks and chin and his salt and pepper hair dishevelled. 'I smell coffee,' he said. 'You know how to use one of these coffee-making machines?'

Harry smiled. 'I'm a man of the world, Len.'

'Me, I'd have just put some instant in a couple of mugs. Would like some breakfast?'

'I don't really like to eat at this time of the morning.'

'Me neither. We'll get something on the way.'

'Is there a newsagent around here? I could do with a morning paper.'

Len rubbed his chin. 'Yes, top of the road, turn left, next to the post office.'

Harry didn't want a paper. It was a convenient excuse to

get to the phone box and call Edge. 'Can I get you anything from the shop?'

Len had opened the fridge. 'Pint of milk wouldn't go amiss, thanks.'

Harry moved to the front door. Len called after him. 'Leave the door on the latch. It's a decent neighbourhood.'

Harry quickly walked to the telephone box, where he called the office. Edge hadn't arrived yet. Harry impressed upon the operator the urgency of informing Edge as soon as possible about the bugs he'd found.

Harry strolled back to Len's house. The morning was bright; a weak November sun shone through high, white, translucent cirrus. The birds chirruped in the trees that retained few brown leaves now. Harry whistled happily to himself as he walked, but was aware of the incongruity of such good spirits when he was about trap a man he liked in the tangled web being weaved by intelligence services in at least two countries. A web, he thought, whose weave began with Peta Shepherd. His whistling tailed off as he remembered Peta.

The journey to the Midlands passed by without incident. Harry had memorized the journey a few days beforehand so he could act as if he knew the area from trips to visit his cousins. Hagley, Peta's hometown, was just on the outskirts of the West Midlands conurbation. They had reached it by late morning. Len pulled up at a café.

'It's been a long drive,' Len said. 'Let's have a cuppa.'

This was the same café, Harry realised, in which he had talked to Molly. He remembered her smile. 'Yes please.'

The tea was strong, and at least the cups seemed clean. They both had a bacon sandwich. Len lit a cigarette. After a few minutes he asked, 'So, how far now?'

Harry opened up his sandwich and poured thin tomato sauce onto his bacon from a red plastic bottle, shaped like a tomato with a black spout around which was a fringe of green plastic leaves. 'Well, we're about three miles from Stourbridge,' Harry said. 'She was buried in a cemetery on the outskirts of Stourbridge, in an area known as Norton, so I'd say ten, fifteen minutes, twenty tops.'

The weather had taken a turn for the worse, and wind blew rain against the windows of the café. 'We're going to get wet,' Len said.

Harry bit into the sandwich. The bacon tasted good, and the vinegary sweetness of the cheap ketchup was a delight. For Harry, who travelled a lot, this was one of the pleasures of the wayside café. No other tomato sauce tasted quite like this.

They chatted amiably about the weather and the club, until they had finished their tea and sandwiches, and then returned to Len's car. Len started the engine, and eased out of the car park and into the traffic. Harry navigated. Soon they were on the long Norton Road, heading towards Kidderminster. Harry glanced down at the map on his lap. 'It's just up here on the right.'

Len indicated, crossed onto the wrong side of the road, and pulled up. 'Here we are then,' he said. 'The dead centre of Stourbridge.'

Harry looked at Len blankly, wondering what he meant.

'*Dead* centre. *Cemetery*. You're slow today, Colin.' Then Len shook his head. 'Sorry, mate. Bad taste.'

Harry provided a wan smile for Len. 'Don't worry about it. We English never quite know how to approach Death.'

Harry looked around. He'd noted the last time he was here how tranquil the setting seemed. Over the quiet road, fields stretched into the distance. He opened the door and exited the car. The rain had slowed to a drizzle. Birds in the trees and hedges twittered and whistled. The countryside reminded him of the long, peaceful hours he had spent with Peta on Copsehill in Dereham. He looked over the low wall surrounding the cemetery. There was nobody else in the small cemetery.

'Come on, let's find her,' Len said. He spoke quietly, almost reverently.

Anxiety, Harry now realised, had squeezed out Len's poor joke. They walked through the gates and onto the path through the graveyard. At the far end of the cemetery the trees and bushes had been cut back to provide a new area for burials. Harry knew Peta's grave to be there, and he subtly guided Len towards it.

Len read the new gravestones and temporary markers as he walked. A few graves in front of him a man stood before a shining new marble headstone around which lay faded floral tributes. The man had in his hand a bouquet of fresh flowers, which he placed on the ground. 'Sorry, Peta,' he said. 'It was my fault. All my fault. I should have been more of a father to you.'

Len moved quickly. Harry moved more slowly. Len grabbed the stranger by the shoulder, and spun him. The man slipped, and the punch Len had aimed at his jaw lost most of its force, merely stunning the recipient. The man stumbled backwards.

'Len! What the hell are you doing?' Harry cried.

Len pulled the man back towards him. 'You bastard! You child-molesting creep! Because of you, Peta's dead!'

Harry arrived beside Len a split second too late. Len launched a blow that this time connected with the man's face. The man's head snapped back, and he fell to the ground. There was a crack as his skull hit a headstone. Harry shoulder-barged Len out of the way. 'You crazy bastard! What the hell was that about?'

Len stared at the man on the ground. He whispered hoarsely. 'It was him, Colin. It was... Peta's father...'

Harry knelt down beside the crumpled figure, and put two fingers on the pulse point at the neck. 'Shit. You're right. He *was* Peta's father.' Harry stood up. 'He's not any more. He's dead.' Len said nothing, swaying as he stood motionless looking down at Peta's father.

Harry looked around. Tall yew trees and evergreen shrubs hid him and Len from the road and the few neighbouring houses. But somebody could arrive at any moment. Harry grabbed Len and dragged him away from the graveside. 'Come on, Len, we need to get out of here, now!' Harry dragged Len towards the waiting car. As they approached the cemetery gates, Harry whispered urgently. 'Keys, Len, where are the car keys?'

Len mumbled something incoherent, and Harry was forced to dig into the pockets of Len's overcoat. He found the keys at the first attempt. Propping Len against the wall, Harry unlocked the car, leaned in and opened the passenger door. He hurriedly bundled Len into the passenger side of the car. With a last, furtive glance around to ensure nobody had seen them, Harry started the engine, gunned the motor and smoothly executed a three-point turn.

As Harry drove back towards Stourbridge, Len rocked gently backwards and forwards in his seat, giving voice to a low, pathetic moan every now and again. He suddenly looked up. 'Stop the car.'

Harry did as ordered. They'd pulled up next to a Mobil petrol station. Len opened the door, and noisily vomited into the gutter.

Harry put a comforting hand on Len's back, and spoke softly. 'Look, Len, there's a pub at the end of this road. I think we stop there and get you a drink, and clean you up. I could do with a stiff drink myself.'

Len straightened himself, and nodded his assent.

It was past midday, and the car park of *The White Horse* public house was sparsely filled. Harry pulled in, and turned off the engine.

Len reached behind them and found the box of tissues on the back seat. 'One of the useful aspects of being with a woman. Always bloody well prepared.' He pulled a wad of tissues from the box, and wiped his mouth. He then turned to Harry, the colour returning to his face. 'Sorry, Colin. Shock, I guess,' Len said, quietly. 'Everything's a blur. What happened back there? Did...did I kill him?'

11

Edge exited the taxi. The streets were wet, the pavements brown and grey. He was late. Very late. He had worked long into the night, and when he finally arrived home, sleep eluded him. Worry about what Harry planned to do today, most likely had already done, had nagged at him. Edge liked his job. It gave his life meaning. He didn't want to lose it because Harry had fouled up. He crossed Curzon Street and passed through the doors of Leconfield House. He debated whether to use the stairs or take the lift. The stairs won, and after a slow climb on tired legs to the third floor, he stopped at the duty officer's desk to collect his messages. He made himself a coffee, and then unlocked his office. Settling down at his own desk, he sifted through the messages that had arrived during his absence. Harry's caught his eye.

So, Stone's house was bugged. Edge put the other reports, and the problems they presented, to one side. Why would anybody bug Stone's house? What information had Emily Freeman carried from the States with her? The Freeman case became more complex and mysterious with each passing day. He picked up the telephone handset and dialled the operator. 'Get me James Pritchard at SIS, please.' Edge waited for the call to be answered at the other end. The phone rang for some time. Edge imagined Pritchard eyeing his telephone with disdain. Finally, ringing stopped and Pritchard's plummy voice greeted Edge.

'Michael, my dear fellow, what an unexpected and, may I say, pleasant surprise. What can we do for the junior service this morning?'

Some personnel in MI6 regarded the Security Service as nothing more than a glorified police force that dealt with trifling national concerns, while they performed the real business of national security. Edge was tired, and in no mood for nonsense. 'Cut the bullshit, James. I have one question for you. I expect the truth.'

'But of course! We *are* batting for the same team, after all. What do you wish to know?'

'Have you, or have you not, sanctioned a listening operation on home turf without getting our permission first?'

'That depends. What part of the country were you interested in?'

Edge sighed. Pritchard was obviously in a playful mood. There should be no listening operation in any part of the country outwith the Security Service's knowledge. Pritchard liked to pretend that there were operations Edge didn't know about. It was a joke that was wearing thin.

'London, Jimmy,' Edge said, knowing that Pritchard hated the name *Jimmy*. 'The suburb of Hayes. That's all I'm prepared to say at the moment.'

'Sorry to disappoint you, but we currently have no such operations within the confines of the mainland.' There was a pause, and then Pritchard continued, his voice now hard. 'And, of course, if we felt the need to run such an operation, we would be polite enough to run it past your service first. Good day, Michael.'

Edge slowly replaced the receiver. He hated having to ask MI6 – and Pritchard in particular – such questions. It implied weakness, of gaps in his knowledge. And Pritchard was a tit.

If MI6 weren't bugging Stone's house, who was? He knew it wasn't anybody in his service; if it were, he would have been told. Edge picked up the phone to talk to his secretary. 'Has Morrow arrived in the building yet?' He waited for the reply. 'Right, find him. If he's at home, get the bugger out of bed and tell him to get in straight away.

Morrow arrived just after midday, dishevelled and with heavy-lidded eyes. Edge looked him up and down. 'Och, you look like shite. Out on the town last night, were we?'

'In a manner of speaking, boss. I was in Slough, at the top of a multi-storey car-park.'

Edge remembered. He had sent Morrow there, after all. 'Ah, yes. Sorry. What time did you get back home?'

'I handed over to Davies at five-thirty and got back just after seven this morning.'

Edge frowned. 'I really am sorry. But you're the best man for this.' Edge showed Morrow the note.

'You want me to check out Stone's house?'

'Of course. But get yourself a coffee first. I don't think the bugs are going anywhere.'

Morrow arrived back at Edge's office late in the afternoon. 'No doubt about it, sir. The house is bugged. Modern stuff, as well. One in the hall, and two in the kitchen. I'd hazard a guess that each room in the house is wired.'

'There were no problems with Freeman?'

'She didn't suspect a thing. I gave her the usual flimflam.'

'We know it's not MI6. Who has the kind of resources to mount such an operation?'

'The Russians would be an obvious choice. She was in the United States Air Force, after all. They might think she had access to secrets.'

'No, I can't see that. The Russians are good at some things, but electronics aren't one of them. They still use valves. Transistors are a pretty new concept to them. My gut feeling is the Yanks.'

'Not so fast, boss. It could be any of the Western agencies. DGCE, Mossad, the Bundesnachrichtendienst.'

Edge laughed. 'You like saying that, don't you, Morrow?'

Morrow smiled in reply. 'You know I do.'

'Say *BND* like the rest of us.'

'No.'

'What did you learn about the signal?'

'It's pretty strong. The bugs could transmit a mile or so.'

'Any suspicious vans in the street?'

'Not that I could see. But they wouldn't need one with that transmitter. They could rent a house within a mile radius, perhaps two, and set up the receivers there.'

'So, we need to find if there's any rented accommodation in the area.'

'There's bound to be. This is London.'

Edge picked up the phone, called Liz Carter, and asked her to come to his office. 'It's the Yanks, Morrow. Trust me. And that means a whole heap of trouble for us.'

'And them,' Morrow added.

Carter knocked the door and then entered. Edge smiled up at her. 'This is a bit of boring job,' Edge said. He knew the girls got the boring jobs, and was doing his best to help women within the service. Yet, boring jobs had sometimes to be done. 'We need to find out which premises have been recently let within, say, a two mile radius of Mr Stone's house.'

'Flats, houses, shops, offices, garages, lock-ups?' Carter said.

She was quick, and efficient, Edge thought. She'd go far. She was already ahead of the rest of her intake. 'Yes, all of them,' he said – and then added, 'Of course.' He wouldn't like Carter to think he hadn't also thought of all possible types of rentable properties in the area.

'As soon as possible?'

'Yes, but get others to help you. Oh, and Liz, I know you're due to finish your shift at five o'clock, but...'

'Could I stay on and ensure this is carried through?'

'That's the gist of it, yes.'

'Overtime?'

'If you must.'

Carter gave him a smile. 'I like this job almost as much as you do, Mick. Still, I'm not about to give my time to the firm for nothing.'

'Fair enough, Liz. I'll sign off the paperwork.'

After speculating for another twenty minutes about who might have planted the bugs, Morrow went back to his office to write up some notes on the Slough job. It was another three hours before Liz Carter returned to his office.

Carter sat on the chair across the desk from Edge, and pushed her straight black fringe away from her eyes. She frowned. 'Do you know how many rentable spaces there are in that area?'

Edge shook his head. 'Of course I don't. Are you telling me this will take even longer?'

Carter crossed her legs and broke into a smile. 'It's already done. I discounted those houses with tenants who had elected to put their names on the electoral roll. I also discounted properties tenanted for less than a month – Stone only moved in this month. That only left three properties. The agents for the second house told me it had been let to a man with an American accent, but that it was actually occupied by three Brits.'

'Interesting,' Edge said. 'So there *is* a Yank connection.'

'Indeed, boss. I know you already have suspicions about our American friends.'

'Good work, indeed, Liz.'

'Is there anything else you need before I go home?'

'Send Morrow in here.'

'Will do, boss.'

Carter pushed her chair back and stood up. 'Are you sending Morrow out to do some real spying?'

'Yes, I think I am.'

Carter looked uncertain for a moment, and then said, 'Can I go too?'

Carter fancied Morrow, Edge knew. It would be amusing to put the two of them together. 'Getting bored with paperwork, Liz?'

'I am a bit, yes.'

'You'll only get time, not time and a half.'

'I can live with that.'

There was a sprightliness to Carter's step as she left the office that belied the ten hours she had already worked. She was a bright woman, and some experience in the field would be useful, Edge thought. Morrow came through the door. 'Liz has an address for a house near Stone's. She thinks it might be our house. I want you to watch it, and see who goes in and out.'

'Photographs?'

'Of course. And take Liz with you. She needs to get out into the field.'

'That's fine by me.' There was a wry smile on Morrow's face.

So, he fancied her as well. He was playing matchmaker here, Edge thought. Perhaps this wasn't such a good idea. 'Try to keep your eyes on the door to the house, not anything else.'

'As if.'

'She can watch the house when you fall asleep.'

'I could do with a kip.'

Morrow left to requisition a camera, and find Liz Carter. Edge hoped he had moved a little closer to discovering what the Yanks were doing.

12

Over the past week, Carl Cleaver had made a few telephone
calls. Firstly, he'd contacted an old school friend, who had
told him that Archie had indeed gone straight into the Army
– the infantry, in fact – from school. Carl had then pursued
Archie's name through a maze of military bureaucracy until
he finally reached an adjutant at Archie's regiment, the Royal
Regiment of Wales. Carl was surprised to hear that Archie
had entered the regiment as a soldier; with his education
and background, Carl had supposed Archie to be a
commissioned officer. The adjutant noted that Archie had
been quickly promoted to corporal. If Archie had remained
in the army, he would have soon reached the rank of
Warrant Officer. However, Archie had, the adjutant said,
become something of a crook, and had been, as he put it,
'Encouraged to leave the regiment.' The adjutant also
remembered being asked on a number of occasions for a job
reference for Conn. He said he would ring back when he
had the information. An hour late, Carl's telephone rang. A
secretary had at last found Archibald Conn's file. The last
reference request on file was from a nightclub owner in
London. Carl had a name now, *The Purple Parrot*. That would
be a starting point at least.

Carl had telephoned Companies House. Requests for
information about a nightclub called *The Purple Parrot* had
drawn a blank. During the week, he had also visited the
national newspaper archive. He had no idea what he was
looking for. It was a fishing trip more than anything. He
hoped he'd be able to find something about Archie's

ignominious exit from the Royal Regiment of Wales. He had found nothing, however. Carl had used up the so-called compassionate leave his editor had given him, and was returning to the office this morning.

Natasha squealed. Carl put down his morning paper with an exasperated sigh. 'Rhys, stop picking on your sister will you?'

His eight-year old son pulled a face, and mumbled, 'Didn't do anything, dad.'

Natasha spoke between slurps of her cereal. 'Did so too. You pinched me on my leg.'

Rhys's response was curt. 'Didn't!' He followed up with a taunt. 'Liar, liar, pants on fire!'

Carl glared at his two squabbling children. He didn't need this first thing in the morning. Jenny had her back to him, busy preparing packed lunches for the school trip the twins were about to embark on. The quiet family breakfast Jenny had hoped for was degenerating into noisy squabbling. Carl knew if that happened, he and Jenny would quickly be at each other's throats. Their marriage was full of ups-and-downs, and they were currently going through a rough patch. Jenny put the lids on the kid's lunch boxes, and turned to face the table. 'Right you two, get yourselves ready for school. You don't want to be late. Miss Williams did say the coach would leave on time. She'll go without you if necessary.'

Rhys sullenly got out of his chair and went out into the hall. The sound of his footsteps on the stairs told Carl that he, at least, was doing what he was told. 'And you, young lady?' Carl said.

Natasha pulled a face. 'But he did pinch me, hard and it did hurt...'

Carl scowled. 'Do as your Mother says and get ready, otherwise-'

Natasha cut him off. 'You'll stop my pocket money, Dad, yes, I know.' She too left the room; her footsteps on the stairs were slow and dramatically heavy.

Carl sighed. 'God, Jenny, were we so damned cheeky when we were that age?'

Jenny gave Carl a small smile, the first for days. 'Well, I know I was a precocious little madam at that age'

Carl looked up and winked. 'Glad to see you haven't changed then.' The only reply he received was a playful slap across his head.

'Any chance of me getting *my* lunch made?' Carl said.

Jenny looked at him, with a stony expression, although there was playfulness in her eyes. 'Don't push your luck, sonny Jim. You'll get a peck on the cheek as you leave, and that's it. You've plenty of fences to mend and bridges to build.'

Carl took a last bite of his toast, then rose from the table and put his arms around his wife. She didn't shrug him off, which he thought a good omen. 'Okay, you win, give me that kiss then. I'm late as it is. I'll get a sandwich from the guy on Union Road.'

Jenny's response was a quick kiss on his left cheek. As he walked to the front door, she called after him. 'Have a good day at the office. I'll see you tonight.'

The morning was bright and brisk, like his mood. He thought he would take advantage of the weak sunshine and walk the mile and half from Sketty into Swansea town centre, rather than catch the bus as he normally did. The walk made him peckish. As he turned into Union Street, he could smell the food frying in the café. The thought of a sausage, egg and bacon sandwich made his mouth water. It was only a short walk to the office from Union Street and he relished the thought of tucking into another breakfast. He gave into desire and bought a sandwich. He was tempted to start eating as he walked, but reasoned that it would taste all the better once he was in the building, with his first cup of tea of the day.

The smog that normally hung in the air of the pressroom was thinner than normal, partly because, despite walking, Carl was one of the first members of staff to arrive that day. The door to the editor's office was open; Tom Hughes was on the telephone. Carl sat at his desk, and took one half of the sandwich from its brown paper bag. He had only taken two bites when there was a crunch, and then pain, as if somebody had jabbed at a tooth with a knitting needle. He yelped and dropped the sandwich onto his desk. The few other people in the room looked in his direction. Taking his handkerchief from his pocket, he spat the contents of his mouth into it. Sitting there, amongst the semi-masticated food, was a sizable chunk of one of his molars.

'Shit,' Carl moaned. He balled up the handkerchief and threw it into a waste bin. The pain was intense.

Hughes came out of his office to see what had happened. 'What the hell is wrong with you?'

Carl spoke slowly. Moving his jaw caused little stabs of extra pain. 'Broke a bloody tooth on a sarnie from that damn café we use, didn't I.'

Hughes tutted. 'I've always said that fast food is bad for you. Eating on the run and all that... Let's have a look then.' Carl obediently opened his mouth. 'Ooh, that's right nasty. Better get that seen to as soon as possible.' Hughes straightened up. 'Look, my brother's a dentist. Shall I give him a call and see if he can fit you in today? Chances are you'll have to wait to see your own dentist, and Clive owes me a few favours.' Carl nodded, mutely. 'Leave it with me,' Hughes said.

Hughes had been true to his word. Just under an hour later, Carl sat in a waiting room, looking nervously around him. The receptionist had warned him that he might be waiting a while, so he began to scan through the pile of aging magazines. He was always on the lookout for potential stories, and leads and insights into current and forgotten news. He picked up an old, well-thumbed copy of *Reveille*, and skimmed through the pages.

All thoughts of impending dental work suddenly vanished. There, in the pages of the magazine, was a photograph of Archibald Conn. Carl read the article next to it. Archie had been involved with some crazy UFO group in the small Wiltshire town of Dereham. He wondered if Archie might still live in the town. There was a credit beside the photo. He didn't recognise the name. He knew the photograph might have come from stock. The door opened and a man with a frozen frown came through it, followed by the dental nurse. 'Mr Cleaver?' the nurse said. 'The dentist will see you now.'

He entered the surgery in a daze. What a co-incidence, he thought. He would never normally read *Reveille*. The next thirty minutes flashed by. His mind raced; and any pain he felt occupied only a small part of his consciousness. One thing that puzzled him was that the article referred to Archie as *Archibald Franklin Conn*, rather than *Archibald Conn*. Carl knew that Franklin wasn't Archie's middle name. It was... Oh, what was it... William. That was it; or one of them, at least. *Archibald William David Emlyn Conn* – A. W. D. E. Conn, as he'd been listed in the school's rugby programmes. Why *Franklin*? The only Franklin he had known had been at school, Johnny Franklin. He and Archie had hung around together sometimes. Carl hadn't been out to the big house where Archie lived very often – he and Archie had been friendly, but had never been close. They had shared an interest in sport and had played on the same cricket and rugby teams. He had seen Johnny Franklin's dad at Archie's house once. He felt sure there was no relationship between the Conns and Franklins. He had little idea why Franklin's dad would be there, and had never questioned it. Perhaps there was, after all, some obscure family tie. Perhaps Johnny Franklin would know. If only he knew where Johnny Franklin lived now. The family had moved after Johnny had finished at school.

It was only when the dental nurse tapped him on his shoulder that he realised the treatment had finished. Clive Hughes smiled at him. 'You hardly made a sound! I wish all my patients were as calm as you, Mr Cleaver.'

Despite the numb feeling around his mouth, Carl knew he was grinning. He slurred out some words. 'Believe it or not, today is my lucky day. There's a magazine in the waiting room – would you mind if I took it with me? It contains an article that would be of great use to me, and to your brother.'

Hughes smiled. 'No not at all. If it's for the paper, please, take it.' The dentist explained that he had given Carl a temporary crown, but he would need a full crown very soon. Even the threat of expensive dental work did little dim Carl's eagerness to return to the office.

Carl left the surgery elated. *Archibald Conn... you can run, but you can't hide.*

13

Harry entered Edge's office. Edge looked up at him, his eyebrows raised, his face otherwise composed.

'So, how did your jolly to the Midlands go?' Edge said. 'Please tell me everything went to plan?'

Harry sat in one of the leather armchairs near Edge's desk. 'All done. We have Stone now. He thinks he killed the girl's father. I hope the sacrificial lamb wasn't too badly hurt.'

Edge grunted. 'He's going to be nursing a sore head and bruises for a few days, but apart from that, he's fine. Amazing what an agent will do if you dangle a large enough carrot in front of them.'

There was a knock at the door. 'Come,' Edge said. Morrow entered. 'Hello, Morrow.'

Morrow had an A4 envelope in his hand. 'Good morning, Mick. Harry, good to see you again.'

Edge sat forward in his chair. 'What news have you got for me, canny lad?'

'Rather interesting news, actually. Have you brought Harry up to speed?'

'Not yet.' Edge explained what Morrow and Carter had been doing.

Harry smiled. 'I bet Liz enjoyed that. Being out in the field, I mean.' He also knew Liz had a soft spot for Morrow.

'Yes, she rather did, I think,' Morrow said, innocently. 'I have some interesting photographs here.' He pulled three large black and white photographs from the envelope, and put them on the desk in front of Edge. 'Recognise anybody?'

Edge shook his head. 'I don't think so,' he said.

'I do,' said Harry. He pointed at the photograph in the

middle. 'That's Freddy Barnes. He's a big lad, but good with his hands. He's into electronics, but can handle himself in a barney. And the other guy-' Harry pointed to the photograph on the left. 'That's Brian Britten. Another electronics guy. He's worked for Six, hasn't he?'

Morrow nodded. 'That's right. They're all mercenaries, guns for hire - although in this day and age, communications experts for hire. The third one is Keith Mason. He's also into electronics and surveillance. He's a phone tap expert. I checked the pole near to Stone's house. Sure enough, there's a discreet tap there.'

Edge shrugged. 'I sometimes wonder how you know so much and I know so little.'

'Field experience,' Morrow said. 'And knowing the people to talk to.'

'I feel lacking sometimes,' Edge said.

'But you're good at the analytics,' Harry said. 'Making the connections.'

'Aye, there is that. But sometimes, you know... I feel... inadequate.'

'There's nothing to stop you going out into the field,' Morrow said.

Edge nodded. 'Perhaps I should.'

There was a pause in which, Harry thought, they all imagined Edge out in the field; Edge seeing himself as a dashing hero from a spy film, Morrow imagining Edge blowing his cover within an hour, and Harry... Harry thinking how Edge would soon discover how dull the field could be. Analysis sometimes sounded good to Harry. The field could also be perplexing, and dangerous to the emotions, throwing up the likes of Peta Shepherd and Archibald Franklin Conn. You can leave the paperwork on the desk at night, but not your feelings. Harry hid a wry smile behind his hand. Well, perhaps he should leave the paperwork in a locked drawer, and perhaps he shouldn't work in analysis.

Edge looked at the three photographs again. 'No sign of anybody else?'

Morrow shook his head. 'Not so far.'

Edge picked up the photograph of Barnes, and studied it. 'So they're pros, aye? Any chance they clocked you?'

Morrow shook his head. 'Not a chance, boss.'

'Now we know who these three are, perhaps we can draw out the big cheese.'

'How would we do that?'

'We should invite him round for a cuppa.'

Harry sounded a note of caution. 'We don't know who they're working for. Say it's the Provos. Things might get rough. Mercenary Brits forking a Provo operation? They'd all be dead in a few weeks, and they'd know it. They'd want to fight their way out to prove to their paymasters that they were loyal.'

'We'll need to have firearms officers with us, then,' Edge said. 'I'll contact the Met.'

Morrow frowned. 'How are you going to do this? They're professional mercenaries. They won't simply blab.'

Edge folded his arms, resolutely. 'They will by the time I've finished with them. I'm coming with you.'

Morrow stroked his chin. 'Field work, Mick?'

'Field work, Paul, yes.'

'By the way,' Morrow, said. 'I have some information about that business at the Conn house. You remember I told you about tyre tracks in the lane?'

'Yes,' Edge said. 'The lane was muddy, and there were clear imprints, enough to get a pattern, yes?'

'That's right. Well, the tread pattern fits that of an off-road tyre. Probably on a Land Rover or something like that.'

'Not many of those in rural Wales, I'd venture,' Harry said with a smile.

'Well, Liz did some checking, and as you'd expect, there's a few thousand. But there's only one that might drive along that track, and that's owned by a farmer who uses the field at the end. Liz spoke to the farmer, and he said he rarely used the track – he normally used another entrance. Liz wondered why, and he said that it was because the track isn't his. It actually belongs to the Conns, who had detached land along it. They had given him permission to use the track, but he didn't want to *take the piss*, as he said, so he kept usage to a minimum.'

'Interesting,' Harry said.

'Yes, but of no use to us.' Edge said, 'As it doesn't help us find the elusive Mr Conn. And neither does it tie your Archie to the murder. Send the information to the local police, Paul. They can do with it as they see fit.'

Discretely and quietly, the small team of operatives began to move in closer to the house. Edge led the way. Soon, the house was being monitored by what appeared, to the untrained eye, to be a motley collection of council workers, a courting couple and a guy leaning against a lamp-post smoking a cigarette. Edge knew that at any moment, he'd lose the element of surprise. He brazenly walked up to the front door of the house, and rang the doorbell.

Freddy Barnes opened the door. 'Hello, can I help you?'

Edge gave him a friendly smile. 'I hope so, sir. I believe you are Mr Frederick Barnes?'

'Yes,' Barnes said, slowly. 'And you are?'

Edge continued smiling as he reached into his pocket and pulled out his identification. 'Over the street, Mr Barnes, are two plain-clothes fire officers. You're not going to offer any... *resistance*... if I come in, are you?'

Barnes pushed his hands out, palms down, a gesture of submission. 'Certainly not, Mr Edge.'

'And your friends, Mr Britten and Mr Mason? Can I rely on them not to be... obstreperous?'

'Now you have us, Mr Edge, I can assure you we'll offer no resistance.'

'Nonetheless, I am sure you'll understand if my two friends from the Metropolitan police accompany us into the house?'

'I most certainly will.'

'Your friends wouldn't think of running, would they? Through a window? Out of the back door?'

'They wouldn't be so stupid. After all, they would simply run into more spooks, wouldn't they?'

'Aye, Mr Barnes, quite right. So lead the way.'

Barnes turned into the hallway.

'Wait one moment, please,' Edge said. Barnes stopped. One of the firearms officers appeared from behind the trunk of a London plane tree on the opposite pavement, sped across the road, and positioned himself behind Barnes. 'You can move on now, Mr Barnes.'

Edge followed the firearms officer. The courting couple, Liz Carter and Morrow, broke apart and followed Edge into the house. Harry remained outside with the remaining firearms officer. The other operatives, on a signal from Harry, drifted away into weak winter light. Barnes led Edge and the others into lounge.

Edge looked around the room. 'Where are Britten and Mason?'

Barnes nodded upwards. 'In the back bedroom. The... surveillance room.'

'Could you call them down, please?'

Barnes went to the hallway, to the foot of the stairs. The firearms officer followed him, and went down the hall to the kitchen, out of sight of anybody descending the stairs.

Barnes called out. 'Keith, Brian. Could you come down here a minute? We have visitors.' Edge could hear one set of footsteps moving in the rooms above him. There was a short gap before the other set of footsteps followed. 'In the front room,' Barnes said.

Barnes entered the room, followed by Mason and Britten.

'So here we all are,' Edge said.

Mason and Britten looked sheepish. The firearms officer followed them, and stood in the doorway, his pistol now conspicuous.

Edge looked at the three of them, and their arrangement in the room. Morrow had suggested that, on experience, Barnes would be the *de facto* leader. Their body language suggested it. 'Carter, Morrow. Get upstairs and see what you can see.'

Carter and Morrow edged passed the firearms office and went up the stairs.

'Now, gents,' Edge said, 'let's find out what's at the bottom of all this. Shall we sit down?'

The three mercenaries squeezed onto the sofa. Edge sat in a chrome and canvas armchair. Barnes leaned forward. 'We won't tell you who we're working for.'

'I'd expect as much – professional reputation and all that. However, we have our suspicions. I will seek confirmation of those suspicions, even if I have to get our firearms officer to phone the boys in blue and have you arrested.'

Barnes sat back and folded his arms, causing Britten and Mason to lean against each other on the sofa. Feet came rapidly tapping down the stairs, and Morrow appeared in the room. 'The recorded reel has been removed from the tape recorder and placed on a magnet.'

Edge looked at Mason and Britten. 'Smart. Quick thinking by one of you.'

'We might be able to get something off it,' Morrow said.

Edge shook his head. 'No need, Morrow. Who wants to hear Len Stone and Emily Freeman's pillow talk? Certainly not me.' Edge was gratified by the look of surprise that passed swiftly across Barnes's face. 'What interests me is why these three reprobates would be eavesdropping on Freeman and Stone. After all, Freeman is a blameless US citizen, and Stone... Well, not so blameless, but he's left his days in the underworld behind him.'

'The underworld?' Barnes said.

'Yes, the underworld. Those nefarious rapscallions who operate beyond the law.'

Barnes shifted uncomfortably. 'And which... part of the underworld was he involved with?'

'Let's just say for the moment that he did various jobs for a certain London criminal gang. You know, the kind of gang that'll kick you in the goolies, nail you to the wall, and kick you in the goolies again for good measure, before putting a bullet between your eyes.' Mason and Britten looked at each other, frowning. 'Surely you knew that?' Edge said. 'Surely you have a reason for bugging Stone's house? I can only surmise that some other gang have you listening out for information that might be pertinent to their continuing turf wars. What other reason could there be? And if that's so, Len Stone - and those higher up in his... gang - might be interested to know that you've been listening in.'

Britten shook his head. 'That's not it.'

Barnes turned and glared at him. 'Shut up, Britten.'

Britten returned the glare. 'Sorry, Barnsey. I don't mind getting caught up in inter-agency turf wars, that fine. You give them a bit of information, they pat you on the head and let you go. But the underworld... No, that's a different kettle of fish.'

Barnes sighed. 'We're not working for a gang, Britten.'

'I know that. But you know what Mr Edge is saying.'

'He could be lying.'

Edge intervened. 'Aye, I could indeed be lying, Mr Barnes. Why don't you phone your boss and find out? I'm surprised he didn't tell you himself. Why is that? Perhaps because your boss is lying. Perhaps he wants different information to what he told you. If he told you.'

'No, he didn't tell us,' Barnes conceded. 'He just wanted us to listen.'

'There you are, then. Perhaps your boss wears a uniform, perhaps he wears civvies. I don't know. But the clothes make little difference. Perhaps a Yank with some firepower behind him wants a cut of somebody's action. We see it all in MI5, believe you me.'

Barnes narrowed his eyes. 'What makes you think it's a Yank?'

'I don't know,' Edge said. 'I'm just supposing. It's an example of the kind of thing we sometimes run up against. I'm not suggesting for a moment that your boss is a Yank.' Edge had been watching Mason and Britten as he spoke. Britten had shown a certain twitchiness at the word *Yank*.

'Well, we are in a pretty pass,' Barnes said. 'You don't know who employs us, and we're not going to tell you.'

Again, Edge noted a certain twitchiness in Britten. 'Let's see,' said Edge. 'Let's pretend that, as officers within the agency charged with protecting the security of the realm, we have access to... certain snitches. Perhaps we even have people undercover in certain gangs. What then, if we were to let one of our snitches know, or perhaps instruct one of our agents to mention, that there's a certain house in Hayes that has recording equipment specifically tuned to bugging devices in a house owned by Len Stone who is involved in some way with the Manley Boys.'

Britten's eyes widened. 'The Manley Boys?'

'Yes,' said Edge. 'The Manley Boys.'

Mason spoke for the first time. 'Tim Manley is a nutter.'

Edge had Mason now. 'Indeed he is. A very clever nutter, as our colleagues in the Sweeney have yet to make a case against him. But, yes, a nutter nonetheless.'

Both Mason and Britten were looking at Barnes. Barnes was chewing a fingernail. 'Okay,' Barnes said. 'Assuming that Mr Stone has the connections you say he does, and assuming that if I were to ask my boss who Mr Stone was, his story would match yours, what would you... offer us?'

'If you do not help me with this enquiry, well... You know phone-tapping and bugging is illegal. So the Met would arrest you, and charge you. The evidence is very good, and you would go down. We would tell Mr Stone that his house had been bugged, and voice our erroneous suspicions that this was because of his gangland connections. You would then spend a very uncomfortable time in jail.' Edge gave Barnes a reassuring smile. 'Alternatively, you tell me what's really going on, and you walk out of here, get on a bus, train or plane, and visit a friend or relative some distance away, somebody you've really been meaning to see for some time. We'd really hate to permanently lose somebody who has been so useful to our sister service in the past.'

Barnes looked at Britten and Mason, and shrugged. 'Well, given the options... You're right. It's the Yanks.'

'Name?'

'Skinner. Major Skinner. USAF.'

'Could you phone him and ask him to come here?'

'Yes, of course. I'm not sure he will, but...'

'You must have something that will make him hot-foot it out here. A codeword?'

Barnes shook his head. 'He usually visits once a week. He takes the recordings away with him for analysis.'

'Which day?'

'Not today.'

Edge ran his fingers through his hair. So – it wasn't the CIA. And a USAF major could have no interest in what Stone had to say. His interest could only be in Emily Freeman. There was a connection between Freeman and Stone, however. They had both been caught up in the UFO contactee movement; Freeman through her father, Stone through direct involvement. Assuming that Freeman had been a mere clerk or administrator in the USAF, the likeliest thing that Freeman could talk about with Stone that would interest the USAF would be something to do with UFOs. Such a scenario might seem unlikely to anybody but Edge, who, after all, had been directed to watch Peta Shepherd for precisely the same reason. What could Emily Freeman say, then, that would intrigue Skinner enough to make him come out here today? 'This is going to sound crazy, Barnes. Phone Skinner, and tell him that Freeman is talking to Stone about UFOs.'

Barnes smiled. 'UFOs?'

'I told you it would sound crazy. Tell him that Freeman is babbling on about contacts, and her father, and... oh... and American defence. That should be enough.' It had to involve defence somehow, Edge thought, if it involved a high-ranking USAF officer.

'You're the boss,' Barnes said.

'Aye, I am now, aren't I? Don't go over the top when you talk to this Skinner.'

Barnes went to the phone. He put in a good performance, roughly following Edge's suggested script, improvising where necessary.

Barnes turned to Edge. 'He's coming. He sounded very eager. He'll be about an hour.' Barnes shuffled uncertainly. 'What now?'

Edge winked. 'Don't you all have friends and relatives to visit?'

Barnes moved towards the hallway. 'Come on, lads, we need to pack.'

The three mercenaries climbed the stairs, followed by the firearms officer.

Morrow nodded at Edge. 'Nicely done, Mick. I thought *we* were mad chasing that Peta Shepherd. Looks like the Americans also have an interest in these contactees.'

Edge laughed. 'We're all barking mad. Them and us.'

Liz Carter came into the room. 'I hear we've got our man. That stuff upstairs is really sophisticated. We should take it home with us and have a play with it.'

'The Americans won't like it,' Morrow said.

'Of course we'll take it,' Edge said. 'It shouldn't be here anyway. The Yanks won't ask for it back, if they've any sense. Get Harry and the other firearms officer in here to help you.'

Carter went to the front door, and called to Harry. The three mercenaries came down the stairs. Edge stood and went to the hallway. 'Thanks, Barnes. You've been a great help.'

Barnes handed Edge a piece of paper. 'Here's a number, should you need to contact me.'

'Why would I need to contact you?'

'Trust nobody, Mr Edge. You should know that.'

Harry, Carter and Morrow had soon packed the surveillance equipment into Morrow's car. Edge told Harry to take it back to Curzon Street. 'Right,' he said to Morrow and Carter. 'I want you to get into my car and pretend to be a canoodling couple again.' Carter raised an eyebrow and smiled. Edge sent one firearms officer back to his van, the other he sent upstairs. When everybody else had left the house, Edge sank into the armchair again, and waited for Major Skinner to arrive.

This, he thought, had better not be all about mad flying saucer bollocks.

14

Colonel Skinner drove slowly into St George's Road. He was a careful man. He was also driving on what he felt was the wrong side of the road, which always befuddled him. He had, at least, requisitioned a car with an automatic gearbox. The Europeans still couldn't make an auto transmission like a Torqueflite, though. The auto jerked up a gear as he cruised along the street. There were a few vehicles here he hadn't seen before. That was the problem with a city like London. The population was so transient, and visitors came and went. There was a black van, which could mean nothing. There was a car with a man and woman in it. They weren't watching anything but each other, it seemed. The man in the car traced a line with his finger down the woman's cheek. Skinner stopped watching them – it seemed impertinent, and, as he was driving slowly, they might think him a Peeping Tom.

Streetlights glowed on their stanchions; yet there were still pools of darkness near trees and hedges where ne'er-do-wells might lurk. Skinner felt, as he often did, the absence of his Smith and Wesson. What kind of goddamn country didn't allow a law-abiding, peace-loving citizen to carry a firearm? What kind of freedom what that? The road seemed quiet enough, however. There was only a man walking a poodle; Skinner had seen him before on his weekly visit. The man must walk his dog every night at this time. Skinner glanced up towards number 23. He could see lights in the lounge and the window that gave onto the stairway landing. Somebody was upstairs, working. He wondered if Len Stone and Emily Freeman were still talking about UFOs. Barnes had sounded very confused on the phone. That was unsurprising. Skinner had never really told the mercenaries what they should be listening for. Stone and Freeman talking about flying saucers and little green men from space would have seemed so outlandish, so strange, no wonder Barnes had wanted to contact him.

Skinner found a parking space, and reversed into it with some difficulty – everything seemed the wrong way round, and the damned auto box was so jerky – and then exited the car. He walked the few yards back down the street to the house. He looked around him warily, but all seemed normal. The man with the poodle was nearly at the junction at the bottom of the road, whistling happily. Skinner opened the gate to the house, and walked up the path. He rang the doorbell. He was surprised when an unexpected face opened the door.

'Major Skinner, I presume,' the man said.

Skinner found himself bridling at the impertinent demotion. '*Colonel* Skinner, sir.'

'Come in, come in,' the man said.

Skinner sat on a sofa, facing the man across from him. They both held a cup of coffee, and what the man had called *a wee biscuit*. He had recognised the face, but hadn't been able to place it immediately, such was his surprise. An identity card had been flashed at him almost as soon as he had entered the house, though too briefly to catch the name. But Skinner now knew who sat opposite him. The man had a Scottish accent and worked for the Security Service. Skinner knew it must be Michael Edge. Once Edge felt confident that Skinner posed no threat, Edge sent away the firearms officer who had been eying him cautiously. He assumed now that

144

the courting couple in the car were also operatives, and suspected there were still others in the street – perhaps even the man with the poodle.

'How can I help you, Mr Edge?' Skinner said.

Edge sipped at his coffee. 'So, you know who I am.'

'One likes to know who one's opponents might be. And you are Michael Edge, 35 years old, a head of Section at the Security Service.'

'That's me.'

'What happened to my men?'

'They're helping police with their enquiries, Colonel Skinner.'

Skinner wondered if that were true. Of course, wire-tapping and bugging were illegal, but Edge must have already discovered somehow that he was running this operation. Barnes wouldn't have easily given up his name. Edge didn't seem the hard-boiled type, so he must have used persuasion. Perhaps he had let them go without charges in exchange for his name.

Edge's demeanour was relaxed. 'So, what are you doing over here? Obviously, bugging Miss Freeman... But why?'

Skinner took a silver cigar case from his pocket and opened it. He looked at Edge. 'Would you like one?' Edge shook his head. Skinner lit a small thin cigar. 'Why am I here?' Skinner chuckled. 'Well, that's kind of complicated, and a matter of national security. Suffice to say I'm doing it for a damn good reason. We wouldn't have taken the risk otherwise. I couldn't trust you to do the job for me. Hell, you guys are so liberal, you're almost commies. 'Not that he would have done, anyway, even if Edge and his department had all been members of the National Front.

Edge seemed unconcerned by the slight. 'You do know that this will have to be reported.'

Skinner shrugged, and blew cigarette smoke into the air. 'Go on, then, Mr Edge, report me.'

'There'll be a diplomatic incident, and you'll probably be demoted and out on your ear.'

'I don't care. And no, I won't be.'

Edge raised an eyebrow. 'What does that mean?'

'There will be no diplomatic incident. At least, not the one you expect. Something will be said, sure. Something might even make the pages of your newspapers. But it won't be what you think, and it won't be concerning this, and I won't be demoted, nor *out on my ear*, as you say. I'll carry on, untroubled by this little local difficulty. Sure, I won't be able to bug the lovely Emily Freeman any more–' Skinner smiled. 'Or, at least, I'll be able to bug her until the next time you find out. Even then, I'll have her and lover boy followed and watched by any means possible. You'll have to follow *me* around if you want to stop me. Or throw me out of the country. Then you *will* have a diplomatic scandal all right. A high-ranking officer thrown out of the country on trumped-up charges? Unlikely.'

'Trumped-up charges?'

'Honestly, Mike... I *can* call you Mike?' Edge nodded. 'Who the hell is going to believe all this UFO bullshit? You try getting rid of me and you'll need to explain to people what I'm doing here, and why you're interested in me. And once you start trying to explain *that*, people will think *you've* lost it, buddy. You'll probably be given leave of absence and ordered to make weekly visits to the shrink.'

'There'll be some who believe my story.'

'Yes, Daniel Parker-Martens. He's the honcho who had you following Peta Shepherd.'

Edge looked surprised. 'You know about that?'

'When it comes to the *contactees*, let me assure you, we know everything. Miss Shepherd was of little interest to us.

Daniel Parker-Martens, however... Now, his curiousity about the contactees *is* of interest to me.'

'Still, that does mean Parker-Martens will believe me, even if nobody else does.'

'That's the problem, Mike. Nobody else *will*. Parker-Martens remains in his job due to his successes against the Reds. He's still held in high regard for those operations. His obsession with the contactees is tolerated because of them. However, can you imagine what would happen if Parker-Martens tried to implicate a high-ranking USAF officer in his pet obsession, especially if he were to claim that the high-ranking officer was also obsessed with UFOs.'

The look of confusion on Edge's face showed that he foresaw the outcome. Still, he persisted. 'Yes, but those higher than me could go to those higher than you, and thrash it out there. Because whatever madness we're engaged in, you are still working without authorisation on my turf, and I will not have it.'

'Somebody higher than *me?*' Skinner laughed.

'You *are* only a Colonel, Skinner. I might not understand USAF ranks all that well, but there must be five or six layers of authority above you. Not including the President.'

Skinner laughed again. 'Oh yes, almost certainly not including the president.

Edge's face showed confusion again. 'I don't understand,' Edge said.

Skinner was enjoying tying the younger man in knots. He stubbed out his cigar. 'It means, buddy boy, I'm above the President. I answer to a higher power. You ever hear of *black operations?*'

Edge shook his head.

Skinner smiled, and lit another cheroot. 'Black operations, what a joy they are. Beyond the law, outside of government. That's where I work. Black ops.'

'Let me get this straight. The government doesn't know what you're doing, the executive doesn't know what you're doing, and the President doesn't know what you're doing—'

Skinner held up a hand. 'Stop there, Mike. That's not quite right. Certain members of the executive think they know what I'm doing. There are presidential aides who also think they know what I'm doing. But as you rightly pointed out a little while ago, I am but a lowly Colonel. Why should the President be troubled with the minor tasks I set myself?'

'Somebody must know what you're doing.'

'Of course they have some idea what I'm running, and what I'm protecting. There are agencies providing my department with money. And I have personnel, of course – not many, but enough. I have authority to use assets in other agencies, such as the Company, and the Feds. I have authority to use them, but they have no authority over me.' Skinner winked. 'Sweet business, eh?'

Edge tapped the chrome arm of his chair. Skinner could see the exasperation in his eyes. 'I can't believe this.'

'So, Mike, what you gonna do, eh? Take me down? I don't think so.'

Edge gave Skinner a hard look. 'I'll give it my best shot. You must answer to somebody. I'll find him.'

Skinner laughed. He put his right hand on his chest, above his heart. 'I pledge allegiance to the flag of the United States of America and to the republic for which it stands – one nation under God, indivisible, with liberty and justice for all.' Skinner just had to say it. He believed it fervently. 'God is my highest authority, Mike. He's the only person I answer to. If you want to talk to somebody with higher authority than me, try praying.'

15

Harry returned from the office late. The night was rain-dark, and heavy clouds hung, burnt orange, softly brushing the tallest city buildings. From his carriage on the tube train, now running above ground, Harry watched the mist and rain as it ghosted past streetlights. He alighted at Oakwood, and walked up the stairs to the ticket hall and the street. Students from the education college at Trent Park ran down the stairs, smelling of patchouli, carrying folders and rucksacks, heading towards the cheaper accommodation of Edmonton and Tottenham. Here, in Oakwood, Harry was almost in the countryside, and rents were too high for poor students. They were almost too much for Harry. Yet, after Dereham, he wanted to stay close to nature.

He exited the station, pulled his collar up, bent into the wet, chill wind, and walked around the crescent of shops towards Bramley Road. He stopped at the Chinese restaurant to get himself a take-away that would accompany another night in front of the television, alone. He walked along Bramley Road, one hand cold, keeping his jacket closed, the other warm, carrying the brown bag of hot food. He wondered what was on the television. He wasn't in the mood for reading; he wanted to... what did they say these days? Veg out. The wind lifted the aroma of star anise from his food. That reminded him of Peta, who hated the smell of star anise; her first flat in Dereham was situated above a Chinese restaurant. Small things reminded him of Peta.

He turned down Westpole Avenue towards his flat. He was hungry, and keen to get into his dry, warm, lounge, turn on the television, tuck into the Chinese, and switch off. He let himself in through the front door, and began to climb the stairs. He stopped at the fourth step. At the top of the stairs, next to the door of his flat, illuminated by the dim, sixty-watt light bulb, sat a figure huddled into an anorak. Whoever was hidden by the hood was a woman, Harry was sure. The large, striped bag beside her was definitely feminine.

Harry crept up the stairs, avoiding those he knew to creak. The woman's head was down, her chin on her chest. She was asleep, he thought. He reached the top of the stairs, and put his brown bag of Chinese food on the worn green carpet. He squatted beside her, and pulled back the hood of the anorak. He was surprised by the face he revealed – Molly Shepherd. She stirred slightly, but didn't wake.

Harry opened the door to his flat, took the Chinese into the kitchen, and then came back to Molly. He shook her gently by the shoulder. 'Molly,' he said quietly. 'Molly.' She woke with a start, blinked her eyes, and then rubbed them. She glanced up at him. 'Mr Roberts? Thank goodness you're back. I thought you might be out all night. And I need a pee. Is it all right if I...?'

Harry smiled. 'Of course, of course.' He showed her the way, and then went to the kitchen where he shared his takeaway between two plates.

Molly came to the kitchen, tentatively, finding her way around the place. 'Chinese?' Harry said. 'Chicken chow mein and egg-fried rice.'

Molly looked at the plates. 'I shouldn't,' she said. 'You bought that for your supper.'

'You're hungry, though, I'll warrant. You must have been waiting for a while.'

'You're right there, Mr Roberts.'

'Harry, please, Molly.'

'Okay – Harry. I've been waiting,' Molly glanced at her watch. 'Since about five o'clock. Four hours.'

'How did you get through the front door?'

'The lady in the flat downstairs let me in. I said I didn't know London, and she didn't want me walking around in the rain.'

'Mrs Albright,' Harry said. 'She's a nice lady.'

'She is. She made me a cup of tea.' Molly looked at the plates on the worktop. 'I am hungry, Harry.'

'I thought you might be.' Harry handed a plate and a fork to Molly. 'Go on, eat it. If we get hungry again later, there's always cereal or toast.'

Harry picked up his plate, and led her to the lounge. They sat on the sofa next to each other, and began to eat. The food was good, and he wished he had more of it. If the weather weren't so foul, he'd have returned to the Oakwood Palace to get seconds.

'Thank you, Harry, for this. And I'm sorry to drop in on you unexpectedly.'

'How did you find me?'

'I memorised the address on your driving license, and wrote it down immediately you left the café.'

Impressive, thought Harry. 'Why didn't you ring?'

'I didn't want you to put me off coming. I wanted to talk to you again.'

'What about?'

'What do you think? About Peta, what she was like when you were with her. About that Dereham place, and her silly ideas about aliens and flying saucers. And what happened with Archie. Everything you know, really.'

'I don't know much. I know about her time in Dereham, and that's it.'

'That's enough for now, Harry. Peta and I were very close. I always thought she might run away. She was older than me, of course. When she got to 16, I thought, that's it, she'll go. Well, it took a little longer than that, but one morning I woke up, and found mum in a tizz. She handed me the note Peta had written about why she'd gone. It didn't say much. Mum asked if she should phone the police, but I said, no, she's over sixteen, she can do what she wants.'

'And your mother agreed with you?'

'In the end, yes. I talked her into it.'

'If she was under eighteen, the police could bring her home.'

'I knew that, really, because Peta had told me. But she was seventeen years old. She could pass for eighteen. If she could survive for a year, she would be eighteen. So all I needed to do was convince mum.'

'And your dad?'

'Dad didn't care. Well, that's not right. He missed having somebody to shout at, threaten and bully. Peta was that person.'

'What about you?'

'I was third in the list. First Peta, then mum, then me. With Peta gone, mum got it in the neck instead.'

'You never wanted to go?'

'Of course I did. But as I told you when we first met, I know I'm tougher than Peta. It's only another six months until I go to university. I'm going to a university a long way away – Aberdeen.'

'A fine institution, by all accounts. So what does that make you? Seventeen and a half?'

'Yes. Well, nearly eighteen, really. I didn't want to make Peta's mistake. When she left, she took what little money she had, and, uh... *liberated* some things from the house. Even then, I knew that wouldn't be enough, and if she couldn't find a job, would be living on the streets.'

'Which, apparently, she did. At least, until she got a job at the nightclub.'

Molly put her fork down on her plate. 'That was lovely. Thank you, Harry.' She smiled. Harry's heart moved. If there was one way in particular that Molly resembled Peta, it was in that smile. There were other similarities – the big brown eyes, the nose. The shape of the face was different, however, and the hair was longer, and darker. Still, there was enough in that face to bring Peta constantly to mind.

Harry took the plates away. 'Tea?' he called from the kitchen.

'Yes, please,' Molly said.

Harry returned to the front room a few minutes later with two mugs. 'So, where are you staying tonight?'

'I've got some money with me. I was hoping you could point me in the direction of a decent hotel or bed and breakfast.'

'There are plenty of bed and breakfasts around here,' Harry said. 'No luxury hotels, though. And I wouldn't know which of the B-and-Bs are decent, I've never used them.'

'Oh well, I'll look in your Yellow Pages later.'

Harry couldn't bear to think of this young girl walking out into the wind and rain, this facsimile of Peta once again on the dark London streets. 'You can stay here if you want. I have a spare bedroom.'

'No, really, Harry, I couldn't...'

'Yes, you can. You won't be imposing. I have to be back in the office tomorrow morning. You can hang around here and leave when you want.'

Molly shrugged and smiled. 'Well, if you're sure?'

'Yes, I am. Save your money for a round of drinks at Aberdeen's student bar.'

'I'll blow it before then,' Molly said. 'Probably in London tomorrow before I get the train back home.'

Harry relaxed into sofa, his arm along its back. 'So what do you want to know?'

'Everything.'

Harry told Molly about the time he had spent in Dereham, from when he had arrived until he had left – he told her everything he could, omitting only operational details. He described the small house he lived in with Peta and Archie. He told Molly how much Peta loved Archie, and how broken she'd been when he left her. He described the skywatches, the UFO Centre, and Richard Patterson. He admitted he'd been falling for Peta. All the while, Molly smiled, shrugged, encouraged, and listened. All the time, she looked like Peta.

Finally, Harry arrived at the end of his story. Archie had left Dereham, and Peta fell into a deep, dark depression. And then Harry had been called back to London.

'You mustn't punish yourself, Harry,' Molly said.

'I didn't find out about Peta until I read an article in the newspaper. If Peta hadn't been associated with flying saucers and Rocking Lord Creighton, I doubt she would've warranted any column inches at all. And Patterson probably wrote the stories, anyway. It was... *knowing* that she'd died, and that... despite the closeness we'd shared over those months, there was nobody to tell me. It was only through the hand of Patterson, a link back to Dereham, that I knew about it. If she had been any other woman, she would've died and I would never have known. I find that... weird.'

Molly rolled her mug between her hands. 'Wouldn't it have been better to have never known? You knew you were never going to see her again. All her death has done is kept her in your mind. Perhaps, without her death, you would by now have let her go.'

There was truth in Molly's words, Harry thought. On any other operation where he'd become close to a subject, a recall to London and a few weeks of working on another case had enabled the object of his desire to fade from memory. He could never know, now, whether Peta had been different in this regard. Was he more in love with Peta than he'd been before? Or was it simply the effect of her death that had left the lasting impression?

'And what about Archibald Franklin Conn?' Molly said.

'I still want to see him... To confront him.'

'And what will you do to him?'

'I don't know, Molly. I think I just want to talk to him, to make him understand what he did, his part in it.'

'Will it help? Why don't you let that go, as well?'

'I can't. What makes it worse, what makes it harder to let these ghosts go, is that the organisation I work for has an interest in Archie. He was with Peta, you see. He might... know things.'

'So you will get your chance to confront him.'

'If we can ever find him. He's elusive, Mr Franklin Conn. Anybody would think he had something to hide.'

'Well, I hope you do find him. You'll both have something to talk about, for sure, and it won't be flying saucers or little green men. And when you do talk to him, I hope you can at last close off that part of your life.'

Harry wasn't sure he wanted to close it off. Yet Molly spoke a great deal of sense for one so young.

Molly looked at Harry quizzically. 'One thing I don't understand. Did Peta really talk to aliens?'

Harry shrugged. 'Who knows? I watched her go into a trance once. She had become so practiced at it, she no longer needed drugs or hypnotism to get her into that state. It was a kind of self-hypnosis, I suppose. Anyway, while she was in her trance, she did seem to be talking to *somebody*. She thought it was an alien – her contact, who she called Molova.'

'What do you think?'

'Perhaps it was, perhaps it wasn't. She could've constructed the whole thing. A confabulation, I think it's called. Perhaps it wasn't an alien at all, perhaps it was a spirit, or somebody from the future. Who knows? Whatever it was, it was freaky.'

Molly stood up. 'Well, thank you for telling me what you know.' She looked down, then back at Harry. 'I still miss her, you know. When she went missing, I kept wondering if I'd ever find her again. I still haven't found her, if you know what I mean. But what you've told me is a great help. Now, I must sleep. I spent a lot of time on trains today.'

'Of course. And I'm glad to have helped.'

Harry stood, and showed her to the spare bedroom. He provided her with a towel and a dressing gown. She went to the bathroom to wash, then said goodnight and went to her room.

Harry poured himself a scotch from a bottle in a sideboard. It had been good to talk to her, he thought. It had helped him with his feelings about Peta. He looked over at the closed bedroom door. She was a sweet girl.

The next morning, Molly woke soon after Harry. 'I'm sorry,' he said. 'Was I making too much noise?'

Molly shook her head. 'No. I'm an early bird.'

They chatted about the day ahead as he made tea and toast for her. She wanted to visit the National Portrait gallery before she caught a train back home. They went to Oakwood station together, and rode the Piccadilly line train back into central London. They talked some more about Peta and Dereham. Molly wanted to know everything she could about the sister she'd lost. As they approached Leicester Square station, Harry said, 'You need to get off at the next stop for the gallery.'

'Thanks, Harry. How much further for you?'

'Just a few more stops,' he said. He would actually be getting off at Green Park station and walking to Curzon Street, but habit precluded him from saying so. 'Hey, look, Molly – do you fancy a drink some time?'

Molly smiled. 'That would be nice, but... I live in the Midlands, you live in the Smoke.'

'No problem. I have a car. It's always nice to get out of London.'

'Okay.' Molly took a notepad from her bag, and a pen, and wrote down her telephone number. 'Give me a ring. It would be good to see you again.'

Harry took the piece of paper offered to him. The train began to slow. 'This is your stop,' Harry said.

'Thanks,' Molly said, and stood up, gripping her bag. 'See you, Harry. Call me soon, yes? I'd like to see you again.'

'Sure,' Harry said. He watched her walk down the aisle towards the train doors. The train stopped, and the doors slid open. She gave Harry a wave and a smile, and then exited the train. Today, she looked a little less like Peta.

16

Archie gently closed the door to the solicitor's office. He wanted to slam it and dance out into the street shouting huzzahs. He didn't think that would be seemly, however. All had gone as expected. The wills he had planted had been found. Gribbens and Nuttley confirmed that Archie was, as he had intended, heir to the family estate. They thought it splendid that, before their deaths, Giles and Lucinda had managed to find their long-lost brother, and patch up the differences between them. They were a little surprised that the wills were different from the ones they remembered drawing up previously, and even a little hurt that Giles and Lucinda hadn't returned to them to have the documents redrafted. However, they had been heartened to find they had been instructed to act as executors. That had been as Archie intended. Four per cent of the estate would keep Gribbens and Nuttley sweet and loath to ask too many questions.

He waited until he was at least two hundred yards away from the offices of Gribbens and Nuttley before letting out an excited yell and punching the air in victory. Gribbens and Nuttley would auction the contents of the house and put the house on the market. Archie knew there were valuable antiques, paintings and objects in the house. His father – or, at least, the man who had brought him up by shouting at him and threatening him – had been an avid collector. The objet d'art his father had amassed had ceased to have any sentimental value for Archie when he had finally accepted the fact that he wasn't a Conn, but a Franklin.

The solicitors had already had the estate valued. It would realise, old man Gribbens had said, somewhere around

£200,000. All his worries were over, Archie thought. That the offices of Gribbens and Nuttley were in Swansea was mildly irritating to him. Still, he would have little need to contact them. Everything could proceed by post. Archie was cautious by nature. He would change his address and direct all subsequent post to a PO Box. He still had the cash he'd stolen from the old house; he could afford to move to a slightly more salubrious flat. He began to walk the mile or so to Swansea station. It was a cold, crisp but sunny day. He had never much liked Swansea, but today, in the low autumn sun, it looked for once pleasant. Better, at least, than Reading, which was a dump. He couldn't wait to leave that shitty town and set himself up somewhere more in keeping with the new life he imagined for himself. But where he wondered? Something classy, it had to be. He had always liked the Cotswolds. Close to Wales, yet apart from it. Cheltenham, perhaps – that had class. He could take time out and reassess his life. He could move there now. Why wait? He reined in his excitement. One step at a time, he thought. There was no rush. He should secure the family fortune, and then move.

First, though, he would take steps to cover his tracks in Reading. He felt confident that the police had no reason to connect him with the death of his brother and sister. Still he felt the need to be cautious, especially now the money was so tantalisingly close. The more difficult he was to find, the more difficult it would be to ask him questions. He would find a new flat, out Caversham way, and maintain the one he currently lived in. He could afford both now. Mail would still be delivered to the old flat; he could pick it up once a week. Mail from the solicitors he would direct to the PO Box.

He arrived back in Reading in the early evening. He took a taxi from the station back to Grovelands Road. As he climbed the flight of stairs to his flat, he happily whistled *I'm in the money*. He opened the door and found a number of letters strewn across the floor. He picked them up, and noted they were all final demands for bills he hadn't yet paid; he could now pay them. He would normally ignore such demands, but that would only cause the utility companies to chase him; and his intention now was to leave as small a footprint in the town as possible.

He made himself a strong coffee and sat in the threadbare armchair. He gazed out of the window, at an amber street-lamp, silently congratulating himself on a job well done. There was no remorse, simply a warm, gentle glow of satisfaction.

His ease was disturbed by a knock at the door. He knew who it was: Mrs Eveson, the doddery old widow who owned this flat. She had converted the house into two apartments when it had become too big for her to manage. She was calling through the letterbox as he approached. 'Are you there, Mr Conn? It's past rent day, you know!'

Archie composed himself, then smiled and opened the door. 'Mrs Eveson. I'm so sorry; the payment completely slipped my mind.'

The old lady merely stared at him. 'This cannot continue, Mr Conn. This is the second month you've fallen behind with the rent. I've warned you before about this. I simply must have the money in my hand by Monday next. Otherwise, I'm afraid... well, you know...'

'Don't fret, dear Mrs Eveson.' Archie oozed charm. 'I've recently come into some money. An inheritance. I can pay you what I owe, and I'll also pay you one month's rent in advance. Now, this might sound odd, but I shall be going away for a short while. I have a job in... Cheltenham. I still wish to retain this flat, but I'll only be here at weekends. You might not see me at all, except when I drop the rent in at the end of the month.'

Miss Eveson eyed Archie doubtfully. 'Are you sure you wish to keep the flat on, Mr Conn?'

'I'm certain. There's a chance the employment in Cheltenham may become permanent, in which case, sadly, I shall have to leave.' Archie gave Mrs Eveson one of his most charming smiles. 'But for the next few months, you'll get the best of both worlds, Mrs Eveson - peace during the week, and a monthly rent.'

Mrs Eveson raised an eyebrow; suspicion remained. 'That's if I do receive it, Mr Conn.'

'Dear lady, this is a new day for both of us. I will no longer hide from you, and you will no longer have to chase me.' While the second part was true, the first was not.

Archie went to the living room, found the cash, and counted out the required notes for Mrs Eveson. It hurt him to so quickly lose money he had so recently gained, but he knew he had to take a longer view. Archie finally closed the door on a mollified Mrs Eveson. He returned to his armchair to finish his coffee. He was in danger of becoming lost in quiet contemplation when what he really needed to do, he decided, was to celebrate. A drink would do. He seldom frequented the pubs in the centre of town, but there were pubs on the outskirts that he sometimes visited.

The Fisherman's Cottage was a pub popular with the students at the University. As Archie entered it, his senses were assailed - music on the jukebox, loud voices and laughing, cigarette smoke, and the smell of warm, spilt alcohol. He ordered a pint of lager, quickly finished it, and ordered another. He gazed out of the window, over the Kennet and Avon canal, and took a deep draught of his lager, lost in thought.

Moving to Cheltenham would be no upheaval. He'd already moved many times in his life. While in the army, he had been stationed at a number of towns. After his expulsion from the service, he'd lived in London, where he'd worked at *The Purple Parrot*, and then in Dereham, before moving to Reading. He'd had a number of jobs, as well. The best, he thought, had been the job at *The Purple Parrot*. It was a nice joint, and the people had been cool. In some ways, he regretted stealing Len Stone's stash. Once he'd sold it and spent the proceeds, he'd been as broke as ever. And he felt as if he'd also stolen Peta Shepherd from Len. She might not have fancied Len, but he had a soft spot for her. He wasn't sure if it was a sexual thing, though. It seemed, rather, avuncular, paternal perhaps. Some memories of Dereham and his time there with Peta came back to him. Remorse was a feeling he seldom harboured, yet there was a small part of him that felt bad about how his treatment of Peta. She was a decent girl, good to be around. Sure, he never loved her, but she was a looker, and she was besotted with him. But that's who he was: he used, abused, and left. Some would call him a heartless bastard.

Archie looked at his empty glass. He was maudlin. He shouldn't drink on an empty stomach. Still, he rose from his seat to buy another pint. He was supposed to be celebrating, after all. This mood would pass.

On his way to the bar, Archie bumped into a lad who was deep in conversation with a group of friends. The young man's beer spilt over the floor.

Archie smiled apologetically. 'Sorry, mate, didn't look where I was going. Let me get you a fresh pint.' That was the alcohol talking, Archie thought. *Soon I'll be buying the whole pub a pint.* Normally, he'd blame the youth for bumping into *him* and demand cash for a new pair of shoes, or trousers, or something.

The young man smiled in return. 'Cheers, man.' He glanced down at Archie's almost empty glass. 'Looks like you could do with another yourself.'

A few minutes later, Archie returned, weaving his way through the now packed pub, a pint in each hand, and a packet of crisps clamped between his teeth. He handed the pint over to the grateful student. He glanced over at his seat. It had now been taken. *Sod it!* Well, it was a pleasant enough evening, if a little chill. He retrieved his jacket and took his pint outside. He leaned on the metal fence next to the canal and lit a cigarette. He took a deep lungful of smoke. He was aware of someone standing next to him. He looked up to see the lad he'd bumped into

'I didn't get a chance to thank you for the replacement beer,' the lad said. 'Bit unfair really, as my glass was less than half full.'

'No problems,' Archie said. He smiled his winning smile. 'Do you smoke? You might as well bleed me dry while you're here.'

The young man thanked him, and took one of the offered cigarettes.

Archie studied the young man. 'I recognise that accent? West Country?'

'Yeah, that's right. I hear Welsh in you.' The man put on a Welsh accent. 'Yes, you've a bit of the Richard Burton and the Dylan Thomas about you, dai.' It was a very passable imitation.

Archie nodded. 'That's the beer talking,' Archie said. 'My accent tends to drift back home when I've had a few.'

The youth held his hand out. 'Reese Johns. Pleased to meet you. Guess us foreigners should stick together.'

Archie frowned. 'Foreigners?'

'I have some Welsh in me. My dad grew up in Port Talbot.'

Archie noted that the lad ran the words into one. 'My dad was in the Army. He was stationed around Salisbury Plain, and after he left the army, ended up in Dereham, in Wiltshire. That's where I was born.'

'Dereham, you say? Well, well. It's small world. I was there last year.'

Reese squinted in the dim light. 'Hey, were you one of guys up on Copsehill, with Patterson? The UFO group he has?'

Archie wondered if replacing this lad's pint had been a good idea. He was, by nature, a loner. Yet the hand of fate seemed to have opened and dropped Reese Johns into his path.

'Yes, I was there. I guess I wanted to see what all the fuss was about. But in the end, I thought it was a load of old bollocks.'

Reese looked at him more closely in the light coming out of the pub windows. 'Hey, yeah, you were the charmer with that hot-looking chick, weren't you? What's her name... Peta, wasn't it? You and her split up, right?'

Archie nodded. 'Irreconcilable differences, you could say.'

'Sad what happened to her, though.'

Archie looked at Reese then. 'Why, what happened?'

Reese looked out over the canal. 'You mean you don't know?' Archie shook his head. Reese took a long swig of his beer. 'Well, I don't know how to tell you this. Peta... well, she died. She's dead.'

'How?'

Reese took a deep breath. 'I was up the hill one night, with my mate, Miles. Having a bit of a laugh like we normally do.'

Archie nodded. He remembered Reese now. He and the friend he'd mentioned, Miles, would sit on a gate, apart from the others, chatting to themselves and laughing. But Peta had liked them, even though they were sceptical about the Dereham mystery. Sometimes she had gone over and chatted with them. Peta liked talking to people.

'Patterson was there,' Reese continued. 'He seemed subdued. We overheard him telling one of his friends that he'd found her – in the bath at the cottage. Seemed she'd slit her wrists. There was nobody else there. You'd gone, he said, and so had that other bloke.'

Archie swallowed. 'Colin?'

'Yeah. There was a note. She felt she had nobody left in her life, and just... well... Ended it all. Sad. She was a nice girl.'

'Slit her wrists?' Archie said.

Reese nodded. 'Yes. Patterson said it was very messy.'

Archie remembered now that he had been in such a hurry to leave he had left his safety razor in the house. He had been angry about that. She had obviously taken the blade out of the razor. He imagined her cutting into her veins. It would have been messy. And if Colin had left the house as well, nobody would have known until Mrs Vought, her boss at the farm where she worked, missed her. Which might have been days.

'Are you all right, man? You look like you've seen a ghost.'

He imagined the razor, his razor, biting into the blue veins below the white skin of the wrists he had sometimes kissed. Something lurched sideways in Archie. He moved a few steps from Reese, turned away from him slightly, and threw up into the canal.

Reese laughed. 'Thanks man. You almost put me off my drink.' He drained his glass. 'Are you sure you're okay?'

Archie nodded. He was surprised at the shock he felt, at the sadness. She had been a nice girl. Archie hadn't loved her, but he had liked her. And he liked so very few people, had fewer friends. In the end, he had simply found her belief in UFOs too difficult to take. And he had wanted to distance himself from her. He was, after all, *Archie*, the *loner*, always on the make. Peta had been more serious. She had loved him. That had been dangerous for him. And then there had been the threat of Len Stone.

'You look like you could do with a drink, a strong one,' Reese said. 'Let me repay the favour. I'll get you a scotch.'

While Archie waited for Reese to return, images and memories of Peta and Dereham whirled through his mind.

Reese came back with the tumbler of whiskey. 'Here, drink this. It's a double. I've blown my budget for tonight, but hey, it looks like you need it.'

Archie downed the proffered drink in one slug. 'Never mind that. Let's get some real painkilling done. Fancy a night of heavy drinking, on me?'

Reese gave Archie a careful look. 'No funny stuff – no... catches?'

'None. You're a link with the past, a past that has come back to haunt me. I can't shoot the messenger, can I? We'll go back to my flat and get hammered.' He wiped his lips on his sleeve. 'Let's send her out in style, eh?'

17

Edge stared at the world beyond the window. He hadn't spoken since greeting Harry with a curt 'Good morning.' Harry waited, patiently; he also had things on his mind – Peta Shepherd. Finally, Edge spoke. 'Do you know, Harry, the power I wield? It could go to my head.'

'Sorry, sir?' Harry said. 'Are you all right?'

Edge was silent again for a short time. He then stood and walked to the window. 'Harry, come over here. What do you see?'

Harry joined his boss at the window. 'The usual. The city. People going about their business.'

Edge's laugh was cynical. 'Yes, like good little termites. All part of their social programming.' Edge clutched Harry's shoulder. 'But what if I were to tell you that...' He gestured around the room with his free arm. 'All this, all we do, is for nothing?'

This wasn't the Edge Harry knew. 'Jesus, Mick, what's brought this on?'

Edge turned away from the window. 'I've had my eyes opened for me, Harry boy. There are forces that make all this, all we do, pale into insignificance. They can bring immense power to bear.' He turned to face Harry. His face was red. 'The *fucking* Americans!'

'Oh. The Americans.' Harry had returned home after he'd delivered Skinner's bugging equipment to the office. He hadn't seen Edge since.

'Americans! Working on *my* patch. The *bastards*!'

'We have protocols in place for such operations, they

know that. We can kick them out of the country now we know what they're up to. We can contact Langley, or–'

Edge interrupted. 'Ah, Harry...' He shook his head. 'This goes far beyond the Company. Colonel Skinner works outwith agency control. He is his *own* agency. Well, fuck it. We'll look at what Skinner is doing very closely indeed. And we'll watch our step every bloody inch of the way. One thing we have on our side is that the Yanks don't know who you are, and that you now have Len Stone in our pocket.'

'Did Skinner tell you why he was bugging Len's house?'

'No. I thought in the spirit of inter-agency co-operation he might. But whatever he's doing he's keeping to himself.'

'What did he say?'

Edge frowned 'We were warned off. I should say, *I* was. What's more, I think the powers available to him have turned him into a bampot.'

Edge had caught Harry's attention. 'You mean he's mad?'

'A total head-banger, Harry. He thinks he's untouchable, that the power he has is literally God-given. He has a religious fervour allied to agency powers. That makes him one very dangerous individual.' Edge's fist clenched, unconsciously. 'But, mark my words, I'll get him.'

Edge was confiding in Harry more than he normally would. Perhaps Edge was out of his depth.

'Is he right? Is he untouchable?'

'I had Carter check him out last night. She rang Langley. She was cautious in what she said. She asked if a Colonel Skinner had any executive authority or operational function within the Company. They said no. She then contacted the USAF, said she was worried about the security of Colonel Skinner, and wondered what he might be doing in London. They said he was performing routine checks at various airfields, Woodbridge, Rendlesham you know?'

Harry nodded, although his knowledge of which airfields the USAF used was limited.

'They said his stay would be short,' Edge concluded. 'The Colonel is supposed to be returning to the States *very soon*.'

'We know he's doing more than checking out airfield. He's in charge of an operation of some kind.'

'Yes. And he's not going to cease and desist. That much is clear, laddie. He knows we're onto him, but he doesn't care.'

'Is he dangerous?'

'Aye, if what he says is true. If he's working outside the purview of known agencies, then they have no control, and no idea what he's doing. He could do anything, anywhere, to anybody, and all the official agencies would have clean hands.'

'So we need to be careful.'

'Indeed.' Edge paused. 'Yet he's not so crazy that he simply made Stone and Freeman *disappear*, if you know what I mean.

'Yes, I do.'

'He's waiting for something. He wants something.'

'Perhaps we should get it first.'

'Indeed.' A tight-lipped smile pulled at Edge's mouth. 'He may think he has God on his side, Harry, but he hasn't bargained on a Highland Devil.' He turned away from the window and returned to the chair behind his desk. Edge steepled his hands beneath his chin. 'Go and do some spying, Harry. See what you can find out.'

'What will you do, Mick?'

'For the rest of the day, this Highland Devil will be polishing his dirk. We need to make things happen, and fast, before Colonel Skinner makes them happen. Whatever his plans, however cocksure he feels, I'll use my dirk to cut his legs from beneath him.'

Harry stood. 'I'll go and see Len,' he said. A cheeky grin was forming. 'And Mick? While I'm away...'

Edge looked up at him. 'Aye?'

'Don't be a berk with that dirk.'

Edge guffawed loudly. 'Hie and away with thee, Sassenach.'

Harry walked into *Peta's*, wondering what he could do to expedite events. He was greeted by a solemn-faced Martyn Harris.

'Any chance of seeing the main man?' Harry said.

'He's in his office,' Martyn said. 'Help yourself, mate. Hope you have better luck than we've had.'

'Hey, Martyn. What's up?' Although Harry could guess. Depression. Guilt. Sadness

'He's been a moody sod since recently. He's been in the office most of the time.'

The doors to the club opened, and Emily entered. Harry gave her a welcoming smile. 'Good morning, Emily.'

'Good morning, Harry.' Emily said brusquely. She went behind the bar and poured a glass of cola on ice, then returned to the front of the bar and sat on a stool, twirling the melting ice cubes with her finger, clinking them against the glass. She gave Harry a measured look. 'Well, what the fuck did you two get up to in the Midlands? Len's been a morose son-of-a-bitch since he got back.'

'So Martyn was saying,' Harry said. 'We didn't get up to much. We went to Peta's grave. Then Len wanted to look at some clubs. But they were a bit naff, to be honest. He's probably frustrated. He wants something good, something to make you proud. He has big plans for you two.' Harry said.

When telling a lie, it helped to tell the truth at the same time, no matter how tangentially connected the truth was to the lie. Len did have big plans for Emily, that was true –

except Len himself didn't know about them, because his plans would be Harry's plans.

He and Len hadn't, of course, spent the afternoon in the Midlands looking at clubs; Harry had driven Len around the countryside, trying to calm him, talking him down, reminding him that he now had Emily to look after, that Peta's father had it coming to him. They had concocted the story about looking at clubs to explain their late return to Hayes.

'I hope he gets his head together soon,' Martyn said. 'I don't often see Len like this.' He looked at Emily. 'Help him along, eh, Em? I can't run this club by myself.'

Emily shrugged. 'I'll try. But I've told him I don't need anything from him. I'm happy as we are.'

'Len *is* ambitious,' Harry said. 'He loves you. He wants the best.'

'Silly fool,' Emily said softly.

Harry had to set things in motion soon. The change in Len was obvious to both Martyn and Emily. Soon they would start asking him different questions. He was grateful that Emily was the woman she was; otherwise she might have already badgered Len, broken him down, made him tell her the truth.

'I'll go to the office and see him,' Harry said. 'I need to talk to him about work, anyway.'

Neither Emily nor Martyn said anything. Emily continued to look absently at her cola while Martyn polished the beer pumps. Harry pulled open the door beside the bar, and walked slowly down the corridor towards Len's office. He didn't like what he was about to do, but do it he must.

Harry found Len sitting behind his desk, looking at the unopened bottle of whiskey sitting on the top of it. He sat down opposite Len. 'You're not considering opening that, are you?'

'I've thought about it,' Len said. 'But if I did, the contents wouldn't last long.'

'It could only be a temporary fix, nothing more.'

'You know, in my time I've beaten seven shades out of villains who crossed the Manley Boys. One or two so badly they ended up in hospital. But I never actually... you know... Killed a man.'

Harry spoke soothingly. 'It was an accident, Len.'

'I wonder what kind of man I am, you know? How much anger and emotion poured out of me to kill that man?' Len shook his head. 'I thought I'd got over Peta. Well, I suppose I don't love her the way I love Emily. But there's something still there. Something...' He looked up at Harry, doubt on his face. 'Fatherly, Harry? Some protective urge?'

'You're a good man, Len. At least, you seem that way to me. I know something about your dodgy past. I've picked that up from you and Martyn. But you've moved on. You're straight now.'

Len smiled at Harry. Gratitude showed in his face. 'Thanks, Harry. It's good to hear that from somebody outside of this...' He waved his hands around to encompass the club. 'Environment. And thank God you kept a cool head. I owe you that.'

'Try to let it go, Len. Peta's father was a shit. He deserved all he got. It'll look like an accident. Middle-aged man falls in cemetery, hits head on gravestone. A tragedy. Very sad for the people who loved him. Which was... nobody. There was no-one else around. There were no witnesses.'

Len smiled grimly. 'You're right, of course. How are things out there?'

'Quiet. But the peasants are revolting.'

Len raised an eyebrow. 'Come again?'

'Emily and Martyn are getting twitchy. They think you're a grumpy old hermit.'

'What do you suggest?'

'We have a story already, it's nice and simple. Stick to it.'

'Yes, I suppose we must.'

'There's another thing, Len. I need something from *you*.'

Len smiled. 'Anything, Harry.'

Harry smiled. 'You might change your mind on that. I need some...' He fished for a word. '*Cooperation*... with a little problem we have.'

'We?' Len said.

Harry nodded. 'Yes, *we*.' He reached inside his coat and withdrew a small leather wallet, and placed it on the desk. He slid it over to Len. 'Open it.'

Len opened the proffered wallet. Inside was Harry's identity card. The colour drained from Len's face. 'What is this?'

'I'm Harry Roberts, a servant of the Crown. We need your help. Events have taken an unexpected turn, so we're reeling you in sooner than we thought.'

'You think I'll help *you*? The system?'

'You will. Not only do you have a murder to keep under wraps, but you could also be arrested on any number of other charges. I could provide the police with information about your possession of drugs, and how you turn a blind eye to the supply and use of Class A drugs in the club. When you add it all up, the information we could supply to the police would add up to a long stretch for you.'

Len moved quickly. He stood and reached across the desk; his hands went around Harry's neck, forming a vice-like grip. Len was strong, as Harry had from a heavy for the Manley Boys, but the grip was inexpert and Len was off-balance.

Harry soon had Len on the floor, his arm around Len's throat. Len struggled, but Harry tightened his arm just enough to show Len why he shouldn't. He hoped the sounds of this struggle hadn't reached Martyn or Emily. Len had to understand the situation quickly, before either of them entered the office. 'Now, now, Len. That's not the way to treat someone who could make your life very uncomfortable for the next few years, is it?'

'What the hell does that mean?' Len gasped. 'Who are you, anyway? Colin or Harry, or some other fucker?'

Harry released his grip a little, to prevent Len passing out. 'As my card says, I'm Harry Roberts. I'm in the Security Service. And we need your help. Think of Emily, Len. All they years you have ahead of you. Do you want to spend them in jail?' Harry felt the release of tension in Len's body. Len had finally accepted that he had no way out of the trap Harry had sprung. 'No more funny stuff, Len. You have to think of Emily.'

'No more funny stuff.'

They both stood and composed themselves. Len glared at Harry. 'I liked you, Colin. Or should I call you *Harry*?'

'You'll like me again, Len. But not for a long time. And continue to think of me as Colin. It'll be easier. Less chance of a slip up.'

'You're not related to Peta then?'

Harry knew he had to be careful. 'No. But I did know her very well. She was very close to my heart for a while.'

Len grimaced. 'Boyfriend? After that prick, Conn?'

'No, but I knew Archie as well. And I have to say that your description of him tallies with mine.'

'So, you were in Dereham with them?'

Harry nodded. 'That's all you need to know for now.'

Len cracked open the bottle of whiskey, and poured himself a large measure. 'I suppose you won't have one as you're on duty?'

Harry smiled. 'I'm MI5, not the bloody police, Len. Pour me a snifter too.'

Len took another glass from one of the drawers of his desk, poured a measure for Harry, and passed the drink over to him. Len took a large gulp from his glass, and sat back in his chair. Some of the old Len began to resurface. 'So, what exactly do your lot want from me?'

Harry placed his hands on the desk, and leaned over, almost face to face with Len. 'Nothing much.' He had to sound determined now, tough even, though it was hard to be this way with Len, and especially knowing what he would need to do. 'Only Emily Freeman. And you're going to give her to us on a plate.'

18

Carl Cleaver alighted from the train and looked around him. So, he thought, this is Dereham. Rain blew in sheets across the two small, tatty platforms of Dereham station. A poster, peeling and faded, lauded *Beautiful Wiltshire*. Carl snorted derisively. He picked up his small case and made his way across the iron bridge to the exit. A sullen railway employee clipped his ticket, and then handed it back to him. Carl wondered where his hotel was. 'Can you tell me where the *White Lion* is, please?'

The ticket inspector nodded. 'Just over the road. Turn left when you go out of the doors, cross the road, and you'll see the beer garden. The back door should be open. If it isn't, come back and I'll tell you how to get in the front door.'

The back door was open. Carl walked down a corridor, towards a small desk next to a flight of stairs. The desk was unmanned. He dropped his bag, and rang the brass desk bell to announce his arrival.

A few moments later, a woman appeared. She had, Carl thought, a homely face. He wondered if the hotel had the same kind of homeliness.

The woman offered Carl a smile. 'Mr Cleaver, is it?'

Carl was surprised. It must have shown on his face.

'Oh, don't worry, love, I'm not psychic' the woman said. You're the only guest booked in tonight.' She held out her hand in greeting. Carl took it. 'Pam Wallace. My other half is the licensee of this place. Welcome to Dereham. Is this your first visit here?'

Carl nodded. 'Yes, and it's been a long day. The train broke down just out of Bristol Temple Meads.'

'Typical British Rail, eh? Well, you're here now. Let's get you settled in. You'll feel like a new man after a rest.'

Carl signed the register, and then Pam Wallace directed him to the staircase. As they climbed the stairs, she continued talking. 'So, Mr Cleaver, what brings you to our sleepy little town? Business?'

'You could put it like that. I'm a journalist. I'm doing some research on the Dereham mystery.'

Pam Wallace chuckled. 'Oh, you mean the little green men and their flying machines?' She stopped, and unlocked the door to Carl's room. 'The man you need to see, Mr Cleaver, is Richard Patterson, our local UFO buff. He often pops in here for a jar or two in an evening. I'll introduce you if you like.'

Carl smiled gratefully. 'That would be most helpful of you, Mrs Wallace, thank you.'

'Not at all, my dear, and please, call me Pam.'

Carl closed the door. He dropped his bag and flopped onto the bed. *One step closer to finding you, Archie my boy.* Within a few minutes, he was asleep.

An hour later, Carl entered the saloon bar. He had expected it to be quiet and sedate. Instead, the sound of a jukebox greeted him. Ranged around the tables appeared to be all the students, hippies and freaks of Dereham. Logs burned orange in the fireplace. A number of what Carl assumed to be regulars had seated themselves around the fire. There was a thin, gaunt man behind the bar. 'Ah, Mr Cleaver,' he said. 'My name's Josh Wallace, Pam's other half.'

Carl smiled. 'Call me Carl. And how did you know my name? Oh, of course, I'm your only guest, and everybody else is a regular.'

'I can tell you've been talking to my wife. I hope she didn't talk the backside off you. Tends to be a bit of a chatterbox, my missus, bless her. Now, what can I get you? Pint of bitter, lager or our own local scrumpy?'

'Yeah, well, as they say, when in Rome...'

Josh Wallace began pulling a pint of cloudy liquid. 'Now be careful mind, or like some of our locals, you'll be seeing lights in the sky all right!' He handed the glass over.

Carl held the glass up to the light. 'I'll need to strain this through my teeth first!' He smiled. 'Thanks, and have one for yourself.'

Carl sat at an empty table and looked at the menu. It contained, as he expected, basic fare. He was hungry though, and would settle for almost anything.

'Well, Mr Cleaver, has anything taken your fancy?' He looked up, and found Pam Wallace smiling at him.

'Just the scampi and chips, I think. Thanks.'

The door nearest Carl opened, and a tall man entered. He appeared to be in his forties. He wore a flat cap and an overcoat.

Pam bent down and whispered in Carl's ear. 'You're in luck tonight, my dear. That's old Patterson – or Potty Patterson as some of the locals call him. I'll let him get a couple of pints down his neck, and then introduce you.'

While Carl waited for his food, the saloon bar slowly filled with more students and hippies. Carl smoked and sipped at his scrumpy. He wouldn't be having any more of that. He observed the people around him, chatting, eating, drinking, and flirting. After a while, Pam brought his food to him. As he ate, he thought about Archibald Conn and the death of his brother and sister, and wondered if this could be the story that finally provided a way into a national daily newspaper. It would be a big story with his name on the byline. When he finished eating, Pam quickly returned to collect his plate.

'Dessert?' She said. 'Or a coffee?'

'Just a coffee, please Pam.' Carl glanced around him. 'It's a bit weird in here,' he said. 'All these youngsters in the saloon bar. Usually this is the place where the posh people go, isn't it?'

Pam laughed. 'Yes, it *is* odd, isn't it? Josh, my husband, has a theory. All these hippie types want a new world order. And yet they want to be different to the common man, he says. So while they sympathize with the common man, they don't actually want to mix with him and his pursuits, like darts, and cribbage and dominoes.'

'Don't you mind? Hasn't it driven away the clientele you'd prefer, the ones with more money?'

'We welcome it, actually.' She smiled benevolently over the heads of the drinkers at the tables, as if she were a vicar surveying his flock. 'They're nice enough people. And the middle class who used to come in here? They only used to have a couple of G and Ts, or a sherry or two, and then go home. We make more money from this lot than we ever did from the others. The real drinkers are in the public bar over the corridor.'

Carl nodded. He understood. He had left university himself only five years ago, and remembered that need to be different, the excitement of entering a new world of ideas and wanting a place and a group in which to express them.

At one of the tables, Carl could see a young lad glancing in Patterson's direction, and then laughter coming from the others at the table. Obviously, Patterson was the butt of the conversation and jokes.

'What's going on there?' Carl said to Pam.

Pam sat down next to Carl. 'That young lad is Terry

Dyson. Rumour has it that a lot of the lights Patterson sees are because of him.'

Carl didn't understand. 'How? Why?'

'Young Terry is a hoaxer,' Pam said. 'That's what some say. He sends up balloons with torches on them, or something.'

There was renewed laughter at the table Carl watched. Patterson began to look uneasy. 'Looks like your man Patterson is getting itchy feet,' he said to Pam. 'I think it's time you introduced us.' Pam nodded, went over to Patterson and spoke quietly to him. Patterson looked over, and smiled. He said a few words to Pam, and then stood up, put on his flat cap, and left. Carl felt disappointed that he wouldn't meet Patterson tonight after all. Perhaps Pam had said something that had made him wary. She walked back over to Carl.

'Cheer up, me dear! Old Patterson is on his way up to Copsehill to look for his beloved UFOs. He said if you wanted to join him, you'd be most welcome. I said you were tired after a long journey, so he suggested you meet him here at lunchtime tomorrow. Is that all right by you?'

Carl smiled. 'That's wonderful, Pam, thanks. I think I'd appreciate a good night's sleep. Besides, I'm not that interested in his UFOs to be honest. I'll bid you goodnight.'

The following morning, after a light breakfast, Carl explored the small town. As he suspected, there really wasn't much to see. By late morning, he'd purchased one local guidebook, and a small mimeographed pamphlet called *The UFO Newsletter*. He wasn't at all interested in UFOs, but at least he could claim these items on expenses.

The day was warm for November, and dry. Carl strolled down to the local park, and sat on a bench overlooking a now-empty raised flowerbed. He opened the UFO pamphlet and began to read. The pamphlet might provide insights into Patterson's world. The prose style was idiosyncratic, Carl noted, wordy, florid, groping after profundity. After reading twenty pages of reports about local UFO sightings and some speculative theorising, Carl glanced at his watch. Already quarter to one. *Shit!* He assumed Patterson would have his lunch at around one o'clock. He put the pamphlet in the bag and walked quickly back to The White Lion. When he arrived, he found Patterson nursing a pint by the unlit fireplace.

Patterson looked up at Carl. 'I thought you weren't going to turn up.'

'Sorry, Mr Patterson. Pam didn't actually tell me what time you'd be here. I assumed one o'clock.' He held out his hand. Patterson took it. Patterson's grip was firm. 'My name's Carl Cleaver.'

'Yes, I know. Pam likes to talk. She also told me you were a journalist. So, young man, what are you? An earnest seeker after truth? Or a hack from London, come to take the piss out of a poor deluded local journalist?'

Carl took out his press card. 'I'm neither, Mr. Patterson. I'm from a regional paper myself, in Wales. I've come to ask you some questions about a something that happened here a few months ago.'

Patterson relaxed a little. 'So, which of our wonderful, mesmerizing, meandering sightings do you want to talk about? The shimmering spheroid over Red Post Hill? Or perhaps a red rambler over Derebury?'

Carl shook his head. 'I'm sorry. It's none of those, as impressive as they sound. No, I'm here about an article I found in a copy of *Reveille*. The one with the photograph of you and your friends.'

'Ah, yes. *That* article. Dear Peta. Such a lovely, sweet girl.'

Carl didn't want to hear about Peta; he wanted information on Archibald Conn. He decided to keep the conversation away from Archie for the moment. Patterson seemed taken by this Peta, so Carl encouraged him to talk about her. 'Peta... Peta Shepherd, isn't it? What happened to her?'

Patterson frowned, and sipped at his pint. 'Well, that was the talk of the town for a few days. She... died.'

Carl was surprised. 'She died? She looked so young in the photograph.'

Patterson shrugged, and then took another sip at his pint. He looked around at the bar, where Josh Wallace was cleaning glasses. 'Josh, get Mr Cleaver a drink.'

'A pint of bitter this time, please, Josh.'

Josh brought the drink over, and then went back behind the bar.

Patterson composed himself before speaking. 'Peta... Peta was a lovely girl, but towards the end, she became very depressed. She...' Patterson looked at the empty fireplace, then at Carl. 'She killed herself, Mr Cleaver.'

'Why? How?' Carl thought he shouldn't ask, but couldn't help himself. He was a journalist. Why, how, what, where, who – that's what he was interested in. It had become second nature. Patterson certainly seemed to understand, and continued talking.

'The *how* is a matter of record. She opened the veins on her wrists, in the bath. There were no suspicious circumstances. As to the *why*? That's a difficult question to answer. I wasn't privy to Peta's secrets, or the nature of her affairs. I was interested in Peta because she was interested in our flying friends. My concerns with things *out there*-' Patterson raised his eyebrows heavenward. 'Often means my concern with more mundane matters is... *underdeveloped*. I am not as close to people as I perhaps should be.'

'Why do you think she was depressed?'

'Ah, as I say, I'm not one for human relationships, Mr Cleaver.'

'Please, call me Carl.'

'Of course.' Patterson shook his head. 'Look, Carl, I don't know what you want to know. I talked to Peta's mother soon afterwards. She came down to see me. She asked similar questions. I couldn't tell her anything. All I know is this – her boyfriend left her, and then her friend Colin also left. She was alone. Perhaps that was enough to tip her over the edge.'

This was all fascinating, Carl thought, but it wasn't getting him closer to Archie.

Patterson smiled ruefully. 'Luckily, I didn't have to speculate on her emotional state for the newspaper reports.'

Of course, Carl thought, Patterson was probably the local reporter for the nationals. He would have wanted the lineage for a human-interest story about the death of Peta. Carl was wondering how to move the conversation onto Archie when Patterson did it for him.

'But, really, I don't think Archie helped.'

'Archie?'

'Archibald Franklin Conn. Peta's boyfriend.'

'She was his girlfriend?'

'Yes. Didn't you know?'

'No, I didn't. The pictures in *Reveille*... Peta is on one side of the page, and Archie on the other.'

Patterson nodded. 'I remember the article. They were photographed side by side, but for page layout they cut the photo in half and pasted them up in different columns.'

'So they were an item?'

'They'd come down from London, for the UFOs, they said. They set themselves up in a cottage, funded by some music mogul from up north. Philip Creighton. Do you know him?' Carl shook his head. 'He was into the UFOs as well, and wanted a finger in another pie. So, they lived in a small farm-worker's cottage on the way up to Copsehill – that's our favourite hill, where we skywatch. They were doing it up, Archie and Peta, in lieu of rent. After a few months, Archie walked out on her. There was another chap living there, Colin. He was the lodger.' Patterson paused, looked into his half-empty glass. 'And then Colin left soon afterwards. Peta was on her own. She seemed to become depressed then. It got the better of her. She killed herself one afternoon. Nasty business all round.' Patterson swigged the last of his pint down.

Carl's glass was already empty. 'Do you want another, Richard?'

Patterson nodded. Carl took the glasses to the bar, and ordered two more pints. Now Patterson had begun to talk about Archie, he wanted the conversation to remain on course. Carl carried the two pints back to the table and handed one of them to Patterson.

'This Archie... He sounds a bit of a lad.'

'Not so much a *Jack the Lad*, no. He had a swagger to him, sure enough. Girls liked him. But he never chased after any other skirt while he was here. Peta never said that about him. No, it wasn't that. He treated the girl with disdain. I really don't know what she saw in him. Well, he was a big lad, handsome. Love is blind so they say. He was just...' Patterson seemed to struggle for words. 'A cold fish. Gave the impression that he was always calculating, always thinking ahead of everyone else, always plotting.'

'Yes,' Carl said. 'I knew him.'

Patterson looked at him in surprise. 'Why didn't you say?'

'I didn't know how he was related to all this. I wanted to hear from you what he was like. He might have changed.'

'He was the sort of person you couldn't get close to.'

'Yes, always an acquaintance, never a friend.'

'You were an acquaintance?'

'We both went to school in Swansea. We shared some time together. We played in the school rugby team. I went back to his house for coffee sometimes. I liked him well enough back then, but once I moved onto university we lost touch.'

'I don't know why he was here. He didn't really believe in the UFOs, like Peta did. He was a people pleaser I think. Not to make himself feel good, or to make friends. It always felt like there was a scheme going on his head. I don't know what his scheme was.'

'That sounds like Archie. A charmer, a schemer. He was probably planning a way to make money down here.'

'Well, he never made any money that I know of.'

'That's probably why he left.'

'Peta told me Archie blew his top when his picture appeared in the papers.'

'*Reveille*?'

'No, the *News of the World*.'

'A national, then.'

'Yes. He was running away from something, I thought, though Peta never mentioned anything.'

That was interesting, Carl thought.

Patterson spoke again. 'I suppose Archie would make an interesting new angle on the story. I don't know where he went after Dereham. I did hear that he had family in your part of the world.'

'I'm pretty certain he's not in Wales,' Carl said. 'His family...' Carl wondered what he could say. 'Well, they're dead. A tragic situation. Archie's brother killed his sister, and then died himself of a heart attack.'

185

Patterson nodded. 'Tragic.' Then he smiled. 'You have a journalist's instincts, Carl. Do you suspect Archie was involved?'

Carl smiled in turn. 'Wouldn't you be suspicious, Richard? Wouldn't you want to follow the story?'

'Of course. If I read the Swansea newspapers, I might have started following this up myself. Too late now. This is your story.'

'Do you have any idea where Archie and his girlfriend had come from before arriving here?'

'London. They'd both been working in a nightclub in London, and had to leave in a hurry. I never understood why. Oh, what was it called?' Patterson clicked his fingers. '*The Pink Pelican*! Or something like that. Something trendy.'

'Yes, *The Purple Parrot*. But I couldn't find any such club listed at Companies House. Is there anything else you remember?'

'Somebody called Len owned the club. Len... Stone, that was it.'

Carl had at last a new nugget of information. And, as he'd suspected, mystery still swirled around Archibald Conn. He was indeed worth further investigation. He thanked Patterson for his help. Before the older man left, they exchanged telephone numbers. Carl sheepishly asked Patterson to sign his pamphlet. At least he'd have something to remind him of his trip.

As he made his way back to the railway station later that afternoon, he looked at the downs that rose above the town. He hadn't been to the hills while he'd been here; they looked like a nice place for a walk. Patterson went to Copsehill nearly every night, Pam Wallace had said. Carl wondered what it looked like, and what the views were like from the hill. Perhaps his kids would enjoy a night on the hills looking for flying saucers. Dereham wouldn't be too bad a place to revisit. The people had seemed nice too, certainly the Wallaces, and Richard Patterson. Carl made a mental note; perhaps Dereham should be the next holiday destination. He'd visited worse places.

'Christ on a bloody bike, Carl!' Tom Hughes wasn't in the best of moods. 'More expenses! A nice jolly to Wiltshire?' Hughes was worrying about the money, as Carl had suspected he would. 'Where do you think you work, the bloody *Daily Mail?* Get real, Carl. And where is this story going? You still haven't found anything that would tie Conn to a murder. I suggest you drop the story.'

Carl frowned, uncertainly. 'I know, I know. But look, there might be more mileage in this. I've been in contact with Companies House again. The *Purple Parrot* did exist, but the owner, Leonard Stone, changed its name a short while ago. Guess what he changed it to?' Hughes remained silent, favouring Carl with a stony face. He would need convincing that the continued pursuit of Conn was worthwhile. '*Peta's*,' Carl continued. 'And that was the name of Conn's late girlfriend.' Carl sat down in a chair, emphatically, as if the act of sitting in such a manner would reinforce his point.

Hughes's square face remained, however, impassive. 'So, you're telling me that Archibald Conn is, in fact, a triple killer, and that the boys in blue have yet to make the connection you so obviously have?'

Carl thought for a moment. 'Well, I'm just hypothesizing here, right? I don't think Conn actually killed the ex-girlfriend. But his actions contributed to her death. He's a cold, hard, uncaring man, who wouldn't have given a toss about this Peta. If there was foul play involved in the death of his brother and sister – and in my mind, there was – then he would be the prime suspect. '

'But you have no concrete evidence, Carl. How on earth are you going to progress your enquiries?'

Carl shook his head. 'I'm not sure. But small pieces of the puzzle keep falling into place. I'm slowly building a bigger picture. Patterson said this Peta kid was a lovely girl. The complete antithesis of Conn. God knows what she saw in the man.'

'I'm sorry, Carl. I just can't justify the expenses you're chalking up. You either drop this, or bankroll the investigation out of your own pocket.'

Carl wasn't surprised. He knew the paper's proprietor was constantly on Hughes's back to keep costs and expenditure down. He scratched his head absently. 'Well, can we at least afford a telephone call to that place Conn worked, *Peta's*? If I draw a blank there, then I suppose I'll have to call it a day.'

Hughes nodded. 'Fine. Then you can go back to writing about local vegetable shows and baby beauty contests.'

Carl had rung *Peta's* three times now. The two previous times, he had let the phone ring for over five minutes. The monotonous beeping of the phone at his ear was beginning to get on his nerves.

Finally, the phone was answered. A Birmingham accent snapped at him. 'Yes? *Peta's* nightclub. Can I help you?'

'Is that Leonard Stone?' Carl said.

'No, it's the assistant manager, Martyn Harris.'

'When will Mr Stone be in?'

'I don't... know.'

Carl noticed the hesitation. He suspected Martyn Harris had been about to unleash a swear word.

'Any idea at all?'

'He's been off for three days with an illness. I'm doing everything while he's away. Including answering the phone.'

Mr Harris wouldn't win awards for his telephone manner, Carl thought. He sounded harassed. Not unnaturally, Carl supposed; if Leonard Stone had need of assistant manager, it implied the club was a busy one.

'Perhaps you can help me,' Carl said.

'I'll try,' Harris said.

'I'm a reporter, and I'm trying to find out the current location of Archibald Conn.'

Harris's reaction surprised Carl. 'I haven't got time to talk about that shit-head!' The phone went dead. Carl took the phone away from his ear, looked at it as if the phone itself had offended him, and then dialled the number again.

The phone was answered more quickly this time. Martyn Harris must still have been standing next to it. 'Mr Harris? Carl Cleaver here. All I need is an address if you have one. I don't know what Mr Conn has done to you, nor his connection to your club. I'm doing a story-'

'Every time trouble rears its ugly head,' Harris shouted down the phone, 'it has something to do with either Archibald Franklin Conn or Peta Shepherd. It was a bad day when we got involved with her. I don't know where Conn is. I couldn't give a fuck. I don't care what your story is about, or what you want to know. What I want is for you to bugger off and leave us alone.' Carl heard the dial tone again.

The last sentence had been so emphatic. Carl felt as if a small bomb had gone off in his left ear. He could almost see Harris slamming the handset back into its cradle, swearing at it. *That's it then. Dead end. I'm going to have to drop the story.* With a sigh, he replaced the handset and began to sift through his in-tray.

19

Archie sat at the bar in a pub in Reading town centre. He had no inclination to visit The Fisherman's Cottage again, where he might bump into Reese Johns. They had both been very drunk the other night. Archie worried that he might have said too much. He knew many things about himself. He was strong, tough, and street-wise. But he also knew he couldn't handle his drink. Hopefully, Reese remembered little of that night. He certainly looked worse for wear the next morning, before Archie had bundled him into a taxi back to his halls of residence.

Peta. She had been the problem. Hearing her name had disturbed him in some way. He had never loved Peta, but her easy nature and adoration of him had engendered warm feelings towards her. Peta had reflected his own virility and manhood back at him and that made him feel good. His egotism was another of the things Archie knew about himself. He knew it was a weakness, that the need for such positive reinforcement was a result of the treatment he had received from his father and Giles.

Reese had also represented a link back to Dereham. Much as Archie despised all the flying saucer nonsense and the people associated with it, he had liked living in the town. It had a certain... *atmosphere.* It pulled gently at him now. He remembered the hills, the trees on Copsehill, and the green downs falling away to the valley floor on a warm summer's day. It had been a pleasant.

He felt a hand on his shoulder. 'Archie Conn?' His heart sank for a moment, fearing that Reese Johns had decided to slum it in town. Yet the voice was different. He turned to find a face he couldn't for a moment put a name to.

'You never write, you never phone,' the man said. 'Anybody would think you were avoiding me.'

Archie laughed as he finally recognised the man. 'Jeff Briggs. What are *you* doing here? Let me get you a drink.' Archie ordered a pint of bitter, and a shandy for himself. 'What are you doing these days?'

Briggs smiled and winked. 'Not here.' He led the way to an empty table in a quiet corner of the bar.

They sat down. Archie laughed again, and shook his head in disbelief. 'Jeff bloody Briggs. I haven't seen you since... well, since we were drummed out of the Army together.'

'That seems a long time ago now,' Briggs said.

Briggs, like Archie, had grown his hair. He had also shaved the moustache he had worn when he was in uniform. He wore a greatcoat over a cable knit sweater, and faded jeans. 'You look a bit like a hippie,' Archie said.

Briggs made a peace sign. 'Peace and love to all, man.'

'Now, that I find hard to believe.' Archie and Briggs had been friends in the Army. They both had an interest in money, and obtaining it by whatever means possible. It had been Briggs with whom Archie had been fiddling NAAFI accounts and off-loading hot NAAFI goods; the swindles that had led to their eventual expulsion from the regiment.

Briggs gulped at his drink, and then wiped beer away from his top lip with the sleeve of his greatcoat. 'I am a brother to my brothers,' he said, then looked over at the bar, then around him. He grinned mischievously. 'Basically... do you want to buy some Mary Jane?'

'Hah!' Archie slapped the tabletop. 'Same old Jeff!'

'I follow the money, Archie. I follow it down the path of least resistance, the path that offers riches with little graft. I realised there was an eager market out there for illicit substances.' Briggs pulled at the lapel of his greatcoat. 'Think of this as my business suit... Or my uniform. It gets me into places I might not otherwise be allowed to go.'

That explained the long hair, Archie thought. 'Your hair... you could... Uh...Wash it.'

'Oh, don't be ridiculous, man.'

'Is it lucrative, your line of work?'

'Oh, yes. I don't just deal in weed. Anything, Archie, I can get you anything. Do you need anything?'

'Not at the moment, thanks.'

'You used to like the dexies.'

'Only to keep me awake at night while we waited for deliveries.'

'Yes. That was a good scam. Shame it all went tits-up.'

Archie shrugged. He lit a cigarette, and offered one to Briggs. 'You win some, you lose some,' Archie said.

'*You've* won some, I hear,' Briggs said. 'You've won *big*.'

Archie became cautious. 'What do you mean?'

'Relax, brother. I'm still in touch with a few of our pongo friends. Some of them are actually Welsh, and some have read the Swansea papers. It seems your brother and sister died in some kind of freak ... *event*.'

'Yes, it's most sad, and unexpected. I can't imagine what possessed Giles–'

Briggs held his hands up in front of him to interrupt Archie. 'Enough with the grieving, brother,' he laughed. 'It doesn't sit well on you.' He drew on his cigarette, examining Archie's face closely. 'I take it somebody benefitted from the estate?'

Archie nodded. 'You guess correctly.'

'Which is odd, given how you often told me your brother Giles was a little shit. I can't imagine he would've put *you* in the will. He'd rather have left any money to a dog's home, I'd have thought, given how much your sister loved her dogs.'

He had a good memory, Archie thought. It had stood them in good stead when they had been swindling the army. Briggs had never forgotten how many pallets of butter, or kegs of beer, they had liberated, or which drivers needed a pay-off, or when a new shipment would be dispatched from the NAAFI stores at Amesbury. 'I'm saying nothing that would implicate me,' Archie said.

'No need. Are you set-up for life now? Or are you still looking for work? Or should I say, *easy money*.'

'It's always the easy way for me, Jeff.'

'And your inheritance?'

'It's enough to keep me going for a long while, but it's not unlimited wealth. It will run out.'

Briggs fingered his beer glass, swirling the bitter, looking at it ruminatively. 'You were destined for big things in the army, Archie. Special services, officer... You were a tough fucker.' He looked up, eyed Archie. 'Still are, by the look it.'

'Yes, I suppose I was. I suppose I still am.' Archie supposed nothing. He knew what he was.

'You also lacked a certain... how shall I say it... *emotional* response to situations.'

'Yes. I was a cold bastard. I still am.'

'Have you ever thought...' Briggs leaned across the table, his hand partly against his cheek, partly hiding his mouth from the rest of the bar. 'Have you ever considered that your training and your emotional ... qualities... make you well-suited to a certain profession that operates ... well... at the fringes of society?'

Archie smiled, sipped at his shandy, and shook his head. 'I've no idea what you're talking about, Jeff.'

Briggs continued to talk quietly. 'You were a top-class marksman in the Army, right? You were always the best of our group at the hand-to-hand stuff?'

'Well, yes. That's why I thought I was being lined up for special services.'

'The rest of us knew you were. You were the obvious man from our intake. I knew it from the day we were handed our uniforms.'

Archie thought he knew where the conversation was leading. 'So, you're suggesting I become a hitman.'

Briggs looked furtively about him. 'Not so loud, brother. Yes, of course I am. You have the aptitude and little emotion.'

It amused Archie to favour Briggs with a cold, hard stare. 'Are you saying I'm a psychopath, Jeff?'

Briggs also stared back coldly. 'Good one. But the Archie stare won't faze me, man.' He laughed, finished his pint and asked Archie if he wanted another. Archie nodded.

While Briggs was at the bar, Archie pondered Briggs's suggestion. He'd never considered becoming a hitman before. Hitmen were something you read about, or saw at the movies. Contract killing wasn't a *career* – after all, just how did you set about becoming a hitman? Briggs was right, of course. He *did* lack empathy, sympathy, attachment. He had a strong stomach. He was a top marksman, he was good at hand-to-hand combat. Everything he had learned in the Army he put to good use. He had *already* put it to good use, he remembered. He had, after all, murdered his own brother and sister, in cold blood, for money. Except – it wasn't cold blood; he had hated Giles. There was, then, one emotion he still carried with him that he could put to use – hatred.

Briggs arrived back at the table with the drinks and sat on his stool.

'I'm not a psychopath, Jeff,' Archie said. 'I'm a sociopath.'

Briggs smiled. 'It's good you have a path to follow, however we name it.' Briggs took a gulp from his glass of bitter and wiped his mouth on his greatcoat again.

That sleeve, Archie thought, must reek of stale beer.

Briggs leaned across the table conspiratorially once more. 'I have contacts, Archie. I can put you in touch with people who have need of a talent like yours.'

'What's the money like?'

'Good, so I've heard.'

'Haven't you been tempted?'

'I don't have your abilities, Archie boy. I do have rather a weak stomach.'

Archie remembered Briggs once fainting during training when a member of the platoon had badly cut his hand on razor wire. 'Yes, you do.'

'Unlike you, I think I was being groomed for a desk job.'

'Yes. Intelligence, I thought.'

'So did I. I blew that, though. Still, selling gear helps keep me in luxuries.'

'You look like shit, though.'

'We don't all feel the need for a Saville Row suit.'

Archie looked down at the beer-stained and cigarette burned table for a moment. His inheritance wouldn't last forever, he knew that. He would need to work again, eventually. He didn't want a nine-to-five job. He wasn't cut out for it. But he *did* want a Saville Row suit. Archie made his decision. 'Set up a meeting.'

'Good man,' Jeff said.

But there lay his strength and his weakness, Archie thought. *I'm not a good man.*

20

Len and Emily sat at a table in the revolving restaurant at the top of the GPO Tower, looking out over a neon- and sodium-lit London evening.

'This is fantastic, Len,' Emily said. 'What have I done to deserve this?'

'Well, I know I've been a pain in the arse over the last few days,' Len said.

'*Ass*, Len, *ass*. When will you ever learn to speak English?'

Len laughed. 'Anyway, this is my way of saying sorry.'

Emily reached across and gently touched Len's hand. She spoke softly. 'Well, if this is your way of making up, honey, let's fall out more often, huh?'

Len smiled, but it was a false smile. He loved her deeply, but now he had to do the one thing he said he would never do: hurt her. The hurt would not be physical; but it would perhaps be a deep and lasting hurt. It might spell the end of their relationship. It was a gamble he had to take. If he were sent down for life for murdering Peta's dad, it would be the end of his relationship with Emily anyway. He would explain everything to Emily once MI5 had finished with her. Until then he could only hope she would understand why he had done what he was about to do. The Security Service wanted information from her.

Harry had told Len that the house in Hayes was bugged; there was only one place they could do what needed to be done, he said: *Peta's*. Memories of Peta began to resurface. He remembered her lying on the couch in his office, deep in a hash-induced trance, communicating with aliens. His thoughts were interrupted by Emily announcing she needed to visit the little girls' room to freshen up. When she was out of sight, Len reached into his jacket pocket, and withdrew a small paper wrap. He quickly opened it, and sprinkled white powder into her glass of white wine.

When Harry had explained what he wanted Len to do, he had smiled reassuringly. It was only a mild tranquilizer, he said confidently. It would act quickly. Emily would probably mention a little dizziness, and then become drowsy. She'd fall asleep in a controlled way. Len had eyed Harry coldly. If it did anything else to her, he said, Harry too would die.

Emily soon returned, looking, as always, radiant. He raised his glass to her. 'Here's to us. I still find it slightly odd that a vivacious and beautiful woman could see anything in an old crock like me.'

Emily chinked her glass against his. 'Bottoms up, Len.' She winked. 'If you're lucky.' She took a long sip of the doctored wine, and then became serious. 'I came to you after dad died because you were one of the few links I had left with him. You know that. Because you'd read the book, you understood. You had similar experiences to his. Then I got to know you better. I saw beyond the tough guy you try to project.'

As she spoke, Len began to loathe himself. Emily loved him, he could hear it in her voice, see it in her eyes. And he loved her so much. Yet here he was, doing what the Security Service asked, jeopardising her life perhaps, their relationship certainly. He didn't yet even know why MI5 needed Emily so badly. He wanted to tell her the truth – or, at least, some of it. 'Em, something happened while I was up in the Midlands. Something that has got me into a whole heap of shit.' He stopped, composed himself, and then lowered his voice. 'I killed a man.' It sounded now, inconsequential, almost absurd. But he felt a huge weight lift from his shoulders.

Her eyes widened. 'Did I hear you right?' She stopped, looked around, and then she too lowered her voice. 'You *killed* a man?'

Len nodded slowly. 'Yes, but please believe me when I tell you it was an accident.'

She shook her head. 'You killed a man?' She repeated. 'How...who..?'

He took a deep breath. 'Peta's father. We met him by chance, Harry and me. I wanted to visit her grave, and Peta's father was there. I lost it, and lashed out at him. He fell, and hit his head on a gravestone. Harry and I panicked, I guess, and ran. No-one saw anything, and we just drove away.' He looked into her eyes, pleadingly. 'It's the truth, that's why I've been so-' Emily's eyes began to defocus, a sign that the drug was taking effect. 'Distant, I guess.'

Emily's head drooped. Len gestured for the waiter, who came over. 'May I have the bill, please? And would it be possible for you to call a taxi for me? It seems the lady isn't feeling too well.'

The waiter looked at Emily with concern. 'It looks like she's about to faint, sir.'

Len looked sadly at Emily. 'She's a narcoleptic, I'm afraid. She'll be right as rain soon enough.'

How Len wished that were true.

Harry and Edge waited in Len's office. Harry had been surprised at first that Edge wanted to join him and Morrow at the club. Len had ensured that the questioning – none of them liked to use the word interrogation – was to be done on an evening when the club was closed. Len had persuaded Martyn to take a couple of day's holiday back in the Black

Country. Harry and Morrow had entered the club an hour earlier with a small counter-surveillance team. Morrow led the team in a sweep of the club, searching for bugs and any other surveillance devices. Rachel Heathcock, a doctor seconded from Army Intelligence, had arrived a little while later. Harry knew Heathcock; he had met her before on similar, delicate, operations. She was petite, dark-haired, mild-mannered and efficient. Harry set up two tape recorders and microphones while Heathcock prepared the drugs she would need to first bring Emily back to consciousness, and then to make her talk.

Edge turned up half-an-hour later. 'Ah, Harry, Doctor Heathcock, good evening to you. There's nobody out there,' he said.

'No,' Harry said. 'I didn't see any spooks either.'

Edge laughed. 'I think Skinner is a modern kind of spook who believes in electronics and bugs and comms.'

'Nothing beats leather on the street,' Harry said.

'Not when they're good, like you, Harry.'

Harry smiled wanly in reply. The compliment was well meant, and well received, but Harry didn't feel good; he had involved people he liked in the machinations of the intelligence services. Such conflicts of friendship, emotion, loyalty, and duty were always ready to confound. He nervously paced the floor.

Morrow entered the office, and slumped on the settee across from the desk at which Edge sat. 'There are no bugs inside the club.' He said. 'The phone is tapped at the junction box on the wall outside.'

Harry wasn't surprised. 'Martyn Harris hardly ever leaves this place. There are bars at the windows and alarms everywhere. It would be nigh on impossible for the Yanks to get in here without him knowing.'

'Yes, I know,' Morrow said. 'I wasn't expecting to find anything inside. Best to check though.' He shrugged. 'After all, Skinner might have got to Harris.'

Harry shook his head. 'Never. Martyn would never betray Len.'

Morrow looked at Edge. 'Do you want me to disconnect the tap, Mick?'

Edge merely grunted a negative and shook his head.

Morrow stood and tapped a microphone. Needles on the VU meters moved. He smiled at Harry, which, in itself, was a rare occurrence. 'Good job, Harry.'

'Thank God for that,' Harry said. 'I find it difficult enough to set-up my hi-fi.'

A member of Morrow's team entered the office. 'Stone has arrived, sir. Miss Freeman looks well out of it.'

'Thanks, Samuels,' Edge said. 'Tell the others they can high-tail it back to their pretty wives. You hang around in the street and have a smoke. Make sure we're not being spied on.'

Harry left with Samuels. He returned a few minutes later with Len, carrying the unconscious Emily between them. They placed her carefully on the settee.

Len looked at Harry menacingly. 'If she comes to any harm, I'll make sure you pay.' He looked at Edge, then at Morrow, then at the Doctor. 'All of you,' he added grimly. 'Who the hell are these people, anyway,' he said to Harry.

Edge spoke. 'I'm Michael Edge, Mr Stone. I'm Harry's section head, his boss.' He introduced Morrow only as Paul and Heathcock only as The Doctor. 'Don't worry. Miss Freeman will be fine. Once this is over, we'll leave you in peace. Although we may, of course, call upon your somewhat unique services from time to time.'

'You mean I'll become a high-ranking grass for you. I

thought the deal was that I would help you get information from Emily, and that would be the end of it.'

Edge shook his head slowly. 'Aye, Mr Stone, that's what we said. But think on this. Once we have ... *teased*... whatever information we can from Miss Freeman, you will, like us, be in possession of highly-classified material. You will, in effect, become one of us. But I do promise you this, unconditionally – the tragic incident that occurred in the Midlands will be dealt with. No finger will ever be pointed at you. I may be a devious bastard, but I am a man of my word.'

Len looked down at Emily. Her head was moving from side to side, her eyelids fluttering. 'Just don't hurt her, will you?'

Heathcock spoke then, softly, reassuringly. 'I have no intention of hurting Miss Freeman,' she said. 'I am a doctor.' She injected something into Emily's arm. 'That is a stimulant,' she said to Len.

The office was crowded, Harry thought. Too crowded. Morrow was sitting on Len's desk. Edge was sitting in Len's leather desk-chair. Harry was pressed up against some filing cabinets. Len stood with his back to the door, his face miserable. Harry would leave, if he could; but he thought he should be here, for Len.

Emily's eyes opened wide. 'Where am I?' She saw Len against the office door. 'Len, what happened?' She turned her head, and looked at Harry.

'Hello, Emily,' Harry said.

'Colin,' Emily said, dreamily, dopily. 'Hello, Colin.'

'Don't worry,' Harry said. 'You've had an accident. The doctor will help you.'

Heathcock smiled reassuringly at Emily, and then gave her another injection. Emily's eyes fluttered and closed again. Heathcock looked at Len. 'This drug, Mr Stone, will open her mind, make her more receptive to our questions. She'll be a little disoriented afterwards, but it's otherwise harmless.'

'A truth serum,' Len said.

'Yes. A few moments, Mr Stone, then it's over to you.'

Edge picked up several sheets of paper from Len's desk and handed them to Len. 'These are the questions that need to be asked, Len. If you want, Morrow and I will leave the room. But Harry and the Doctor must stay with you. Harry knows almost as much as I do, and if the questions need reframing, then he'll be the one to ask you to do it.'

Len shrugged. 'Do what you like.'

Heathcock turned to Edge. 'I think it would be best if you and Morrow did leave. This room is becoming rather stuffy.'

Edge looked at Morrow. 'She's right. Let's go.'

Len stood aside to let them out, and then closed the door behind them. Len looked measuredly at the Doctor. When he spoke, his voice was hard. Harry recognised the tone. 'I assume that you know what you're doing then, *Doctor*?'

'Please, Mr Stone, let's not get off on the wrong foot here, shall we? Call me Rachel, if that helps. And yes, I do know what I'm doing. I've conducted many of these...' She paused before continuing. 'I was going to say *interrogations*, but that, in this instance, is perhaps too strong a word. The drug I've given her is mild, and very safe.'

'So what exactly would you call it then, *Rachel*? An examination? A grilling?'

'A conversation, I hope.'

'Well get on with it. Whatever you call it, the sooner we start, the sooner we finish, and Emily and I can try to patch up our relationship.'

Heathcock's smile seemed warm and genuine. Her bedside manner was always impeccable. 'Let me reassure you, Mr Stone. Whatever story you choose to tell Miss Freeman will appear plausible in the few hours it takes for this drug to wear off. I also know what you did in the Midlands. Did you tell Miss Freeman about that?'

Len nodded.

'You have exculpated yourself, then. Good. She'll remember nothing of what you told her in the few hours before she arrived here. I advise you to keep it that way. Your relationship will quickly be on the mend.'

Len's tight mouth finally curved down, and he closed his eyes. His big frame sagged, and appeared somehow smaller. Heathcock checked Emily's pulse. 'Everything seems normal. I suggest we begin.'

Harry sat on the chair behind Len's desk. Len pulled a chair over, and sat next to the prone Emily. 'Emily, can you hear me?'

Emily replied in a dreamy voice. 'Yes, I can. Len, what's happening to me?'

'Relax, sweetheart, you're safe. You're... dreaming. I'm going to ask you some questions.'

Emily moaned again, and tried to move; then she spoke. 'Len, please, you don't understand. You must stop this now, please...'

Harry had watched this procedure before and was surprised at the urgency in Emily's voice. The drugs usually flattened such emotions. Her body shook slightly, and Harry saw a tear form and run down her cheek.

Len spoke again. 'I'm so sorry.'

Harry stood, came around the desk and whispered into Len's ear. 'We have to start the questions. The drug is only active for half an hour.'

Len nodded, and looked down at the first of the type-written sheets. 'Emily, what was your role in the United States Air Force?'

She smiled. 'Public relations, you know that.'

'Why did you leave the job?'

Her smile widened. 'Because I love you, lover boy...' She giggled.

Doctor Heathcock looked at Harry. 'This isn't right. She sounds drunk. She's either fighting it, or-' She broke off. She looked at the floor, and stroked her chin. She began again. 'Perhaps...' But her voice tailed away uncertainly on that one word.

Len looked up. 'What? Is everything all right?'

There was doubt in Heathcock's bright blue eyes. 'She might have been conditioned in some way... Perhaps to resist this type of questioning. But that would mean she was something more than a public relations officer. The Americans wouldn't go to those lengths to block access to the memories of a mere pretty face. I think Mick is onto something here. I'll be back in a few minutes.' Heathcock left the office.

Len and Harry were alone. Len shifted uneasily, and looked at the floor, not at Harry.

'Len,' Harry said, soothingly. 'This is important, you must believe me. Edge gets no pleasure in doing this. He's acting in the best interests of the country.'

Len's only reply was a stony silence. The door of the office opened. Heathcock returned with Edge and Morrow. Emily began moaning.

Len stroked Emily's cheek, concern on his face. He turned to Heathcock. 'What the hell's going on?'

Heathcock squatted beside him. 'Don't worry, Len. Everything is under control. We sometimes see a little discomfort. If you could just talk to her softly, and reassure her...'

Len bent closer to Emily, and began to whisper words of love and comfort. Heathcock took the opportunity to jab a syringe into his exposed neck.

'What the fuck?' Len said. A few moments later, he slowly fell forward until his head rested on Emily's breasts.

Edge walked over and touched the unconscious Len's shoulder. 'Sorry, big man, but this is more serious than we imagined.'

Morrow, Edge and Harry sat at bar stools, each holding a glass of whiskey. Heathcock came through the door beside the bar. 'Are they okay?' Harry said.

Heathcock nodded. 'They'll be fine. Sleeping like babies. I had to give Freeman another tranquilizer.'

'Would you like a wee dram, Rachel?' Edge said.

'I think I would,' Heathcock said. She pulled one of the bar stools closer to the others and sat down. Harry went behind the bar to get Heathcock a whiskey.

'Right, Doctor,' Edge said. 'Let's get this straight. You think that Freeman's memories have been deliberately blocked, by drugs, or some form of advanced hypnotism, right?'

Harry returned to his stool and handed Heathcock the glass. She took a sip before speaking. 'I read a paper a few years ago by an American, Edward Straker. He and some other psychologists developed techniques and drugs he thought could alleviate the effect of shell shock and other traumatic syndromes brought on by the conflict in Vietnam. They were, as far as I'm aware, quite successful. It was cutting edge stuff.'

'And?' Edge said. 'How does this to the current situation with Miss Freeman?'

Heathcock took another sip. 'Sorry, I forget I'm not at a colloquium of my learned colleagues. Well, if you have a technique that can successfully hide traumatic memories from the conscious mind, you also have a technique for hiding *any* memory from the conscious mind.'

Harry considered the consequences of what Heathcock had said. 'But wouldn't that mean Emily would remember nothing *at all*.'

'No. I assume you've heard of partial amnesia?' There were half-hearted nods from her audience. 'You know amnesia can be caused by bumps to the old noggin, right?' She looked at Morrow. 'I believe Paul himself has cause one or two cases of temporary amnesia.' The three men smiled. 'Well, trauma can also cause partial amnesia; the patient only loses particular memories while retaining others. The beauty of Straker's technique – if beauty is the right word – was that it caused permanent partial amnesia. Subjects only forgot what Straker wanted them to forget.'

'So, the trick cyclists are out of business, then?' Edge said. 'If you can effectively block traumas, then the causes of psychological problems can be hidden away. No more Freudian nonsense with the unresolved past.'

Heathcock shook her head and smiled. 'Ah, Michael, if it were only that simple. Straker and his associates published one paper, outlining the techniques and hinting at the processes required. Test results on small groups were suggestive. The thing is, though, Straker never followed up. There were no more papers from him. I know that other researchers have attempted replication, but without success. '

'So you think,' Edge said, 'somebody succeeded where Straker failed?'

'Oh, no. I think Straker *has* succeeded. After his paper was published, Straker left the hallowed halls of academe.'

'Where is he now?'

'You'll like this. He went freelance. Rumour at conferences suggests he works for the Company.'

Edge stood then and began pacing the dance floor. 'So, the block applied to Freeman could be a far more advanced version of the treatment you described?'

'Yes. If so, the drug I administered won't do the job for you.'

Harry asked the question that everyone was thinking. 'But you do have *something* in your bag of tricks that *can* do the job?'

Heathcock's animation subsided. She frowned. 'Yes, I think I do. It's not with me now. It's in my other bag of tricks back at the office. It's highly experimental. Giving it to her so soon after the first drug... Well, I can't be sure of the consequences. There could be a physical reaction, but far more likely is a mental one.'

'Are you talking about C21?' Edge asked.

Heathcock nodded.

'Jesus!' Edge said. 'I remember using that wee bugger on a Russian sleeper a few months ago. Tore his mind to shreds. He was a basket case after that.' Edge paced the floor some more.

'It's your call, sir. Remember this, though – Orlov was an ordinary agent. He hadn't been conditioned to resist this kind of interrogation. The drug opened his mind too wide, and let in too much. We were using a sledgehammer to crack a nut.'

Harry shifted uneasily on his stool. 'What will it do to Emily?'

'Truth is, I don't know,' Heathcock said. 'I don't think it'll affect her in the same way it affected Orlov. He had no doors to kick open, no blocks to breakdown. What Orlov experienced was like... Well, something like the worst LSD trip you can imagine.'

Harry stood. His heart raced. 'If something happens to Emily, it will be on my conscience. I like her. I like Len.'

Edge stopped pacing, and re-entered the circle of spies. 'Who you like is of no interest to me, Harry. I suggest that we transfer Miss Freeman to The Sanatorium. She'll need much better care than we can give her here.'

Heathcock nodded. 'That's where she needs to be.'

'Right, Morrow,' Edge said. 'Get outside and ask Samuels if it's still all clear.'

'The Yanks are watching Len's house, Mick,' Harry said. 'If Len and Emily don't come back tonight, they'll get suspicious.'

Edge thought for a moment. 'Can you do an impression of Len?'

Harry shook his head. Then he said, 'I can do a passable Brummie accent though. I shouldn't think the Yanks would pay Martyn much attention.'

'Call our friendly spa. Book a weekend for Len and Miss Freeman.' Edge took a small black book from his pocket, opened it and handed it to Harry. Harry went behind the bar and picked up the telephone. He could see Edge and Heathcock smiling at his imitation of Martyn Harris.

Morrow returned. 'Samuels says the street is dead. There's no sign of anybody at all.'

'The street is quiet when the club's closed,' Harry said.

'Right,' Edge said. 'It's time we took our love birds on holiday.'

They went to the office. Morrow and Harry carried Len to one of the cars, while Heathcock and Edge carried Freeman to a white van.

Three hours later, Harry sat next to Len in the back seat of Edge's Cortina. They drove though darkness into quiet Berkshire countryside. Morrow sat in the front passenger seat. They were followed by the plain Ford Transit containing Emily, Heathcock and Samuels.

There was a groan next to Harry. Len was coming around. He shook his head, blinked, and finally said, 'Where am I?'

'We're going on holiday, Len,' Harry said.

'Where's Emily?'

'Don't worry, she's fine. She's in the van behind us. She's with the doctor.'

Len looked behind him, frowning. 'With the doctor? Is she all right?'

'Like I said, she's fine. She'll probably be waking up like you about now.'

'Where are we going?'

Edge's voice came from the front of the Cortina. 'That's for us to know and you to find out, as my gran used to say.'

As my gran used to say. Peta, too, had been full of sayings she'd heard from her gran, Harry remembered. Peta was a ghost at the edge of his mind. He needed the technique Heathcock had described, he thought.

Edge picked up the handset fitted to the dashboard of the car. He drove with one hand as he radioed ahead with their current location and estimated time of arrival at The Sanatorium. He replaced the handset. 'This must all seem very James Bond to you, eh, Len?' Edge's mood had lightened when they had left London.

'No, Edge, more surreal than that.' Len said. 'A cross between *Department S* and *The Prisoner*.'

Edge gave a short laugh. 'Ha! I would've thought you too busy for such drivel.'

Len scowled. 'I do have a life outside the club you know. I was hoping to live it with Emily,' he finished quietly.

The car slowed, and then turned to the left, through a set of wrought-iron gates, and continued along a gravel drive.

'Welcome to our little spa,' Harry said to Len.

Len was surly. 'I'm sure it will be *lovely*.'

'It's our own special cottage hospital. A rest home. State of the art.'

Len said nothing, and turned to look out of the side

window. Harry also looked out of his window. The Victorian brick building was a gothic apparition against the dark sky. There had been a sign at the gate, *The Sanatorium*. That is what the building had been before the war, and how most locals remembered it. Now it was an inter-service, inter-agency medical facility in which doctors fixed the broken, broke the fit and healthy, and experimented with psychological and pharmacological techniques. Harry would rather be anywhere but here.

21

Carl Cleaver sat at the table in the dining room, reading a story in the *Daily Mirror* about a murder. He glanced down to the bottom of the column and found a by-line giving the name of the journalist. He felt envy. He was capable of better things than working on a regional local paper for a pittance. He yearned for a by-line, a big break, a story that would set him up alongside the big boys. He'd have a flash car, and a flash lifestyle. Jenny would love him. The kids could go to private schools. He chased Archibald Conn because, if his intuition was correct, that story was his one chance to break a *big* story – the kind of story that would look good on any journalist's CV.

The kids were in bed, and Jenny was cooking the evening meal for her and Carl. He'd offered to get a takeaway, but she'd already begun preparing the food. She thanked him for the offer anyway. Things were looking up, he thought. She had even smiled at him when he returned this evening.

The high-pitched tweeting of the telephone interrupted his thoughts. He hated that new bloody Trimphone. Its ring – if it could be called that – irritated him. He'd acquiesced to Jenny's demand for one. Trimphones were trendy, she'd said. She liked to be trendy. 'I'll get it,' Carl said. He closed his paper and folded it on the table, then went to the hall. As he lifted the handset, the tangled cord lifted the phone off the shelf. He held the phone down and said hello. A soft Wiltshire accent replied. 'Hello, Carl. Richard Patterson here. How are you?' Carl mumbled some pleasantries

'I've some rather interesting information for you.' Patterson said. 'I recently bumped into a local lad, Reese Johns. He joins us sometimes on our trips to Copsehill. He's currently at university in Reading. One night last week, he went to a local pub. You'll never guess who he bumped into.'

Carl's heart missed a beat. 'Please tell me it was the elusive Archie Conn?'

'Spot on, Mr Cleaver. Apparently, young Reese found Archie in a mood to get hammered. Seems he's Flash Harry at the moment. Bought young Reese drinks all night, then took him back to his flat to continue the carousing. Reese said news of Peta's death had come as a complete surprise to Archie. He never knew a thing about it.'

'If he left her and never looked back, that's not surprising.' Carl looked around the shelf for a piece of paper and a pen or pencil while trying to stop the Trimphone sliding around. He really needed to screw the base to the wall, as he'd promised Jenny so many times.

'No, I suppose it's not. Because Peta committed suicide, there were never any suspicious circumstances. The police wanted to talk to Archie, but only to fill in her background for the coroner.'

Carl couldn't help wondering how Peta fitted into the story. Her name came up so often. She seemed to be a rather large and important piece of a jigsaw of which he only ever saw an Archie-shaped corner. Still, no matter how she fitted into the puzzle, he had no time to indulge Patterson's reminiscences about her. He needed to know about Archie.

Patterson continued. 'When Reese went back for a drink, Archie came over all nostalgic, and talked about the old days, about being on the hill, the skywatchers, and Peta.'

This intrigued Carl. 'Interesting. I never really thought of Archie as the sentimental sort.'

'I suppose even the likes of Archie hungers for human contact sometimes.' There was a soft chuckle. 'But then I am a sentimental sort myself. I always believe there's some good in our fellow man – even the likes of Archibald Franklin Conn.'

Carl noticed the name Patterson had used. 'You might not know this, Richard, but *Franklin* isn't Archie's middle name.'

'Oh! Really? I didn't know that, no. I always assumed it was a hyphenated family name.'

'He's actually from a wealthy family, the sort that gives its children a lot of middle names. 'Franklin' isn't one of them. Do you know why he calls himself that?'

'I've no idea. In the end, I began to suspect it was an affectation. Something to make him seem more interesting and mysterious.'

'That's possible,' Carl said. 'Anyway, thanks, Richard. At least I now know he's in Reading. I'll visit the pubs and see if I can bump into him myself.'

'No need to do that. My young friend imparted one other nugget of information – Archie's address. Reese awoke the next morning with what he called *a really shit hangover*.' Carl smiled. Patterson continued: 'Archie rang for a taxi to take Reese back to halls, and gave his address over the phone. Luckily, the number stuck in Rees's head, as it was the same as his birthday, and he knew the road anyway because some of his student friends live out that way.'

Carl had patiently waited for Patterson to stop rambling. 'And the address is?' He nodded as he wrote the street and house number down on the back of a cigarette packet. Smoking came in useful sometimes, he thought. 'Thank you, again, Richard. Did your friend Reese share anything else?'

'Yes, one interesting thing. Archie has, it seems, come into a great deal of money. Reese didn't know how this change in fortune had come about, but I'd guess it was illegitimately.'

'I think I might pay Archie a visit.'

'You'll have to move fast, Carl. Archie told Reese he was moving out. He's already given his landlady notice of his intentions. He's only there at weekends now.' There was a pause. 'There. That's about all I can tell you, I'm afraid.'

'That's fantastic, Richard. It's the best lead I've had for... well... ever. I owe you one for this. The next time I'm in Dereham, the drinks are on me.'

'Are you thinking of visiting our small town again, then?'

Carl laughed. 'Don't worry, I'm good for the drinks. I was charmed by your town.'

'It has that affect, Carl. People are drawn back here again and again by its mysterious atmosphere.'

Carl knew where the conversation might now head, so quickly curtailed it with effusive thanks to Patterson, and a promise to visit soon.

He put down the handset, as Jenny came into the hall. 'Anything important, love?'

Carl gathered her up in his arms, planted a kiss on her cheek, and then spun her around the hall. 'Important? I'd bloody say so!'

As he let her down, she placed her oven-gloved hands on his neck. 'Hmmm, kinky, ' Carl said. She smiled, and then kissed him.

The taxi driver was more than chatty. By the time they reached their destination, Carl had the whole man's life story. He stifled a sigh.

'Here you are, pal. Grovelands Road.' Carl paid the driver. 'Want me to come back?'

Carl looked up at the house. 'No, thanks. I don't know how long I'm going to be, anyway.' He walked up the short pathway. Large laurel bushes hid the house from the road, and shadowed the front door. He rang the bell, and waited. There was no answer, so he knocked the door. After a few moments, a small, elderly woman opened the door.

The woman looked at him from head to toe. 'Yes? Can I help you?'

Carl framed his face into the boyish smile he knew charmed little old ladies. 'Hello. I was told that an old friend of mine was lodging here, chap by the name of Conn, Archie Conn.'

'Yes, he's moving out soon. He's only here at weekends.'

'Is he here now?

'Yes, he's upstairs, I think. I heard him walking around last night. He's probably still asleep.'

'Do you think I could...'

'Oh, you go on up, dear. I'm waiting for a friend to take me into town. I thought you were him when you knocked. Do be sure to bang heavily on Mr Franklin Conn's door. That should wake the lazy-bones.'

Carl climbed the stairs with mounting excitement. After all this effort to locate Conn, he was now only a few feet away. He composed himself, and knocked on the door. There was no answer. The woman who had answered the door shouted up the stairs. 'What did I tell you? Knock harder.'

Carl knocked again, and shouted through the door. 'Archie? An old mate from school come to see you.'

The door opened a crack, and in the dim light, Carl could see Archie measuring him through heavy-lidded eyes. Archie spoke quietly. 'Who the hell are you?'

Adrenaline enabled Carl to adopt a jovial mien. 'Carl Cleaver, we were in the same year at Swansea School, remember?'

Archie's eyes narrowed. 'Carl, yeah. You were that skinny

runt, played in the back row. Could never run through a prop forward. Haven't seen you in years.'

Same old Archie, Carl thought. He'd have to tread carefully.

Archie smiled. It was a delightful smile; warm, friendly. 'Come on in.'

Carl entered the small flat. A studio flat, Carl noted. Bed and sofa in one room, a separate kitchen, and probably a small bathroom with a shower.

Archie took some clothes from the sofa and put them on a side table. 'Sit down, Carl. Coffee?'

Carl nodded. 'Yes, please.' Archie walked to the small kitchen. He was bare-chested and barefoot, wearing jeans.

'Sorry, I took so long to answer the door,' Archie said from the kitchen. 'You woke me up, to be honest.'

'No problem. It's been so long since I last saw you, I couldn't resist popping in.' Carl watched Archie through the kitchen door where he filled the kettle and rinsed out mugs. Archie's smile had seemed inviting, but Carl knew that smile. Carl had himself used it on Archie's landlady. It was a constructed smile; genuine enough to the uninitiated, but false nonetheless.

Archie poured hot water into the mugs. 'How did you know where I lived?'

'I bumped into an acquaintance of yours a while ago, and he knew you, much to my surprise. Richard Patterson?'

'Patterson? The UFO nut?'

'That's the one.'

Archie came back into the room, and sat on the edge of the bed. 'Potty Patterson, eh? Still looking for his flying saucers?'

'Oh yes. He still believes they're buzzing the town every night.'

Archie looked absently around him, patting the bed. He was looking for his cigarettes – Carl recognised that behaviour.

'And how do you know Richard Patterson?' Archie said. 'Dereham is a long way from the valleys.'

Carl had expected this question, or one similar. 'I was intrigued by those *things*, too.'

Archie finally found his cigarettes and a lighter. He smiled archly. 'Not another bloody UFO nut? Cigarette?'

Carl took one. 'I've been trying to give up.'

'Don't bother,' Archie said. He lit both cigarettes. 'It's not worth the pain. And we all have to die sometime.'

'No, I'm not a UFO nut. I'm sceptical I suppose, but interested.'

Archie bent forward, found the soup bowl he used as an ashtray under the bed, and placed it on the floor between him and Carl. 'I'm surprised Patterson knew where I was.'

'It's a small world, I suppose. I was in a dentist's waiting room and picked up a copy of *Reveille*. Imagine my surprise when I found a picture of you inside it.'

'Me?' Archie seemed genuinely surprised.

'Yes. There was an article about Dereham in there. There was a picture of Patterson, and you, and some girl, Peta.'

'I don't know anything about that article.'

It was Carl's turn to be surprised. 'Really? But your picture was there.'

Archie shook his head. 'Old Patterson was always knocking out articles.'

Carl quickly understood. 'It was probably a cut and paste job. A word with Patterson on the phone, a photo from stock, lines nicked from other articles.'

'Yes, that was probably it. How do you know so much about that sort of thing?'

'That's what I do now. I'm a journalist.'

'Oh,' Archie said. He looked down at the soup bowl, half-full of last night's crumpled dog-ends, and flicked the ash from his cigarette into it. He looked up again, all innocence. 'And which paper do you work for?'

'A regional,' Carl said carefully. 'In Wales.'

'Swansea area?'

'You could say that. It's part of my beat.'

'So you know about...' Archie turned to look out of the window. 'The terrible tragedy involving my brother and sister?'

Carl believed for a moment that Archie's bottom lip was about to tremble. The voice had been pitched beautifully. The abstracted stare was perfect. Carl remembered all this from school and college. Fragments of the younger Archie came back to him, memories awoken by Archie's actions now. The hurt frown when accused of lying. The winning smile for the girls. The look of cunning when on the make. The new Archie wasn't so different. Still the same handsome man, with the big brown eyes and the square jaw. The stubble he grew now looked rugged rather than scruffy. His hair was longer, sure, but so was everybody's. Broad shoulders, and tight stomach muscles. Carl still felt feeble next to Archie. The pot-belly he was developing was tight against his top trouser button.

Carl sipped at his coffee, and took a long drag on his cigarette. 'Obviously, I heard about what happened to Giles and Lucinda. It was tragic. It was in our paper, of course, and other Welsh papers. I always liked Lu.'

'I thought you had a soft spot for her,' Archie said. He stubbed out his cigarette, stood up, went to the other side of the bed, and pulled on a shirt. 'Can't say I'm unhappy to see them dead. I never liked them.' He paused, stopped

218

buttoning. 'Perhaps Lucinda a little. But Giles was a bastard to me. Well, I was a bastard to him. Literally.' Archie finished buttoning the shirt and returned to sit on the bed.

Carl knew that the last statement had been loaded. There was bitterness in Archie's voice. 'You were a bastard to him?'

'It's in the name, Carl.'

'What name?'

'In the article, the one in ... what did you say? *Reveille*? What did they call me?'

'Archibald Franklin Conn.'

'Do you remember Johnny Franklin?' Archie smiled. 'He was even weedier than you.'

'Yes, I remember Johnny.'

'You used to come over my place for coffee sometimes. Didn't you ever wonder why Johnny's dad was there so often?' Archie lit another cigarette and stared at Carl. He's waiting for me realise something, Carl thought. And then Carl did realise. 'Johnny's dad was your....'

'That's right, Carl. I'm a Franklin. Thank God.'

'But your old man - your dad... uh... Mr Conn. He was all right, wasn't he? You benefitted from the family fortune.'

'The man I called father for fifteen years was fine until he realised that I was another man's son. Why he tolerated my real dad at the house is something I don't understand. Somebody must have had some hold over somebody. Franklin only came around when father was out, anyway – which he was, a lot. But father made our lives - mine, and mum's - misery for the rest of his existence. He drove mum to drink and an early death and he treated me like shit until I joined the Army and moved out. I was glad when he died.'

Carl thought back, quickly. How had Archie's father died? He tried to remember if there had been anything in the paper about it. If Archie's father had died of natural causes –

or had appeared to – then the paper wouldn't have carried a story about it. 'And Giles and Lucinda?'

'Giles carried on my father's good work. He bullied me. He was bigger than me for a long time. When I finally got to be bigger than him, I beat the shit out of him – that was the day before I left to join the army. Lou was sweet Lou – but she never once stood in Giles's way, and I resented her for that.' Archie picked up his coffee, sipped it and looked Carl straight in the eye. 'That family made me the man I am today.' There was something unnerving in that look.

'And what are you today?' Carl said.

Archie waved his arms. 'Look around you. This is what I am. This shitty little flat. Or rather, I *was* this. For some odd reason, Giles and Lou left the old man's money to me. I expect Lou talked Giles into it. Or Giles thought the money should stay attached to the name Conn. I'm tempted to change my name by deed poll to spite Giles.'

Carl wondered how much of this was true. Archie lied so often, Carl couldn't begin to guess if Archie was lying now; in all likelihood, he was. Perhaps Giles *had* done an about face, accepted Archie back into the family, and left the inheritance to him. The family were military all the way back to before the time of Napoleon, when a minor aristocrat had enlisted as an office. That small hereditary wealth and various pensions had been handed down, generation after generation, accruing interest. Carl imagined that the house, the antiques, and the other assets would amount to a small fortune to Archie – certainly worth killing for. Yet how could he tempt Archie into confessing to such a crime? The coroner had already passed judgment on the deaths of Giles and Lucinda; and that judgement had not implicated Archie in any way. Yet, Archie was ex-military. He probably knew some tricks.

Moreover, Archie undoubtedly had among his acquaintances those who could teach him ways to kill without obvious trauma.

Carl lit a cigarette and passed one to Archie. 'I guess the money makes up for some of the shit you put up with.'

'Yes, it does. It was almost worth being born a Conn.'

'I suppose you knew how much the estate was worth?'

'Of course. Not the exact amount. But there was the house, the cars, the antiques. I knew it was worth more than I'd ever see in my working life. When I joined the army, and left home, I missed that easy access to money, the *cachet* associated with being... not rich, but *well-off*.'

'So your inheritance will allow you to be the person you think you should be?'

Archie's eyes narrowed. 'You ask a lot of questions, don't you?'

Carl looked innocent, although his heart began to beat rapidly. 'Sorry, force of habit. Goes with the job, I suppose. Being a reporter does have its drawbacks – we ask questions like a policeman.' Carl gave a short laugh.

Archie relaxed a little. Carl still didn't have what he wanted. He would have to spin Archie along, play him – appeal to his egotism, perhaps. He involved Archie in what he thought was inane chit-chat for the next few minutes, reminiscing about their time together at school. Archie laughed and joked, and Carl wondered how he could direct the conversation back to the deaths of Giles and Lou. Archie opened his cigarette packet, sighed, and tossed it over his shoulder. 'I'm out of cigs,' he said.

Carl reached for his packet, but Archie said, 'I never took to Benson and Hedges.' He looked at his watch. 'Almost midday. There's a pub a few streets away, fancy a jar? I can stop off at the newsagent and pick up a pack of JPS.'

Carl thought that alcohol might loosen Archie's tongue. 'You're on. I'll buy the first round.'

'Don't be ridiculous. I'm in the money. I'll stand you a couple first.'

Carl wondered if he'd managed to gain Archie's trust. Would Archie open up to him now?

The sun was shining but offered little warmth. Carl and Archie crossed the road, and walked down a short street, beyond which Carl could see the park Archie had mentioned on their way down the stairs. The park was heavily wooded on this side, Archie had said, and they needed to follow a well-trodden path through the trees to get to the shop and pub. They walked through a deep thicket of trees. There was nobody else in sight. The park was obviously one of the town's less popular green spaces, Carl thought.

'We'll have to go in single file,' Archie said. 'After you. Just follow the path.'

Carl began to feel uneasy. But his instincts had warned him too late. All he heard was a faint whooshing sound, and then his head felt as if it had exploded. He staggered, and put his hand to the back of his head. He tried to turn, but the thick broken branch Archie now held slammed into his cheek. Carl fell into the bracken and grass. Archie stood over him. Carl could feel blood running down his cheek and onto his neck. Archie gave a grunt, and then lashed out with the branch again. 'You ask too many questions, Carl,' he said. Archie hit him again. 'You're a tougher son of a bitch than I remember.' Another blow to the head followed. Carl began to lose consciousness, but not before he registered, rather than felt, a kick in the groin. Carl didn't even groan at this final kick. His breathing was laboured and ragged. At the periphery of his consciousness, he thought he heard the bright laughter of children, and the barking of a dog. Carl felt, rather than saw, Archie turn him over, and removed his wallet. Then he finally lost consciousness.

The first sense that returned to Carl was that of smell. He registered the distinct aroma of disinfectant. Pain arrived next, at the back of his head, and he gave a loud groan. Hearing was the next sense to arrive. 'Carl! Thank God!' He recognised Jenny's voice. He tried to open his eyes, but all he could see was diffuse light. 'Don't panic, love. Your head is wrapped in bandages. Oh, I thought you'd never wake up.'

Carl's voice was thin and croaky. 'How long have I been here?'

A male voice close by, slightly above him, spoke. 'You've been unconscious for nearly a week, Mr Cleaver,' the voice said. 'Normally, the wounds visited upon you would have been fatal. Not only do you have the constitution of an ox, but a thick skull.'

Carl felt his wife's hand on his. 'He will be all right, won't he, doctor?' He felt hands at the back of his head, and flinched, almost in panic.

'Steady now, Mr Cleaver,' the doctor said. 'I'm going to remove some of the bandages, so at least you'll be able to see.'

The gauze covering Carl's eyes peeled away, one layer at a time, and the world became slowly brighter.

The doctor spoke again. 'You have a displaced retina in your right eye. You'll have trouble seeing with that eye. Things will be blurry for a while.

Carl blinked, and looked across to his wife. She was softly crying.

The doctor addressed them both. 'As far as we can tell, there's no brain damage. We'll keep you in for a few days, to make sure you don't have concussion. With rest and care, you should be back on your feet in a few weeks.'

Carl looked around him. 'Where am I?'

The doctor smiled reassuringly. 'The Royal Berkshire Hospital, in Reading. You were very lucky, you know. You were found, by all accounts, only minutes after the attack. If you hadn't been, then...' The doctor's words trailed off, and he shrugged. 'The police tell me it was a vicious mugging. Sadly, we get far too many victims of that crime in here these days. Do you remember anything?' Carl merely grunted. The doctor continued. 'If you're feeling up to it, the police have some questions for you, I'm afraid.'

'Surely not now,' his wife pleaded.

'I'm sorry, but given the severity of the attack the police are itching to speak to your husband.'

The doctor said he would be back around later in the day.

Police officers arrived within the hour. They were understanding, and kept the questions to a minimum. All they needed was a description or a name, and Carl had one for them. Archibald Franklin Conn.

A few days later, Carl was able to move around the ward. He was surprised to find his editor, Tom Hughes, sitting patiently at his bedside when he returned from a visit to the toilet.

'Jesus, Carl, you look like death warmed up, man!'

Carl gently sat on his bed, and looked at his boss. 'Thanks. What the hell are you doing here?'

Hughes leaned forward, and whispered. 'Whatever you've been up to, it's got big, very big. We've been officially warned off the Conn investigation.

'Really? By whom?'

'By the Security Service. They visited us late last night. They took away all your notes. They quoted national security, and basically, old lad, I'm shitting myself.'

Carl looked at the floor, then at Hughes. 'What about the police. Can't they pull Conn?'

Hughes shook his head. 'I used some of my contacts, tried to find out what had happened. It seems that the officer in charge of the investigation reported back to his superior. The first line of investigation was obviously to visit the house where Conn was staying. They sent a panda car, and found that Conn had left.'

'Yes, Archie said he was moving out.'

'The police asked Conn's landlady for a forwarding address, but he never left one.'

'He wouldn't be so dumb.'

'Then an observant officer connected the name to an old bulletin from MI5. So, the police contacted them. The plod were told to drop the case and forward all the paperwork. As far as the police are concerned, the case is on hold until such time as MI5 find Conn and ask plod to pull him in.'

Carl touched the scar on the side of his face, as he'd been doing habitually now for the last week. 'So, it's over. What the hell is Archie involved in?'

'I don't know, but whatever it is, it's too damn sensitive for us to keep digging.' Hughes reached into his jacket pocket, and produced an envelope. 'And far too dangerous. There's this. It arrived for you a couple of days ago, and because of what happened, I opened it. I'm not sorry, pal, because if I hadn't, the spies would have it now. You'd better read it.'

Carl opened the envelope, extracted a single sheet of writing paper, and read it.

> Cleaver – That was just a sample of what I can do. Stop hounding me, or next time, it'll be your family. Conn

Carl screwed up the paper and threw it across the ward, earning for his trouble a look of reproach from a nurse.

'No story is worth all this, Carl,' Hughes said. 'You have to think of Jenny and the kids. Tell me it's the end of the line.'

Carl sighed, and twisted a blanket in his hand. He didn't want to be beaten this way, by a thug, before justice could be done. And it was obvious now that Archie was more than capable of murdering his brother and sister, and had probably done so. Why else would Archie attack Carl, unless he was getting too close?

'Carl, please tell me, you'll stop,' Hughes said,

Carl looked up at Hughes. 'Yes. End of the line.'

22

Len Stone walked listlessly around the well-manicured grounds of the Secret Service clinic, smoking. He didn't smoke often, and when he did, it was mainly weed. But there was no weed here; the pack of twenty Embassy was all he had. There were a couple of gardeners working on a topiary yew hedge in the distance, and he idly wondered if they too were members of the Service. He was aware that two minders followed him at a discreet distance, there, no doubt, in case he decided to do a runner. Where could he go, anyway? He was stuck in the middle of rural Berkshire, and the nearest village was miles away.

He worried about Emily. He'd been refused access to her time and time again. The goons minding him almost certainly had instructions to lock him up if he made even the slightest move towards the secure medical wing.

He stubbed out his cigarette on the gravel path with his shoe. Turning sharply, he headed back the way he had come. He called out to his minders. 'Get Edge on your walkie-talkie, tell him I want to see him now!' He obviously sounded angry, or aggressive, although he was hardly aware of his own state of mind, because one of the minders held up a hand, attempting to placate him. The tension was getting to him, Len thought – the waiting, the frustration.

'Mr Edge went back to London, Mr Stone, the minder said. 'Harry Roberts is still here. Do you want to talk to him?'

'Harry bloody Roberts.' Len could hear the aggression in his voice this time. 'He'll have to do, won't he?' Len stormed past the two minders, who then hurried to follow him.

When they entered the building, one of the goons led Len to a small office on the second floor. Harry was sitting behind a large, antique writing desk. He seemed uncomfortable there, out of place, which took some of the edge off Len's anger.

Harry looked up at Len, smiled without conviction, and then shifted uncomfortably in his chair. 'Hello, Len. What can I do for you? You wanted to see Edge?'

'You bastards have stitched me right up, and... and I can accept that. But what you are doing with Emily is *totally* unacceptable.' Len's voice rose. 'She's an innocent party in all this for God's sake!'

Harry sat back and looked Len in the eyes. He looked less uncomfortable behind the desk now, more in command of the situation. 'As our friends in the police might say, Emily is helping us with our enquiries. For that, unfortunately, we need to keep her away from London, away from your home.'

Harry's answer wasn't good enough for Len. It was empty of content, meaningless. Emily had never done anything wrong. He put his fists on the desk, and leaned over, glowering at Harry. 'Just what the hell are you sneaky sons of bitches up to here? Just why is Emily so bloody important to you?'

Harry picked a pen up from the desk and rolled it between his fingers. He looked down, then looked back up at Len and sighed. 'Ah, Len. You should know better than to ask a question like that. I can tell you that Emily is in protective custody. She needed protecting from... well, I can't tell you that. Emily was in danger, Len – and so were you. You didn't know it, and neither did she. Of course, there are things we'd like Emily to tell us while she's here.'

Len sat down in the chair opposite Harry. He shook his head, completely confused now. 'Come on, Harry. Stop drip-feeding me information. Either put up, or shut up. Be warned, though... If all this is for nothing, I'll go to the press and tell them what happened. I'll make sure MI5 ends up on the front pages of the nationals. I'll keep slinging shit in this direction until some of it finally sticks.'

Harry shook his head, and nibbled on the end of the pen he had been playing with. Then he said one word. 'Molova.'

Len almost started in surprise.

Harry smiled. 'I thought that might get your attention, Len. We know all about Emily Freeman and her father, and what happened to him. We know all about you and your little, how shall I put it, *experiments* – the alien contacts at the club, the drugs, Peta, Archie, and Dereham.'

Len's mind raced. It had all happened, of course it had – the long nights at *The Purple Parrot*, smoking dope, hypnotising Peta, all in the hope of getting another brief contact with the aliens. Molova – that had been the name of Peta's contact. Of what interest were these alien contacts to the secret services? Len was no longer entirely sure that he and Peta *had* contacted aliens. The contacts might have been simple, psychological reactions to certain experiences and stimuli. Len knew what he was: a hippie nightclub owner with a mystical bent. He believed in karma, yoga, Qi, and all that jazz. Nevertheless, the alien contacts had begun to tax even his credulity. To find MI5 also had an interest in contactees was a surprise. 'Jesus, Harry. Are you guys into witches' covens and Ouija boards too?'

'If they affected the security of the realm, yes. Probably.'

'How do you know this stuff? About me and Peta, I mean? Molova?'

Harry stroked his chin, and then sat forward, his forearms on the desk. 'I can't tell you everything, Len. Of course I can't. But you do deserve to know something. I did know Peta, and, for my sins, fell in love with her. I was watching her–'

'Why?' Len said. 'She wasn't dangerous.'

'I can't tell you that. But, getting emotionally involved with someone in an operation is an unacceptable risk, and Edge pulled me...' His voice trailed off. Clearing his throat, Harry continued. 'If Edge hadn't called me back to London, the chances are that Peta wouldn't have... killed herself. This is something that I live with, day in, day out.' Harry sighed, picked up the pen and fiddled with it, looking out of the window. 'Believe me when I tell you there will be retribution for Peta.'

'What? How? And who's to blame for all this?' Len growled.

Harry gave another sad little smile. 'Well, that's a moot point. I blame Archie for what happened to Peta. He used her for his own ends, and then just threw her away. Now, Edge... Well, he blames an outside party for what has happened to Emily. Mick has his agenda and I have mine. They coincide. Trust me. Everything will work out.'

The telephone on the desk rang. Harry picked up the receiver. 'Hello. Harry Roberts here.' He listened for a few seconds. 'I see, thank you. We'll be right down.' He replaced the handset, and stood up. 'Come on, Len, Emily's awake. She's asking for you.'

The room was dimly lit. In one corner was a hospital bed with Emily propped up in it, her face pale and waxy. Len rushed over to her, and took her hands in his. 'Emily, it's so good to see you.'

She looked at him through half-closed eyes. When she spoke, her voice was low. She sounded tired, very tired... 'Hiya, honey. Guess you ain't seeing me at my best, huh?'

Len's eyes were misting over. He squeezed her hands. 'It's okay. I'm here now.'

She gave him a wan smile. 'Nice to see you, babes.' She turned her head to one side, and fell asleep again.

Len looked Harry, anger boiling in him. 'What the hell have you done to her, you bastards?'

The door to the room opened, and Doctor Heathcock entered. 'Keep your voice down, Mr Stone. Emily needs rest.' She put her palm on Emily's forehead, and then felt her pulse. She turned back to Len. 'The psychotropic drugs we were forced to administer to Miss Freeman have, as I warned, had an adverse effect on her. But we simply had to do this to break through the conditioning.'

'Conditioning? What conditioning?'

Harry spoke. 'She knows things, Len. Important things. She was conditioned by somebody to ensure the secrets she has stay locked away.'

'What the fuck are you two blabbering about?' Len said angrily.

'We should leave Emily to sleep,' Heathcock said.

Harry put his hand on Len's shoulder. 'Come on, big man. She's fine. And we have the best doctors here.' He guided Len towards the door.

Len and Harry drank coffee in the office. Evening had overtaken the room, and Harry had switched on a desk-lamp.

There was sadness and quiet desperation in Len's voice. 'I don't understand, Harry. What has Emily ever done?'

Harry spoke quietly. 'I shouldn't tell you this, Len. But I like you. You're a good man, and I think you deserve an explanation. You know that Emily was in the United States Air Force, yes?' Len nodded. 'And what was her job, Len?'

'Mainly P.R. Making sure the American public was kept happy with the Air Force, that sort of thing. Of course, it was part time. She also worked with her father–'

Harry placed his hand on Len's arm. 'That was her public face. I'm afraid she never told you the whole truth. We're not *actually* sure what the whole truth is. We do know she was working in Air Force intelligence. Except... it appears not to have been your everyday intelligence section. This was something... very secret. The Yanks have an expression for it – *black operations*. She was working for this bloke named Skinner. We think he heads up a multi-million dollar project. Although she acted as her father's literary agent, we think she babysat him. You know, to make sure he didn't say anything he shouldn't. We think her father knew things... secrets. Because of that, Emily also had to know those things, so that she could keep watch over what he was saying.'

'What were these things they knew?'

'We've no idea, Len. That's the problem. Crazy as it sounds, we think it had *something* to do with UFOs. But what that something was, we have no idea.'

'You were watching Peta, weren't you? Surely that gives you some idea.'

'No, unfortunately, it doesn't. We watched Peta just in case...' Harry's was uncertain for a moment. 'Well, just in case what people like she and you were saying turned out to be true. That they might reveal... *something*... of importance. Also, we were worried that agents or subversives from other countries might infiltrate sky-watching groups. Dereham is on the edge of Salisbury Plain, as you know, and even I don't know what the military is testing out there.'

Len nodded. 'So what do you want to know from Emily?'

'The problem appears on the surface to be one merely of protocol. No friendly power should undertake electronic surveillance on sovereign territory without our consent, that kind of thing. We discovered that somebody was bugging your house. We later established that the buggers, so to say, were the Yanks; none other than Colonel Skinner, Emily's ex-employer.'

'Why would they want to bug the house?'

'Edge met Skinner. Edge thinks he's mad. We think – and this is mere speculation – that Emily is going to tell you things that Skinner wouldn't want you to know.'

Len shrugged. 'She's never said anything, nothing that would be... incriminating. We've talked about her dad, of course, and his contacts, but there's nothing she's said that's not in the book.'

'Ah. The book. *Panlyrae - A Message for Mankind.*'

Len smiled. 'That's the one. I suppose you saw it at Peta's house?'

'Yes, I did.'

'That was my old copy. I bought a new one and got Ed Freeman to sign it.' Len stood up and paced the room. 'But I still don't see what this has got to do with Emily.'

'Neither do we. Edge was worried about two things, however. Firstly, the unauthorised activity on British soil. Secondly, that Skinner was, as I said, mad.'

'In what way?'

'A patriot. Overly zealous. Crazily religious.'

'So?'

'He feared for your safety, you and Emily. The only way to counter Skinner was to find out why he had an interest in Emily, take that information through channels, and then get Skinner kicked out of the country. That would also alert Skinner's paymasters to his unorthodox activities. However, we're dealing with people who have no scruples and will stop at nothing to protect their interests. We think that, before she left the States, Emily was conditioned... Brain-washed, if you will.'

Len sat down again, and ran his fingers through his hair. 'So all of this, everything you're doing here, is to protect us?'

'Yes. And I'd be grateful if you mentioned none of this to Edge. He'd kick me in my Sassenach goolies if he knew I'd told you this much.'

'But Emily? The aftermath? What happens now?'

'We've only seen the tip of the iceberg. We're certain there's more buried in Emily's mind than we've found so far, but-'

Len jumped out of his chair. Harry stood as well. 'You want to pump her full of drugs again, don't you?' Len said. 'But what will it do to her? How can you be sure she'll be safe?'

'I can only tell you what Heathcock has told me. What the Americans have done can never be reversed.'

'But she seems all right to me.'

'She wasn't all right, although you might never have known it. There are, even now, parts of her life she can't remember. In time, that might have come out. According to Heathcock, depending on the amount of memory already *erased*, Emily would have become depressed, paranoid – schizophrenic even. It would have taken time, but it would have happened.'

Len shook his head, angrily. 'How can you know that? How? How do you know that what you're doing isn't the cause of that?'

'Because I trust Doctor Heathcock. She's one of the best there is, and certainly the best in this country. She's seen all kinds of attempted brain manipulations in veterans of Korea and Vietnam, and in agents we've uncovered. She knows what will happen to them in the long run.'

'And yet you're making it worse.'

'We hope not. We're trying to recover memories, trying to restore her. That is the only way we can find out what the Yanks are trying to hide. But yes, after her experience here, she will need to recuperate. Her mind will need to make sense of what has happened. She will need your love and support, Len. However, the bigger issue is – can you restore her faith in you? You handed her over to us. We will, I promise you this, look after her, and she will get the best possible care for the rest of her life. And, of course, we will ensure that you, too, will be looked after.'

'Back at the club, you said Emily wouldn't remember what had happened when I brought her in for you. You said she'd have no memory of it.'

'That was before Heathcock began her deeper procedures. Remember, now we think we know what the Yanks have done, we're trying to piece Emily's memory back together. There's a chance she'll now remember what you did.'

Len walked back to his chair and slumped in it. 'Shit, Harry. I betrayed her. How will she ever trust me again?'

'I don't know, Len,' Harry said. 'But remember this - we are doing this to protect you from Skinner. We can't be sure, but Emily might have died if it wasn't for you.' A sadness crossed Harry's face, Len noticed. 'Such are the moral dilemmas we so often have to face in this business.' Len wondered if Harry was thinking of Peta.

Sleep didn't come easily to Len that night. He lay in the cot a nurse had placed next to Emily's bed, thinking about what Harry had said, trying to assimilate everything.

Heathcock had given Emily another sedative. Len could hear her breathing, which was shallow but steady. Every now and then, just as Len was drifting into sleep, she would give a small moan, instantly jarring him awake. What most worried Len was that whatever Heathcock was doing she would do once again, later today.

The room had visibly lightened in the last hour. Len looked at the clock on the wall. It was eight o'clock. Within a few hours, he hoped, Emily would be through the worst. He stretched, and stood up.

He sat on the metal folding chair next to Emily's bed, held her hand, and watched her. Heathcock returned about ten o'clock to administer a sedative. 'She needs sleep, Len,' Heathcock said. Just after midday, he fell asleep, despite the uncomfortable chair. He heard Peta's voice. *What goes around, comes around. It's karma, Len. You hurt people for the Manley Boys. Now you're being hurt in return.* He awoke with a start, his heart racing. Emily was still asleep. Len shook his head, as if to shake Peta's presence away. Had she contacted him? He believed in what she said – in karma, in yin and yang, the whole Eastern mysticism thing. Perhaps Peta was right.

He was hungry, and even though he didn't want to leave Emily, he thought he should eat. Because even if he watched over Emily all day, that would not be enough, he suspected, to balance the scales, refill the karmic well, remove him from the wheel of rebirth.

The smell of the food frying in the small canteen made him feel hungry, yet when he looked at the bacon frying on the hotplates behind the counter, he also felt nauseous. Still, he asked for a bacon sandwich, which he took to an empty table. He tried to eat the sandwich, attempting to alleviate the hunger while ignoring the faint nausea. A few bites satisfied the pangs. He remained alone, deep in thought, drinking coffee after coffee. He sat there for an hour, only leaving the table to refresh his cup, and gazing out of the large window over a wide expanse of lawn. The road into and out of the clinic curved beyond the lawn, hidden by trees and shrubs.

A voice said, 'Penny for them?'

Len looked up. Heathcock was standing next to his table, in the white coat she seemed to have permanently worn since she had arrived at the Sanatorium.

'Sorry, I was miles away,' Len said. 'Didn't even see you come in.'

Heathcock took his reply as permission to sit with him.

She pulled out a chair; its metal legs scraped dully across the linoleum.

Heathcock smiled at him. It was her professional, bedside smile. 'So, how are you bearing up?'

'Not too bad.'

Heathcock study him intently. 'Dark rings around the eyes. Stubble. Heavy lids. I'd say, not too *well*, actually. Have you been getting any sleep?'

'What the hell do you think? You've got Emily locked up, doing God knows what to her, and I'm supposed to be *bearing up?*'

Heathcock spoke quietly. 'Look, for what it's worth, I'm not happy with what's going on. I'm just following orders here.'

'So the Nazis said at Nuremburg. *I was only following orders.*'

'I'm going to prescribe sleeping pills for you. Make sure you take them. You're no good to Miss Freeman in this state. She'll need you at her side, once this is over...' her voice trailed off.

Len instinctively knew something was wrong. 'What's happened to her?' he growled.

Heathcock was choosing her words carefully. 'While you've been sitting in here, I administered the drug again. Edge was insistent that we proceed as quickly as possible. We managed to get more information from Emily, before...'

Len stood up, his fists clenched, while the world fell from under him. 'She's dead, isn't she?' He felt his legs weaken him; he collapsed back onto his chair. He buried his head in his hands.

'No, she's not dead, Len. But she is in a coma.' Heathcock stood up and turned to face the window. She crossed her arms. Weak autumn sun lit her worried face. 'She's suffered some kind of mental breakdown. The drug has been too bloody successful. Before she became unconscious, she was babbling like a child, Len. Childhood memories had reformed and become established.' She sighed. 'But not what we needed to know. Whatever steps the Americans took to keep their secrets locked away has been very effective.'

'Can she recover?'

'Only time will tell. I know what I need to do to keep her alive. I believe her brain has shut down in response to what we were doing. A defence mechanism. I think – I hope – that Emily will return to us once she is *certain* that what she is unconsciously defending herself from has ended.'

'Has it? Has it ended?'

Heathcock turned back to Len, her arms still folded across her breasts, a wall against his anger. 'Yes, of course it has. There's nothing I can do to elicit memories if she's unconscious.'

Anger boiled up in Len, and then exploded out of him. He flung back his chair and ran out of the room. He wasn't sure if he was running towards Emily to comfort her, or towards Edge to kill him. Heathcock had obviously also been unsure, as three security officers quickly caught up with Len. He tried to battle his way towards the medical wing, but was finally subdued. A beefy security officer sat on Len's back, pinning his arms behind him.

He heard Heathcock's voice again. 'Sorry, Len.' There was a sharp, stabbing pain at the base of his neck, and he slowly lost the will to fight. 'That should keep you calm for a few hours.' Len felt himself being lifted. Two of the security officers remained on the ground where Len had put them, one unconscious, the other sitting, feeling his nose.

Heathcock came around to stand in front of him. 'We're going to put you in a secure cell for now, Len. You can see Emily when you've calmed down.'

Edge seemed to arrive from nowhere. He looked at Len. 'Are you all right, Len?'

Len could only nod. His anger still burned but it was distant, and something soft surrounded him, something like cotton wool. Everything was fuzzy, indistinct, and somehow remote.

Edge turned to Heathcock. 'Your office, Doctor, right now. And get Harry.' Edge looked over Len's shoulder, to the officer holding him up. 'Take him down to a holding cell.'

Len felt the pressure in his back and at the collar of his shirt as the man behind him pushed him forward. He thought about Emily. He wanted to hold her. But what would he be holding? Would Emily even know he was holding her? He felt as if he should be crying, but knew Heathcock's drug was keeping even that release at bay.

Harry and Doctor Heathcock sat on the opposite side of the desk to Edge. The light of the late November day was slowly fading. The lamp on the desk filled the room with a weak yellow light. The atmosphere in the office was tense.

Edge steepled his fingers under his chin. 'Well, people, we're in a fine pickle, aren't we? We have a man on the brink of a breakdown, the girl nothing more than a vegetable, and a folder full of information that makes little sense.' Edge opened the thick manila file that contained the notes taken during Emily's interrogation, looked at the first page blankly, and then closed it again.

The last few days had taken their toll on Edge, Harry thought. His eyes were heavy; he was tired, world-weary.

Harry cleared his throat. 'Rachel, what are Emily's chances?'

Edge's look was impatient. 'Laddie, we have to sort through all this information, and you're concerned about the girl?'

Edge studied Harry. His voice became soothing. 'Relax, Harry. Rachel will do everything she can for Emily.'

Heathcock put a hand on Harry's forearm. 'I will, Harry,' Heathcock said. 'She's only in a coma.' She glared at Edge. 'She's not a vegetable, as Mick so unfeelingly put it. I think she'll come out of it. The only question is when.'

'It's not just Freeman, Mick,' Harry said. 'It's Len. Everything Len touches seems to end in tragedy. Peta and Archie, now Emily. Everything!' Poor Len, Harry thought.

23

Skinner had spent most of the night on the telephone. The US embassy had provided a desk and access to secure lines to the States.

Emily Freeman and Len Stone had disappeared. Where had they gone? Edge was involved, Skinner was sure of that. The Brits were certainly backward in many things, Skinner thought, but, by God, they could teach Uncle Sam a thing or two about being sneaky. But he too was a wily beast. He always had a back-up plan. He had spent the night setting wheels in motion. The calls had been difficult, but his contacts knew better than to cross him. Now he dozed in the chair behind his temporary desk, waiting for a call from his contact in New York. Once the word had been given, he could forge ahead, and the Limeys would be taught a lesson they'd not forget.

Two hours later the phone rang, waking Skinner from a dream in which God blessed him for his patriotism and devotion to his country. Despite his lack of sleep, Skinner was onto the dinning instrument like a pouncing cat. 'Yeah, what's the outcome?' He listened intently for a few moments and then placed the handset back on its cradle. He smiled contentedly.

The breakfasts in the embassy weren't to Skinner's taste. The cooks seemed to be enamoured of the English way of cooking, which seemed to him all grease and fat. Skinner took a few slices of toast and a pot of strong coffee to his regular table, away from the bureaucrats that staffed the building.

He opened the broadsheet paper he had delivered to him every day since he'd arrived. He never ceased to be amazed just how damn stupid and naive the press was. Place a well-crafted story, and watch the dumb-asses bite. He'd seen it happen time and time again – Vietnam, Apollo, and soon, that sweaty moron, Nixon. He allowed himself to revel for a moment in his position as a major player on the world stage. Few other people were aware of his power – *very* few. That was how he wanted it to be – how it *needed* to be. Leaders would come, and leaders would go but Project Flashlight would go on forever. Skinner was untouchable – he knew too much, after all – and controlled everything and everybody. I am almost a *God*, he thought. He caught himself. No, not a capital G god. A minor deity – no, not even that. There was, after all, only the Father, Son and Holy Ghost. Minor deities were far too pantheistic. An angel, then, doing the work of God.

A waiter approached Skinner's table. He let the jumped up little asshole wait a few moments. The menial Americans here were deferential, polite. They were turning native. Skinner continued to read his paper until the flunky cleared his throat. 'An urgent call for you, Colonel Skinner, on line one. If you'd come this way?' Skinner carefully folded the paper and placed it on the table. 'Who is it?' He asked gruffly.

'How would I know, sir? I'm merely a waiter. I was only told to pass the message on to you.'

The waiter's accent placed him in Omaha, his deference in Orpington. Skinner sighed. 'Where's the nearest secure phone?

'All the telephones within the building are completely secure, sir.'

Reception was quiet. The young woman at the desk chewed gum and read a magazine. A security guard stood a few paces away, watching the door. Skinner glanced at the magazine cover: a grainy photograph of Prince Charles and some woman the press had decided was the bride-to-be – for the moment at least.

'Line one?' Skinner said, curtly.

The receptionist looked up, chewed her gum absently, then pointed at a telephone and pressed a button on her desk before returning to her magazine.

Skinner picked up the phone. 'Skinner here. Who the hell is this?' There was a slight pause at the other end.

'Ah, Lieutenant. It's Mr Edge here. I take it you remember me?'

The demotion riled Skinner. 'Yeah, I remember you, Mr MI5. What the hell do you want? I thought I made it clear that you were to leave me and my operation alone.'

There was a soft chuckle from the other end of the line. 'Now, now, laddie. No need to take umbrage. I thought I'd made it clear that unauthorised operations on my patch were strictly *verboten*.' Good grief, Skinner thought, he even talked German. 'I may be in a position,' Edge continued, 'to help you out of a rather sticky situation. If, of course, you help me. Tit for tat, and all that.'

There was something in Edge's voice that alarmed Skinner. Edge was playful, and self-assured. Something was amiss.

'Okay, Edge. I'm listening. What's so goddamn important to you?'

'It's not what's important to *me*, Colonel Skinner. It's what I know is important to *you*. Have you heard of, uh, *Project Flashlight*, by any chance?'

The plastic of the handset dug into Skinner's palm as he involuntarily tensed. 'I don't know what you're talking about.'

'Oh, I think you do, Colonel Skinner. You explained black operations to me in our first conversation. The only thing I didn't know, of course, was the nature of your operation, and whether you were a threat to the inhabitants of our fair isle. I have since learned of course, that you *are* a threat. I have also learned the nature of your operation. Project Flashlight. An ultra-secret operation, which, I understand, has been funded by the unknowing American tax-payer, for what... Nearly twenty years?'

'Go on,' Skinner snapped.

'Your people did a marvellous job of brain-washing Emily Freeman, you know. But not quite good enough. With enough drugs pumped into her, she told us everything she knew. It's taken us a while to piece it all together, but we got there in the end."

'You know nothing. Freeman was nothing more than a Press Officer for the Air Force. A pen pusher–'

Edge broke in. 'With unrestricted access to information secret information. Such access hardly seems to tally with her job description. Interesting, eh? As for what you did to her father, well... Given that you supposedly live in the land of the free, I think even you'd be hard-pressed to defend yourself against prosecution. Brain-washing, indeed. So, before I send all this rather juicy information over to the Secret Intelligence Service, and to the British and US embassies and... oh... whatever other embassies take my fancy, and, hey, perhaps the newspapers as well, would you be prepared to do a little bartering?'

Skinner thought fast. He hadn't foreseen this. None of it would be happening if he'd only taken the easy option and quietly disposed of Emily Freeman. But she'd been loyal to the project, and that bastard Straker had talked him into trying a new procedure on her he claimed would work. The procedure hadn't been as effective as Straker had thought it would be.

There was a now a gaping hole in security, and that had to be dealt with. He sighed, knowing, for the moment at least, he had to go along with Edge. 'Okay, what do you want?'

'Good lad. What I want is this. The people who conditioned Miss Freeman are to come over here and undo the mess you created.'

Skinner thought for a moment. 'I'll see what I can do. I suggest we meet face to face to thrash things out.'

'Fair enough. Ever been to Trafalgar Square, Mr Skinner? The tourists seem to like it. There'll be little chance of you pulling one of your nasty little tricks. Say, at three this afternoon? And do come alone. We can't have mercenaries tramping all over the place. One on one, Mr Skinner, or the deal is off.'

With that, the phone went dead. Skinner replaced the handset and found the receptionist looking at him. 'Trouble, sir?'

Skinner smiled at her, although he didn't feel like smiling. 'Nothing to trouble your pretty little head about.' The receptionist smiled sourly back.

Three o'clock, huh? Skinner thought. Plenty of time to do a little business.

Two hours later, after another series of calls to the States, Skinner stood outside a dreary London pub and waited until the team he'd sent in were ready. This was likely to be a prickly negotiation, even though his contacts relied on money from the State. He opened the door and entered. The pub was half-full, and the stench of stale cigarettes and beer assailed him. He looked around; his men were quietly drinking in a corner. He ordered a small bourbon and then sat down at a vacant table to wait for his contact. Skinner was just finishing his drink when the door opened. A large man entered the bar and, like Skinner had done, looked around him. He nodded at Skinner, who returned the the gesture. The man's voice was gruff. 'Colonel Skinner?' The accent was Irish.

'Larry Behan, I assume?'

'I might well be, today, at least...'

Behan walked to the bar. Skinner watched as Behan ordered a drink, judging what kind of man he was.

The Irishman sat down opposite Skinner, a pint of stout clasped firmly in his large hand. Skinner noticed that the pub had been silently emptying since Behan's arrival; only a few customers remained. 'What have your officers told you, exactly?' Skinner said.

Behan sipped at his drink, and then lit a cigarette. He eyed Skinner. 'There's something so important to both of us that we should meet up.'

Skinner studied the face across the table. It was a round face, yet hard. He had taken an instant dislike to Behan, and was glad he'd brought back-up with him. 'Your continuing skirmishes with the British Army are funded, in the main part, by sympathisers in the States, yes?'

Behan's eyes narrowed. 'Skirmishes? Our struggle for freedom, you mean, our fight for unification.'

'Call it what you like, Behan'

'Be careful what you say, Colonel Skinner.'

'And be careful how you respond, Mr Behan.'

Behan drank some of his stout, studying Skinner over the rim of the glass. 'Without certain funding, we'd be in the shite, to be sure. What of it?'

'I want some help from you – some ordnance and some information. In exchange, I'll ensure your funds never dry up. A mutually beneficial exchange you could say.'

'Sounds more like blackmail to me, Skinner. Now why would you want to go threatening me like that?'

'Do you really think I' d come here alone?'

He took out his silver cigar case, the prearranged signal for his team to make themselves known. To his puzzlement, nothing happened.

Behan gave a huge guffaw. 'Who do you think you're dealing with here? A bunch of bloody amateurs?'

Skinner glanced across the room. The team he'd sent into the pub before him were surrounded by at least six burly men. Skinner now recognised them as drinkers who had already been in the bar when he'd arrived.

'My boss warned me you were a sneaky bastard, Skinner, so I took precautions. Your boys might as well have *security services* stamped on their foreheads.'

Skinner looked around him. The only people left in the bar were the members of Behan's Skinner's teams. 'They don't need anything stamped on their heads when you can frighten the rest of the clientele away.'

'This is one of our pubs, Skinner. The good folk here know when to give me privacy.'

'Or when to get the hell out before trouble starts.'

'Aye, that too.' Behan looked at Skinner's glass. 'You're empty.' He looked over at the bar. 'Mick, get him another.'

'So, we've reached an impasse,' Skinner said.

'No, not exactly. I have explicit instructions to help you if I can. I just don't like being threatened. So, Mystery Man from the other side of the big pond, what exactly do you want from the IRA?'

'Now we're talking,' Skinner said. He held out his hand. The big Irishman grudgingly shook it.

The barman brought over Skinner's drink. Skinner took a swig, and then looked at Behan. 'What I need is twofold,' he said. He took a brown envelope from inside his jacket pocket. 'We know you have a man inside MI5. I want information on the guys in these photos. Any dirt you can come up with. Any information on their recent work.'

Behan took the photos from the envelope. 'And who are these people?'

'Michael Edge, a senior MI5 officer, and people from his team, we think.'

Behan's thin lips set in a tight, grim line. 'That may be difficult. Our man hasn't been inside for long. He's supposed to be getting information for *us*, not you. His cover might be blown if he starts to dig around somewhere else.' Behan pocketed the envelope. 'And the second request?'

Skinner took a small sip of his drink. 'I want enough explosive to get rid of a rather irritating vermin problem I have.'

Behan tutted. 'You're asking rather a lot, aren't you? Any ordnance we have is supposed to be used in the struggle.'

Skinner stared at Behan. 'Unless you co-operate with me as your masters instructed, I'll become the bane of your existence. I need only make a few phone calls and your struggle against the Brits will become almost impossible. Without money your rag-tag army will be fighting with pitchforks and bare hands.'

Skinner clenched his fist and raised it. His previous signal had indicated only that his men should come to readiness. This signal indicated that they should take action. There was the sound of a brief scuffle. Skinner's men had acted. Behan glanced across at the unexpected sounds. His shoulders slumped. Skinner's team had easily incapacitated Behan's minders. Heckler and Koch MP5s kept them under control. One was pointed at Behan.

Skinner rose from the table. 'I think, Mr Behan, I've made my point. If you cross me, the consequences for you, your men, your families and, of course, the IRA, will be catastrophic. Get me explosives. Find out about Edge.'

Skinner exited the pub and crossed the road to his waiting car. He opened the door and climbed into the rear seat. Fucking papists, he thought. His driver, Oldrey, turned around. 'Where are we going now, boss?

Skinner again glanced at his watch. There was time to make the appointment. 'Trafalgar Square.'

Twenty minutes later, after they had struggled through the heavy London traffic, the car stopped. Skinner climbed out, walked to the centre of Trafalgar Square, and waited. Edge was on time.

'Let's admire the fountain, shall we?' Edge said.

'So, no chance of us being recorded as we natter away?'

Edge laughed. '*Natter*? Why, Mr Skinner, I do believe you're becoming a native of our small island. You're picking up some of our quaint expressions.'

Skinner stopped walking. Cut the crap, Edge. If I wanted to, I could have you taken out here and now.'

Edge shook his head, smiling. 'When will you learn, sunshine? The Met have arrested the men you had deployed, who are already helping with enquiries. And–' Edge gestured around him. 'A number of the buildings you can see have police marksmen in them. One wrong move from you, and you will be ferried home, wounded, incapacitated, a failure.' Edge sat on the low of the fountain. 'Here's what I want. The man behind your mind control programme, Straker, is to fly out here and repair the damage done to poor Miss Freeman. I also want you off my turf, and all listening operations to cease. I also want to make it clear that any future listening operations must first be cleared with me. A small price to pay for the unbridled and unexamined maintenance of your precious *Project Flashlight*, don't you think?'

Skinner gave a snort of derision. 'That's why you goddamn Limeys will never amount to anything, ever again. It's all fair play, tea on the terrace and good old Queensbury rules with you guys. It's like you lost an empire but not your manners. Why worry about some woman you don't even know? Especially when you don't even know who's side she's on.'

'I'd say she's not on your side. That's good enough for me. What was done to her by your people was reprehensible.' Now, Edge seemed uncomfortable 'Sadly, we compounded the damage when we tried to elicit information from her.'

'And what do you get out of this?' Skinner sneered.

'Healing? Absolution? I do what I do as zealously as you, Skinner, but I have a conscience. When I can, I try to fix any *unintended* consequences.'

'See, that's exactly what I mean. There's no room in our business for sentiment.'

'Not in yours, perhaps. Now, from what Miss Freeman has told us so far, you've cannily used the flying saucer incident at Roswell to cloak your real project. You're creating myths and stories that cloak in mystery any object your project wishes to put in the sky. In pursuit of that project, you've ridden roughshod over anybody who stands in your way. People are merely tools to you, discarded when they've served their purpose without any thought of the consequences. You have one goal in life and that is to maintain your project. Nothing else.'

And you feel sorry for Emily. Poor Michael.'

'Project Flashlight has the smell of a religious crusade,' Edge said. 'That scares me.' Edge was suddenly angry. 'Somebody has to draw the line with you,' he barked. 'And, by God, I'm the man to do it!'

Skinner was surprised by Edge's passion. This was not what he expected from fellow players in the long game. He knew, though, that he had to give a bone to Edge. 'Okay, Edge. I'll arrange for Straker to fly out here. I'll contact *you* via the Embassy when they arrive. Let there be no misunderstanding, though – if you cross me, you'll rue the day!' He turned and walked away, blending into the crowds around the historic monument.

Edge didn't really care about Project Flashlight, Skinner thought. That was a problem for Six. All Edge wanted was the Yank to go home, and Emily Freemans fixed. Skinner walked towards the side street where Oldrey waited in the car. Edge knew too much now. And so did Edge's team. Too many people knew.

Skinner settled into the back seat of the car as Oldrey nosed it out into the London traffic. Whatever Straker did would ultimately be of little consequence. Once Emily Freeman returned from wherever MI5 were holding her, and began working at Mr Stone's club, she and Stone would no longer be a problem to him. It was appalling that the IRA would target innocents in a London nightclub simply for the sake of their *republic*. Still, that was the modern world of terrorism and asymmetric warfare. And if Behan's mole could find and destroy Edge's file on Project Flashlight, all Skinner need do was eliminate Edge. If Edge were to die at the same time as Freeman and Stone, so much the better.

24

Harry sat at his desk in the office. Although a field operative, he was still sometimes required to perform mundane tasks. Today was one of those days. He collated information that had arrived from various sources, sifting through what appeared to be a mountain of paperwork, assessing reports and assigning them to appropriate section heads, desks and departments. He'd been scanning folders and pieces of paper for a good hour when one report caught his eye. It was terse, probably written by somebody over the weekend.

> Reading Police have reported to us an assault on Carl Cleaver, a newspaper reporter. The prime suspect is Archibald Franklin Conn. We have a request out to all constabularies to forward information on Conn. Conn is peripherally linked to one of Edge's assignments.

Harry's stomach turned a somersault So Archie was in Berkshire. He went to Edge's office, where he knocked the door and entered. Edge was behind his desk, reading reports that Harry or Morrow had already sifted. He looked up as Harry entered. 'What can I do for you?'

Harry handed Edge the report. 'I think you'll like this.'

Edge read it. 'Thank goodness for the boys in blue.'

Harry nodded. 'So, we have a lead at long last. Do you want one of our local agents to interview this Cleaver?'

Edge chewed one of his fingers. 'I think not,' he finally said. 'You're as interested in Mr Conn as the Service. Take a train down to Reading and see what you can learn.' Edge looked at the report again. 'I wonder if this man is still in recovery?'

'I'll phone and check.'

Edge smiled. 'Well, let's hope he is. Who knows where he might live. I don't want to fork out for an overnight stay in Scunthorpe, or Torquay,'

'It would be nice to have an overnighter by the seaside.'

'Aye. I'm sure a hotel would be much nicer than your flat.'

Harry's mind wandered for a moment to an imaginary hotel room in Scunthorpe. Molly was also there. He collected himself quickly. 'So, I'll interview Cleaver and find out where Archie is.'

'Yes. Get whatever information as you can. 'Edge looked at the report again. 'It seems Cleaver was pretty badly beaten. You should be careful Harry.'

Harry shrugged and smiled. 'I've got nothing to worry about. Archie and I are old chums.'

'Perhaps they're the ones who should be most worried.' Edge put the report down to one side of those he'd already read. 'Well, get going then. Don't bother me with your travel arrangements. If you need to go to Scunthorpe, phone in and I'll sign off the paperwork.'

'I'll call when I've talked to Cleaver.'

'Ach, leave it until you get back. I have bigger fish to fry at the moment. I'm leaving you in charge of this. Move quickly, though. If news of our interest somehow gets back to Conn, the trail will run colder than an Eskimo's shower in midwinter.'

Harry turned to leave the office. Edge's voice stopped him. 'Harry. Don't let me down. I know there are personal issues between you and Conn. But the only thing Conn is guilty of is breaking off his affair with Miss Shepherd.' Edge looked down at his desk for a moment, and then continued. 'We've opened a big enough can of worms as it is, and we're sailing close to the wind.'

Harry laughed. 'In a sea of worms?'

'What are you on about?'

'In the good ship Mixed Metaphor?'

'Oh, aye. Very good.' Edge smiled, but then regarded Harry seriously. 'There are risks in what we're doing. I can't afford to have you behind bars because of a vendetta against Conn. We're only interested in him because he knew Peta.'

'You're worried about the Americans?'

Edge grunted. 'Aye. Now away and boil yer heid.'

Harry phoned the Royal United Hospital in Reading, and found that Cleaver was still there. Edge was right. If Conn found out that MI5 were after him, he would quickly cover his tracks. Yet, Harry felt sure that if Conn did run, it wouldn't be very far. Harry now had Archie's address. It had been in the report. He was tempted to phone Archie first, but thought better of it. He would first talk to Cleaver. After all, if Cleaver was telling the truth, he had been attacked by Archie. Why? Cleaver, he had learned, was a journalist on a local newspaper based in Swansea. Harry knew, from their days together in Dereham, that Archie had grown up in South Wales. There must be a connection there. What had Cleaver discovered?

There had been no information in the report about why Archie had attacked Cleaver. The police file would have that information, of course. Harry preferred to talk to Cleaver himself, and get the information first hand. One thing he had noticed from the report, though, was that Cleaver was both the victim of and the only witness to the attack. Proving that Archie had attacked Cleaver could be difficult without further evidence. Harry would quite like Archie put away – for any reason, on any charge. What Archie had done to Peta still rankled with him. He knew his feelings were ridiculous. Lovers had tiffs all the time. People used people.

Such behaviour hardly warranted imprisonment. He felt like this, he knew, because he'd loved Peta. And there was a kind of quiet horror in knowing that she had died alone. He had difficulty letting that thought go. Somebody had to pay for that, somehow. If Archie went to jail for beating up Cleaver, that would be something. Harry could perhaps be a character witness for the prosecution, somebody who knew what a bastard Archie had been. At least Archie's appalling behaviour would then be a matter of public record. At the same time, though, Harry knew he felt this way because *he* also felt guilty. Because he too had left Peta.

Harry sat on a train to Reading, vaguely disappointed that there'd been no need to travel to Scunthorpe, or anywhere else for that matter. An image of Molly came to him again; she smiled at him. He should phone her, he thought, and tell her he had a lead on Archie. He would tonight, he decided. He would also invite himself up to the Midlands for a drink at the weekend. She had, after all, seemed keen to meet him again.

The journey to Reading had passed quickly, and he was now in a taxi on the way to the hospital. The taxi driver managed to tell Harry his life story in the time it took to do the trip. Harry wondered how many people a day heard that story.

A nurse took Harry to Carl Cleaver. Harry introduced himself. Cleaver's face still showed bruises, although they had lost their lividity. There was a bandage wrapped around his head, covering his right eye.

'I've had an operation,' Carl said. 'To fix the retina.'

'That sounds serious.' Harry said.

'It is. The doctors said it was for the best.'

'Would you like some water?'

'Yes, please.'

Carl took the offered water. His one good eye examined Harry closely. Harry said nothing.

'I've already told the police everything I know.'

'Yes, I understand that, Mr Cleaver. I'd just like to hear your story myself.'

'Who did you say you worked for?'

'I didn't.'

'No, you wouldn't. You work for the Service.'

Carl was astute, Harry noted. 'I can neither confirm nor deny such a question. As a journalist yourself, you can understand the need for... discretion.'

Carl shook his head sadly. 'Ah, if only it was so.' Harry noted the Welsh accent, still there but soft. Carl had obviously spent some time out of Wales, probably at university. 'Unfortunately,' Carl continued, 'I don't get to do undercover reporting on my paper. Council budgets, dockyard strikes, town politics, that's my game.' He smiled sadly. 'I was hoping that a story about Archie would get me out of there. Onto the *News of the World* or the *Sunday Mirror*, or something.'

'Why were you interested in Archie?'

Carl explained about the deaths of the Conn brother and sister, and his pursuit of the story.

'Yes, we know about that,' Harry said.

'I always thought Evans dropped the case too quickly.'

'Oh yes, Owen Evans, the detective. '

'Yes. Usually he's like a dog with a bone.' Carl's one visible eyebrow lifted. 'Did you lot...?'

'Yes, we did. We could understand why people might suspect Archie Conn. But proving that Conn had murdered his brother and sister would be difficult. We were worried that if the police pursued the case, Archie would fall off the map. Not that we knew where he was on the map. How did you find him?'

Carl explained about Patterson. Harry smiled. 'Old man, Patterson, eh?'

'You know him?'

'Yes. Not well. But I met him once or twice.'

'So you were in that town... Dereham? What were you doing there?'

Harry shook his head. 'As they say in the films, I ask the questions. You'll have plenty of time when I leave you to join the dots. Perhaps you will, perhaps you won't. But you managed to find Archie. The best minds in my... office... never managed that.'

Carl nodded slowly. 'So, what do you want from me?'

'Tell me what you were doing in Reading, and why Archie did this to you.'

Carl told Harry everything.

'You know it'll be difficult to prosecute Archie,' Harry said. 'It's your word against his.'

'Yes, I know. I don't want them to arrest Archie, anyway.' Carl frowned. 'Look, I can tell you, right, because I know you won't do anything about it. Archie sent me a note, through my editor. He threatened to harm my family if I pressed charges or continued to follow this story.'

'So you're not pressing charges?'

'No.'

'And the story?'

'Officially, it's dropped. But, you know...'

'Yes, I know. Be careful, Mr Cleaver.'

'I will be. What will you do now?'

'Visit Archie, I think. I have his address.'

'He won't be there. He's only back at weekends. He works in Cheltenham during the week. He was keeping the flat on down here for a while in case the job didn't work out. That's what he said, anyway.'

'Well, this is Archibald Franklin Conn we're talking about. I wouldn't believe a word of it.'

'Be careful, Mr Roberts.'

'I will be.' He shook Carl's hand, and then went to hospital reception where he phoned for a taxi. He exited into fresh air and waited. The day was dull and cold. It was the last day of November, and dusk was already falling. Harry breathed deeply. It was time to resurrect Colin Butler.

25

Archie sat in the worn armchair of his second flat, smoking a cigarette. He cleaned his rifle carefully. Jeff had been true to his word. Within a week, he had passed Archie a message. It was a test, Jeff had said, to see if he was up to the job. The hit was easy; out of town, at a posh house in the Surrey countryside. Archie had no idea who he'd killed, and wanted to keep it that way. Jeff had said he could find out, but Archie didn't want to know. It was safe to assume that the mark had been a criminal. That was the game, wasn't it? Double-crossers, territorial disputes, grasses; that was his world now. He'd earned a couple of grand. The amount seemed paltry in comparison to a life. Although, of course, the life wasn't being valued; his abilities were. He intended to become good; sought after. Then he would demand more.

Archie finished cleaning the rifle, gave the stock and barrel a quick wipe down with his rag, and then put the rifle in its case beneath the bed. The rifle had been down payment on the job. A MAS 49, Archie believed. Accurate enough, but heavy. He would look for something more suitable if the job kept coming in. He pushed the case to the very back, against the wall, and stood up. The bed was low, and the counterpane wide. He straightened it, and pulled it to one side, so that it almost touched the carpet.

He looked at his watch. It was three-thirty. He decided to visit his old flat. The old biddy, Mrs Eveson would be out with her friend, shopping now. He looked out of his window. Evening was already falling on this grey day. Mrs Eveson would be back about five o'clock. He had plenty of time to get down to the flat and pick up any mail before she returned. He wasn't expecting any letters, but it was always possible that his solicitors, Gribbens and Nuttley, might forget to send mail to the post office box he had specified – especially old Gribbens, who was, Archie thought, going senile.

As Archie approached the flat in Grovelands Road, he was surprised to see a dark figure at the door. It was a man, Archie could tell. The man bent down and looked through the letter box. Archie approached the path to the house quietly. The man knocked at the door again. In the months he'd lived in Reading since leaving Dereham, he'd never had two visitors to his flat within a few days of each other. In fact, he'd had no unexpected visitors at all. As Archie put his foot on the path, the man, obviously expecting no answer, turned. Archie recognized that face, although he couldn't place it immediately.

'Well, well. Hello, Archie,' the man said.

The voice was familiar, and it identified the face for Archie. 'Bloody, hell, Colin Butler.' He remembered how Cleaver had found him. 'Don't tell me. Richard Patterson?'

Colin laughed. 'Yes, you got it one. I was in Dereham the other day, and saw old Patterson. He gave me your address. I was in Reading on business and I thought I'd look you up.'

Fucking Patterson, Archie thought. Fucking Reese. He stopped himself. It wasn't Reese's fault. Archie had invited him back here. And now here was another reminder of his Dereham days, Colin Butler. Archie didn't really want to talk to Colin. Yet, when Archie had lived with him in the cottage at Dereham, they had always been civil. To send him away might invite suspicion. 'Come on in. Do you want a coffee?'

'I'm parched,' Colin said. 'That would be great.'

Archie opened the door and led Colin in. 'You're lucky you caught me,' Archie said. 'I'm not here most of the time.'

'Yes, Richard told me. Reese Johns told him you'd found yourself a job in Cheltenham.'

Archie wondered again what he'd told Reese Johns that night. He'd been too smashed to remember much. He hoped he hadn't said anything stupid. The police hadn't arrested him yet, so he supposed he hadn't. Despite his drunkenness, he can't have mentioned the grisly demise of Lou and Giles. There was always a chance he might still be arrested for the assault on Cleaver; but his threats seemed to have had their effect.

At the top of the stairs, Archie opened the door and allowed Colin to enter first. 'Sorry it's so... spartan,' Archie said. He switched a table lamp on, and went to the kitchen. 'Milk? Sugar?' he called.

'Milk, one sugar, please, Archie.' Colin said. 'It's good to see you again.' Colin leaned against the frame of the kitchen door.

'Did you hear about Peta?' Archie said.

'Yes, yes, I did. It's very sad. I read it in the papers.'

Archie was genuinely surprised. 'It was in the papers?'

'Yes, a couple of them. Just short articles. Patterson probably wrote them.'

'I don't read the papers much,' Archie said. 'Only *The Observer*, on a Sunday.'

'It wasn't that sort of paper,' Colin said. 'A tabloid.'

Archie handed Colin a mug. 'Well, come into the lounge and sit down.'

Archie followed Colin, who sat on the small sofa. Archie sat in the threadbare armchair.

'Colin fucking Butler.' Archie laughed. He wondered if the entire ufological fraternity of Dereham would pass through his lounge and drink his coffee in the next few months.

'Archibald Franklin fucking Conn,' Colin said, and smiled. He lifted the mug in a salute. 'Cheers.'

'Cheers,' Archie said. He sipped his coffee, and eyed Colin. He wondered if there was an angle. Why would Colin visit him? They had shared a house in Dereham for six months, and Colin was a nice enough guy, exactly the kind of person, Archie suspected, who would look up an acquaintance and rehash old times. Perhaps there was no angle at all. Archie could never stop looking for one, because he was the sort who always had an angle; he thus suspected everybody else of having one. Yet he knew not everybody did. Peta had never had another angle. She had only wanted to love and to be loved.

'That was a sad business with Peta,' Archie said, neutrally. Archie noticed a moment of sadness pass across Colin's face. Of course, Archie thought, Colin had fallen for Peta while he was living in the house with them both. He remembered suspecting it. Not that he had cared.

'She was a nice girl,' Colin said.

'She was that,' Archie said.

'Peta missed you when you left her.'

Archie feigned sadness 'I'm sorry about that now,' he said. 'Of course I am. But it wouldn't have worked. She wanted more than I could give.'

'Yes, she said you were...' Colin smiled. It was a conciliatory smile, Archie thought. 'Flighty. Not ready to commit.' There seemed to be no malice in his words.

Archie sipped at his coffee again, thought for a moment. 'That's true,' he said. 'She wanted... marriage, I think. A car. Happy ever after. You know?'

'You had a car though, didn't you?'

Archie smiled. 'That crappy little Mini.'

'Have you still got it?'

'No, I sold it on. I have a Land Rover now. A proper car.'

Harry nodded. 'But everything else... Steady relationship, marriage?'

'I wasn't ready for that. But then I didn't know she'd do... well, she'd do what she did.'

'Don't blame yourself,' Colin said. 'You can't have known that she was unbalanced.'

'Didn't you... ever... I mean, I thought you had a soft spot for her too.'

'Who wouldn't?' Colin said. 'But no, I never... tried it on with her. She was too depressed after you left.'

'You're not making me feel good, Colin.'

Colin shrugged. 'After you left, she was depressed, it would be silly not to expect that. And then I left her too.'

Archie looked into his coffee cup. He did feel guilty, even if that guilt lay deep below the surface. He felt more guilt about Peta, he knew, than he ever would about Giles and Lou.

Colin looked around the room vacantly, a little sadly. 'Perhaps I'm as much to blame as you. We talked a lot, after you left. I said I'd be there for her. But then I got a job offer in London. The money was good, and... well, it talked. I left her alone, in that house.'

'I see,' Archie said. He was somehow cheered that Colin seemed to feel worse than he did.

There was a pause before Colin spoke again. There was a wry smile on his face. 'She told me about the... peccadillo that caused your rapid retreat from London.'

'Stealing Len Stone's stash, you mean?'

'Yes, that was his name. Len Stone. At... *The Purple Parrot?*'

'Ah, yes. What a dumb name for a night club. What did you think? When she told you?'

'I'm not lily-white, Archie. Okay, stealing a Manley Boy's stash is a bit out of my league.' Colin laughed. 'Stealing pens from work and purloining the odd fiver is about my limit. Still, I'm not the sort to question people's motives. We all like a bit of bread, don't we? And it's not as if you were interfering in... uh... the legal activities of Mr Stone.'

Archie was warming to Colin. He made him another cup of coffee. Colin's visit seemed innocent enough. So far, there had been no questions about his time in Wales, and his family. Not that Colin had known much about his family, of course. Archie had said very little about them when he had lived with Colin in Dereham. He hadn't thought about them much, either, except when considering schemes to get at the family fortune. Unless a burning hatred of Giles counted as thinking. Archie supposed not; it was feeling, not thinking.

Colin leaned towards him conspiratorially. 'I didn't say anything at the time, but I thought you were trying to work the ufologists. What were you trying to do?'

'Oh, them. I thought they might pay to watch Peta perform, you know? She liked to go off into a trance and contact aliens.'

Colin corrected him. 'Alien. She only contacted one. Molova, that was her name, wasn't it?'

'That's right. Of course, you believed in that stuff.'

'Well, I believed in Peta. And we saw some weird stuff on Copsehill. But some of the ufologists... well, they were intense.'

'Mugs,' Archie said. 'Ripe for a con. I thought we could set up some kind of... I don't know, foundation, or group, or something. They'd pay some dues, subscriptions, and I'd pocket the money and fuck off.'

'It didn't happen.'

'No. They were always suspicious of Peta. I worked it out in the end. Down in Dereham, they saw lights in the sky. They expected aliens to land and shake them by the hand and talk to them. Peta's contacts seemed... a bit... mystical, spiritual. Like talking to the dead. It was something from a different era.'

'Yes,' Colin said. 'I see what you mean. So your plans came to nothing.'

'Oh, I don't know. I didn't have to pay rent. I worked on that house for Creighton. It didn't need much work, really. I exaggerated my hours, and the cost of materials. You know that. I wasn't short of money. More would have been nice. Still, I think I could have kept at it. Until my picture appeared in the paper. Then I knew Len Stone would find me. And the one thing I couldn't risk was Len Stone finding me.'

'You're a hard man,' Colin said.

'Yes, but Len is harder. And he has the Manley Boys as back-up.'

Colin changed the subject. 'If you thought the ufologists were crackers, why did you hook up with Peta?'

'You saw what she looked like, didn't you? You had the hots for her.'

'Well, yeah, but I was into that crackpot stuff, too.'

'True. Well, Peta was just... hot. I had the hots for her big time. And...' Archie stopped.

'And you thought that with her... uh... talents, she might be a meal ticket. Sex and money. That's fair enough.' He put his mug on the floor beside him. Archie reached for the cigarettes in his breast pocket, and offered one to Colin, who shook his head.

Archie lit a Rothmans, and blew smoke into the air. 'Okay, I was using her. That *is* what I'm like.'

'I know. I think I always knew that. It's a shame Peta didn't, otherwise...'

The unstated assertion silenced them both for a moment.

Archie sat forward, dragged on his cigarette. 'Yes, it is sad, don't get me wrong. If I'd known the consequences...' That was true. For once Archie knew he was neither lying nor acting. Much as he had used Peta, he wouldn't have wanted her to die. She was a nice kid. Needy and insecure, but nice. Pleasant to be around. Intelligent and quick.

Colin brought him out of his reverie. 'As I said, don't blame yourself. Sometimes I blame myself for bailing out so quickly. But we can't blame ourselves, can we? She told me about her father and her life on the streets. She was messed up before we even met her. We couldn't know how things would turn out.'

Archie nodded. That Colin didn't blame him he found oddly reassuring. His guard came up again, however, when Colin returned to the subject of Peta's contacts.

'Did you ever learn anything from Peta? You know, about what Molova told her?'

There was something about these questions, Archie thought. They seemed harmless enough, and connected to their mutual lives in Dereham, but there was also an obsessive return to the same subject. In the same way that Cleaver had returned to the subject of Archie's family again and again, alerting Archie to Cleaver's objective, so Colin seemed obsessed with Peta's contacts. Yet, Peta's contacts were something that both Archie and Colin shared, having witnessed them together. Still, when Archie had invited Reese Johns back for a drink, their conversation had ranged much wider than Dereham, UFOs, Peta and her contacts. Reese, though, had been a sceptic, while Colin had always been into UFOs – that was why he'd visited Dereham in the first place.

'Nothing,' Archie said. 'It always seemed so much nonsense to me. She never came out with anything except platitudes and mystical shit. That's what I thought, anyway. My mind usually wandered while Peta was in contact.'

'That's a shame,' Colin said.

'Why?'

Colin smiled. 'Suppose Molova had told Peta about an infinite energy source. Or how to build a time machine. You could have made millions.'

'That's true. And all my money worries would be over. But no, she never said anything like that.'

'Never? Nothing at all?'

'No, nothing.' Archie was suspicious again. 'Why do you care?'

'Oh, imagine Archie. I was into sci-fi before I got into flying saucers. I wanted it all to be true, you know. Travel between the stars. Infinite, cheap, energy. Time travel. I love all that stuff. UFOs, if they exist, are an embodiment of all my hopes and dreams.'

'So you hoped you'd find out something like that through Peta.'

'Yeah. I really hoped Molova would tell Peta something that we could use to improve the world.'

'She did.'

Colin sat forward eagerly. 'Oh?'

Archie smiled. He spoke sarcastically. 'Yes. Be nice to each other.'

Colin sat back again, disappointment evident on his face. 'That's it?'

'I'm afraid so. So if that's why you came to find me, you're out of luck.'

'I'm sorry, Archie, I didn't come to see you about that, honestly. But it did fascinate me. It still does.'

They talked about Dereham for a while longer, about Patterson, the journalists who visited, about the ufologists and Reese Johns and Miles Stephens, the two jokers on the hill, and the town itself. Archie was surprised to find himself strangely moved by the conversation. The town had affected him more than he'd thought.

Eventually, Colin looked at his watch, and then stood. 'I'd better get going, I want to catch the last train back.'

'I'll call for a taxi.'

The taxi took ten minutes to arrive. They talked about their jobs while they waited. Archie's was, of course, imaginary, but he knew how to spin a yarn. Watching Colin, he wondered if *his* job too was imaginary. Something about his story didn't quite ring true. Then again, Archie knew nothing of the workings of high finance, so what seemed incredible was possibly true.

At the door, they shook hands. 'It's been good to see you again, Archie.'

'And you, Colin,' Archie said. 'If you're ever in Reading again, pop in.'

'I will. Thanks for indulging me.'

'No problem. I enjoyed the trip down memory lane. And I hope you find your science fiction dream-world sometime soon.'

Colin waved as he got into the taxi. Archie shut the front door, and walked up the stairs, back to his flat. He decided to stay here for the night. If he bumped into Mrs Eveson in the morning, he could always tell her that he had a day's leave from work and had come into town for the night. It was, after all, still his flat.

It had been good to see Colin. For once, Archie felt light, happy, free of suspicion and doubt. And he felt better about Peta, knowing that Colin didn't blame him. He should visit Dereham again, he thought.

He'd almost forgotten about the man he'd killed.

26

The taxi driver that drove Harry back to Reading station was mercifully taciturn. Harry had enjoyed revisiting Colin Butler's persona for an evening. Perhaps, he thought, he was simply a frustrated actor. And he felt *free*. He had harboured a hatred towards Archie for months now, since before Peta's death. Yet what was Archie? He wasn't the devil incarnate, the son of Beelzebub. He was just a *bloke*. A Jack the Lad, a chancer, a man's man. He had never loved Peta. So what? Harry had met plenty of people like that. There were people in the Service like that. And, if truth were told, *he* was like that. He fell in love with, or sometimes simply slept with, women he met when undercover, and then left them when the job was over. What line had Archie crossed that Harry hadn't himself crossed more than once? So Archie had tossed Peta aside. It wasn't Archie's fault that Peta had been so weak, so emotionally unstable. It wasn't Harry's fault, either. While talking to Archie, Harry had felt grief and guilt dissolving, the tears that had remained unshed drying. Peta was an affecting girl, there was no doubt. No, he thought, *woman*, as Molly had said.

He needed to get in touch with Molly. He wanted to tell her about his meeting with Archie, and about their conversation. He wanted to tell her how he now felt about Archie, Peta, and himself. He looked at his watch. It was too late to phone her. She would, he assumed, be in bed.

The taxi drew up outside the station. Harry paid the driver, and then walked through the concourse. He stopped to check a timetable, and then crossed to the platform at which the next London-bound train would arrive. The wind was cold, and whipped dust from the platform and the gravel ballast between the rails. Harry had ten minutes to wait until a train from Swansea arrived. A Welsh connection, Harry thought, like Carl Cleaver and Archibald Franklin Conn. Harry wondered if Archie had killed his brother and sister, as Cleaver suspected. He pulled his jacket tight around him, and wished he'd worn his black Crombie. He folded his arms across his chest to keep the warmth in. A station past midnight was a cold and soulless place. The buffet was closed, and the waiting room locked. Harry walked up and down the platform, attempting to keep himself warm.

On the opposite platform, a late-night reveller, worse for wear, slumped on a hard, slatted, wooden bench, his head down, his chin on his chest. Harry wondered where the drunk was heading. A remembered phrase ran through his head – *Newbury, Pewsey, Westbury, change at Westbury for Dereham, Southleigh, and Weymouth*. The house in Dereham came to him. Archie, Peta, and Harry. Harry the spy, Archie the chancer, Peta the innocent. Harry couldn't imagine Archie as a murderer. A petty criminal, an embezzler, a fraudster, yes; but not a killer. And yet... When Archie had offered him a cigarette, he had noticed the distinctive blue and white packet of Rothman's King Size, the same cigarette as the butts he had found in the gravel at the Conn house. However, Rothman's was a popular brand; perhaps the postman smoked on his round.

The red-framed train arrival/departure indicator, bolted to a girder in the platform roof, clattered as it updated information. Harry turned to look at it. The Swansea train would be five minutes late. Harry heard the throaty roar of an engine in the distance, and the singing of the rails. A British Rail diesel engine, pulling six dusty blue and white carriages, pulled into the westbound platform. He wondered where it was heading. He thought all westbound trains arrived at the platform on which the drunk fitfully snoozed. He looked up at the indicator, now quiet, and saw that the train was going to Birmingham. The Black Country, Harry thought. Molly crossed his mind. He did need to talk to her. He *wanted* to talk to her.

Harry looked at the train. It was nearly empty. There were only a few weary travellers dotted along its dimly illumined interior, half-asleep like his friend the drunk, or reading newspapers and books. There were three minutes until the train departed. He wanted to see Molly again. He had her number. He didn't know where she lived, but knew it was somewhere near Stourbridge. He looked at the train again. There were now only two minutes until it departed. He would be able to square it with Edge in the morning. Edge would be okay. He could buy a ticket from the guard on the train. He walked across the platform, and boarded the Birmingham train. He moved along the aisle between the seats towards the first-class carriage, calculating, optimistically, that the Service had already paid for at least part of this trip. The carriage was empty. The train pulled out of the station. A gruff voice crackled over the intercom. *Next stop Oxford, then Banbury, Leamington Spa, Coventry, Birmingham New Street.* The train would arrive, Harry calculated, at about 2.30 in the morning. He would find the first hotel he could and get a room. And then, in the morning, he would find Molly.

Molly, of course, didn't live in Birmingham, but she'd arranged to come into town to meet Harry. She sat with him now, drinking a glass of wine at a bar. Harry was drinking a strong coffee, with sugar. By the time he'd found a hotel and fallen asleep, it had been four in the morning. He'd been woken early by the arrival of a maid with a continental breakfast – croissants, small pots of jam, and a pot of tea on a tray.

'I found Archie,' Harry said.

'Well done,' Molly said. 'How did you manage that?'

Harry explained about Carl Cleaver.

'Is this Cleaver all right?' Molly said. His injuries...?'

'He's recovering.'

'Mr Conn sounds like a nasty piece of work.'

Harry nodded. 'He is. But charming at the same time. I understand why Peta fell for him.'

'But not for you.'

'No, not for me. But it was the wrong time. Anyway, I would probably have hurt her too. It's in the nature of my job. And perhaps in the nature of me. It's difficult to form long-lasting relationships, particularly with those you're watching. Things become complicated.'

'Have you forgiven Archie?'

'Yes, I have. He's a nasty piece of work, sure enough, but he's no different to a hundred and one other men out there.'

'I'm sure of that, Harry. I know it. So why did you hold such a... grudge... against him?'

'Because of how I felt.'

Molly smiled at Harry. 'And I'm sure of that. So how do you feel now?'

Harry smiled back, weakly. 'I forgive myself too. I couldn't know she was so depressed she'd kill herself.'

Molly placed a hand over Harry's. 'None of us could. I knew she'd been badly affected by what happened with Dad, but I never believed she'd go that far. She was young, she had her life before her. She was bright and beautiful.'

It was, Harry thought, time to stop talking about Peta. She was in his past. Nothing he could do would bring her back, and he had forgiven himself. The quest for retribution was over. Archie was a bad lot, anyway, and would undoubtedly come to grief eventually – which would be some form of retribution, at least. Karma, as Len would say. For now, though, Archie would live his life, and Harry his. It was possible – indeed, most likely – that their paths would never cross again. Archie knew nothing, and there was little point in the Service maintaining an interest in him.

Molly's hand still rested on his. It felt warm, comfortable there. Harry looked down at it. Molly must have noticed his glance, because she then slowly withdrew the hand.

Harry sat forward then, his elbows on the table, his hands clasped together under his chin on his hands. 'What are you going to do next?'

Molly leaned back in her chair. 'When?'

'After college, sixth-form, whatever it is you're doing.'

'A-levels, at college. I suppose I'll be going to university.'

'Are you academically inclined? Are you studying for the love of learning, or because you want a good job?'

'Because I want a good job. Although whatever I study, I intend doing well. I can be very determined, Harry.'

Molly was resourceful, Harry thought. He imagined she would throw herself into whatever course she chose, and obtain a first-class degree. 'What are you going to study?'

'Politics or law. Perhaps both. International and domestic.'

Harry was intrigued. 'Politics? You have an interest in politics? Left or right?'

'Neutral. I'm not studying politics because I have an *ideology*. I want to work in politics because it interests me.'

Harry sat back, mirroring Molly, and stroked his chin. 'An interest in politics and law, hmm?'

Molly laughed. She now sat forward. 'Why are you so interested?'

'If you could get a job that involved politics and law *now*, a job that would be interesting and fulfilling, a job that would make full use of your intelligence, would you take it, rather than going to Uni?'

'Well, of course, I'd think about it, but one has to think of the future, you know, and how would I know the job would last, that I wouldn't be–'

Harry smiled. 'Oh, the job would last, Molly, believe you me, and you'd get first-rate training.'

Molly's face creased in puzzlement. 'What kind of job do you mean, Harry?'

'It was very smart, what you did, when you memorised my address on the driving license and wrote it down when I left. That was... quick thinking. It showed foresight. You're bright. You look big and strong, too, for a woman. How tall are you?'

'Five-foot eight or so. And I play badminton, swim and jog. It used to get me out of the house when we lived with Dad.'

Harry made a decision. 'We're looking for people like you, Molly.'

'Who are?'

'We are.'

Harry saw the realisation slowly creeping across Molly's face. 'Oh.'

'This is how we recruit. Through contacts, through friends and acquaintances, or by getting to know somebody. We don't advertise our jobs.'

'Who is it you work for?'

Harry smiled and wagged a finger. 'You don't find out until the interview, when you've signed various... papers.'

'Secrets?'

'Yes, big secrets. You've guessed before the organisation I work for. I continue to neither deny nor affirm that I work for that kind of organisation. However, if you were interested...'

Molly looked around the quiet bar. She was thinking. There was also excitement in her eyes. 'Yes,' she said. 'I'm interested.'

'Great,' Harry said. 'I'll put the wheels in motion. You don't have to accept the job, you can still go to Uni. It's up to you. And, of course, my superiors might not be interested in you. Sometimes even I don't understand what makes a recruit acceptable.' Harry looked at his watch. 'I'd better get going. My boss will wonder what I'm up to.'

Harry stood, took his jacket from the back of his chair, and put it on. Molly also stood, and picked up her handbag. She had said earlier that she was going to stay in town for the rest of the afternoon, and look around the shops. They left the pub, and stood facing each other on the pavement.

'You go that way for the station,' Molly said, nodding her head to the left. 'I'm going up town.'

'Well, I hope we see each other again, soon,' Harry said.

'So do I.' Molly leaned forward, and kissed Harry softly on the cheek. 'Because, you see, now I know you've left my sister behind, I can tell you I'm also interested in *you*.' She smiled, and walked away up the street. Harry watched her tall, lithe form as it slowly disappeared between the other shoppers. He had left Peta behind him, he felt sure enough of that. Relieved of guilt, he could see Molly as something other than a replica of her sister. He wondered, however, if it would be madness to become involved with another Shepherd.

27

Straker was the man Skinner called in when the somewhat delicate issue of security raised its ugly head. People could leave Project Flashlight, but not with their memories intact, not as they person who had joined the project. Not that people often left. Whether that was because of the handsome remuneration or because they knew about Straker, Skinner wasn't sure. On those rare occasions when a project member insisted on leaving, Straker was the man Skinner entrusted to protect Flashlight. Straker called the procedure *Preparation* - preparation for a world outside the project, a world with no reason to know about Flashlight. Skinner knew what his staff called it - *Operation Mindfuck*.

Skinner looked at his watch. It would soon be midday - early morning in California, where Straker undoubtedly slept the sleep of the righteous. Skinner had things to do later in the afternoon, and couldn't care less whether he woke Straker or not. Besides, Straker's incompetence had led to the current mess. He picked up the phone, and dialled the numbers. The phone rang for a while before Straker answered.

'You fucked up, Straker,' Skinner said without preamble.

'Colonel Skinner? Is that you?' Straker sounded confused, his voice thin, his words slow. He had obviously still been asleep.

'It is, Doctor Straker.'

'How have I *fucked up?*'

'It appears Emily Freeman's conditioning has been broken. A meddling British secret service team has been trying to extract information from her about Flashlight.'

'Her conditioning has been broken, you say? Very impressive.'

'I thought the conditioning was watertight.'

'It is. Or, rather, it *was*. It was state of the art. Others have caught up with the art. It was bound to happen, I'm afraid.'

Those who had been *mindfucked* were supposed to forget everything about Flashlight, and should, under interrogation, fall unconscious or gabble nonsense. 'About two dozen people' Skinner said, 'are currently at liberty outside the project, walking around with highly sensitive, top-secret information locked away in their heads. If the Brits can access the information, so can the Russians. So get your team together and get your ass over to Patterson Air-force Base. A plane will be waiting.'

'What do you expect me to do?'

'Clear up one hell of a mess.'

'How?'

'Well, first you can find out what MI5's specialists did to get around your conditioning, and learn from it. And then... Well... Then we have to fix Miss Freeman.'

'Fix her?'

'She's supposed to be a fucked-up mess, isn't she? That's what a mindfuck does, isn't it? Well, sadly, Freeman isn't fucked up enough. She talked.'

'You might be disappointed that Emily is still *compos mentis*, Colonel, but I am not.'

'Hell, no, I suppose you're not. You never liked that part of Preparation, did you? You're surprisingly soft, all things considered. The deal with the Brits is this – either we return Freeman to something resembling full mental health, or they blow open Project Flashlight.'

'I don't know if I can.'

'You'd better try, Straker. If you don't, we're all fucked.'

'We'd all be candidates for Preparation if that happened.'

'Yes, we would. Or something far more permanent.'

Perhaps it's something genetic,' Straker mused. 'Her father was also difficult to control.'

'Yes, another failure,' Skinner snarled. 'You turned him into an alcoholic who needed continual supervision by his daughter. If you'd been more successful we wouldn't have needed Emily to babysit him.'

Straker sounded bitter. 'I did the best I could with the techniques I had available at the time. He died in the end, anyway. That should have made you happy.'

'Not so, *Herr* Doctor. Ed Freeman had an important part to play in the psyops.'

There was a pause. When Straker spoke again, he changed the subject. 'Who is the psychiatrist for the British?'

'Doctor Rachel Heathcock.'

'And who is she working for?'

'MI5. The Security Service.'

'I'll see what I can find out about her. I think I know the name.'

'You do that.'

Skinner put the phone down. Mention of Ed Freeman led him back down the murky byways to the origins of this current crisis. Ed Freeman had witnessed one of Flashlight's early prototype airplanes when it made a forced landing at his farm. With Straker's help, Skinner had turned what could have been a disaster for the project's secrecy into something else. They had abused public interest in unexplained and unusual aerial phenomena by creating stories about flying saucers that enabled Project Flashlight to fly exotic aircraft in plain sight. Ed Freeman had been central promulgating these stories. He'd already convinced himself he was in contact with aliens. He helped maintain the mirages Skinner constructed. Freeman's own beliefs, in conjunction with wacky contactee stories concocted by Straker and his team, and Freeman's book, *Panlyrae–A Message for Mankind* – which Skinner and his psychological operations team had actually written – had been used to sow disinformation into the ufological field. Emily had been a child when all this happened. When she left college, Skinner recruited her to keep an eye on her increasingly unstable father, and to work on Flashlight. In the end, Ed Freeman had died from chronic alcoholism, and Emily had met a man: Len Stone. For some reason, these two events had changed everything. Suddenly, Emily – who until then had been a solid *Flashlight* operative – wanted out. For a while, Skinner had given serious thought to Emily meeting with an *accident*: but he had agreed to her request to be Prepared. Skinner sighed. *And that had led to the current mess.* How he wished he'd arranged that accident instead.

Skinner picked up the telephone handset on his desk and asked the operator to put him through to Edge at the Security Service. Edge's gruff hello indicated that the operator had told him who was calling.

'I've done it, Edge,' Skinner said. 'My team will be arriving as soon as possible. Can you authorise the arrival of a C-9 Nightingale as close as possible to London?'

'I'll get my embassy to contact your embassy and arrange for a landing at Northolt.'

'Where are you holding Miss Freeman?'

There was a laugh at the other end of the line. 'Wouldn't you like to know?'

'What are you going to do, then, blindfold us?'

Skinner's question was greeted with silence. Edge was obviously calculating how the operation should proceed. Skinner understood. He wouldn't want anybody seeing his secret facilities, either. 'I'll tell you what. We'll do it in town. I'll have a word with Mr Stone. We'll see if we can use his nightclub. When Miss Freeman comes around, she'll be in familiar surroundings.'

Skinner nodded. 'That sounds reasonable, Mr Edge. When would you like this to... happen?'

'Phone me when your team has arrived. I'll need to speak to Mr Stone first. I'm sure he'll understand.'

'Good. I'll be in touch.' Skinner put the handset back in its cradle. He smiled. He had been wondering how he could take out Edge as well as Emily Freeman and Len Stone. Edge had inadvertently simplified matters. He looked at his watch. There was plenty of time before the arrival of the flight carrying Straker. Skinner picked up the phone again and called Oldrey.

At five o'clock, Skinner sat next to Oldrey in a Company Jaguar. They were heading to a run-down area of the London docks. Skinner had arranged to meet Behan in a disused warehouse there. Skinner looked at the run-down buildings they passed through. This had once been was the centre of the world's trade, Skinner thought. Now the USA - the country he was proud to serve and to protect, through the grace of God, by any possible means - was the leader of the free world.

Oldrey had said little during the journey. For a Brit, he wasn't bad. He knew when to keep his mouth shut, and was efficient. 'So, Oldrey,' Skinner said. 'Do you know much about explosives?'

The driver smiled. 'You could say that, sir. I like nothing more than a good clean explosion.'

Skinner nodded. 'Excellent. In that case, I have a job for you. And, rest assured, no finger will ever be pointed your way.'

'My services don't come cheap, Colonel.'

Skinner grunted. 'You'll be paid handsomely enough.'

'Now you're talking my kind of language. I assume the kit is coming from the Micks, then?'

'What makes you think that?'

'It makes sense. If the kit I'll be using is supplied by the IRA, the finger of blame will be pointed in their general direction.'

'You catch on fast, Oldrey. Ever thought of moving to the States? I could use a man like you.'

Oldrey blushed slightly. The car slowed to turn into a gateway. Once white gates rusted and hung off their hinges. A faded sign on the gates read *Parsons, Ltd. Import/Export*.

'I've got nothing to keep me here now,' Oldrey finally said. 'Wife buggered off with a salesman a while ago. So, yeah, always open to offers.'

The car pulled up outside a derelict building. Oldrey reached under his seat and pulled out a gun. Skinner recognised it as a Walther P38. 'Nice pistol,' he said.

'Merely insurance, Colonel.'

Skinner opened his coat to show his Smith and Wesson tucked into its lovingly polished shoulder holster. 'Once we have what I want, there are to be no witnesses, understand? The fewer people who know about this, the better.' Skinner winked. 'Let's look upon this as your interview, shall we? Do a good job, and you're in.'

'And the Provos?'

'They'll know why we did it. They're soldiers like us. So, do we have a deal?'

Oldrey nodded. Skinner exited the car and walked a few yards towards the building. Doors hung from their hinges; windowpanes were cracked and broken; roof tiles had fallen to the ground and shattered. There was, as far as Skinner could see, nobody else around. Oldrey joined him at the front of the Jaguar.

Skinner looked back at Oldrey, who tucked the Walther into his belt, under his great-coat, and then followed Skinner towards the large double doors of the warehouse.

'Would've been better to have had a few of the lads here as back up,' Oldrey whispered.

'We'll be fine,' Skinner quietly replied.

Perhaps the Walther and the Smith and Wesson would come as a surprise, but probably not – Behan would expect them to be armed. When they were a few feet from the doorway, Skinner discerned movement. A flashlight blinded him. A voice said, 'Skinner?' Skinner nodded. 'Follow me,' the voice said. Skinner and Oldrey followed the dark shape, which itself seemed to follow a dim yellow pool of torchlight that bobbed in front of it. Skinner could see a lighted doorway ahead of them, and the torch was turned off. They entered a large storeroom, its dark spaces weakly illuminated by a single, bare, sixty-watt bulb. Behan stood with another heavy-set man beside an upturned packing box. That made three of them, Skinner thought. He wondered if there were others lurking in the shadows. On top of the box was a large, metal, military-green, ammunition case. That was the Semtex, Skinner thought. Beside it was a brown envelope, and Behan's revolver. The other heavy had some East European submachine gun slung casually over the shoulder. The heavy who had led them into the bowels of the warehouse had his hand in his overcoat pocket. The right-hand gripped a small pistol, Skinner surmised. He assumed a pro like Oldrey had also noted the likely disposition of firearms.

'Here we are, then, Skinner. The explosives and detonators you requested.' He tapped the envelope. 'And some rather interesting information for you as well.'

Skinner deliberately looked around the room. 'We've come alone, Behan. Have you honoured that part of our agreement?'

The thickset man nodded. 'High command said that if I crossed you in any way, they'd kill me and my family. So, aye, it's just me and the boys here.'

Skinner smiled. 'Good. I'm going to reach inside my coat for the money, okay?'

Behan didn't say a word, but he moved his hand towards his revolver. Slowly Skinner's right hand moved inside his jacket. He gripped the stock of the Smith and Wesson and whipped the gun out, yelling, 'Now!' Skinner dropped to one knee, sighted quickly along the barrel, and pulled the trigger twice, before rolling away. Two reports close to him indicated that Oldrey had followed his terse order. Beside the sound of three bodies falling, there was no other noise. Skinner stood and quickly moved behind a red metal pillar. Oldrey had moved into the shadows. Skinner waited for a few moments, the Smith and Wesson ready. He moved his head from behind the pillar, and looked around.

'What do you know,' Skinner laughed. 'The thick Mick was telling the truth. They were alone after all.'

Oldrey emerged from the shadows like a ghost. Skinner walked over to Behan, his gun pointing at the body. He poked the fallen man with his foot. Blood seeped from two wounds in the chest. He turned to look at the heavies Oldrey had taken out. Each had a bullet hole in the centre of the forehead. The man was an excellent shot, Skinner thought. 'Two shots, Oldrey, two dead. Good work.'

Oldrey nodded. 'Thank you, sir.'

'Mind you, they were amateurs. Right, let's get the kit out of here before the police arrive. Somebody must've heard the gunshots.'

Skinner waited with Oldrey in the upholstered comfort of the Company Jaguar outside Len Stone's club. It was now midnight. Nobody had entered or left the club. He could see no lights in the building.

'What do we know about this place?' Skinner said.

'Stone's assistant manager lives on the premises,' Oldrey said. 'In a basement flat. But he's out of town at the moment, so my contact tells me. Since the business with Emily Freeman started, the club's been closed.'

'Are you sure it's empty?'

Oldrey nodded. 'As sure as I can be.'

'We might as well move in,' Skinner said. 'If this assistant manager is on the premises... well, he'll regret he came back.'

Oldrey and Skinner exited the car, and quickly but quietly moved across the narrow street. Oldrey carried a rucksack that held the explosives and detonators. They went down the steps that led to the main doors. Oldrey quickly picked the lock. Opening the doors slightly, he slipped inside. Skinner followed, pulling the door shut behind him. Oldrey took a small torch from his coat pocket and illuminated the stairs. Oldrey moved stealthily forward. Skinner didn't need to be here, of course. He wanted to be sure everything was done properly. He also enjoyed working in the field.

Skinner and Oldrey reached heavy double fire-doors. Oldrey swung one of them open. His torch swept across the wide expanse of the dance floor, illuminating tables, chairs, and then the bar. Next to the bar was a door. 'We'll try there first,' Skinner said. They crossed the dance floor, opened the door, and found themselves in a corridor. They walked down it. The first door off the corridor revealed an office. Oldrey and Skinner entered. Oldrey shone his torch around it. A desk, a sofa, filing cabinets, shelves. The beam from Oldrey's torch retraced itself, revealing a dark rectangular line in one of the blue-painted walls. 'There boss,' Oldrey said. They crossed the office. The door, the handle, and lock had been painted blue. Oldrey tried the door. It was locked.

He raised an eyebrow at Skinner, and then quickly picked that lock.

They made their way through the door, and found the flat Oldrey had mentioned. Skinner quickly found the bedroom. There was a kitchen close by. If Edge were bringing Freeman to the club, this would be where the treatment took place. 'Here,' he hissed to Oldrey. They examined the bedroom. Under the bed were three shoeboxes.

'Perfect,' Oldrey said. He opened his rucksack, and took out a slab of Semtex. He removed a pair of loafers from one of the boxes, and placed the Semtex and detonators inside. 'What time will our victims be here?'

Skinner thought for a moment. Straker wouldn't arrive in London until the early hours of the morning. Straker would need time to rest. Freeman would need to be transported from wherever she was located. Skinner imagined that Straker, Edge, Heathcock, Freeman, Stone, and other members of Edge's team would all be here to ensure that Straker did his job.

Straker's recent displays of compassion had disturbed Skinner. If Straker also died, well, he would be a casualty of war. He knew that Preparation took around six hours. He surmised that Straker's attempts to undo that processing, and fix whatever damage Heathcock had done, would take at least as long. He had, therefore, at least a six-hour window. Skinner knew that he controlled Straker's arrival at the club. If he aimed, therefore, to deliver Straker to the club at midday, and detonate the Semtex two hours later, he would remove most, if not all, of the thorns in his side. 'Two o'clock tomorrow afternoon,' Skinner said.

Oldrey nodded, set the countdown timer and connected it to the detonators. He packed it carefully into the box and pushed it back under the bed. He shone his torch on the loafers he had placed on top of the bed. 'Hey, size nine,' he said. 'Waste not, want not.' He smiled and placed the shoes in his rucksack.

'Let's get out of here,' Skinner said.

As they left, Oldrey locked the doors he had picked. Out on the street, Skinner said, 'Good work. Let's hope the bomb goes off.'

Oldrey reached into his bag, and pulled out another block of Semtex. 'Insurance,' he said.

Peta's was a cellar club, beneath a block of Victorian shops. Oldrey eyed the doors to the club, and the shops above. He moved one shop down. 'We're at street level here,' Oldrey said. 'You keep your eyes open, Colonel. I'll go in alone.'

Skinner nodded. Oldrey skipped up three steps, picked a lock and was in. Skinner expected an alarm to sound, but there was none. While he waited, he looked through the scissor-arm metal shutters that were drawn across the windows. He could see cheap bric-a-brac, hardware, crockery. He looked up at the sign above the window. *F. Denison, Ironmongers and Haberdashery.* He heard footsteps. Turning, he saw two lovers walking arm in arm down the street. He smiled pleasantly at them as they passed, then returned to examining the items in the window. He saw the shape of Oldrey inside, returning to the door. Skinner shook his head. Oldrey stopped. The lovers continued walking down the street, and disappeared down a path at the end. Skinner nodded, and Oldrey slinked through the door. He locked it, and he and Skinner headed back to the Jaguar.

Oldrey started the car, and executed a three-point turn. 'I'm pretty certain that I've placed the other device above, or somewhere near, the flat,' he said.

'Near enough?' Skinner said.

'Oh yes.'

'Well-hidden?'

Oldrey nodded. 'I can't imagine anybody will find it before the big kaboom.'

Skinner smiled. 'Good work.' He trusted Oldrey. It would be a pleasure to move him to the States and introduce him to Project Flashlight. He took a cheroot from his cigar case and lit it.

It was three o'clock in the morning when the C-9 touched down at Northolt. It was nearly four o'clock by the time Oldrey had ferried Straker and his team back to the US Embassy.

Straker stood in front of Skinner's desk. The rest of the team were resting in the empty canteen, drinking coffee. Skinner felt very tired. He looked up at Straker. Despite travelling for twelve hours - including a short stopover in Newfoundland - and despite being woken early by Skinner, Straker looked as fresh as a daisy. Probably some secret drug, Skinner thought. 'I'll have some of what you're having,' Skinner said.

Bafflement passed across Straker's face. 'Pardon me?'

'A joke, Straker. A joke. Like your Preparation technique. After all the money I've poured into your research, you've failed me at a critical moment.'

Straker shook his head. 'You know very well that my work isn't one hundred per cent effective, Colonel. It never has been. There is always room for error when working with the mind. No, not *error*. That's the wrong word. There was no error in the application of the technique. No two minds are the same. There will always be grey areas-' Straker smiled. 'In the matter of the grey matter.'

'Bullshit!' Skinner shouted. He was in no mood for wordplay. He moved from behind the desk and stood in front of the nervous scientist. 'Doctor Heathcock has followed your *public* work closely. She is, so to say, a *fan* of yours. Seems she has access to all your published articles and theses. She's put two and two together, come up with four, and added one to crack a mindfuck.'

Straker shrugged. 'As I say, nothing can be completely effective. When do I start trying to... uh... repair Miss Freeman?'

Skinner gave a grim smile. 'You will not *try*, you will *succeed*. Do you understand?' Straker nodded. 'You'll begin work tomorrow. We're all meeting at some psychedelic club in the city.'

'Most apt,' Straker said.

Skinner afforded Straker a hostile glare. 'The club belongs to Freeman's boyfriend, Len Stone. Seems the Brits don't want us looking inside their secure medical facility. If she was in some ordinary hospital, I'd arrange a little accident for her, but she's beyond even my reach.'

Straker glared at Skinner in turn. 'That's a little extreme, isn't it?'

'Don't be such a pussy, Straker. Anyway, rest for a few hours. And Doctor, if you fail me, heads will roll. If that is so, yours will be the first to fall into the basket.'

Skinner dismissed Straker. When the doctor had gone, Skinner picked up the file supplied by Behan's mole, and read through the contents. He'd underestimated Edge. The man was no fool. The sooner he was taken out, the better. Later today, the righteous sword of God's justice would chop, cleave, and lacerate the meddlesome Edge and his team.

28

Edge had told Harry his plan. Len had, as expected, agreed to the use of the club for Emily's rehabilitation; he seemed vaguely cheered by the prospect of returning to familiar surroundings. Emily's condition hadn't improved. Len sat in the back of Harry's car, biting his fingernails. Edge sat next to Harry in the passenger seat.

Edge obviously felt the tension in the silence, and uncharacteristically attempted to make small talk. 'This is it, Len,' he said. 'Things will begin to look up from here. This Straker, well, he caused the problems with Emily. I'm sure he and Doctor Heathcock will straighten her out.'

Len said nothing. Edge looked at Harry, and grimaced. They continued towards London in silence. Behind them, Morrow drove the van that contained Doctor Heathcock and Emily. Edge had assigned Liz Carter the task of leading Skinner, Straker, and Straker's team to *Peta's*.

After another hour of silence, Harry turned his car into the narrow side street in which *Peta's* stood followed by the van Morrow was driving. Liz Carter had arrived already. She leaned against her car, behind which were two Jaguars. Harry pulled up behind them. Morrow drove up onto the pavement by the steps that led down to *Peta's*.

As Len got out of the car, he looked forlornly at his dark and empty club. 'I hope Her Majesty's Government will provide some compensation for the loss of earnings this fiasco has cost me?'

Edge grunted. 'I'm sure we'll manage something, Len.'

A biting wind whipped along the street. Grey clouds scudded across the rooftops. The occupants of the other vehicles had joined Len and Edge. Len unlocked the doors to the club, and led the now rather large party inside. He flicked switches, and lights came on in the vestibule. 'Wait here for a moment, will you?' Len went through the double doors at the end of the passage. A few moments later, Harry saw the lights above the dance floor and behind the bar flicker on. Len came back, and led them into the club.

They stopped for a moment. Skinner introduced Straker and his team, and then Julian Oldrey. Oldrey had an English accent, Harry noted; probably a mercenary, he decided. Edge introduced Harry and Carter.

Skinner raised an eyebrow when introduced to Harry. 'I know you, don't I?'

Harry shook his head. 'I don't think so.'

Morrow came down the stairs with another man. Between them, they carefully carried a stretcher bearing Emily Freeman.

'I have business back at the Embassy,' Skinner said. 'I'll leave you in the capable hands of Doctor Straker.' He shook Edge's hand, and left with Oldrey.

Straker waited until the double doors had closed behind Skinner and Oldrey, and then said, 'Mr Edge, do not trust that man.'

Edge had also been watching the retreating Skinner. 'I don't.' He turned to Len. 'Lead the way, laddie.'

Len took them through the door beside the bar, down the corridor to his office, and then through the door to Martyn's flat. Len pointed out the bedroom. There was a general shuffling as they all moved aside to allow through Morrow and the other man to carry Emily. Harry noted that Martyn Harris was fastidious. The bedroom was clean and tidy. A large double bed dominated the room.

Edge was standing in the office, looking thoughtful. He called Carter and Morrow over to him. 'I don't like the way

Skinner scuttled away so quickly. Before we begin, I want the club searched from top to bottom.'

'Fair enough, boss,' Morrow said.

Edge looked at the man who had been helping Morrow. 'Thompson, come with me. We'll search the corridors, and the dance floor. Morrow, you and Carter search this flat.'

'What about me?' Harry said.

Edge nodded towards the crowded bedroom. 'You keep your eye on these doctors, and on Mr Stone.'

Edge led Thompson away. Carter began searching through the cupboards and drawers in the small kitchen. Morrow went the office.

Harry went back to the doorway to the bedroom. Straker and Heathcock were talking in psychological buzzwords. The two members of Straker's team were unpacking syringes, drugs, restraints, and other small items of medical equipment. No scalpels, Harry noted with relief. No lobotomies today. Len was looking at the unconscious Emily on the bed. 'Are you all right, Len?' Harry said.

Len nodded. 'I hoped that being in familiar surroundings might help Emily, that she'd know where she was and... I don't know, come back to me.'

Heathcock smiled her bedside smile. 'Sorry, Len. It doesn't work that way. If it was that simple, I wouldn't need the help of Doctor Straker.'

Len leaned across and gently stroked Emily's hair. 'If anything was to happen to her...' The sentence trailed off, a threat implied in the lost words. How Len would revenge himself against the US and British security services, Harry couldn't imagine. 'I lost one special lady in my life,' Len continued. 'I can't lose Emily as well.'

Heathcock gently put her hand on Len's arm. 'Don't worry. Doctor Straker is the best there is. He'll get your Emily back.'

Morrow appeared next to Harry. 'Have you finished?' Harry said.

Morrow nodded. 'Oh, apart from here, of course.'

'Here? You mean the bedroom?'

'Of course. This has to be checked as well.'

Harry leaned through the door, and asked if everybody could leave for a few moments. The doctors all shuffled towards the kitchenette. Len was the last to leave. 'It's as tidy as Martyn always leaves it,' he muttered.

Harry nodded. 'But that, Len, is the problem. Any agent worth their salt would make sure they left the place as they found it.'

Morrow opened the small wardrobe, and rifled through it. Harry helped. He went through each drawer of the chest next to the bed. Morrow was lifting down boxes from the top of the wardrobe. Harry knelt to look under the bed. He found shoeboxes. He took the first one out, lifted the lid, and found canvas deck shoes. He pulled out the second box, removed the lid, and found a bomb.

'Fuck,' Harry, said quietly. 'Morrow, over here.'

Morrow put the box he was holding back on top of the wardrobe, and quickly came around to Harry. He examined the device, checking the timer, looking at the wires, tracing their paths. 'Neat job,' Morrow said. 'But simple.'

'And deadly, I assume,' Harry said.

'Oh yes, very deadly.'

Morrow stood slowly, with the box full of bomb in his hands. 'I'm going to take this outside.'

'Is it dangerous?'

'It has a countdown timer.' Morrow said. 'What's the time now?'

Harry looked at his watch. 'Twelve thirty. How long have we got?

Morrow closed his eyes and was silent for a moment. Harry assumed he was performing some mental calculations. 'Plenty of time,' he finally said. 'An hour and a half. I'll take this to the van, and get Thompson to block off the street. I'll call for bomb disposal.'

'You said it was simple.'

'It has an anti-tampering device fitted.'

'The Yanks?'

'Don't know,' Morrow said. 'Could be IRA. We shouldn't jump to conclusions.'

'Edge will.'

'Let him. Once we've defused it, we can get it analysed.'

Morrow turned towards the door. He almost collided with Edge. 'Careful, boss,' Morrow said.

Edge looked in the box. All he said was, 'Oh.'

'I've got it under control,' Morrow said. 'Thompson, come with me.'

Thompson and Morrow left. Thompson followed Morrow reluctantly; Harry didn't need to be an expert in reading body-language to see that.

'Those fucking Yanks,' Edge said.

'Morrow knew you'd jump to that conclusion. He said to wait. It could be the IRA. Where bombs are concerned, I trust Morrow.'

'Aye, there is that. And Len's club would be a prime target for the Micks.' Edge looked around at the doctors. 'Well? What're you all waiting for? Get your arses back in here and sort out this lovely wee girl for Mr Stone.'

As Straker passed Edge, he said quietly, 'Remember. Don't trust Skinner.'

Straker was skilled, Harry thought. Experienced. A grey-haired man, in his early sixties Harry supposed. A veteran of the Second World War, certainly. Which side had he been on? A beneficiary of Operation Paperclip, perhaps.

Over the past hour, Straker had pumped different drugs at different times into Emily's arm. Len had gone to his office, unable to watch any longer. Straker had put Emily to sleep, returned her to consciousness, put her into a trance, snapped her out of it, and put her to sleep again. There were elements of hypnosis that Harry recognised. Lights were flashed in Emily's open eyes, and against her closed lids. Conditioning, Harry thought. Straker had a notebook with him, passages of which he read aloud when Emily was in particular states of awareness. These passages seemed relevant to Emily's life, to a world she'd been forced to forget. Before Straker induced yet another spell of unconsciousness in Emily, she appeared, despite heavy-lidded eyes and a dopey expression, somewhat like her old self.

Straker looked over to Doctor Heathcock and smiled. 'She's back with us,' he said.

Heathcock looked at Emily doubtfully. 'Are you sure? She seemed so–'

Straker interrupted her. 'I'm sure. The state I put her into will help reknit her memories. The drugs will help. She will remain in this state for half-an-hour or so. I will then inject a stimulant, to bring her round. This will be quite a high dose, to jump-start her brain, if you will.'

Harry heard Len's voice beside him. 'Like speed?' Len had entered the room quietly, while Harry had been absorbed in what was happening.

'Exactly like speed,' Straker said. 'In fact, it will be quite a high dose of amphetamines. I want her mind to work fast, very fast. I want her to remember things very quickly, like a waterfall of memories. You understand?'

'I understand,' Len said.

'You can help here,' Straker said. 'While she is... speeding... take her back through her memories, encourage her to talk about her past.'

'And then?'

'Tonight, and for the next few nights, we will give her sedatives, to allow her to sleep, and especially, to dream. When dreaming, we rebuild and stabilise our neural connections, Mr Stone. Sleep will be good for her.'

'But the speed... A high dose?'

'Don't worry, Mr Stone. We have four doctors here, one of whom specialises in cardiac emergencies. But Emily is young. She'll have no problems. I expect you took without knowing it even higher doses when you were young and-' Straker smiled. 'Grooving to The Beatles and the Rolling Stones.'

For a moment, Len looked uncertainly at Straker, and then Emily. 'So everything will be all right?'

'I am sure it will. Even now, while she is resting, her neurons are firing together, and becoming reordered.'

Heathcock turned to Len. 'I trust him, Len. She was much more lucid in her last period of consciousness. Try not to worry; you're getting your Emily back.'

'Thank God for that,' Len said. He looked at Harry. 'Let's have a drink, Harry, or Colin, or whatever your name is.'

Harry put a hand on Len's shoulder and squeezed it reassuringly. 'You can call me Harry, now. And I'd love a drink.'

Len led Harry back along the corridor to the bar. Edge and Morrow were sitting on bar stools. 'I didn't think we should disturb,' Edge said. 'How goes it?'

'Very well,' Harry said. 'Both Heathcock and Straker seem certain that within a couple of days, Len will have Emily back pretty much as he remembers her.'

'That's excellent news,' Edge said. He looked at Len. 'I apologise for ever getting you both into this mess.'

Len shrugged. 'If what you say is true, your Yank would have got us into an even bigger one.' He asked what they all wanted to drink, and then went behind the bar.

Harry looked at Morrow. 'What happened with the bomb?'

'The anti-tampering device was easily dealt with by the bomb squad,' Morrow said. 'It smells like an IRA device. While I was back at the office, I quickly looked through reports of suspected arms imports. This looks like it was from a batch smuggled through various ports earlier in the year. Special Branch have been chasing this package for months, and always suspected it was destined for the IRA. They didn't want to detain it, you know, but...' Morrow shrugged. 'They lost track of it.'

'Aye,' said Edge. 'And we shouldn't give them stick for that. It's in the nature of our business. Still, they know where it is now, and who's been using it.'

Len called from behind the bar. 'Hey, perhaps the docs would like a drink, coffee, or tea, or something.'

Morrow slid from his bar stool. 'I'll go and ask them.'

Harry glanced at his watch. Quarter to two. If he hadn't found the bomb, in another quarter of an hour they might have been dead.

Len brought the drinks from behind the bar. He began to chat to Edge and Harry cordially, for the first time in days, it seemed – about the club, and about Harry's time in Dereham. Morrow appeared in the doorway next to the bar. 'Mr Stone. Doctor Straker suggests that you join him in a little while. They'll be bringing Emily around for the final time. Oh, and the Yanks would all like a coffee, and Heathcock a good old English cuppa.'

Len smiled. 'I've only got instant.' He went behind the bar again. A door to one side of it led to a kitchen at its rear.

Harry could hear an electric kettle being plugged in and switched on.

'All's well that ends well, eh, Harry?' Edge said.

'It seems so,' Harry said. He looked at his glass. 'Fancy a top up, sir?'

'Yes, please. It seems Mr Stone has a rather fine malt.'

Harry went behind the bar, shouting to Len that he was getting another. Len pushed his way through the door from the kitchen. Harry held the bar door open. Len was carrying a tray with four mugs, a milk jug and a sugar bowl. 'Thanks. I hope the Yanks like my cheap coffee,' he said.

Edge came behind the bar and looked at his glass. 'Put a bit more in there, man.'

Harry pushed Edge's glass up against the optic. The door to the corridor creaked as it opened and closed. He should have helped Len with that door, Harry thought.

Harry glanced at his watch again. Two o'clock. The wall behind the bar bent inwards, and optics shattered. There was a painful roar, which quickly changed to a muffled silence. Bottles silently fell and smashed around him. Edge staggered and fell over among the shards of glass. Harry turned and saw the door beside the bar fall off its hinges. Len was lying on the dance-floor, the silver tea tray beside him, smashed cups and mugs around him. There was blood on Len's face. Harry staggered, put a hand out to lean on the bar, and cut his hand on broken glass. Edge stood, looking confused, cuts across his face. Harry looked at Edge's hands. His, too, were bleeding, after he'd lifted himself off the ground, numb, and cut them on shards of the shattered optics. Harry walked unsteadily around to the front of the bar, bent down to Len. He felt for a pulse at Len's neck, listened for breathing. The pulse was faint, and the breathing ragged. Harry looked down the corridor. Flames billowed from the office doorway, on the threshold of which was the blackened body of somebody who looked like he had once been Morrow.

29

Harry's hands were bandaged. There were surgical plasters over cuts to his face. The doctors had found a sliver of glass that had punctured the skin in his neck, close to a carotid artery. He had been lucky, they had said. Edge had also been lucky, suffering similar injuries to Harry's, though he also had a minor fracture to his leg. The concussion from the explosion had knocked him off his feet; as he fell, he had kicked out a leg to steady himself and caught it on a stanchion behind the bar. Otherwise, he was a mass of minor cuts. For a while, he had looked worse than Len, as blood trickled from the wounds and stained his clothes.

Harry and Edge had Len to thank for the mildness of their injuries. The bar held valuable stock; alcohol and cigarettes. When it had been remodelled a year ago, Len had asked for a wall of brick to replace the stud and plasterboard at the back of the bar. It wouldn't keep out the determined thieves, but it would deter opportunists who hadn't come armed with sledgehammers. The blast had buckled the wall, no more. It had blown all the fire doors from their hinges, however, which had allowed shock waves to reverberate around the club.

Len had been walking down the corridor to the office when the bomb had exploded. There were brick supporting walls on each side of him. The blast had ripped the door from the office, spilled the broken and burned Morrow across the threshold, and, channelled by the walls, propelled Len backwards onto the dance-floor. Len had lacerations and burns to his face. Glass and shards of wood from the doorframes had penetrated through his clothes and into his skin, peppering his shins and thighs. He'd cracked two ribs when he'd landed heavily on the floor.

Emily Freeman had died. Whoever had planted the bomb in the shop above had known how to cause maximum damage to the club below. Straker, his team, and Heathcock had also died.

The newspapers were condemning an IRA outrage. The IRA denied any involvement, though that was to be expected. If the IRA were responsible, they had been aiming at an economic target, and terrorism in its purest sense – instilling fear into the citizens of London. The bomb had gone off at two o'clock, when the club would normally have been empty of all but Martyn Harris. They hadn't intended multiple deaths, as would have been possible had the club been full of revellers at eleven o'clock at night.

Harry, and Edge, suspected Skinner might have been responsible. But how would they prove it? The method, the materiel, pointed to an IRA connection. Even with the IRA denial, the waters were sufficiently muddied.

Len had shouted and cried and blamed everybody, and then become mute and hardly moved for a day. Edge had ordered that Len be taken back to the clinic in Berkshire, where all his wounds – physical, mental, and emotional – could be tended. Len had gone willingly.

Harry, on a week's sick leave, watched the evening news. After only two days, the explosion at *Peta's* had been relegated to the last item. Special Branch and the Security Services were looking for the perpetrators of the act, the newsreader solemnly declaimed. Harry knew that Special Branch and the Security Services were doing very little. Special Branch had lost track of the smuggled package. The Security Services had no leads. After a perfunctory investigation, the bomb would be assigned to the IRA; but little would be known about the motive for its placement. Even less would be known about those who had died, even if the number and identities of the victims were now known. The media reported that Michael Edge, a civil servant, and various friends, including visiting American civil servants, had been having a private party at Leonard Stone's club, *Peta's*, where Colin Shepherd, an ex-civil servant and friend of Michael Edge, worked. Nobody could ever know, of course, that everybody who had died, apart from poor Emily Freeman, had been a current member of or contractor for the security services.

The weather forecast came and went. Tomorrow was to be a cold, late November's day. Harry wouldn't be able to stay indoors again. He would go for a walk tomorrow, in the afternoon, around Trent Park.

There was a soft knock at the front door. Harry wasn't expecting anybody. He carefully levered himself out of his armchair, and walked to the door. He opened it to a beaming Molly Shepherd. She held an overnight bag. 'Hello, Harry,' she said. 'I thought you might need somebody to make you soup.'

Harry smiled back. He was pleased to see her. 'Come in, come in. Why didn't you phone first?'

'I wanted to surprise you.'

'You did.'

'And I hope it's not an unpleasant surprise.'

'Of course it's not.' Molly shouldn't, of course, know that he was one of the victims of the explosion. 'Let me take your coat, sit down, and then tell me how you knew?'

Molly shrugged her coat off and passed it to Harry. 'Oh, come on, Harry,' she said. 'A bomb in a night club called *Peta's*? Well that can only be Len Stone's nightclub, right?

Then a list of the injured includes Colin Shepherd. *Colin. Shepherd.* Honestly, I know you use the name Colin, but *Shepherd*? That was a dead give-away.'

'Yes, I suppose it would be to somebody as quick as you. I had to use that name. Colin Butler is my usual pseudonym. However, to get in quickly with Len, I used Shepherd, and claimed to be Peta's cousin. In Len's current state, we couldn't confuse him with another handle. It was better, we thought, if I remained Colin Shepherd.'

'Mum thought it was fascinating that there was a Shepherd in the explosion. She wondered if it was a relative. I suppose you are a pseudo-relative.' Molly laughed.

'You didn't say anything to your mother?'

'Of course not. When I realised it was you and Len Stone, well, I put two and two together, and realised you probably weren't at a civil servants' convention.'

'You're a clever girl, Molly. You'll be an asset to the service.'

'Yes, I got a letter from the service yesterday. I've been invited for an interview. Guess who signed it?'

'Not Mick, surely.'

'Yes, it was. Michael Edge. The very same civil servant who had also gone to the civil servants' ball.' Molly laughed again, but she cut it short. 'I shouldn't laugh. People died.'

'Yes, one of my colleagues, who was also a friend. There were some American... contractors. And of course, Emily Freeman. She was named in the papers, so you know that.'

'Len Stone's girlfriend?'

'Yes, indeed.'

'Why? Why were you targeted?'

'What you read in the papers, about the IRA? That's as good an answer as we've come up with. There are other people in the frame, but we could never prove it. It's as likely to be the Provos as anybody else.' Harry shrugged. 'In our game, it's good to know when to give up. You can't chase every lead. Chasing them might lead you all over the place and take up valuable time. The simplest solution is usually the right one. Mind you, at the same time, you never forget. Something you overhear on a case, or something another team brings to you, may connect. Then you might start chasing again.'

Molly smiled. 'Free lessons in the art of espionage already.'

'Tea?' Harry had been pacing around the room as he talked. He'd been cooped up all day, on doctor's orders, and was full of energy.

'Oh, do sit down, Harry. I've come to nurse you. I'll make the tea.'

'No, no, I'll do it.'

'Look at your poor hands! How can you hope to hold a kettle and mugs in that state?'

Molly was right there, Harry thought. Making tea for himself during the day had been difficult. It would be a pleasure to let somebody else do it for him. 'I'll show you where everything is.' Harry led her to the kitchen. 'You can see for yourself where the kettle is, and the teabags are right next to it.' He placed a bandaged hand on a cupboard door. 'That's where the crockery is kept.'

Molly took the kettle, filled it, and placing it back on the worktop, switched it on.

'Treat the house as your own, Molly,' Harry said. 'You'll soon learn where everything is.'

'Have you eaten?'

'Not much. A bit of toast. A biscuit or ten.'

'Shall we have one of those scrummy Chinese take-aways later?'

'Well, yes, but I can pay.'

'No, Harry, my treat. For the invalid. You can walk down there with me to protect me. You look like you could do with a walk. Burn off some of that energy.'

A Chinese meal did sound good. 'Why don't we actually go out? To the restaurant, for a proper meal?'

Molly reached up and touched the plasters on Harry's face. 'Have you forgotten what you look like? You'll frighten away the clientele.'

Harry smiled. 'That's true.'

'Besides, after you've walked to the restaurant, you might not feel so... lively.' The kettle boiled. 'We'll go down after our cuppa.'

Two hours later, Harry realised Molly had been right. After they had walked to the restaurant, sat around while the meal was prepared, and then walked back, Harry had felt very tired. 'It's the shock,' Molly had said. After the meal, and the painkillers he had been instructed to take, even though his pains were slight, he felt pleasantly relaxed. Molly sat beside him on the sofa. It was nine o'clock. They watched television together. A play had just started, and Harry was relaxing in Molly's quiet company. She was a girl who didn't say much. She wasn't taciturn, but neither did she waste words. She knew Harry was tired, and made no attempt to engage him in conversation.

There still existed a thorny hedge between them, he knew, a subject that must be approached carefully, and got over with delicacy and skill. *Peta*. She was still there. Harry had to metaphorically kill her and show Molly the corpse. It was different for Molly. Peta would always be her sister, to be fondly remembered. Harry could only fondly remember Peta once he had set her adrift. When he could show he was free, everything would change; he would be allowed fond remembrance. After his conversation with Archie, Peta *had* started to fade away. It was only Molly he needed to reassure. Harry wondered what he could say. He *could* say something like, 'You're so much prettier than your sister, you know.' But that would indicate that he had once thought Peta pretty, and Molly would soon wonder *how* pretty Harry had thought Peta, and whether the statement was only a convenient lie. Molly and Peta were probably aware of their prettiness, anyway, so comparisons would be invidious. And given how much Molly had loved Peta, such a statement would be met with a flat refusal of such a preposterous notion. Perhaps, then, the approach would not be to compare them in their looks, but to compare them in some other way, some way that would not be so obvious to the Archies of this world, the lads' lads, the blokes' blokes. 'I'm glad you got the interview,' Harry said lazily, playing to his sleepiness.

'It was quick,' Molly said. 'Somebody put in a good word for me, I'll be bound.'

'Yes, I did. You're very bright. *Very*. We need people like you. Astute. Quick thinking. Level-headed. Dare I say it, even mature for your young age. I think you'll fit right in, and do well.'

Molly turned to look at him, smiling. 'Why, thank you sir.'

'This isn't just flattery. You know, you're different to Peta. Deeper. More interesting.'

'Well, Peta was lovely.'

'I know, I know. Of course she was. But you're... not her. And I like it that way. Look, you'll find it goes with the job, if you do field work. You're alone, in a strange place. You want something that looks like love, to help you fit in, to help you feel like you belong somewhere. The thing is, though, at some point afterwards, you realise it's only... It's like a crush.'

'Peta deserved love.'

'Yes, I know. I couldn't give it, though. Not in those circumstances. Who knows, in other circumstances I might have been able to. But the truth is, I didn't love her. I couldn't.'

Molly touched one of Harry's bandaged hands. 'Yes, I know. I don't blame you for anything.'

'That's the thing. I realise I've nothing to blame myself for. Peta was lovely, a sweet woman. But that was in another country.' And then Harry thought: *And beside the wench is dead.* Harry hoped Molly didn't know the quote.

Molly picked up the bandaged hand, and looked at it. 'You poor boy. Look at your hands.'

'You said the other day that your weren't just interested in a job, but you were also interested in me. I'm interested in you, too, Molly. Not because you're Peta's sister, not because you look like her.' He put a finger of his free hand on her forehead. 'But because of what's in here.' He moved the finger towards her chest, a bare fraction above one of her breasts, pointing at her heart. 'And because of what's in here.' He felt Molly clutch his bandaged hand tighter. It didn't hurt. 'The more I've seen you, the better I've got to know you, the less you look like Peta, and the more you look like *you*. Simply, adorable *you*.'

Molly had been leaning slowly closer to him as he had talked. Finally, she kissed him. A gentle kiss, on the lips. 'Thank you, Harry.'

'Are you staying the night?'

'Yes, but in the spare room. I don't sleep with people on a first date. Not that I've slept with anybody at all, but you get my point.'

'I do.'

She leaned in and kissed him again. This time, they kissed more passionately. Harry tried to run his hands gently across Molly's face, but was impeded by his bandages.

Molly broke away from the kiss. 'It feels like I'm being stroked by marshmallows. We'll save the kissing for another day.' She turned back to the television programme. 'Put your head on my lap, Harry.'

Molly shuffled up to the end of the sofa. There was just enough room for Harry to bend his knees, put his legs up on the sofa, and rest his head on Molly's lap. She stroked his head, slowly, pulling his hair away from his eyes and flattening it along the side of his head. Occasionally, she traced the intricate whorls of his ears, gently, softly. He didn't think he'd ever felt so relaxed, with anybody.

Soon, he was asleep.

30

Len looked down at the yellow head of one of the teddy bears he held tightly to him. Grief can have a strange effect. He'd been a hard man for the Manley Boys, but here he was, lying on his bed, clutching two of the teddy bears he'd once bought for Emily. The one in the crook of his right arm smelt faintly of her. She'd once sprayed it with her perfume, telling him that if he took Bubbles away on business trips with him, she'd never be far from his heart.

The tears began to well again. Today was her funeral. It was the final goodbye. He rocked slowly backwards and forwards on the bed, weeping silently. How could he carry on? Emily, the woman he had loved so deeply, had gone. He felt alone. He'd lost Peta through his own stupidity, blinded by his beliefs then. After Peta's death he'd gone to Dereham and visited Copsehill, where he'd heard her voice, as clearly as if she'd been standing next to him. Would Emily's voice come to him? He would like to hear her voice. A balm to soothe him.

He wanted closure, and closure would come. The grief would pass. He also wanted revenge. He could feel that emotion side-by-side with his grief. But revenge on whom, exactly? Tossing Bubbles and Betsy aside – all the bears' names began with B – he stood and walked to the window. Everything he touched or saw reminded him of Emily.

A sad smile tugged his mouth as he looked out over the garden. That was to have been Emily's next project. The sky was a clear deep blue. A weak November sun shone from it. 'Well if you're going to go,' he muttered to himself, 'go on a good day.' He limped down the stairs, rubbing his chin, deep in thought. His legs were hurting. The lacerations throbbed and itched, and his right leg had been heavily bruised when the fire door came off its hinges and hit his thigh.

He knew that after he'd made it through today, he'd need to focus on something. The club? No, the club was tainted now, too many memories. Perhaps it was time to leave the scene. Martyn might like to buy his share in the club. It was a thought, at least – a sensible thought, about the future. But now his mind coiled back on itself, thinking about revenge.

As the kettle boiled for his first coffee of the morning, he absently prepared two mugs. When he realised what he'd done, he grabbed one of the mugs and hurled it against the far wall. As it shattered, he realised that it was Emily's favourite mug he'd thrown, and he dropped to his knees, crying again.

Then he heard Emily's voice telling him to get a grip. The voice hadn't come to him in the same way he'd once heard Peta's, or the voices of aliens during a contact session with Peta. His own imagination had supplied the words he knew Emily would say. He so wanted to hear Emily's voice in the way he had once heard Peta's; but now, it seemed, wasn't the time. The letterbox rattled, interrupting his thoughts. With a sigh, he stood and went to the front door. Half a dozen envelopes lay on the mat. Picking them up, he knew at least half of them were cards of sympathy and condolence. He placed those on the small telephone table in the hall with the other unopened cards. The rest of the mail looked to contain bills, which he was in no mood to open.

He glanced at the clock. Nine thirty. Ninety minutes until the car arrived. He looked around the living room, satisfied that if anyone came back to the house after the service it was, at least, tidy. He sincerely hoped nobody would engage him with well-intentioned sympathy. He wanted to be left alone with his grief. Slowly and heavily, he climbed back up the stairs, towards the bathroom, preparing himself for the ordeal ahead.

Len's suit felt loose on him. After his four-day stay in hospital, recovering from the injuries he sustained in the bomb attack, he'd eaten very little, surviving mainly on coffee and the odd meal. Still, who would see his suit anyway? Emily knew few people over here, so the funeral was only to be a small affair. Len had decided on a cremation. He knew Emily had few friends in the States –she had spent so much time looking after her father and then working for the Air Force, she'd had little time to call her own. She had no family to speak of in the States, either; both parents were dead, and her brother Ed Jr. was lost somewhere on the hippie trail. Len had left a message for Ed Jr. with a surviving aunt – the one relative Emily had mentioned – who seemed grateful that Len was handling the funeral and that it was happening four thousand miles away. Len and Emily barely knew the neighbours – they had kept themselves to themselves. Martyn would be at the chapel, along with a smattering of club regulars, Harry perhaps, and one or two other acquaintances, but that would be it. He was straightening his tie when the doorbell rang. 'What now?' he said, as he descended the stairs. As he approached the door he could make out the caller through the frosted glass. By the build, it could only be one person. His heart lifted slightly as he opened the door to Martyn Harris.

Martyn threw his arms around Len. 'Jesus boss, you look like shit!' He hugged Len tightly. 'Forgive me if I'm intruding, but I just thought... Well, you know... I couldn't let you do all this alone, mate. '

'Get off me you queer bugger!' Len laughed. 'The neighbours will talk. Come on in.' He ushered Martyn into the hallway. 'You're the *only* person I could put up with right now.' Len looked Martyn up and down. He hadn't seen Martyn in a suit for years. 'By God, you do scrub up well, you Brummie scruff.' They both smiled. Len felt more at ease now Martyn was here. They went back a long way. If anyone could offer him support and comfort in the difficult hours ahead, it was Martyn. They talked about the club and life in general, until, just before eleven o'clock, the doorbell rang again.

Martyn looked at Len. 'Ready then, mate?'

Len nodded. 'As ready as I'll ever be, Martyn.'

As they left the house, Len's injured right leg almost gave way. He grabbed Martyn's arm to support himself.

Martyn frowned. 'You sure you shouldn't have that looked at again?'

Len pulled a face. 'You can talk, peg leg.' Martyn, too, limped after an accident at the club in the days when Peta worked there. The days of Peta, and Archie, the days when he had first met Emily. Len and Martyn were silent as they sat in the black Daimler, the only mourner's car that Len had ordered. With the smoothness possessed only by a funeral cortege, the car quietly pulled out into the street, following the hearse. Len's stared over the shoulder of the black-coated driver, at the coffin in the vehicle ahead of them.

The journey to the cemetery was short. As they drove in through the gates, Len was surprised to see a knot of people waiting respectfully outside the chapel of remembrance. The car drew up next to the doors. Len recognised some club regulars, and saw the Manley Boys, Edge, Harry and Liz Carter. Len and Martyn entered the dimly-lit building, followed by the others. Len, lost in his own thoughts, heard little of the service. Neither he nor Emily believed in God. If they both believed in anything, it was something more universal, more numinous. He spoke a few words about Emily; about the stresses of her fractured family, but also about her beauty and sense of fun; and about how she had been looking forward to her new life with him. Martyn and Harry contributed their memories. Martyn, a Catholic, had suggested they sing a couple of well-known hymns, so everybody could feel part of the mourning process. They sang as the coffin slid behind the doors to the furnace. Len sang through his tears.

Only when Martyn put an arm around his shoulders did Len realise the service was over. He allowed himself to be guided out through the doors and onto the path. Mourners shook his hand, or hugged him, and offered condolences. Martyn walked away quietly, to say goodbye to some people from the club, leaving Len alone with his thoughts. After a short while, he heard footsteps on the gravel path. He looked up. It was Harry.

Len, I'm so sorry,' Harry said. 'I never wanted anything like this to happen. I regarded you both as... friends.' Harry looked uncomfortable. He looked around him, and then reached inside his coat; he took an envelope from an inside pocket and held it out to Len. 'It's not policy, but you might be interested in this.'

Len looked over at Edge. 'Does he know?'

'Yes,' Harry said. 'He knows. This is just between the three of us.' Len mutely took the offered envelope. Harry winked. 'Open it when you get home, eh?' Harry placed a hand on Len's shoulder. 'If I can do anything, let me know.' He turned away then.

Martyn rejoined Len. 'Time to go, mate.'

Len stuffed the envelope into his jacket pocket. 'Yeah. Come on, let's go back to our-' He stopped himself mid-sentence. 'My place.'

The winter sun was warm on their backs as they made their way to the waiting car.

Len woke up the following morning with a raging headache and a burning stomach. He slipped into his dressing gown, and slowly walked down the stairs into the living room. Both he and Martyn had seen Emily out in style. Empty bottles littered the floor. He couldn't remember much about last night. There was the sound of retching from upstairs, and then the toilet flushed. Martyn was also awake then. *And like me, a little fragile.* Len ran a hand through his tousled hair.

He prepared coffee. He heard footsteps on the stairs, and then Martyn arrived in the kitchen.

'Christ alive, man!' Martyn exclaimed. 'You look as rough as I feel.' He slumped onto a chair at the kitchen table.

Len poured coffee into mugs, and then joined Martyn at the table. They looked at the mugs of steaming coffee, not saying anything. Finally, Len broke the silence. 'Martyn, I want to talk to you about the club. It's too painful for me to go on with it. There are too many bad memories. If you can get some finance in place, you can have my half, for a hefty discount. I'll help you get a loan from the bank if you need it, but I'm out of it.'

Martyn nodded slowly. 'Yeah. It's one of the many things we talked about last night. I didn't think you were serious.'

'I am, old pal.' Len reached for a bottle of aspirin, and took four with a slug of his coffee. 'What else did we talk about? Your memory seems to be better than mine this morning.'

'That envelope you were given at the funeral yesterday, for one thing.'

Len looked at his friend closely. 'Why? What did it say?'

'Not so much *say*, more what it contained. It took me half

an hour of talking to stop you doing something about it there and then.'

Len's memory began to come into focus. 'Where is it? The letter?'

'Where you left it, I expect, screwed up in the fireplace. Man, you were talking evil things after you opened it.'

Len pushed his chair back, and went to the living room. He retrieved the ball of paper from the fireplace, straightened it out, and read it again. 'Shit, Harry, you son-of-a-bitch!'

Martyn came slowly into the living room. Len read the letter again.

> Len. This is for your information, and your eyes
> only. Edge says he will deny any knowledge of
> your receipt of this - thus, if anybody else finds out,
> I'm for the chop. Archie Conn's last known address
> is 102, Grovelands Road, Reading. Do as you see
> fit with this information.

Len looked at Martyn. 'Did I tell you what was in it?'

'Yes. Archie's address. You said Harry gave it to you. I didn't know who Harry was.'

'Oh. You know him as Colin. Colin Shepherd.'

'Colin gave it to you?'

'No, Harry. Colin is Harry.'

'What? Colin is called Harry? You tried to explain all this to me last night, but it was all very confusing.'

Len shook his head. 'If I was too drunk to make sense, that might be a good thing. Forget it all, Martyn.'

'So what happens now, Len?'

Len looked up. His voice was low and steady. 'Revenge for all that man has done.'

31

Harry arranged the cushions on the sofa, and looked around the room. He nodded. The flat was tidy. He had spent the last hour dusting, vacuuming, and cleaning. His hands had been re-bandaged. The cloth only covered his palms and the backs of his hands now. His fingers were unfettered. The plasters on his face had been removed. There were small weals and scars there, but they looked better than the plasters. He'd been to the office today for a short while. Despite everything that had happened, work at the Service continued. He and Edge had spent the day wondering if Colonel Skinner had at last left the country. They had heard nothing from him, and enquiries to the US Embassy had been rebuffed. They continued to wonder whether Skinner had been behind the bomb at *Peta's*. They would never know for sure, which frustrated Edge.

There was a knock at the door. Harry opened it to Molly. She smiled, then dropped her bag and put her arms around his neck. 'Hello, Harry,' she said, softly. She kissed him. Then, she kissed him again. After a few moments of her soft, warm lips on his, she stopped, 'Good to see you again.' She bent down, picked up her bag. 'Well, this won't get the baby's bonnet knitted.'

Harry laughed. 'A saying of your gran's?'

Molly walked into the sitting room. Harry followed, admiring her walk. 'Yes, it is. How do you know?'

'Peta was always quoting your gran, too.'

Molly sat down on the sofa, and struggled out of her grey duffle coat. 'Not as green as she was cabbage-shaped, our gran,' Molly said. 'Be a love and make me a cuppa, will you? I'm parched.'

Harry went to the kitchen, and put the kettle on, and then took some mugs from the cupboard; as he did so, he felt warm, excited, nervous, tingling. He wanted to kiss Molly again.

When he returned to the sitting room, and placed the mugs on the stripped pine coffee table, Molly was already curled up on the sofa. 'You look relaxed,' Harry said.

'I don't feel it. I'm not looking forward to the interview tomorrow.'

'Don't worry about it. You'll breeze through it.'

'Tell me again what happens.'

'You'll be interviewed by a couple of section chiefs. They'll ask you questions about, oh, political matters, about your home life, your relationships–'

'This – you and me – won't be a problem, will it?'

'No – there are married couples in the service. And then,' Harry continued, 'they might give you a test or two, to see if you have analytical skills.'

'What kinds of tests?'

'They vary, so I can't tell you. Perhaps an IQ test. Perhaps some logic puzzles.' Harry shrugged and sipped his tea. 'It depends.'

'On what?'

'I've never been quite sure.'

Molly bit a nail. 'Oh, I'm not sure I can do this. I'm not sure I have the ... qualities.'

Harry pulled her hand away from her mouth. 'You can do it. I have faith in you.' He kissed her hand. 'I can see many qualities in you.'

'Yes, but you're biased. I hope.'

Harry kissed her hand again. 'Yes, I am. But I can also see *particular* qualities in you. You'd fit right in. You'd be a good match for Liz Carter. There aren't enough women in the Service. There's a drive to recruit more. And women have qualities that men don't.'

Molly laughed. 'Sex, you mean?'

'No, not that. Or, not *only* that. Women chatter. They talk. They can get men to open up to them.'

'Like you do.'

'I hope not. I should be the soul of discretion.'

'Hah! I only need to say one word to you to get you babbling like a brook.'

'What's that?'

'Peta.'

'Not any more. You can talk about Peta all you like. But for me, she's finished, if that doesn't sound too harsh. The thing is, I never knew her that well, not really. She was Archie's girlfriend. She never told me anything... personal, until Archie left her. Then it all came out in one sad, miserable torrent. She had allure, you know, a patina, because I watched her all the time. Finally talking to her about her feelings, well that felt... Well, it felt, special, you know?' Molly was nodding. 'But I could tell her nothing about me that wasn't a lie. I was Colin Butler, not Harry Roberts. My hometown was made up, my life was a lie, my interest in UFOs was.... Well, not a lie, but exaggerated. Everything about me was a falsehood.'

'I learned a new word yesterday, Harry. *Dissembling*. That's what you were doing.'

'Yes, that is what I was doing. I'm good at it. You might become good at it, too. But between you and me, there will never be need for it.'

'Good,' Molly said. She leaned over and kissed him. Her tongue was warm and sweet from the tea. His fingers free at last, Harry traced a line lightly down Molly's cheek. The kiss lasted a long time. Finally, they broke apart. 'I don't mind if you talk about Peta, you know. She was my sister, and I loved her. And I know that whatever dreams you might have had Peta a few months ago, I know you never kissed her like you just kissed me.'

'I know. I never did. Can I kiss you again?'

'Of course.'

They spent the rest of the evening talking idly between kissing, stroking, and caressing each other. Harry wondered if he might be falling in love. She was young, of course, younger than Peta, but he was only twenty-seven. She was nine years younger than him. That wasn't too great an age difference. They were both young. His hand slid under her sweater, under her shirt, and slipped across her stomach towards her breast. His fingers lifted the elastic of the bra across her chest; he slipped his hand beneath the cotton cup, feeling a nipple beneath his unfettered fingers.

'That's nice,' Molly murmured. 'Very nice.'

Harry kissed her again. After a few moments, she broke away. She spoke softly. 'Hey, Harry... As lovely as this is, I have an interview in the morning. What's the time?'

Reluctantly, Harry looked at his watch. 'Nearly midnight.'

'Crikey. What time are we getting up?'

'Half seven.'

'Oh, Harry. I must get to bed. I want to be bright-eyed and bushy-tailed in the morning.'

'Oh, don't worry about that, you're always bright-eyed and bushy-tailed.'

Molly gently eased him away. 'Now, Harry, what's the point in setting me up for a job interview, and then getting me all flustered the night before?'

Harry sat up. 'You're right, damn you.' He smiled.

Molly winked. 'I'll be here tomorrow night, as well, don't forget.' She stood, straightened her clothes, and went to the bathroom. A few minutes later, she came back to Harry, and kissed him on the forehead. 'Good night, Harry. I'll see you in the morning.'

'Yeah. We'll travel into town together.'

'Lovely,' Molly said. She tousled Harry's hair, laughed, and then headed towards the spare bedroom.

Harry watched her slip through the bedroom door. She gave him a little wave as she went.

Harry, hot, frustrated, picked up a book. He needed to calm down before he went to bed.

After ten pages, he heard the door to the spare bedroom open. He looked up. Molly's head poked around the frame of the bedroom door. "Won't you come into my parlour?' said the spider to the fly.'

Harry smiled. 'Pardon?'

'Don't you think I make an attractive spider?'

'Well, yes, but...'

Molly opened the door wider, and came out of it. She stood before him, five foot eight of sleek, toned, naked, loveliness. 'Don't be so dense, Harry.' For a moment, Harry simply sat there, struck dumb by her beauty. Then he stood wordlessly, and made his way towards her bedroom door. She grabbed one of his hands, and dragged him inside. 'You know,' she said, 'for a fly, you're pretty good looking.'

'What about the interview?'

'Fuck it,' Molly said. 'I'll never get in, anyway.'

Afterwards, Molly looked up into Harry's eyes. Harry was leaning on his hand, his elbow on the pillow, admiring her nose. There was always something new to admire.

'So that's what all the fuss is about.' Molly said.

Harry was confused for a moment, then remembered that Molly was – had been – a virgin. He wondered if there would be blood on the sheets. 'It... didn't hurt, did it?'

'No, it didn't. It was really.... Something different.'

'Because, you know, err...'

'Harry, don't be so coy.' She stroked his cheek, brushed some hair away from his eyes. 'Yes, I was a virgin. But there was no pain. I do a lot of exercise, remember. My hymen was probably broken already.'

'That's true,' Harry said. He had never slept with a virgin. The first woman he'd ever slept with had been experienced, had already had lovers.

'It was good,' Molly said. 'Can we do it again?'

'Erm, in a little while,' Harry said. 'One thing you'll learn – men can't do it again, straight away. We need to... recover.'

'How do you recover?'

'With some help from you.'

She kissed him. 'Like this?'

'Exactly like that. And anything else you feel like doing.'

They kissed and stroked each other. When they broke apart, Molly's mind had momentarily turned to matters more mundane. 'What did you do today?'

'I went to work. Boring stuff that you don't need to know about yet.'

'What did you do this week?'

'Not much. There was Emily Freeman's funeral, of course.'

'Oh, god, yes, I'd forgotten.' Molly sounded concerned. 'How was it?'

'Sad. I didn't know Emily well, but I liked her. Len was cut-up, of course. I gave him–' Harry wondered if he should tell Molly this. 'I gave him Archie's address.'

Molly thought for a moment. 'Are you sure that's wise? He had a thing for Peta too, didn't he?'

'Well, yes. But I thought if he met up with Conn, he might feel like I did afterwards. That it was Emily that mattered, that Peta had just been a passing fancy. Like you matter to me now.'

'But what about the other stuff?'

'What other stuff?'

'Didn't Archie steal from Len? You told me he'd taken some pot, or something.'

'Oh, yes. He did. About a grand's worth.'

'Don't you think Len might still be angry about that?'

'Well, he never *seemed* angry about it. He only mentioned it once to me, and kind of dismissed it.'

'He's very angry now, though, isn't he? About the death of Emily? Don't you think he might want to take his anger out on somebody, anybody, if he can find an excuse? Okay, Archie didn't kill Emily, but I can imagine Len thinking that all his woes began when he met Peta. And Archie is part of that whole... *situation*. He took Peta away, he took the stash, Peta died, Len met Emily, everything was rosy, and now it's most certainly *not*. Don't you think that setting up a meeting between Archie and Len might, you know, end in tears?'

Harry hadn't thought that. He'd thought a different way. He thought that if Archie and Len met up and talked about Peta, and about stealing the weed, Len would understand Archie a bit better, understand him as Harry now understood him. Yet, Molly had a point. 'Damn it, Molly Shepherd. You might be right.' He scratched his head. 'Now I feel a proper Charlie.'

'You only did what you thought was right. That's all anybody can do.' She smiled at him, generously. 'You tried to do the right thing. But you and Len are different people. You haven't lost somebody you loved the way Len has. He must be heartbroken. I know I would be.'

Harry stroked Molly's long dark hair, wondering if he had made a mistake. But then Molly kissed him, and all thought receded before a torrent of desire.

Later that night, Harry looked at Molly's sleepy face,

admiring now her exquisitely-shaped eyebrows. Her eyes were closed. Molly quietly said, 'I love you, Harry.'

Harry smiled. He thought about Molly, as he drifted into sleep himself, and what a strange world it was that first brought him into contact with Peta, and then through her, with Molly, and then his thoughts inevitably drifted towards Dereham, and the hills, and Peta and Archie, and he found himself recalling fragments of his conversation with Archie, and he remembered the green Mini Archie had owned in Dereham, and how Archie had said it had been replaced now with a Land Rover.

And then Harry sat up, his eyes wide in the darkness. A *Land Rover.*

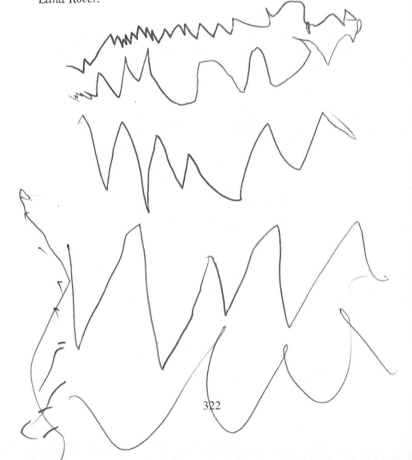

32

Len Stone had been knocking at the door to the house in Grovelands Road for an hour. There was obviously nobody in, but still he knocked. Somebody would have to come home, or wake up, or whatever, at some point, and he was going to stand here and knock until they did. The leg that had been injured in the bombing began to hurt: the bruise began to throb, and each stitched laceration tingled and itched. He sat down on the door-step to rest and to wait. He lit a cigarette. He'd been smoking more since Emily's death.

He must have dozed off despite the pain, and the chill. The pain-killers were strong. He was woken by a voice above him that seemed to come from a dream. The voice came again. 'I said, who are you looking for?'

Len lifted his head, and opened his eyes, which focussed only slowly in the dim light of a December afternoon.

'Holy fuck,' the voice said. 'Len Stone.'

The figure above Len came quickly into focus now. Archibald Franklin Conn loomed over him. The hair was longer, the cheeks were stubbled, but it was Archie, still looking big and mean. Len slowly stood up. His leg pained him as he did so. 'Yes, Archie. It's Len. How are you?'

Archie looked both puzzled and amused. 'I'm fine, Len. What the hell are you doing here?'

'It's funny, really. I took on a temporary barman at the club. His name was Colin. He said he'd been to Dereham. We got chatting, you know. Turned out he knew you.' Len didn't mention a surname. He wasn't sure what name Harry had used when he was in Dereham.

'Colin Butler?'

'That's the guy,' Len said. 'He said he'd visited you recently. So I asked where you live.'

'What are the chances of that?'

'It's karma, Archie.'

'You always did believe in that mystical bullshit.'

'I still do.'

Archie shook his head, still smiling in bemusement. 'Len fucking Stone.' He opened the door to the house. 'I guess you'd better come in for a coffee.' Archie led Len up the stairs to the flat. 'Jesus, I swear if I live here long enough, everybody I've ever known will come to visit me.'

'Apart from Peta,' Len said.

Archie opened the door to the flat and ushered Len in. 'Yes,' Archie said quietly. 'Apart from Peta.'

Archie threw the keys of the flat onto a small table by the front door. Len followed him into the sitting room. 'Find a seat,' Archie said. 'I'll make you a coffee. You still take it the way you used to?'

Len slowly settled himself into a battered armchair. 'Yes, please.' He looked around him. The flat was small, but it was clean and spruce. Archie had always been a bit rough around the edges, a mixture of ex-military and weekend hippie, bruiser and lover; Len had thought Archie's flat would reflect that. He had expected joss-sticks and overflowing ashtrays, half-empty vodka bottles and coffee mugs with mould growing in them; but Archie was a tidy man, disciplined. Len wondered if this had remained with him from his days in the Army.

Archie brought the coffee mugs in, and sat on the sofa opposite Len. 'So what do you want from me, Len?' He lit a cigarette, and blew smoke out towards the ceiling. 'We don't know each other that well, and I stole your stash. I can't imagine you're here to discuss the old days.'

The coffee was hot and welcome. Len had become very cold while waiting on the step. He didn't speak, but sipped his coffee and eyed the man opposite him.

Archie returned his look. 'If I had any money, I'd pay you for the stash, Len, just to close this thing between us.'

'I don't care about the value of the stash,' Len said quietly. 'What I do care about is that you *took* it. I trusted you. I gave you a job when nobody else would.'

Archie flicked ash from his cigarette into an ashtray on a small coffee table. 'You always were a bit of a softie, Len.'

'Yes, I took Peta in, got her a flat.'

'And then I came along and took her away.'

Len wondered how much Archie knew, what Peta had told him. 'She was never mine. You took nothing except my stash.'

'You must have felt something, Len. She was hot stuff.'

'We shared... beliefs.'

'Yes, in all that UFO mumbo-jumbo.'

'And other things. She had a... spiritual side to her.'

'She did. It annoyed the fuck out of me. She talked shit all the time.'

'So you never felt anything for her?'

'She was a good lay. She had a great body. Apart from that... nothing. I thought she might be a meal ticket. She was, for a while. After all, I got a free house in the country. But she drove me nuts with all that contactee nonsense.'

Len wondered if Archie were telling the truth. 'That's all you felt for her?'

'That's all, Len. She was a frivolous, empty-headed, shit-talking, hot piece of skirt. She meant nothing to me.' Archie leaned forwards. 'Between you and me, man to man, as it were, she was surprisingly good in bed, though. Especially after I taught her a few tricks. Don't you wish you'd had that experience?'

Len felt something stir in his belly. Envy, jealousy. Hurt. Pain. Emily had been good in bed. She and Len had been good together.

'You know, you spent all that time with her,' Archie continued, 'hypnotising her, getting her to contact fucking aliens. You should have used your talents more wisely. You should have hypnotised her into bed and given her a good shagging.'

Was Archie goading him deliberately? It worked. Len threw the remainder of his hot coffee into Archie's face, forced himself up out of the armchair and across the coffee-table, and punched Archie. His momentum carried him onto Archie and tipped the sofa backwards, tumbling them both onto the floor.

Archie let out a low moan, felt his nose, and then said, 'Nice to see you too, man.' He wiped coffee from his face. 'You'd better be certain you can take me down, because if you don't, I'll kill you here and now.' Archie aimed a fist at Len. He caught Len on the jaw. Len rolled away. Even lying down, Archie's punch had weight. Len tried to stand. Archie snaked quickly across the floor and pulled Len down by his legs. 'You're a fucking amateur, Len. You're too slow. You're not strong enough. You've gone soft. You've been living the good life for too long.'

Archie was a trained killer. But Len had something on his side, something he thought was stronger – the need for vengeance. Payback for everything that had gone wrong since he'd met this slippery bastard. Archie now tightly gripped Len's head and neck in the crook of his arm. Slowly, he began to squeeze, choking Len. Through gritted teeth, Archie whispered, 'You're old Len, out of shape, out of practise.'

With a strength that surprised him, driven by anger and adrenaline, Len managed to break free and stagger to his feet. At the same time Archie stood up. They faced each other.

'So, you cocky little shit,' Len gasped. 'You think I'm past it? Let's see shall we?' One thing Len while on the payroll of the Manley Boys was to fight dirty. At that, he was good. Time may well have dulled his reflexes, but now in front of him was a target for all his sadness, his failings, his need for revenge, his desire for retribution. If only he could get close enough. Len launched a punch. It was fast, but not fast enough. Archie moved his head and received only a glancing blow to his face; he merely shook his head. 'Nice try, Lennie boy.'

Archie's left kicked out, and his foot connected with Len's chin. Len went down. He felt as if he were about to pass out. Archie grabbed him by his shirt, and pulled him up. 'You know, I just came to see if there was any post for me. Instead, I found you. In other circumstances, I might be amused to see you. But too many people from my past have been popping up recently, and this... This is just too much of a coincidence.' He kicked Len hard. 'You're after revenge, aren't you? For poor little Peta?'

Len loudly spat out a mouthful of blood. His body was wracked with pain, but he still had fire in his belly. 'You wouldn't understand, couldn't understand, you heartless shit.'

Archie crouched down, almost face-to-face with Len. 'Like I said – old, and soft.' He rabbit punched Len on the leg, the leg that had been bruised and lacerated. Len moaned and clutched at it. A stitch had opened, and he could feel the warm blood beginning to stain his trousers. Archie looked down. 'Well, well, Len,' Archie said. 'It seems you have a weakness.'

Despite the stabbing pains in his leg, Len managed to stand. He back-pedalled towards the kitchen. Like a predator sensing that its prey was weakening, Archie slowly moved in for the kill. Len feinted, collapsing against the doorframe, and then fell through the doorway, hoping that Archie would be confused for a moment or two. He quickly looked around him for a weapon, any weapon.

Archie followed him through the door, with an amused smile. 'You really should have thought this through, you stupid little man.'

There was a bottle of cooking oil on the work surface. Len knocked it to the floor, where it shattered. The broken glass and pool of oil slowed Archie only for a moment. Images of Emily and Peta returned. 'You might think you're the hard man, Archie,' he snarled. 'But I've a few tricks left!'

Archie carefully skirted the oil and broken glass. Len backed further into the small kitchen. He found himself beside a block of cooking knives. He reached over and pulled out a knife, which he threw at Archie with all the force he could muster. Archie twisted to avoid the knife hitting his chest, but inadvertently turned his face towards the spinning blade instead. The knife slashed his cheek before hitting the wall and bouncing into the sitting room.

Archie wiped a sleeve across his cheek, and looked at the blood. 'Now *that* has *really* pissed me off. Why can't you die, old man?'

Len glanced down at his injured leg. His trousers were now soaked in blood. More than one stitch had obviously broken. At the sight of his own blood, he began to feel faint.

Archie followed Len's gaze, and saw the blood. 'You *are* going to die after all. Pronto, Tonto, as the lovely Peta might have said.'

Len was weak now, too weak to offer further resistance. Archie grabbed a knife from the same wooden block. 'So,' Archie said. 'How would you like to die? Quickly or slowly?' He moved towards Len, but then, suddenly, his feet took on life of their own. If the situation weren't so serious, Len would have found it comical. Unseen by Archie the cooking oil had spread further across the kitchen floor. Archie grabbed onto the edge of the kitchen worktop. The top half of Archie came to a halt, while the bottom half continued on its way. Archie was pitched to the floor. As he fell, he lashed out wildly. The knife caught Len's so far unbloodied leg, gouging a sizable wound. Len could just make out Archie through his blurring vision as he slowly crumpled to the floor. Blood began to mingle with the oil.

Archie looked across at him. 'Can you stand, Len?'

Len shook his head, too tired to speak.

'Good.' Archie carefully stood up, and made his way to the kitchen door. He turned to look at Len. 'Thanks for the entertainment, shame I can't stop. Things to do, people to kill.'

'Why don't you kill me?'

'It looks like you're going to die anyway, Len. If the fuzz ever do haul me in for this, this looks more like self-defence.' Archie changed his voice, pretended he was frightened. '*He was a strong man, your honour. I had to run away while I had a chance.*' He smiled then. 'Be seeing you.'

Len's vision slowly dimmed; at the centre was a bright spot containing Archie's face. Archie was the Cheshire cat. His face slowly dissolved into greyness. The last thing Len saw was a sardonic smile.

Len felt a slap on his cheek, and then cold water splashing across his face. He sat up, gasping. His eyes blinked open to find a concerned face, old, wrinkled, and haloed with curly white hair, looking into his.

'Are you feeling all right, my dear?'

Len began to feel dizzy. He slowly lay back down.

'You stay where you are. What's your name?'

'Len. Len Stone.'

'I'm Kay Eveson, Mr Stone. I'm the landlady.'

'What are you doing, how did you...'

'Mr Franklin Conn is most inconsiderate. When he tries to kill people, he should remember that the blood will stain my ceiling.'

'Blood?'

'Yes, Mr Stone. You've lost a lot of it. I've put tourniquets on both your legs and rung for an ambulance.'

'Are you sure you've done it... right?'

'I was an ambulance driver during the war, young man. I know how to apply a tourniquet. Now, you close your eyes and rest.'

Len did as he was told. Behind his eyelids, he could see a bright light. And he could hear an argument. Women's voices. It was Emily and Peta. Emily soothed him, cajoling, asking him to let go and join her. Peta's voice was the more dominant, urgent, telling him to fight, to hold on. He had unfinished business, she said.

Len thought about karma. 'Where am I on the cycle?' he weakly asked.

'You're not on a bike,' an unfamiliar male voice answered. 'You're in an ambulance, on your way to the hospital. Hold on there. Everything will be all right.'

33

Archie arrived back at his other flat, had a shower, and put on clean clothes. He bundled up the clothes covered in blood and cooking oil, put them in a carrier bag and took them outside to the next-door neighbour's dustbin.

He was towelling his wet hair when the phone rang. He put down the towel and picked up the receiver.

'Hello,' a voice said. 'Mr Archibald Franklin Conn?' The man had said enough for Archie to identify an American accent.

'Yes,' Archie said. 'This is he.'

'Good. I might have some work for you.'

'What kind of work?'

'You know what kind of work. A friend of a friend of a friend suggested your name. I have an irritant that needs removing. I believe you provide a solution for those kinds of problems.'

'I do. But why are you contacting me directly? Normally, I have a go-between who–'

'I don't like too many people to know my business. Meet me tonight. London.'

After his fight with Stone, Archie was in no mood to travel to London at such short notice. Still, money was money. 'Where will we meet?'

The American gave him the address of a pub in London. 'I'll see you there, sir. Will eight o'clock be suitable?'

'Yes. How will I recognise you?'

'Don't worry about that. I'll know you. Eight o'clock, then.'

Archie put the phone down. How would the Yank know him? He finished towelling his hair, then pulled on a coat and made his way slowly to the door.

The pub was close to the centre of town – nowhere near, Archie was happy to note, Stone's old club. He looked at his watch. It had already gone eight o'clock. The Yank was late. He went to the bar and ordered another orange juice and lemonade. He wanted to be sober. A voice behind him said, 'I'll have a bourbon. And a shandy for my friend.' The voice was American. Archie turned to the look at the man behind him. He was stocky, powerful, with a military bearing. Beside him was a smaller man.

Archie ordered the drinks. He carried them on a tray to a table in the corner of the pub, near the jukebox. The adjacent tables were empty. Archie sat on a stool opposite the two men.

The American wasted no time on preliminaries. 'I trust you're discreet? You can be trusted in such... missions?'

Archie smiled his winning smile. 'Of course. I'm a professional.'

The American turned to the man beside him. The man nodded. The American spoke again. 'My name is Skinner. Colonel Skinner. This is... Well, we'll just call him Oldrey.'

'Pleased to meet you both,' Archie said. He noted the rank. *Colonel.* So that's how Skinner had been able to identify him. Secret Squirrel stuff. A phone call from one agency to another, his military records pulled up, a photograph, some identifying features. Bingo. But who was Oldrey? He hadn't spoken yet. Another Yank? Secret Service?

Skinner looked at Oldrey. 'Do you trust him?'

Oldrey finally spoke. 'I do, Colonel.' Archie noted the London accent. 'I've heard good things about our man here.'

Skinner looked back at Archie. 'Oldrey is one of the friends of a friend I was telling you about. He knows... people.' Skinner sipped his bourbon. 'I hear you're new to the game.'

If Oldrey was one of the friends of a friend, and Skinner was in military intelligence, there was no point denying it. 'Yes, I've only done two hits.'

'But they were well-executed, by all accounts,' Oldrey said.

'I like to think so,' Archie said.

Skinner took a thin cigar from a silver case. 'Good. I can be assured of your absolute discretion?'

Archie nodded. 'Absolutely.'

'You're bleeding, Mr Franklin Conn,' Oldrey said. 'Your face.'

'Oh, yes. Sorry. I was involved in a small *contretemps* earlier.' Archie took a handkerchief from his pocket and dabbed at his cheek.

'How's the other guy?' Skinner said.

'Dead by now, I should think,' Archie said.

Skinner blew a smoke ring into the air. 'Good, good.' He reached inside his coat, and pulled out an envelope. 'Take a look at the faces in there. I will arrange to meet those people tomorrow night. You'll be there, suitably hidden, of course. You will identify them, and then take them out. You understand?'

'Of course,' Archie said. He took the envelope and opened it. The face in the first photograph he didn't recognise.

'That is Michael Edge,' Skinner said. 'He works for the Security Service. MI5. I want you to kill him, and anybody who comes with him to the meet. Anybody with him is likely to be working on the same project.'

'Understood,' Archie said. He moved the photograph to one side, to reveal the next photograph. He was surprised, the kind of surprise that made him want to laugh out loud. He resisted the urge. He looked down, smiled, and then looked back up at Skinner with a serious face. 'And this man is?'

'Leonard Stone.'

Colonel Skinner would be surprised, Archie thought, when informed by this Michael Edge that Mr Stone couldn't come to the meeting because he was already dead. Archie wasn't about to tell Skinner this though; it might affect his fee. 'So how much are you going to pay me?' Archie said.

'Mr Oldrey will confirm that I pay very handsomely for absolute discretion and a job well done.'

Oldrey nodded. 'Very handsomely, indeed.'

'Are you willing to do the job?' Skinner said.

Archie smiled. 'Of course.'

Skinner looked around the bar, reached under the table, and pulled out a small attaché case. He placed it on the table. 'As a token of my faith in your abilities, here is a down-payment on your services. It is five thousand pounds. You'll get the other half on completion of the job.'

Archie let out a low whistle. 'Very nice, Mr Skinner.'

'*Colonel* Skinner.'

'Apologies.'

Archie turned the attaché case towards him, and flicked open the catches. He lifted the lid a little. He could see wads of fifty pounds notes. Archie had no need to count them. It was obvious that Skinner was serious. Archie closed the case. 'All right, Colonel Skinner. What happens next?'

'I'll phone you with details. I expect you to be securely and covertly emplaced before the meeting. I'll arrange the meeting to take place after darkness has fallen, on a well-lit street in London, to make your job easier.'

Archie stood and shook hands with Skinner and Oldrey. 'Thank you. I won't let you down.'

Oldrey looked at Archie, coldly. 'It would be inadvisable to do otherwise, Mr Franklin Conn.'

Archie laughed. 'Ooh, I'm scared.' He winked at Skinner, picked up the attaché case, and left the pub.

Archie arrived back at the flat in Reading at midnight. He wondered if Len had died yet. Mrs Eveson would have a surprise if she snooped around the other flat. He had decided some time ago that Mrs Eveson was the snooping type. Still, there was nothing to connect him to the death of Len Stone, even if it did unfortunately occur in his flat. After all, he worked in Cheltenham during the week. He had broken windows and doorframes on the way out of the flat to confuse matters. He'd have to make up some obscure job there that involved him working alone, if anybody asked. Perhaps he should start buying and selling antique books. There were some he could pick up from the old house. He thought he should phone Gribbens and Nuttley and see how they were getting on with the estate. He'd heard nothing from them since he'd found a letter from them a few of weeks ago confirming that probate had been granted.

He reviewed the meeting with Skinner. Who was that little jerk Oldrey? A mercenary, certainly, and thus not to be taken lightly. He thought he should phone Jeff Briggs. It was late, but Jeff was probably awake and sucking on a bong. Jeff took a while to answer the phone.

'Jeff, it's Archie.'

'What do you want, brother?'

'Are you stoned? I need some clear answers from you.'

'Not very. Not yet. Fire away.'

'Do you know anybody called Skinner? Colonel Skinner?'

'From the Army days?'

'No, this was a Yank. I met him tonight.

'Never heard of him.'

'He wants me to do a hit.'

'What? I'm offended, man. I'm your broker.'

'Yes, I know. I'm as surprised as you are. He said he got my name through a friend of a friend of a friend. You get the picture. Do you know anybody called Oldrey?'

'Ah, now that name rings a bell. Oldrey. Yeah. A merc. I don't know him, but my friend Motorhead knows somebody called Mason, who moves in those circles... Hold on.'

'What?'

'Chick. The other day. I *was* stoned then. He asked me about a hitman, whether I knew of any.'

'You trust Chick?'

'Absolutely. Fundamentally. We're blood brothers.'

'Okay. What did Chick want?'

'I don't know. Like I say, he asked if I knew any hitmen, I thought he was looking for somebody, so I gave him your name, said we were brothers in arms, that you could be trusted. Then we ended up arguing about whether brothers in arms were more important than blood brothers, started laughing a lot, you know, we were very stoned, and then Marta came around looking for love, and you know what happens then, brother.'

'So this Chick had my name.'

'Yes. But I trust him.'

'Fair enough. Skinner must have got my name that way. Either him or Motorhead.'

'So, are you cutting me in on the deal with this Skinner?'

Archie laughed. 'No way, Jeff. I got this job without your help.'

'Not true, man. I gave your name to Chick. Keep me sweet, or no more work for you.'

Archie sighed. 'Okay. How does a grand sound to you?'

'Sweet indeed,' Jeff said. 'You're a good man, brother.'

'A couple more questions. You know I don't like to personalise my hits. I don't like to know anything about them, beyond a face and an address.'

'Sure. Keep it clean, impersonal, I understand.'

'Well, Skinner didn't know that. He handed me the photographs, told me some names, what they did. Does the name Michael Edge mean anything to you?'

'I'm not sure.' Jeff paused. 'But there is *something* ringing a bell in my brain.'

'That'll be the dope.'

'Don't mock me, brother. Hang on a minute...' Archie heard the sound of the receiver being placed on a hard surface. He lit a cigarette while he waited. After a minute, Jeff came back on the line. 'I knew I'd heard the name somewhere. Don't you ever read the newspapers?'

'Not if I can help it. My name might be in them.'

There was a snort from the other end of the line. 'Good one. Never watch the news on the tellybox?'

'No, you know me. I prefer to curl up with Radio 3 and a good book.'

'Right then. I'm looking at a paper from last week. Michael Edge is a civil servant. He was in a nightclub that was bombed by the IRA. That was why it stuck in my brain, brother. You know what the nightclub was?'

With a sense of increasing anticipation, Archie said, 'No, go on, fill me in.'

'It was called *Peta's*. Now, you used to work in a nightclub in London, right, and–'

Archie made the connection. 'Shit. And guess what? Michael Edge isn't a civil servant. He's in intelligence. Skinner told me. The guy works for MI5.' He paused, dragged on his cigarette, thinking. 'And guess what... The other guy Skinner wants me to hit is only Len fucking Stone.'

'Your old boss?'

'That's the one. What the fuck is this all about? What does the rest of the article say?'

'Seems there was a private party at this club. A bunch of civil servants having an afternoon snifter or two in town. Somebody who worked there was an ex-civil servant, invited them all to the club.'

'Well, for civil servant, I think you can read secret service.'

'Let's see. He was called Colin Shepherd.'

'Colin Shepherd?'

'Mean anything to you?'

'No. I know a Colin, but his surname is Butler.'

Archie dragged on his cigarette again, thinking quickly. 'Did anybody die?'

'A couple of the civil servants. And some woman, Len Stone's girlfriend it says here. Emily Freeman.'

'Freeman? I know that name from somewhere.'

'The paper says it was an IRA bomb.'

'Freeman,' Archie said. 'Freeman. Why does that name mean something to me?'

'No idea, brother.'

'Well, you've earned your grand now. Drop by tomorrow afternoon and pick it up.'

Archie put the phone down. What the fuck was all this about? Len Stone entertaining secret agents? What a coincidence. Talk about karma. Did Skinner know all this? He couldn't, surely.

Colin Shepherd, Emily Freeman. Shepherd. Freeman. Peta's surname was Shepherd. Colin Butler. Colin Shepherd. The paper said that Colin Shepherd was an ex-civil servant. For which read one-time member of MI5 or MI6. Shepherd. Another coincidence. Archie had never believed in all that new age crap, but shit, what a huge collision of significant coincidences. Freeman. He remembered now. Ed Freeman had written that credulous book, *Panlyrae – A Message for Mankind*. Peta had made him read it, *to understand her better*, she had said. Ed Freeman's daughter had been Emily Freeman. She would be an adult now. Had Len Stone hooked up with her? He had loved that book, too. Stone, Freeman, Peta. They all had that connection with UFOs. Why the hell would a bunch of intelligence agents be interested in them? It made no sense. Yet, here they all were, part of the same jigsaw. And now some Yank wanted to rub out two of the players. They were all, Archie decided, connected in some way. Emily Freeman, Peta, Skinner, Len Stone. But how? It addled his brain thinking about it.

Oh well, Archie thought. No need to wonder why. He didn't care about any of these people anyway. Why worry? *Just take out this Edge, job done, and the money is mine.*

He walked over to the attaché case and opened it. He looked at the money. Five grand. Amazing. It was twice or more what he'd normally get for a hit. It really was a lot of money. So much, it would make a man greedy enough to blind him to reality. And another five grand afterwards? Suspicion began to nag at him. So much money had been provided in down-payment, he really had no need of the money he would purportedly receive after the hit. He went to his bedroom, bent down, and slid the MAS 49 out from beneath the bed. He took it to the front room, sat on the sofa, and began to clean it.

34

The hit had been arranged for a day later than originally planned. There had been an unfortunate hold-up, Skinner had said when he'd phoned.

Darkness had already fallen. The street Skinner had picked for his meeting was well-chosen. The light was good; it was a commercial area, with few houses, and offices that began to empty as darkness approached. Christmas would be here soon, and workers were leaving early to buy presents for their loved ones. The only present Archie would be getting this year was a bottle of scotch from Jeff Briggs. He didn't mind that. The sooner Christmas was over, the better. He wondered if Michael Edge had a family. If so, their Christmas would be miserable.

Archie had found an office block, five stories high, from which he had a good line of sight to the junction where the meeting would take place. He was concerned that if Michael Edge was secret service, armed officers would be present. Still, he knew what he had to do. One, two or three quick shots, then dump the rifle. If there *were* armed officers close by, Archie would already away down the fire escape before they realised where the shots were coming from. He knew he could be down the ladder within a minute. He'd be a couple of streets away within a couple more minutes. His only concern was if a firearms officer also chose to use this rooftop. He kept alert, listening for boots on the fire escape or on the gravel of the roof. He was lying between two air-conditioning units. He wore black jeans, black boots, a black greatcoat and a black balaclava. He would be difficult to target, even if he drew fire.

It was a cold, moonless night. Archie looked up at the sky. The stars shone fitfully, struggling to pierce the amber haze that always domed London. It was a fine night for a killing, Archie thought.

He looked down the street again. There was movement at the junction. He peered through the telescopic sight. He could see Skinner and Oldrey. He didn't like Oldrey. He didn't trust him. A few minutes passed. Oldrey obviously felt the cold. His coat collar was up, he rubbed his hands together, and he bounced from foot to foot. If Michael Edge didn't hurry up, Archie would shoot Oldrey simply for annoying him.

Finally, three people came around and the corner, one of whom was in a wheelchair. Skinner greeted them. Archie quickly scoped their faces. Michael Edge. He looked at the man in the wheelchair. *Len fucking Stone!* He hadn't died. He moved the sight to the third figure. He couldn't believe it. Colin Butler. None of this made any sense. Colin Butler, Len Stone, Michael Edge. Then he remembered what Jeff had told him the other night. The ex-civil servant, Colin Shepherd. Archie quickly pieced together some of the jigsaw. Colin Butler, Colin Shepherd. Perhaps Colin Butler had ingratiated himself with Stone by claiming to be a member of Peta's family. Len's soft heart would have bled. So who *was* Colin, really? Obviously, he was also Security Service. And what *was* his real name? Archie would never know. The little shit, Archie thought. He came to my flat, talked about the old days, and made me *like* him. What was he doing with us in Dereham? Why was he there? Archie surprised himself. He pulled the trigger.

That's for making me like you, Colin Whatever-your-fucking-name-is. He quickly sighted Edge. One thing Archie didn't

341

like about Skinner's choice of location was the amount of street furniture and the number of ornamental trees. Edge's head was hidden by branches and a street sign. Still, two shots to the heart would be enough, and Archie had an unobstructed view of Edge's torso. He pulled the trigger twice in rapid succession, and Michael Edge fell to the ground. He moved the sights to Len Stone. Stone sat in his wheelchair, looking up at him. He had worked out where the shots were coming from. Archie looked at Len's face through the sights. It was impassive. Accepting. Waiting for the final deliverance. Archie's attention focused on that face. Poor Len Stone. So much shit had happened to him.

Time passed. How much, Archie didn't know. He opened his left eye. He could see Oldrey and Skinner looking up at him. Ten grand was a lot of money. It was an amount deliberately chosen to blind. He trusted neither of them. Nobody else knew about this job. He was out on his own.

Two more shots rang out. Skinner and Oldrey fell to the ground. Archie looked through the sight one more time. Len Stone still looked up at him, towards his vantage point. Did he know who was here? Did he have some of that psychic sixth-sense he believed in? Did he know that Archie was peering down a telescopic sight at him, weighing his life? *Len Stone. I treated you like shit when you handed me a chance. I treated Peta like shit when she never deserved it.* He was wasting valuable time now. Even if there were no firearms officers around, the silenced shots would still have attracted attention. The fallen bodies would soon attract more.

Len Stone. What do I owe you?

Life, Archie thought. He dropped the rifle, and ran towards the fire escape.

35

Edge was grateful he'd had the sense to wear a bulletproof vest. He had never trusted Skinner. Harry, though. Poor Harry.

Skinner had said he only wanted to talk about Project Flashlight, how important it was, and how he was now going to pull out of the country. Harry had believed him. *What had Skinner to gain now*, Harry said. But Edge still believed, deep down, that Skinner had been responsible for the bomb in the club, despite what Special Branch and forensics had told him. He didn't trust Skinner. He would never have trusted him. And now Skinner was dead.

That was a puzzle. Who had shot Skinner and Oldrey? And why? Edge could only presume it had been somebody with even more power than Skinner. Somebody – not quite Skinner's beloved God, but *almost* that exalted – had wanted him dead. Somebody who thought that Skinner had gone, or was going, too far. Somebody else who believed in the survival of the project, and saw Skinner now as a liability it.

Yet Len Stone had survived. Not a single shot had been fired at him. And it had been because of Len Stone and Emily Freeman that all this madness had begun; the idea that Emily would tell Len about Project Flashlight, and thus compromise it. Madness, all of it. But if somebody believed Skinner to be a liability, that person must also have known of Skinner's belief about Emily and Len. So why wouldn't this unknown person also want Len Stone dead? Why save him? So many dead, Edge thought. Emily, Skinner and

Oldrey, Straker and his team, and Morrow and Thompson. So many injured. Len Stone, other agents, even himself.

Edge swallowed two aspirin with a sip of sweet tea. One of his ribs was cracked, and his chest bruised from the impact of the bullets. The police had found the rifle, but there were no fingerprints on it. Special Branch, forensics, even his own experts, would be able to tell him the ammunition fired, might possibly be able to trace the route of the ammunition through the country, might be able to trace the journey of the rifle through a dealer. But without the fingerprints, any association with an individual would be circumstantial.

Edge pinched the bridge of his nose. He had a headache coming on. He'd been up late last night, filing reports, talking to the police. The pain in his ribs had then woken him early in the morning. It had been not only the pain, though – his brain was in overdrive, connecting and disconnecting facts and ideas, and then connecting them again. Not but an hour ago, Edge had been contacted by a spook from Langley who had provided another snippet of information he felt should somehow fit into the puzzle, although where he couldn't yet fathom. On Skinner's desk at the Embassy, among all the other pieces, the agent had found name and a telephone number. The name had been Archibald Franklin Conn. The telephone number written beneath the name, however, was different to the one that had been provided by Carl Cleaver. Why would Skinner have Archie's name? It made no sense, except that Archie had been Peta's lover and had known Len. True, Archie had been connected to everybody, to all recent events, but only tangentially, and only because of Peta.

Edge knew one thing. No matter how Archie was connected, he had assaulted Stone, grievously injuring him. Archibald Franklin Conn was going down, whatever Len thought about it. Mrs Eveson disliked Archie, and would testify against him. He had only to convince Carl Cleaver to press charges and Edge would have Archie. A clever lawyer would probably get the charges reduced, but Archie would be jailed for a couple of years. That wouldn't be much, but it would be something.

The door opened. Len Stone came in, pushed by Liz Carter. 'Len wanted to see you, boss.'

'You're welcome here any time, Len. You're almost part of the family.'

Len smiled wanly. 'I'd rather I wasn't.' He looked at Edge. 'Oh, not because of you. I grew to like Harry. But if Skinner hadn't arrived, none of this would have happened. Emily wouldn't be... dead.'

'You think it was Skinner?'

'I know it was Skinner. We survived the bomb. That hadn't been the plan. So he arranged to have us killed another way.'

'Perhaps, but then who killed Skinner?'

'You've never moved in the circles I have, Edge. Whoever was hired to hit us found it worth his while to take out the paymaster. Who knows why? Perhaps he didn't like Skinner.'

Liz Carter's laugh was ironic. 'Who would? He was slippery as an eel.'

Len looked out of the window, spoke quietly. 'I know who was on that rooftop, anyway.'

'Ach, laddie,' Edge said, 'how can you know?'

'I just know.'

Len added no more, and there was silence for a few moments. Edge wondered if Len would reveal who he thought the assassin was, but he only rubbed his chin slowly, and continued to look through the window.

Edge looked over at Carter. 'Make Len a cup of coffee, please, Liz. And then phone Carl Cleaver.'

'Cleaver, sir?'

'Yes, I'm going to convince him to press charges against Archibald Franklin Conn. I know Len won't. But he can't refuse to be called as a witness against Conn.'

Len looked back at Edge. 'I don't want to do it.'

'But look at yourself, laddie. You're in a wheel-chair because of that man. You'll be recovering for months.'

Len shrugged. 'Them's the breaks.'

'Well, I'm not going to stand by and let him get away with it. Refuse all you want. I'm going to do something.'

Liz Carter returned with Len's coffee. 'Cleaver's not at home, boss. He must be back at work. I'll phone him there in a moment. Meanwhile, you have another visitor.'

Edge looked over towards the door. 'Molly. Come in.'

Molly came in, her eyes red. 'I had to come down. I hope you don't mind. I didn't know where else to go.'

Edge had phoned her last night, to tell her that Harry had died. It had broken his heart to listen to her. 'Of course I don't mind. We wouldn't normally have let you in, but... Well, you'll soon be part of the family. Who gave you clearance?'

'Liz Carter.'

'Yes, she was a strong advocate for you. Normally you would have received a letter next week. Officially, you still will. But for now, welcome aboard, from me.'

'You mean, I've been accepted?'

'You have. Harry always had faith with you.'

A small smile broke the sadness of her face. 'Thank you.' She looked at Len for the first time, then back at Edge. 'Oh, sorry, I didn't realise I was interrupting, I'll-'

'Hold up there, Molly. You need to meet this man. I don't think you've met before. Molly Shepherd, meet Len Stone.'

Molly and Len both looked at each other for a moment, taking in the relevance of the other's name. Len was first to speak. 'Good grief. Molly! Peta's little sister.' He looked her up and down. 'Though not so little anymore.'

'I never was, Mr. Stone. So you're the exotic night-club owner?'

'I am. I was. I don't know what I'll do now.'

'I was sorry to hear about... your girlfriend, Emily.'

'Thank you. I'm sorry about your friend Harry. I was beginning to like him.'

'Beginning?'

'Well, he did come to my club under a false name.'

'Ah, yes. But with the best intentions, I assume.'

'Possibly. I think he first came there looking for Archie.'

'Yes, he did. But he got over the need for revenge.'

'So have I.'

Molly looked at Len's legs. 'What happened to you?'

Before Len could speak, Edge interrupted him. 'Mr Stone was attacked by Archie. I'm trying to convince Len to press charges against him. The evidence is good, and we have another person who was assaulted by Conn who will make the case even stronger.'

'I can't.'

Molly spoke. 'But you should, Mr Stone.'

'Len, please.'

'You should, Len. You know, in the end Harry forgave Archie. Or, at least, he understood him. I never told Harry, but I didn't. I didn't forgive Archie, nor understand him. I thought he was a total pig to my sister, a conniving, mean bastard. It's weird. The more we talked about Archie, the more forgiving Harry became, and the less forgiving I became. It's as if we swapped emotions. And he's a murderer. Harry was sure of it. Did he tell you, Mr Edge?'

'Yes,' Edge said. 'A Land Rover, some tyre tracks and some Rothmans cigarette butts. I'm afraid it's all very circumstantial. I'll pass on Harry's thoughts to the police in Wales, but nothing will come of it, of that I'm sure.'

'Don't make life easy for Archie, please Len,' Molly said. 'He doesn't deserve it.'

Len sighed, and looked out of the window again. 'I know this will be difficult to believe. I know it'll sound weird. But I owe Archie one.'

Edge scratched his head. 'What?'

'I know, I know.'

'Why, laddie? He cut you up good. What do you owe Archibald Franklin Conn?'

'My life.'

'What do you mean?'

'When everybody was falling around me last night, I looked up to the rooftop, and just knew that looking right back at me was Archie. He was up there, staring down a telescopic sight at me. I was supposed to die as well. You, Harry, and me. It made sense; the three remaining people who knew about Project Flashlight. For some reason, he decided to kill Skinner and the other guy. He had plenty of time to kill me, yet he didn't.'

'Ach, laddie, how do you know it was Archie?'

'Call it a sixth sense, call it intuition. I just know it was.'

'I'm sorry, Len. I deal in cold, hard facts. I've no time for psychic mumbo-jumbo.'

'He'd make an excellent hitman,' Len said. 'He's a military trained. He's a sociopath. This is the job that has been calling out to him without him even knowing. I think he has finally realised his true vocation.'

'We have no evidence that Archie is a hitman.'

'I only know what I feel.'

Molly broke in. 'And I only know this. He has harmed you, Len, and Peta loved you. In a different way to the way she loved Archie, sure, but she still loved you. Harry knew, and he told me. Archie seems to have affected us all in different ways. Something needs to happen to him Len, if only to close off the influence of Archie on us all, for good.'

Len shook his head. He was frowning. Edge knew he was conflicted. Finally, he said, 'I'll do it. I'll be a witness, if you can get Cleaver to press charges. I'll do it for Peta, and Harry, and you, Molly. But I owe Archie my life. I'm sure of it. I can't be the one who presses charges.'

'You've done the right thing, Len,' edge said.

Molly took Len's hand, squeezed it, and smiled at him.

36

Three months later, Archie was being moved from his remand centre to Dartmoor. Archie didn't blame Len, who had never pressed charges. Cleaver had pressed charges, and Len had been called as a witness. Cleaver had been scared of what Archie would do to his family. He'd obviously been offered protection. Archie had sent word through his solicitor to Cleaver's solicitor to let Carl know he and his family were safe – he would never have harmed Cleaver's family. He could never physically harm any woman – except Lou, of course – or a child. He did have some ethics. Besides, despite everything that had happened, Carl was still a connection to Swansea. And he knew Jenny, Cleaver's wife, from old. She was a lovely woman. There weren't enough of them in the world.

Archie was only being jailed for two years. He'd admitted his guilt, which had gone down well with the judge. With good behaviour, he would be out on parole within eighteen months. He would find work when he was released, Jeff Briggs would see to that. Archie found the job of paid assassin most *congenial*.

After his trial, the mail in his PO Box had been forwarded to him. Gribbens and Nuttley had swiftly auctioned everything; the house, books, knick-knacks, antiques, the car. Archie had been surprised and gratified to find he had three hundred grand in the bank. With the jobs Jeff would find him, Archie would never have to do a proper day's work again. That was all he'd ever wanted from life, really. That simple desire had created the tangled, interlocking web of causes and consequences, the lines that had crossed and weaved together and led to this point

He was willing now to accept imprisonment, *wanted* it, really. He hoped that, by going to jail, by taking eighteen months away from the world, the chain of events would finally be broken, the chain that, looking backwards, led from this moment to the moment he had first met Peta Shepherd.

CPSIA information can be obtained
at www.ICGtesting.com
Printed in the USA
LVOW01s0116150616

492566LV00031B/745/P